Fic
V

Vine, Barbara,
1930-

Gallowglass

$19.95

DATE			

© THE BAKER & TAYLOR CO.

GALLOWGLASS

Also by Barbara Vine

A DARK-ADAPTED EYE
A FATAL INVERSION
THE HOUSE OF STAIRS

GALLO

BARBARA VINE

NO NIGHT IS TOO LONG

HARMONY BOOKS ⟆ NEW YORK

Copyright © 1990 by Kingsmarkham Enterprises

Published by Harmony Books, a division of Crown Publishers, Inc., 201 East 50th Street, New York, New York 10022. Originally published in Great Britain by Penguin Books Ltd. in 1990.

HARMONY and colophon are trademarks of Crown Publishers, Inc.

Manufactured in the United States of America

Library of Congress Cataloging-in-Publication Data
Vine, Barbara
    Gallowglass / by Barbara Vine.
    I. Title.
  PR6068.E63G35 1990
  823'.914—dc20 89-29026
CIP

ISBN 0-517-57744-5

10 9 8 7 6 5 4 3 2 1

First American Edition

TO PAT KAVANAGH

Much of the information on kidnapping in Italy which contributes to the background of this novel derives from *The Kidnap Business* by Mark Bles and Robert Low, Pelham Books, 1987.

The merciless Macdonwaid . . .
Of kerns and gallowglasses is supplied;
And Fortune, on his damned quarrel smiling,
Show'd like a rebel's whore.

Macbeth, Act I, scene ii

GALLOWGLASS

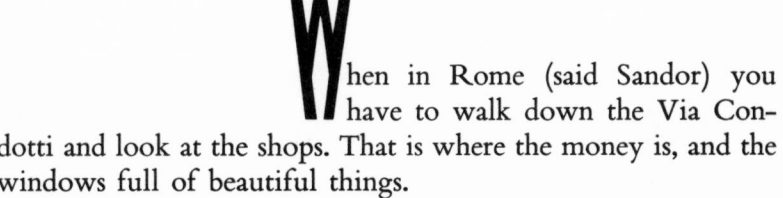

When in Rome (said Sandor) you have to walk down the Via Condotti and look at the shops. That is where the money is, and the windows full of beautiful things.

"What does that mean?" I said. "The Via Condotti, what's that?"

"Kidnap Street."

"Really?" I said. "Is that what it means?"

He only laughed, the way he does. Then he went on with the story, the first one he ever told me. If you've got a shop in the Via Condotti, he said, you've arrived, you're rich, a window on the most fashionable shopping street in Rome is a sure sign of wealth.

Bulgari the jewelers are there. One of the Bulgari family was kidnapped in 1975 and released on payment of a ransom of

£650,000. Well, it was in Italian money, Sandor said, but that's what it was in pounds. Eight years later two more members of the family were taken and let go when £1.75 million was paid. Keep on down the street and you'll come to Piatelli. It's men's clothes they sell. Barbara Piatelli was kidnapped and held for nearly a year before being released for £500,000.

On the opposite side is Prince Piraneso the perfumer. Sandor asked me if I'd ever heard of the perfumes called that. I had to say no, I've never heard of things like that, of course I haven't, let alone used them.

"Was he kidnapped?" I said.

"Not him, his wife."

"What happened to her?"

His voice was dreamy as if his thoughts were a long long way away. "It was at the end of the Kidnap Era. It was only five years ago. The Golden Age of Kidnapping was past—even in Italy."

I looked at him, waiting for more. It wasn't a story really, was it? More a sort of account, a history. It wasn't a story like the ones about Señora Santa Anna or Lichnikoff that had a beginning and an end. But somehow I already knew it wouldn't be any good asking Sandor to go on if he didn't want to, I knew I had to leave it to him to tell it in his own time. If he wanted to tell it or if he never meant to mention it again. He lit a cigarette and lay back with his eyes half-closed. I watched him, three or four days into love. Even then I could feel my love trembling inside me, and as I watched him the trembling bubbled up and got stronger as if it had to come out of my mouth in a cry. I covered my mouth and sat there watching.

Next day we went out together. It must have been the first time Sandor took me about, showing me the town I was born in but never saw before. We went in the tube to get me used to it again, and I could see him looking at me to check if I was all right. Oxford Street and snow flying in the wind, melting on the warm pavements.

"Hardly the Via Condotti," he said.

I don't know what he meant. It was full of shops and people. Perhaps it was money he meant, you could feel the hunger for things, but not the money to buy them. We went into a big store. You could smell the department where they sold the perfumes and powders and creams and things long before you got to it. It was the way I imagined it must be in one of those foreign places when you're coming to a tropical garden but you can't see it yet. Sandor led me up to a counter where all the stuff they sold was called Prince Piraneso. There were things for women on one side and for men on the other. A girl with a cut-glass bottle in her hand sprayed perfume on me and on Sandor, and Sandor, much to my surprise, didn't seem to mind or get cross. He even lifted up his wrist and smelled it and smiled a bit.

The women's stuff was done up in very pale blue and the men's in red. It was so expensive you wouldn't want to waste it on your face, you'd have to eat it. There were no pictures of this prince, only of girl models and one man model I thought looked a lot like Sandor, but he frowned and shook his head when I told him so. What he drew my attention to particularly was a small photograph in a golden oval surround. It was on the lid of a big powder box, a tiny picture of a blond girl with masses of golden hair done up on top of her head and with strings of pearls wound in it. Sandor sort of pushed my face right into it so that I could get a good look.

We were there so long that the girl with the cut-glass bottle sprayed us again, but this time Sandor wasn't pleased anymore. He scowled at her.

"Come on, little Joe," he said to me. "That's enough for now."

I'd been living in Sandor's room in Shepherd's Bush for getting on for a week when that happened. It gave me something to think about in the evening while he was reading. That was when I got into the habit of thinking about the day that was past and maybe the day before, and sort of reviewing everything that had happened and the things Sandor had taught me. Most days I'd learned new words too and I'd run over them in my mind. It was quite a big room on the top floor of the house with a double bed in it and a chair and a thing called a chaise longue. Now that I'm talking about first times, I think that was the first new word Sandor taught me, that a funny kind of settee, very hard and uncomfortable, with a back like a padded bedhead, is a chaise longue. I had to sleep on it those first few nights, but when I'd been with him a week, give or take a little, Sandor said from his bed, "You may as well come in here with me."

I slept on the edge of it, so as not to touch him in the night. I would very much have liked to touch him in the night, just to hold him, nothing nasty, nothing sexual. I would have loved that beyond anything, but it wasn't possible. Once in spite of myself I did roll against him. He woke up and said terrible things, made accusations that cut me to the bone, and then he struck me in the face, a blow on one cheek and then the other, hands as hard as the side of a gun slapping. I think something in my unconscious keeps the memory of those words and those blows on alert, so that in the night if my body grows weak with sleep and longing, a warning bell rings in my head and a grip charges my muscles and holds them back.

By that time I understood how I felt about Sandor. It was gratitude, of course, and admiration for the way he looked and the way he talked, but it was love too. I felt that I'd been looking for someone to love all my life, that that someone had been waiting and it was Sandor. Of course I'd loved Tilly and still do, though I haven't seen her for months, but the way I love Sandor—it sounds mad because he's only two years older than me—well, I think that's the way a child might love his father. At home with Mum and Dad we didn't talk about love, the word wasn't used. You liked people or were "fond of" them or, in extreme cases, in Mum's phrase, were "devoted to them," but love, no. I think they thought of "love" as something sexual and sex to them was for darkness or for jokes.

Much harder to understand is what Sandor sees in me. I don't really want to think just at this moment about the main things that have made me what I am, notably the last thing that Sandor rescued me from, but it's not hard for me to admit that I've had no education to speak of, I've got no background and, frankly, I've nothing to give. Nothing to offer, that is. I've got my love to give, but I don't think it's exactly that which Sandor wants. Perhaps it's my devotion—that word of Mum's again—and my willingness to obey him that he likes. Or perhaps he wants a servant. I owe my life to him, of course, because he saved my life that time, and he explained what that meant: being his person and doing what he tells me.

The latest thing he has told me to do is grow a beard. I'm not sure if he first mentioned it before he told me the next story or after he told me the first part of the next story. I don't suppose it matters anyway. At the time I took it for an example of Sandor reading my thoughts. I'd been feeling a bit self-conscious about shaving with one of those Bic razors, orange-colored plastic things that come in packets of ten, while Sandor shaved so elegantly and expertly with his great-grandfather's cutthroat razor. It was as if he was giving me a way of getting out of it.

"I've never had a beard," I said.

"All the more reason to start one, little Joe," he said.

It brings me a sort of warm glow when he calls me that. No one else ever did. I'm not little, I'm as tall as he is, nearly six feet, but it's like a fatherly thing to say, a son's name to call me. I went and looked at myself in the mirror.

I'm very skinny and long legged. A forked radish, Sandor says, which is a funny way to put it. My hair is as dark as his, but it's thin and wiry-curly, not thick and smooth like his, and my skin is too pale for my hair. I've got pale blue eyes with pink rims to them and Sandor says I'm "sore-eyed and tender," which is the way some woman is described in the Bible. Not exactly flattering, but I know I'm not good-looking. A very tall weasel with a long neck is what I look like.

I'd been shaving since I was thirteen, fourteen years ago. Dad took me into the bathroom one day and shut the door on us as if he was going to show me something dirty. He gave me one of those plastic razors and said to start shaving next morning. I never questioned it, I just shaved every day after that, though my naked face with my small chin might have been better for a bit of covering up. It must be about a week since I threw my razor away, and now I have a dense dark furring on my chin and cheeks and top lip. Hairiness is the way animals are, but I think my beard is making me look more human.

We'd had three stories since Prince Piraneso, the one about hiding the Hanoverian crown jewels when the Prussians came, and the one about the old couple who had a monkey's paw to wish on and made their dead son come back but were too scared to let him in. Next Sandor told me about Señora Santa Anna. She was the wife of the dictator of Mexico, and while she was out in her carriage with her lady-in-waiting and her flunkeys some bandits caught her.

"What's a flunkey?" I said.

"A kind of servant in a fancy uniform," said Sandor, "and a powdered wig too, I expect."

The bandits wanted revenge on General Santa Anna, so they made the lady and all the people with her take their clothes off and drive naked back to Mexico City. They didn't hurt them, just made them strip. The General was so angry he offered a reward for the head of the chief bandit so that he could lay it at his wife's feet. But he never caught him, only hundreds of innocent people, who got executed just the same.

It's a cruel story, isn't it? All Sandor's stories are, full of dark things and pain, but exciting too. Four days went by and I was wondering if there'd ever be another. I wondered if I'd ever hear any more about Rome and Kidnap Street and the Prince. Indian takeaway was what we'd had for supper and a bottle of red vino, and Sandor was lying on the bed reading a book called *The Golden Bough* by Sir James Something. He had the old pinkish-gray bedspread pulled up over him. Have you noticed that when curtains and covers and things in places like furnished rooms in Shepherd's Bush get old they always end up that color? It must come from dust and bad washing and sunshine and more dust. Tilly's boyfriend Brian, the one who had been to India, told me pinkish-gray was the color of all the beggars' rags.

Sandor has a face you'd never forget. Once you've seen Sandor, no one else will do. Or that's the way I feel. Not good-looking—and then you ask yourself, if he's not good-looking what do I mean by good-looking? I mean this, don't I? A big mouth with full lips, a big nose, and long cheeks, hollow for a man not yet thirty, sunken eyes the darkest brown you ever saw, and a hard clean jaw like the blade of something sharp. It's wonderful when he smiles, especially if the smile is for you, and it's been a lot for me lately. His hair is quite short, very dark and thick, and a lock of it falls down over his forehead. He has marvelous hands, long and thin but not like a woman's because the joints are big and the fingertips blunt.

He put the book down, laid it face downward because he never uses bookmarks. Mum used to have bookmarks for *magazines*—can you imagine? Sandor just put his book facedown on the floor and looked at me smiling and said it was time to tell me a bit more of the story he'd begun but never finished.

"It can be our serial," he said. "Our soap opera, if you like, remind you of what you're missing."

He knows I miss TV, though I've never said so, only that watching TV is what I used to do. That's what I told him when he asked me what I did. What else could I say? But I like stories just as much, better really, and being next to him strengthens the idea of the bedtime story. Sandor couldn't tell it without smoking. I like that too, though I don't like the smell, because that's just what it might have been when I was three or four, say, and my father lit a cigarette before he called me over and took me on his knee. Sandor inhaled very deeply so that the smoke took a long time coming out of his mouth, so that it seemed it would never come out but stayed in the depths of him as if he could live on fire and brimstone.

He rested his head back against the wall, there wasn't a bedhead, and closed his eyes. The smoke trickled out from his lips. "The Prince," he said, "was an old man when our story begins."

I've learned to know when he wants me to ask a question. "What's old?"

"We're young," he said, and I could tell he took a lot of pleasure saying that. He sort of rolled the words round his mouth. "We're young, little Joe. I want to stay young forever, don't you?" I didn't answer, I'd never thought about it, staying alive and in my right mind had been enough for me. "He was old not just by our standards, by anyone's. He'd had two wives already. One of them was divorced and the other one was dead. He'd got children too and they were pretty old by that time. They were old enough to be the Princess's parents."

"What Princess?" I said.

"She was the most beautiful woman in the world." He looked at me as if I might be going to argue. I just nodded. "And she was just an ordinary little girl too," he said, "or she had been. She was born in a little village by the seaside. You're going to ask me if that was in Italy too, but no, it wasn't. It was here, in England. She was English. When Prince Barnaba di Piraneso first met her she was a famous model and her face was on all the magazine covers, but she was still only twenty-two. He was sixty-eight but he was very, very rich. Have you ever heard of a Gila monster, little Joe?"

"I reckon," I said. "In a nature program on TV."

That made him laugh. "Then you'll remember its scaly face and its beady eyes, its fat body and the pink and black blotches on it. It's got a wonderful name in Latin, the Gila monster. It's called *Heloderma horridum*. Our Prince looked just like H. Horridum, but the Princess married him just the same. It was a case of Beauty and the Beast, but this beast never turned into a handsome young prince. He was a prince already, you see, and it takes more than marriage to do the rest. It's supposed to take love and I don't suppose there was much of that."

"Was she the one that was kidnapped?" I said.

"Oh, yes, but not yet. Not for a few years." Sandor lit another cigarette and sat silent for a few moments. I thought this might be the end of episode one. It almost gave me a shock when he started again, this time in a harsher voice. "They had three homes. One was in Paris. Then they had the apartment in Rome and a house in the Tuscan hills not far from Florence. The Prince was nearly seventy and his heart was bad but he was still boss of the business. He was still chairman or whatever they call it of the Piraneso perfume empire, with offices in Rome and Florence and shops in London and New York and Paris and Amsterdam and one, of course, in the Via Condotti, in Kidnap Street. He was there, in Rome, when it happened, when they took her."

I asked when who took her. Some Calabrians, he said. Did I know Calabrians made the best kidnappers? It was a well-known fact in Italy. I don't even know what a Calabrian is—something like a Gila monster, for all I know. But I didn't say so. I said to go on and Sandor said, "No more for now. It's to be continued."

"You ought to write your stories down," I said. "You could be a writer, Sandor."

He looked sad and shook his head. "I haven't the gift of originality." And then he said something flattering, something that made me want to hug him, but of course I couldn't. "I wish I had your imagination, little Joe."

But he does write sometimes. He writes letters. His handwriting is very beautiful, thin on the upward strokes and thick on the downward ones, and sort of pointy and very even. He sent me out to buy paper and envelopes, though he wasn't very pleased with what I got. The letter he wrote he posted himself and then he went to the library. He was a long, long time in the library, he told me that much, though not what he went there for.

We never got letters. That's not quite true because sometimes, not very often, Sandor got a letter from his mother. She lives in Norwich. When one of her letters comes he takes his time about opening it and his face goes blank as he reads what she's written.

"I'm a remittance man, little Joe," he once said after reading one of her letters. "D'you know what that is?" I didn't then. "It's someone their family pays to keep away. Would your lot pay you not to go home again, d'you reckon? It's worth a try."

"They haven't any money," I said, which wasn't to deny that they'd do it if they had. If you could get a grant to make your son a remittance man they'd be the first to fill up the forms.

Letters from Sandor's mother were the only ones we ever got. We'd hear the post come but we didn't bother to go down unless we were going anyway. But Sandor started watching the posts after he'd written his first letter. I don't think he ever got a reply, though I can't be sure. He wrote more letters in the next months, but it wasn't until March that he said he was going to move. Not "we" but "he."

"Up into East Anglia, to be nearer."

I asked him nearer what. Sandor doesn't like being questioned, except on what he calls "academic" things. And when he's telling a story and he pauses and sort of half raises his eyebrows. He doesn't like being asked to explain what he's said, but he seems to provoke questioning just the same. He didn't answer me.

"I ought to have a car. How can I get hold of a car?"

"You have to buy them or steal them," I said.

"Or borrow them." He stared at me and there was a grin in his eyes. "What's wrong with you? Why the long face?"

"What about me?" I said. "What's going to become of me?"

"You're coming with me, of course."

That was when I first saw the peculiar things Sandor carried around with him: his property, his movable baggage. He had a carrier bag full of car registration plates and a suitcase full of bits of newspaper. Well, not just newspaper cuttings but photographs as well and whole magazines. The case came open, which is how I knew.

"That's private."

Sandor said it in the harsh, sharp way I hate him using. But he calmed down when I fastened it up again and locked it and he told me a story about someone called Prince Lichnikoff being strung up on a lamppost in a revolution. It's no wonder I sometimes don't know the difference between fiction and truth. In an old bag like a briefcase I found his passport. He was reading again and didn't see me looking at it. Finding out his name wasn't really Sandor but Alexander was a bit of a shock. The passport had a lot of stamps in it, mostly from places in Italy, but the most recent was over four years ago.

We left London the next day with all our possessions. They were mostly Sandor's possessions because I hardly have any. I was weighed down with them, like a donkey—or a flunkey.

"It sounds like a Mayfair pub," said Sandor. "The Happy Flunkey, Bruton Street, West One."

"Well, I am happy," I said.

He smiled. "I should be so lucky."

The train from Liverpool Street took us up through Essex. I've hardly traveled anywhere, hardly been anywhere. Of course I haven't a passport of my own and I haven't even got a driving license, though I can drive as well as anyone else. The thing is, I'm not the sort of person who takes tests, exams, that sort of thing, let alone passes them. Darkness was coming down over the countryside, though it was only late afternoon. It looked gray and windswept and unfriendly.

We had to change at Colchester and we had half an hour to wait. "It's the coldest station in East Anglia," Sandor said. "Really, it's a well-known fact."

He told me a story he said came from *The Thousand Nights and a Night.* It was about an old Eastern man who wanted to protect his daughter from men, so he locked her up in a box and locked the box inside a casket and the casket inside a trunk and then he threw the key to the trunk into the sea. But she still escaped and met her lover and they ran away together and lived happily ever after. Sandor said the point of the story was to prove that no matter how much you lock a person up they'll still escape if they really want to. I didn't say anything but I didn't think it could possibly work out in practice. If it did hardly anyone would stay in prison.

While we were standing there, the Norwich express came through. It goes to Norwich nonstop from London and it travels at about a hundred miles an hour. The first we knew of it was the voice that comes on and tells you about trains arriving. The voice said, *Will passengers on platform two stand clear of the edge. Stand clear of the edge, please.*

And then it came thundering through. That doesn't describe what it was like, I don't think I could describe it. It roared past and the whole station shook. Everyone fell back like a wave and the extraordinary thing was they were all smiling and grinning at each other. Sandor was smiling and so was I. I don't know why unless it was that there was something triumphant about that express, something marvelous and exciting, as if it was bounding and charging off to new worlds instead of the ordinary old city where Sandor's mother lives.

"It's a great train!" Sandor said, or rather yelled, above the roaring.

Our own train was lumbering in on the other platform. The contrast was a joke and that made people smile too. Sandor was looking carefully at me.

"Did that bring back something you'd rather forget?" he said.

"No," I said, "oh, no," though it had.

2

Sandor saved my life. That was how we met.

I was sick for a long time. Not sick, Sandor would say, ill. You're not an American. It's all right for Americans, it's correct for them, but not if you're English. I was ill, then, though that word *sick* somehow expresses better what I was. On and off, I was in hospital for years.

People talk about being depressed when they really mean they're feeling low, pissed off, under the weather. They don't know what depression is. Real depression is something else. It's when you haven't got anything, when everything goes—wants, needs, will, caring, hope, desire. Don't make me laugh—desire! It's when you can't make decisions anymore, any sort of decision, like, shall I get up out of this bed and go to the bathroom or not? Or, shall I pick up this cup of tea and drink some or shall I just go on staring at it? It's when you don't want anything and can't do anything and don't even want the opposite of not wanting anything, whatever that is, and haven't got anger or fear anymore, or even panic.

And that's not the worst of it. You get deeper in. You get to the place where you can't see colors or hear people speaking to you and inside your head is something that washes around when you move. It's water in there, a sink of it, dirty water with oil floating on the top in those rainbow rings. That's the only color left that you can see, the rainbow circles of the oil on the dirty water slurping around inside your head.

But there's no point in going on about it. I haven't had anything like that since I've known Sandor, though I've had other things. Anyway, I was getting better in the hospital. It was slow but I was getting better. Depression is the one thing that goes wrong with your mind that they can do a lot for and they do it with drugs. Talking to the so-called experts, therapists, psychiatrists, and whatever, is worse than useless. But the drugs really help you. The trouble for me was that they discharged me before the cure was complete. It was the cuts which did it, of course. There weren't any more funds and they were closing down four wards.

Not that they said so. It was Sandor who explained to me about the cuts. They said I'd reached a point where it was up to me, they'd done what they could and now it was for me to take over and help myself. I'd have the utmost support from my local Social Services. I said, what did they mean by local? And they said I had a home and parents, hadn't I? That was where I'd be going.

It's a funny thing that your friends like you better if you're a failure in life, if you're not really good at anything much. It means they've nothing to envy and nothing to compete with. For parents the opposite is true. Parents want successful children with plenty of qualifications and preferably high salaries. Sandor says it's because they relive their own lives through their children and want to see themselves succeed. *Vicar-something* is the word he used. You can't be envious of yourself or be your own rival.

However that may be, Mum and Dad didn't want me. Of course they didn't say so. They bent over backward to be cooperative and understanding—at any rate while the social worker was there.

It was a long time since I'd lived at home. Dad had turned my bedroom into a darkroom and they had a lodger in Tilly's. I slept on the couch—sorry, Sandor, sofa—in the living room. It wasn't that I minded, though; I'd have slept on the floor, I'd have slept in the garage. From the moment we were all three alone together they made things plain. The way I was introduced to the sofa, for instance.

"It'll be quite adequate for you, Joe, until you find a place of your own."

What did she mean? Till I got a mortgage? Till I got a job in top management and the house that went with it? I'd have gone to Tilly if I could have. If she'd only had one room she'd have shared it with me, I know that. But Tilly and her boyfriend had gone to Belgium in the camper, I don't know why. I don't know what was there for him or her. She was never mentioned in that house. She had left home to live with a man she wasn't married to and that was enough. They didn't know that she'd lived with a couple of others since then and was even now with the latest one on some camping site. Mum had made her feelings very plain.

"When Matty makes up her mind to lead a decent life and can respect herself again, then she can come back and I'm sure she'll be very welcome."

I was still on my drugs course and perhaps because of that I never quite got back into the oily water. It was what most people call being depressed that I was, low and dispirited and feeling nothing mattered. I didn't know anyone but Mum and Dad and the lodger. My friends had all moved off somewhere. The lodger, who was a mature student at a college studying something called naturopathy, said I had schizophrenia due to a bad diet without enough raw food. I think he was scared of me. He used to jump when I came into the room.

One day Dad said, "I think we all realize the time has come for you to be making a move, Joe. Even if you were our own we'd say the same." *Even if you were our own* . . . "There comes a time in every man's life when he has to stand on his own feet." They wouldn't have turned me out. They couldn't have done it if I hadn't wanted to go. Short of fetching the police. Come to think of it, they were capable of that.

If I'm being strictly honest I must say I wasn't really thinking of suicide. Not, that is, to the point of saying to myself, I'll do it this way, on Thursday, at such and such a time, I'll write a note and then I'll do it. It wasn't like that. But I did feel it was all hopeless. I did feel I might as well not bother, I might as well cross the street without looking, swallow all the pills I've got left and see what happens. I didn't though. I left. I walked out of that house in the afternoon without saying anything, not knowing where I was going, the money in my pocket amounting to around £8, all I had. Sandor says that in that moment I became the stereotype of the person the National Health Service has turned into a beggar through throwing them out of the mental hospitals.

It was November and very cold. After I'd been walking for a bit I wished I'd taken Dad's overcoat which was hanging on the hall stand. He'd gone to work in his raincoat with the lining in. In our family you don't go into proper winter clothes until December and you don't leave them off till May. That is one of the rules. I wished I'd taken it but I couldn't go back. I didn't know where I was heading, there was no one I could think of that I could stay with. It seemed to me that I had to find other people like myself and join them.

I found some on the Embankment. No one said anything to me. They were making arrangements for the night, wrapping themselves up in newspapers and old coats and in some cases blankets. There was an old woman who got inside a cardboard box that had once contained a dishwasher. I hadn't come provided for camping out overnight and I thought of going elsewhere, but there was nowhere to go. The cold was the worst of it. I put on everything I'd got in my backpack but it wasn't enough. Some time in the early hours I bought myself a cup of tea and a Danish pastry in a cellophane pack I couldn't get open because my fingers were too cold. I had to tear it open in the end with my teeth.

When the Embankment tube station opened, which was at five or six in the morning, I hadn't a watch so I couldn't tell, I went in there because I thought it would be warmer. It's funny, isn't it, if I'd decided to go down to the Northern Line platform I probably wouldn't be here now, I'd be dead. I chose the Circle because the trains go round and round, you can sit in the train all day and it'll just go on going round—all that for a 6op ticket, which was what I got out of the machine. At that point I had no thought of killing myself, though I had other ideas. I was thinking that once I'd been round Kensington High Street and Paddington and Farringdon and Liverpool Street and Temple and Kensington High Street a couple of times I'd be warmer and I could do something. For instance, I could steal something from someone and be arrested and then I'd have a bed in a police cell for the next night.

But would I? Maybe for one night. Then they'd have me in court and give me a conditional discharge or a suspended sentence and send me back to Mum and Dad. The only way to be sure of going to prison these days, and that wouldn't be certain, would be to kill someone. I was on the platform by then and there weren't many people about. It was too early.

A train came but I didn't get on it. Seven or eight people did and I was alone. Push someone under the next train—how about that? I had been sitting on a seat under one of those timetables that tell you about first and last trains, but I got up and went close to the edge of the platform. I stood there about three inches in from the edge and a few feet from the opening of the tunnel.

Someone had come onto the platform. I turned round to have a look at who it was. A man a few years older than me, dark, thin, with a hollow face, a rapacious face, and black hungry eyes. Could I really have seen all that then? I don't know. He had jeans on and a denim jacket lined with dirty sheepskin. I'd like to be able to say I knew at once what he would mean to me, that I detected in advance my best friend, but that wouldn't be true. I felt nothing except that this was a man who would be a witness.

The truth was my attitude had altered. The edge of the platform was tempting me, the black mouth of the tunnel drawing me, the light which had turned to green making me tremble. I couldn't yet hear a sound nor feel the rush of air but I knew the train would be there in—what? Thirty seconds? I pushed my feet forward, shuffling them toward the edge. I thought of the news reaching Mum and Dad and that brought me a sort of weird pleasure. The news reaching Tilly I didn't want to think about. My feet were over the edge now, the ball of each foot and the toes over the edge.

I leaned my body forward a bit. My head was hanging. I had put the backpack down on the platform. I was thinking, I can't kill anyone but I could kill me. That only, mark you, I hadn't got farther than that. I hadn't got to the point of saying, I'll do it, I'll kill myself, this is it, goodbye, world; only of Mum crying and saying I was always unstable and Dad saying I hadn't any grit.

Sandor says I was about to commit suicide. I don't argue with him. He knows best anyway, he always knows better than I do, of course he does, he's educated. I'm heaps better than I was because he's educated me in the time we've been together, but then I was pig ignorant, I didn't know what I was doing half the time. So Sandor must be right when he says I was on the point of throwing myself in front of the train. I wouldn't know. A kind of haze comes over my memory at this point, anyway. As far as my thoughts go, that is. I don't know what I thought or what I intended, only that I stood there with half my feet over the edge of the platform and my body bowing.

It was a lifetime before the train came. I felt the breeze of it sweep my hair. I heard it mutter in the tunnel. I didn't see its lights, I wasn't looking. The noise of its coming filled my head, so perhaps there were no thoughts there, they were all driven out by the train coming. I didn't hear Sandor behind me, I only heard the train. His breath was hot on my neck and his hands warm on my waist, they were the warmest things I'd felt since I was a child. They were hard as heated iron and they held me by the waist and pulled me back and I fell over and fell over and we rolled back toward the walls as the train burst out of the tunnel.

A couple of people got off. They must have thought we were drunk. We got up and I retrieved my backpack and we sat on the seat. We looked at each other, not smiling, just staring, and our eyes had got very big. The oily water slurped in my head and gave a sort of hiccup and gurgled away down a plughole in my brain. That was the last of it and the space where it had been was clean.

"Who are you?" he said. "What are you doing here, apart from killing yourself?"

I told him who I was. I told him a lot about myself, my voice low and mumbling, looking down at my hands. When I got to the bit about sleeping on the settee (he didn't correct me and call it a sofa then) and about them saying it was just a temporary arrangement, I started crying.

He said, "You'd better come back with me," and then, when the next train came and we got into it, "I saved your life, so your life belongs to me now."

"All right," I said.

3

Tilly isn't really my sister. But when I come to think of it, no one is really "my" anything. Mum isn't really my mother or Dad really my father or Sandor really my friend. Somewhere I've got parents who are really mine, that is, their blood is mine and their genes and all that, their sex made me, and I know their names. There's no secrecy about it, but if they met me in the street they wouldn't know me and I wouldn't know them. I went into care when I was four and was fostered with Mum and Dad when I was seven. By then they already had Tilly, who they'd fostered a year before when she was eleven.

It sounds sentimental, it sounds like one of those Hollywood movies of the thirties they made to put child film stars in, but in fact it does happen that when you bring two kids together like that they love each other because they've no one else to love.

Mum never touched us, never kissed us, that goes without saying. But she never said anything nice either, never called us "dear" even or praised us or said those routine things foster parents are supposed to say about choosing to have us and taking us to live there because she wanted us. I won't say she never called us by our Christian names because she did very, very rarely, perhaps when she had to call one of us and there was absolutely no other way of doing it. She was brisk, chilly, very dutiful. We were there because it was her duty.

Dad went to work and came home and watched TV, went to the betting shop and went fishing, went to bed and got up and went to work. Sometimes he played tricks on us, like a dead frog in the bed or replacing the egg in my eggcup with a raw one. April Fools' Day was a nightmare. But he never touched us, not in bad ways or good ones. He never had Tilly sit on his knee. Except once, nearly. He was reading something and she was looking over his shoulder, sort of leaning against him, and he put out his arm to pull her onto his lap. She was about twelve. Mum grabbed Tilly by the arm and pulled her away and whispered something very sharply to Dad that I couldn't catch. This was before we ever heard all that stuff about the sexual abuse of children, but I suppose that was what she had in mind.

I can remember my own mother. She wasn't married to my father, that's something else that goes without saying. Various men I can remember and one of them may have been him—the one who smoked so much and sometimes talked to me? I don't think my mother ever hit me or anything, but she used to leave me locked up in our room all day while she went to work and eventually they took me away from her. I got my name Joseph because she was Irish and a Catholic. Tilly's name is Matilda. It was typical of Mum and Dad that they wouldn't let her be called Tilly when she came to them because that was the *unusual* shortening of Matilda, the unconventional one, and you never did unconventional things, you never did things to draw attention to yourself. So they called her Matty. Of course, they hardly ever called her anything, but when they had to, it was Matty.

When I was older and found out she'd been called Tilly in her own home I started calling her that. Mum never forgave me. She behaved about it as if I'd been shoplifting or cursed God or hit an old lady over the head. When I called Tilly Tilly she would snap at me to be quiet, to shut up, never to say that again, and then she wouldn't speak to me for hours.

When people ask me where I was born and grew up I say London. If you say that to a foreigner he'll think you mean Hyde Park or the Post Office Tower. Most people who're brought up in a suburb don't know London at all, they don't go there from one year's end to another. Actually, it's at the year's end that they do go, to see a pantomime or *The Mousetrap* and do their Christmas shopping in Oxford Street.

Sandor showed me London. He taught me about it. We'd go and look at things, and not only stores with perfume departments. We'd visit places I'd heard of but never seen, and sometimes I'd wonder if we'd run into Mum because it was coming up to Christmas, but we never did. We didn't run into Tilly either, though I always hoped we might. The country, where we are now, was a closed book. It was something you saw on TV, the nature programs. Sandor says they've only confused me, those programs, so that walking down a Suffolk lane I expect to meet a rhinoceros and to me a cow looking over a gate is part of a herd of stomping buffaloes.

The Railway Arms is where we are living now, in the middle of a little town. You'd expect it to be by the station but it's a good half mile away. Perhaps there was once a railway station here as well. We walked, carrying our stuff. Sandor says he chose it because it didn't look respectable, which is the funniest reason I've ever heard for choosing anything. We'd passed a couple of houses with *Bed and Breakfast* notices outside, bungalows with nice gardens and polished brass doorknockers. Sandor said they might be in the country but they were suburban just the same. The only indication the Railway Arms gave that it had rooms to let was a card in the window of the public bar that said *Vacancy*. Not *Vacancies* but *Vacancy* and when we got inside we found it was just one room they had.

It was late by then and I was hungry. Sandor had his cigarettes, which are food for him, so I went down to the saloon bar and bought what they had, two Cornish pasties, though you could hardly be farther away from Cornwall, two packets of crisps, and a toasted sandwich that had been so many times in and out of the microwave it looked as if it'd been cremated. When I got back up there he was lying on the bed. The bed cover was another one of those woven affairs and the same color, pinkish-gray, as the one in Shepherd's Bush.

"Maybe there's a shop somewhere you can buy them," I said. "A disabled furniture store. Tables with amputated legs a specialty."

He laughed and said something about my imagination. But it was kind, not scornful. "It's another sort of shop I'm going to tell you about," he said, "or another sort of shopkeeper."

Then I knew we were going to have installment two of the Prince and Princess. He patted the bed beside him and I went and sat there, putting my feet up after a moment or two, but taking good care not to sit too close to him and even more to keep my hands in my lap. The curtains weren't drawn but it was pitch-dark outside, a black sky with a blacker slope of land underneath and little pinpricks of light all over it. I spread out the newspaper between us and put the food on it, opening up the packets of crisps. Sandor lit a cigarette.

"Their country house was in a place called Rufina," he said. "It's all green mountains with trees on them. Not like here, not a bit like anywhere here. The trees are olives and cypresses and the mountains are high round hills. There's a little town in the valley and a station where the train goes through to Florence. The villa's name was I Falci. That means The Falcons. When it was foggy in Florence and the city was all gray and gloomy it would be sunny at I Falci, up above the clouds.

"The Princess lived up there while the old man was in Rome and Milan. She had two servants for company and the truffle dog. The truffle dog was a brown spaniel they kept for digging up truffles in the woods."

"I thought truffle was stuff you got inside chocolates," I said.

That was one of the times it wasn't all right to interrupt.

"Christ God," he said, "I don't always believe you're true." I didn't say anything. I'll learn, in time I will. "Now where was I? Oh, yes. Of course, she went out sometimes. Not to Florence much. It's a funny thing about Florence, how the people who live outside it hate it and never go to it while tourists all over the world can't get enough of it. She used to see her neighbors sometimes, she had friends in Rufina. One day she was driving down the hill from the villa, it's a winding road going round and round the mountain, when she saw a car parked broadside across the road in front of her.

"I don't know if she suspected anything. She wasn't Italian, perhaps she didn't realize. But she saw she couldn't get past and she was reversing the car to turn round and go back when another one came up behind her and cut off her escape. There was one man in the car in front and two in the one behind. They tied her up and the suggestion was to put her in the boot. They had a long way to drive, they were going to Rome, and they didn't want her to see their faces. So far they had dealt with that by keeping the sweaters they wore pulled up as far as their eyes.

"They were two Italians and—a foreigner. The Italians were father and son and the younger of them was a medical student. He solved the problem by giving the Princess an injection in the arm which put her out for the next four hours. None of them was what you'd call a professional kidnapper. They were amateurs and amateurs are far more dangerous, for they are inexperienced, unaware of what the going rate for a ransom is in their area and far more inclined to panic if things go wrong. Kidnappers, when they panic, kill their victims.

"But although these three weren't professionals they had educated themselves in the business of abduction, they had read the newspapers, one of them had researched kidnapping as a purported basis for a newspaper article. They knew, for example, that the kind of ransom it would be reasonable to ask would be eight to nine hundred million lire."

"How much is that in pounds?" I said.

"Four to five hundred thousand pounds. But negotiations were still a way off. They took the Princess to a house twenty miles from Rome that they had rented from a holiday agency and where in the main room they had set up a tent. She never saw the house or even the room she was kept in. All she saw was the inside of the tent."

I asked him what stopped her getting out. A peculiar expression came to his face. It was as if he was going to have to say something he didn't want to say but couldn't avoid it. He caught his lower lip under his teeth. His shoulders moved in the faintest shrug.

"She was chained to the wall," he said. There was a bit of a pause while I digested this. "It was a long chain, one end attached to an ankle ring, the other to an upright beam by the fireplace, and it passed under the canvas of the tent. It wasn't a tight chain." Sandor was looking at me intently. For some reason he was very keen for me to believe that about the chain. "It was a good three meters long, and it wasn't heavy, it didn't hurt her. After the car journey, during most of which she was unconscious, she never saw her Italian captors, though later on she often heard them speak. It was the foreigner she saw and for a while she saw him only masked and hooded.

"Before she regained consciousness the elder of the Italians cut off her fingernails. Her fingernails were very long and varnished pale gold. He cut them off as short as a child's might be cut, or a very macho man's, and sent the parings to Prince Piraneso."

"Was that the first he knew?" I said.

"No. Of course it wasn't. There was no point keeping him in ignorance. The younger of the Italians had spoken to him on the phone, told him they had his wife and that he would be sent proof she was with them. That was the proof. It wasn't proof she was alive, of course." He fell silent and I didn't want to say anything. I watched his fingers move sort of mechanically across that bedspread, reaching for a cigarette. "No more now, little Joe," he said. "I'm tired, and we've got things to do tomorrow."

He didn't tell me what things but next day he went off on his own. A task was set for me. I was to go to the public library and see if they had a book called *Suffolk Houses* by someone whose name I forget but a famous architect. If they had I was to join the library and borrow it, take it back to the Railway Arms and see if I could find a house called Jareds in it.

I found the book but they wouldn't let me join the library on account of not being a resident or a ratepayer or having a job there. I sat down at a table and looked through the book for Jareds. It wasn't there. I was having a second look through when the woman who's the licensee of the Railway Arms came up to the table and said hello to me. The upshot of all that was that she lent me her ticket and they let me take the book out.

Sandor was back by five. He'd been to see his mother and driven himself back in her car. One of her cars, that is, a small gray Fiat.

"She gave it to you?" I said. It's always hard for me to believe people (even Sandor) when they tell me their parents have done something generous or kind.

He gave me one of his sidelong looks. "I just took it, little Joe," he said.

"You mean she doesn't know you've got it?"

"I expect she knows now. But she won't do anything. I mean, she may make a fuss but she doesn't know where I am. I'm still in Shepherd's Bush as far as she knows. Don't look so nervous, she won't set the police on me. I'm her only son, right?"

He forgets I haven't the happiest memories in the world of what's due to only sons. But I showed him the book and said something about Jareds not being in there. He lit a cigarette. He started going through the book very carefully. There were big colored photographs of huge old houses and small black-and-white photographs of huge old houses and other photographs of windows and doors and fancy bits of decoration. Sandor was looking at the pictures.

He said, "Aha!" and pushed the book over to me.

The picture his thumb pointed to was not so much of a house as the way up to a house, a long straight drive with high walls on either side of it and thick trees on the other side of the walls. The caption underneath—my new word for the day—said: *The remarkable walls and drive at Atherton Hall, known as the Flint*

Avenue. You could just see a house at the end of this sort of open-topped passage, rather grand-looking, like the buildings in London along the Mall and in Regent's Park, with long windows and pillars with fancy scrolls and leaves on the tops of them.

"Read it aloud," Sandor said. "Not the caption, the text."

It was all architecture and I stumbled a bit over some of the words. Sandor corrected me and then he said I was a quick learner, which pleased me a lot. The man who wrote it said the house was very, very old but had been "Georgianized" and Sandor said that meant they'd built one of those Regent's Park fronts on to it in the 1700s. All the house and the buildings at the back and the stables had been covered up with things called mathematical tiles that looked like stone but weren't really. There were good things inside the house, a winding staircase called a newel stair with carved roses and poppies on the banisters, and a wall painting upstairs done four hundred years ago and called *The Judgement of Paris.* I said I wouldn't have thought people out here in the sticks would have known about a place called Paris in those days but Sandor said this wasn't a place but a person and he'd tell me a story about him one of these days.

All the time I was reading I couldn't understand what made Sandor so interested in the house. The writer got very keen, quite excited really, about this so-called Flint Avenue, which was unique, and the gateposts with "rare" stone lions, but practically everything in the book had something unique about it. And then when I got to the last line I read: *Atherton Hall is now known as Jareds.*

"We'll go and have a look at it tomorrow," Sandor said. "We'll go in the car."

Asking him what he means by this and that, interrupting him for explanations, really isn't on. I have to let a lot pass by. I let him go on talking and gradually I get a picture, I pick up what I can from what I understand. My confusion doesn't show now I've got a beard. My mouth is hidden. It's funny the way people talk about the expression in someone's eyes, his eyes giving him away, and so on, but it's the mouth that shows the feelings. If my lips tremble or my lower lip drops Sandor can't see anymore. I hide my bewilderment under my thick dark curly beard and feel very comfortable and safe.

Last night we went out and bought our supper at the Indian takeaway and more cigarettes for Sandor and talked about getting my DHSS payment transferred to the post office here. It wouldn't be too far to go to sign on. Then he showed me the gray Fiat in the car park at the back.

"We won't take it far till we've changed the registration plates," he said. "Tomorrow we'll go into a quiet lane somewhere and do that."

Having the car makes me feel quite excited. Mum and Dad had a car but it was only used for best. The inside of their garage was a lot better decorated than Sandor's room in Shepherd's Bush or ours at the Railway Arms, white walls and built-in shelves and a plastic shade on the light bulb. The car had a felt cover like the coats they put on the horses in the fields round here. Dad took it out and—I nearly said "groomed" it—*cleaned* it on Sundays and then he'd use it to fetch Mum's father back to us for dinner. It was like its weekly exercise. Tilly and I got a rare outing in it, but I could count the number of times on the fingers of my two hands.

I lay beside Sandor last night thinking about Mum and Dad's car and remembering them and Tilly and how bad it was when she ran away. Something about those memories must have affected me, made me feel lonely or nervous, for I reached out for Sandor in my sleep. Only half-awake, I cuddled up to him and held my arm round his body—oh, so strong and warm!— and the process that's supposed to stop me doing that didn't work. He didn't slap me this time, only pushed me away savagely and kicked my shin. He's got long toenails and I could see blood on my shin when I got up this morning, but he said nothing about the night before so I thought it best to keep quiet.

He handed me the car keys and I had to drive. It was a good thing Tilly's boyfriend number two had taught me. Sandor had a map on his knees. It was a long way to Atherton, a lot farther than Sandor thought when we moved into the Railway Arms, getting on thirty miles. The sky was gray and a bitter wind was blowing. There were no leaves on the trees, they were skeletons with blue bones, but the fields were a bright hard green. We went through one little village after another, all the same they looked to me, and with all the same things in them: houses like Mum had on calendars with thatched roofs and woodwork on the outside of them, a church with a round tower or a square one, great big sheds more like the things you see outside railway stations, and things standing up like big iron bottles Sandor said were silos. The countryside itself was big fields and small dark woods and here and there an enormous house looking like Hampton Court.

Atherton Hall or Jareds was marked on Sandor's map. He told me when he thought we'd find it in the next mile or two. I could tell he was getting excited about something. His voice had got slower and deeper and there was a strange feeling inside the car. The nearest I can get to describing it is to say it was like the atmosphere before a storm, heavy and as if something powerful and struggling is being pushed down.

"There," he said. "Pull into the lay-by."

At first I couldn't see anything, only a high hedge of something prickly on the other side and a fence. But up the road a bit the hedges bent inward and big trees overhung the grass verge. Sandor and I got out and walked up there. It was miles since we'd passed a car or met one and I've already learned you never see anyone on foot in the country. The place was silent and empty. On the other side the huge fields stretched away to the skyline, one with a horse standing in the middle of it, the other planted with something in rows so that it looked like the ribbing on an enormous green sweater.

Where the hedges turned in were two gateposts built of red brick and between them a pair of iron gates which were closed. I saw what the architect who wrote the book meant by "rare." On top of the gatepost on the left stood a lion made of stone. It was just standing there, staring across the top of the iron gates at its friend or mate—another lion, anyway—and this other lion was also standing up but under its front paws it was holding down a man. The stone man was dressed in clothes of olden times, with a frill round his neck like Henry VIII. It was wonderfully done, whoever had made it was very clever, for there was agony and fear in the stone man's face. He'd stretched his poor hands up and got hold of the lion by its lower jaw and was holding on for dear life, but you could see it wasn't going to be any good, and the lion would eat him just the same.

"Only he never will," said Sandor. "It's the Grecian Urn syndrome"—whatever that may mean. "The lion will go on holding him and he'll keep struggling for all eternity." And then he peered through the gates, which were too high to look over the top of.

The long drive with the high walls on either side stretched away just like in the book. The Flint Avenue, the architect had called it, and you could see why. The walls, which were a good eight feet high, were made of stones, the kind you see lying about in the earth round here. On our way back I saw a plowed field covered with stones just like the ones in the walls at Jareds. Sandor said he could just see the house in the far distance and I looked but I wasn't sure if the grayness was house or a piece of sky.

I don't know why I tried to open the gates. I suppose you always do in a situation like that. They looked as if they'd just push because there didn't seem to be any sort of fastening but I couldn't move them. Sandor said, "You haven't got the key."

"What key?" I said. "There isn't a keyhole."

There was an electronic device, he said, you had to have a special key, a kind of personal transmitter, to break a circuit or complete one or something. You'd wave this thing out of your car window and Open Sesame, hey presto! the gates would open before you.

"He's probably got a security screen in the hall so that he can see people arrive and have a two-way conversation with them. And when you get up the drive after dark there'll be an infrared heat sensor that'll detect anything that comes in its path, man on foot or in a car, a fox or a cat even, and all the lights will come blazing on."

"How do you know?" I said.

"I just know."

We got back into the car and drove on a bit to the village. It was a mile away or a bit more. A hundred yards past Jareds and then again half a mile past, Sandor got me to stop and we looked back to try and see the house, but all you could see were fields and little woods and clumps of tall trees and the line of trees and wall, straight as a die, that was the flint avenue. He had some money, maybe he'd stolen it from his mother, and we went in the pub. Sandor listened to the conversations going on around us and said he'd come back here tomorrow, I would drop him off "on my way."

"On my way where?" I said.

"Tomorrow you start your reconnaissance, little Joe," and he explained to me what the word meant. I was to park where we had parked just now and watch the gates, see who came out and went in, note the car numbers, and if *she* came out, driving herself or being driven, follow her.

"Who's she, Sandor? Who is it lives in that place?"

"The book told you," he said. "A man called Apsoland. A very rich man, about fifty years old and an expert on security. Who else do you think lives there?"

I just looked at him. I couldn't be expected to know.

"Who d'you know that marries rich men and might, after what she's been through, like a safety expert?"

Suddenly it was easy. "The Princess," I said.

4

Next day I dropped Sandor off in the village long before the pub opened and he said he'd get a bus back. There's one that runs twice a day or something crazy like that. I thought he'd have done the watching and the shadowing much better than I could but when I suggested it he refused outright. He said I was lazy. I was outside Jareds by ten, parked where we had been the day before. The first thing I did was get out of the car and have another look at those lions.

They fascinate Sandor, I could tell that, but they upset me a bit, I don't like them at all. The person who made them might be very clever but he was sick, too. I've seen a lot of sick people one way and another and I ought to know. There was a man in the hospital who used to bite people, he'd bite the nurses' hands and once I saw him get down and bite someone's ankle like a dog.

And there was a woman who never used her right arm, she said she'd had her right arm amputated, though you could see it there like anyone else's. If either of them had been clever enough to carve things out of stone I reckon they'd have been capable of making those lions, but not an ordinary sane person like me or Sandor.

This time I noticed a box built of bricks and with a wooden lid attached to the side of the left-hand gatepost, the one where the watching lion is, not the man-eater. It was for the mail to go in and had *Jareds* written on it in iron letters. You'd only be able to see it coming from the village direction. I looked through the gates again. There's something about those gates that attracts you to look through them. I've never seen a drive up to a house like this one before, not anywhere. Of course it's true I haven't seen much, I'm not exactly sophisticated, but I don't think there can be many like it just the same, a corridor of stone and trees without a ceiling. Unless the skeleton branches overhead are a ceiling. When the leaves come on them they'll form two roofs that meet.

It was a bit uncanny what happened. I'd believed the two walls went on unbroken right up to the invisible house but this can't be so, for quite suddenly a dog came walking out of one wall and disappeared through the other. For a moment I thought he'd been there all the time, up against the wall, but even if he had been where was he now?

The dog was the same color as the flints. I was peering, telling myself my eyes had deceived me, when a man came through and another dog with him. They were those dogs that look like wolves. The man was very tall, taller than me or Sandor, and big with it, not fat but with big shoulders and a broad chest. Apsoland, I thought. Then I remembered Sandor had said Apsoland was fifty. Of course I couldn't see the man close to, he was at least a hundred yards away, but you know how it is, there's something about the whole person, the way he walks, the air of him, the way he holds his head, that tells his age. This man was younger than that, maybe more than ten years younger.

Sandor hadn't said anything about trying to get in there and explore and he hadn't said not to. I very much wanted to know if there were gates in the walls, if they too operated electronically, and what the grounds of the place were like on either side of the walls. The gateposts were brick and formidable—I hope I'm using that word right, it's the latest Sandor's taught me—but the wire fence that joined on to them was just thin strands. I knew why when I got hold of the top strand. It was electrified.

My hand jumped off and it felt as if someone had struck me a heavy blow on my upper arm. It's illegal, isn't it, setting up something like that for people? It must be. People aren't pigs or cows. When I told Sandor he said, illegal or not, what would stop him if no one knew or those who got caught on it never told?

"I mean, you're not going to run to the police about it, are you?" he said.

I was walking back to the lay-by, guessing I'd have a long cold wait ahead of me, when I heard a car behind me. I was back by the Fiat by the time it turned left at the top of Jareds' drive. It was a Volvo, one of the small ones, the 343s, in that funny pinkish-copper color you never see in any other make of car. For just a second or two I could see the driver and his hand waving something out of the window. The special key, as Sandor had said. The driver looked young, as far as I could see, with dark hair and a handsome profile.

The Volvo slid into the drive. In a way I wished I'd still been there by the gates so that I could have seen them open and the car go down that flint avenue, but that would have been a mistake, of course. I wasn't supposed to let anyone see me. Time dragged slowly when I was back in the car. I wished I'd brought something to eat but I hadn't thought of it and I started to get very hungry. Eventually, at about three, I drove off into the village, hoping I wouldn't see Sandor. I don't really mean I hoped I wouldn't see him, I can't imagine the time ever coming when I wouldn't want to see him. I meant I didn't want him catching me not at my post.

The pub was closed. When we got round-the-clock licensing hours last year we thought pubs would stay open at all hours but they don't. They close when they feel like it. I found the village shop which had a café part to it where they had stale sandwiches and cans of Coke and Sprite on sale. It was just as well, as it happened, that I wasn't at my post because as I left the café I saw the man with the two dogs who had crossed the flint avenue in that mysterious way. The dogs weren't with him this time. I knew it was him, though I'd find it hard to say how. On TV, in detective serials, the police ask witnesses how they can be sure a suspect is who they think it is, what makes them think so. Well, maybe I'd have to say you couldn't get two men that size and height in such a small place, and you'd never get two with all that and the same large round head covered with bristly fair hair.

He was with a crowd of other people, all the rest women. It took me a minute or two to realize it was outside a school they were all waiting. The kids began to come out. It was just gone 3:30. The one that came up to the big man was a girl with long golden hair down her back, a little girl, I can't tell kids' ages, perhaps she was six or seven.

Suppose she's the Princess's daughter, I thought, and the idea made me feel quite excited. Sandor had said the Princess was beautiful and this kid was too. She and he walked off together, turned down a side street and got into the coppery-pink Volvo I'd seen the other man driving.

Of course I followed them. At Jareds' gates I didn't dare stop. The Volvo driver signaled turning left and I just had to overtake him and keep straight on. I had a lot to tell Sandor. He was lying on the bed when I got back, smoking and reading a book in a foreign language. The room was full of smoke, hanging in the funny way it sometimes does, in thin blue sheets.

"Do you know what a verb is, little Joe?" he said.

It's best to be honest about your ignorance. I shook my head. He explained it was a word of doing and I think I've got the hang of it.

"In the Schwyzertütsch language, that's Swiss-German," he said, "there's no verb 'to love.' " I don't know if he'd just found that out. It made him laugh. "Isn't that amazing? No verb 'to love.' " I told him about the Princess's little girl.

"She hasn't any children," he said, and he sounded cross. "This one must belong to one of the servants. They've got servants, you know, they're rich. They've got a driver called Garnet—Ben Garnet—and a married couple who live in. Did you think the Princess did her own housework and drove herself about?"

I hadn't thought about it. In a way the whole thing was still like a fairy tale to me. "Tell me a bit more of the story," I said.

For a moment I thought my request would be ignored. He had gone back to his book but I could see he wasn't reading it, staring at the print rather, and not seeing it. Then he laid it facedown, took a cigarette, and held it in his fingers for a while without lighting it.

"There can't be much suspense in it for you now," he said. "You know she got away, you know they didn't kill her."

"I still want to know what happened."

"All right." He felt about on the bed for his matches. I took the box off the mantelpiece, lit a match and held the flame to his cigarette. He took hold of my wrist to steady it. Does he know that it's he who causes the unsteadiness? I wonder. "The second time the kidnappers called the Prince he asked them for proof of life."

"Proof of *life?*"

"He might never have been kidnapped nor had any member of his family kidnapped, but he knew all about it. Wasn't he a rich Roman with a shop on Kidnap Street? He practically had a degree in Kidnap Studies. That's why it may have been bad for him, worrying, a horror, but it was never all that much of a shock. It had happened to the neighbors already, hadn't it? He knew the next step was to ask for proof of life. Are you going to negotiate, raise the cash, pay it, for a victim who's already dead?"

"It seems a bit cold-blooded," I said.

"Yes, in a different social climate maybe. When in Rome you do as the Romans do. He wasn't cold-blooded. He didn't go to the police."

"Did the kidnappers tell him not to?"

"I don't think they bothered," Sandor said. "This was Italy where everyone was very sophisticated and blasé about kidnappings. They took it for granted he would but he didn't."

"Why didn't he?"

"He knew that if it became public knowledge, if the police knew and it got into the papers, the investigating magistrate in charge of the case would have frozen his assets. It was generally done to prevent the payment of ransoms and he knew that. What perhaps he didn't know was that as a deterrent it was unworkable, it only upset families and alienated them from the authorities but it never prevented the payment of ransoms. Let's say he only had a third-class degree in kidnap studies.

"They gave him proof of life. They sent him a tape the Princess had made. It was the usual thing, she'd been instructed what to say, the foreigner instructed her, and she told her husband how uncomfortable she was, how they'd threatened it wouldn't just be fingernail parings next time but whole fingernails. They told the Prince to go to the Montemario Observatory on the top of one of the Seven Hills of Rome and there he'd find his next instructions in a cigarette packet in a corner of the statue there. That reminds me . . ."

I handed Sandor another cigarette. He lit it and stared into the distance. Somehow I knew I wouldn't be hearing any more that day.

"Where's the writing paper?" he said. "Get me out a sheet of paper and an envelope, will you? There's a post goes out at five-thirty and you can catch it if you hurry."

I caught the post with Sandor's letter and the next morning I went back to Jareds. We'd put a different set of index plates on the car and I was wearing a pair of dark glasses Sandor bought me in the town. My best friend wouldn't have known me. Well, I suppose Sandor's my best friend and of course he knew me, but Tilly, let's say, she wouldn't have. Things are different now, but that morning my small-chinned face and lips that tremble so easily were covered by beard and mustache and the glasses covered my cautious eyes. I looked older. I looked like a character in disguise in a TV program.

I didn't see the gates open, only the car emerge. Not the Volvo this time but a long, elegant pale-gray car I later found out was a Bentley. The big man was driving, Garnet. There was someone sitting in the back, in the far corner of the backseat. I couldn't see her at all clearly, but I knew enough to see it was a "her," a woman.

I followed them. It was easy to do that because there wasn't much traffic. I expected him to take her shopping somewhere but the Bentley went on and on, round the outskirts of Bury St. Edmunds and on to the big road that goes to Newmarket and Cambridge. The name Newmarket means something to me because of racing, Dad used to go to a betting shop down the road from where we lived, and as for Cambridge, Sandor had been to a college there.

I couldn't have kept up with the Bentley if Garnet had driven it fast, but he kept to the slow lane mostly. Once or twice another car got between it and me, and that was all to the good because it made it look as if I wasn't following but just happened to be there. Garnet was three cars ahead when I saw the Bentley signaling it was taking an exit to the left. The sign pointed to Cambridge.

It had to pull up at the entrance to a roundabout and I could see that the woman in the back had blond hair, neither long nor short. I hoped she'd turn her head but she didn't. It wasn't the center of the city they were making for, I could soon tell that, but a sort of suburb, an estate of big newish houses on the outskirts. Garnet stopped outside the gates of a bungalow, the kind of thing they call ranchstyle, with a garden full of daffodils and little Christmas trees and a big tree in flower. I drove on past, turned right and right again, and parked the car behind where the Bentley was, sort of diagonally opposite and just inside the side turning.

Garnet was holding the rear door open. The woman got out. I knew it was the Princess but somehow I'd expected her to be big and colorful and dramatic-looking, someone like Dolly Parton say, and I'd expected her to be dressed in the kind of showy expensive clothes Tilly would love to have. The woman I saw looked like a young girl. She was very slim and slight and she wore jeans and a sweater with a woolly shawl wrapped round her. Beside Garnet she seemed quite small, or he looked very big beside her. He's a large man, a giant, but thin with it. He looks fit.

She went up the path between the daffodils and Garnet watched her. He watched her till someone invisible opened the door and let her in. Then he got back in the car. I sat there, not knowing what to do next. There didn't seem anything I could do but wait till the Princess came out again. It was so quiet and peaceful, no one about, only the occasional car sliding by. Birds were singing. I was wondering what it would be like to live in a place like this, so tranquil and wealthy and calm, when I saw Garnet get out of the car again. He stood in the roadway, looking in my direction. Then he crossed over, strolling easily, and came up to the car.

He couldn't be coming to speak to me, I couldn't see any reason why he would, so I thought he must be going to call at one of the houses down here, or maybe he was on his way to find a place to eat in, it was coming up to 12:30. When he tapped on the window it made me jump. I wound it down, though I shouldn't have, I know that now. I should have turned my face away and driven off, not looked up at him the way I did.

"You've been following me," he said.

I just shook my head. "No."

"Get out of here," he said. "Get out of here and go back to wherever you belong."

As if I was a creature that crawled out from under a leaf or something. He stood in front of the Fiat and wrote the number down on a bit of paper he took out of his jacket pocket. Much good that would do him. My first thought was what would Sandor say and I wondered if I'd have to tell him.

I got into the habit of eating a lot when I first went to my foster parents. That was being nice to children, unlimited television and unlimited food. As well as the TV downstairs Tilly and I each had a set in our bedrooms and a chocolate biscuit put on our pillows at night like in good hotels. (I've seen that on TV.) It made an amazing impression on the Social Services, who called it love. Mum—I can't call her my mother though I've tried—used to say, "No child of mine will ever go hungry," a funny remark since she had never had a child and never could, which was why Tilly and I were there. Sandor, on the other hand, doesn't eat much. Smokers don't. I don't know why, because it's not as if the smoke goes down the same way as the food. He was writing another letter but he covered it up with his foreign book when I came in. He said to me, "Did you bring any cigarettes?"

"I can go out and get some."

Immediately I knew he wouldn't like that. He doesn't like it when you say something that isn't an answer to his question. "I know you can," he said, and then, "If you knew how tired I get of translating every fucking thing you say. You mean you didn't bring any, right?"

I did it again. It's because he makes me nervous. "I think there's one left in a packet somewhere."

"Christ God," he said.

I found the cigarette and lit it without thinking before I gave it to him. Sometimes he likes me to do that and sometimes he hates it. This time it was all right. I put the ashtray the Railway Arms provided on the night table. The night table, which is the only one and on Sandor's side, is made of wicker, only one of its legs somehow broke off and got replaced with a wooden one. The ashtray has *Lygon Arms, Broadway* written on it. Sandor said, "How did you get on?"

"All right. Fine." He often knows when I'm lying but he didn't know then. I gave myself away when he asked for a description of Garnet, what was he like, and when I'd told him about Garnet being tall and big I said he had a voice sort of halfway between mine and Sandor's own, if you can imagine such a thing.

"How did you come to hear his voice?"

That was it.

"Don't tell me you let him see your face?"

Someone with an accent like Sandor's can be much more intimidating than a person who speaks ordinarily like I do. It's funny, because on television threatening people usually seem to talk cockney or your average south London. They should do something about that. They should be told that the voice of authority talks like Sandor, Received English Pronunciation it's called, REP, that you get from a public school and an old university or learn it in acting school. The way Sandor said that about did Garnet see my face was sort of steely and cold and disgusted and going up to a high note combined with a hiss on that last word, face or "feysse."

"I'm sorry, Sandor," I said, "but I had my glasses on and I only opened the window a bit. He won't recognize me."

"You're damn right he won't when I've finished with you."

A bluish haze hung between us. I've never smoked, though I've tried, I really have, because I think if we had something like that in common it would somehow bring Sandor and me closer. He sat up and threw the pinkish-gray bedspread off him. He was wearing his blue denim shirt and his black jeans and my dark blue Marks and Spencer sweater Tilly gave me for Christmas two years ago. His shoes were by the side of the bed, black leather shoes. Sandor won't wear trainers the way I do, he hates them. He sat there and pushed his long thin feet into his shoes.

"Garnet won't recognize me," I said. "I know he won't. He only caught a glimpse of me for a minute or two. You know— you said—one dark man with a beard looks much like another."

"One fair man without a beard doesn't look at all like a dark man with a beard, so that's the way it's going to be."

"But why does it matter?" I had to ask, though I knew I wouldn't get an answer. "What's it for?"

He shook his head, not the way people do when they mean no but when they're impatient.

"I really don't want to shave off my beard, Sandor," I said, very brave. I have to learn to stand up to him sometimes, I have to.

He looked at me. He gave me one of those smiling looks that make me go cold. "You won't have to. I'm going to do it."

Sandor shaves with a straight razor, a cutthroat. I'd never seen one till I saw his. The double blade folds away into a handle of mother-of-pearl. He told me it was his great-grandfather's and it came from some high-class shop in London, in Jermyn Street. Sandor never cuts himself. He enjoys shaving because of the skill he has to use, the precision involved in passing that terrible gleaming sliver-thin blade along his jaw, which is like a blade itself.

I knew he wouldn't cut me but I didn't like the idea of it just the same. I have a funny idea about Sandor, about what he wants from me and to do to me. I'm not so ignorant that I don't know he wants control. Well, he has control. But I sometimes think he wants to—it sounds mad—well, to turn me into a masochist. He wants me to like pain. He wants me to like him giving me pain and humiliating me. Perhaps I am a bit mad or, as Sandor says, I do have imagination.

"I'd rather do it myself," I said, and realized in saying that that I'd yielded, I'd consented to the loss of my beard. Sandor had done it again, tripped me up and caught me in his strings and tied me.

"Sit in the chair," he said.

There's only one. Black carved wood, very chipped and broken, filthy dark-red velvet upholstery, the seat with a round basin-shaped dip in the middle. Sandor lit a cigarette. He started sharpening his great-grandfather's razor on a leather belt thing he calls a strop. I put one of the pillows on the chair and sat down on it in front of the mirror. The mirror has got an ugly woman called Jane Avril kicking up her legs painted or somehow printed on it, but it isn't genuinely old, just a cheap copy from Homebase. Sandor didn't start with the razor. He cut my beard off with nail scissors and then he cut my hair.

The way I came out from behind my beard when he started shaving me reminded me of something I thought I'd forgotten: the way Mum used to wake me up in the mornings. She'd come into the room, very bright, and say, "Good afternoon," though it was never after seven-thirty, and then she'd pull the covers off me. With one single movement of her arm she'd pull it off and the cold air would hit me. Mum and Dad had four TV sets in the house and more packets of cake and biscuits than Ipswich Sainsbury's, but they didn't have central heating. The cold hit me and made me gasp. It was a bit like that feeling all over again when Sandor shaved my cheeks clean of all that kindly, disguising, *warm,* cuddly, comforting hair.

But apart from that it was all right. The razor didn't hurt. It just tickled a bit, very lightly. I felt myself starting to relax, though I had to exercise control to stop myself from putting my hands up to cover my face, my stripped naked face. I made myself sink a little into the chair, expel my breath, let my shoulders sag. My chin looked bigger than I remembered it. That was good. My cheeks were pink, though that might have been just from the friction. Sandor moved the razor across my upper lip very gently. There are no words, are there, for that bit between your mouth and your nose except upper lip, but the bit below it is really your lip. Sandor was very careful not to graze my actual lip.

I was beginning to think it was all rubbish the ideas I had about him wanting to turn me into a masochist, I was really relaxing. I thought he had finished. I was looking, with a very slowly growing confidence, at my new face, when he lifted the razor off and held it a millimeter from the skin where that little cleft is under the nostrils. Did I move my head a fraction, the better to see my jawline? I don't think so. I think—know—Sandor drew the razor an inch across the tender cleft and it felt like an insect stinging. The blood welled, a row of beads at first, a brooch of beads, then a stream that trickled into my mouth.

5

In the evenings we go out and see what takeaway is on offer. These country towns are strange places. They aren't like what you'd think from the descriptions in guidebooks. You expect them to be pretty and cozy with nice fresh air and happy people leading relaxed lives. You expect shops selling good fresh country food, locally killed meat and free-range eggs and apples and pears from the fruit farms. The reality is different.

For one thing, they have great sprawling industrial estates, at least one in each town and some have two. And even if they're small they have suburbs of little new houses. You never see any people walking about the industrial estates among the factories, but they must be there because at four-thirty or five the cars start coming out, thousands of them, they come pouring out, clogging up the roads and queuing at traffic lights. Sandor says they built those factories to stop the local people going away, and if this is true it certainly worked. You can't really go out in those towns in the daytime, you can't move for people shopping, the crowds of them, though what they find to buy God knows. Every other shop is a bank or a building society and the real shops are run-down branches of unpopular food chains and souvenir knick-knack places and stores selling sports gear.

Each town has about fifteen pubs and one, or at most two, good restaurants where Mr. and Mrs. Apsoland could afford to eat but Sandor and I never could in our wildest dreams. Well, Sandor's wildest dreams, the noisy ones he often has. I never dream. Then there'll be the Chinese restaurant and the tandoori takeaway and the fish-and-chip shop. Only this last is usually closed by the time you want to eat in the evening. The whole of the town is closed and has become a spooky place.

I suppose the hearts of these towns are still pretty, if you like that sort of thing. If you like houses that look like pictures on calendars with the top floor hanging out over the street, and Georgian houses built of pale gray brick the color of cement and winding lanes with walls made of gray and black flints. There are never any people about in the evenings. And I mean not any. It's stuffed with cars and shoppers and cyclists and traffic wardens in the day, but at night it's empty and it's silent. The narrow streets are the gray of a beach and somehow windswept. There may not be any wind but they're windswept. If there was anyone coming you'd hear their footsteps echoing on cobbles a mile off. And sometimes there is, just to give you a shock. Just to frighten you and make you jump, you'll hear the footsteps echoing and a bunch of boys will come out of one of those lanes into the marketplace. They still dress like punks, even now, greasy black synthetics with artificial holes in them and metal studs and weird colors on their hair. Even now. You'd hardly believe it but last week I saw a boy with a safety pin through one nostril.

That doesn't happen much though, the boys I mean. Mostly there's emptiness and quiet, orange light seen through the pub windows, their doors shut, silhouettes of quiet people. You never hear a sound from the pubs. Litter blows about, left behind by the daytime hordes. The Chinese restaurant is so dark from the outside you can't tell whether it's open or not. Sandor and I walk across the marketplace and the stone walls throw back an echo of our footfalls. Our footsteps ring on the old flagstones. The Indian place is open and we order prawn vindaloo and basmati rice and poppadoms. The mango chutney we already have in a jar on the lower shelf of the wicker night-table.

Sandor said while we sat waiting for the curry, "Tomorrow we'll move, little Joe."

"Move where?" I said.

"On. On to nearer where the Princess lives." He named the town that was only a mile away from her village. "We'll go there, see what's going. We'll see what we're offered in the Railway Arms' Yellow Pages."

The tandoori man was looking at me. When he saw I saw him looking he dropped his eyes in that meek way Indians have. We may all look the same to black people—Afro-Caribbeans, that is—but we don't to Indians. They're Caucasians like us, Sandor says. I could see the tandoori man was wondering if I was the same person Sandor had been in there with before. He was looking at my hair, now a dull mustard yellow.

"I wish you'd take that plaster off your lip," Sandor said. "It would heal more quickly if you didn't cover it."

He had never apologized for cutting me. He had never said anything about it till now, two days later. I knew what he had been thinking though, what he would have said if he had spoken: there, that's for letting Garnet see your face, that'll teach you not to do it again. I'm keeping the plaster on because I don't want to see what's underneath. Not yet. I don't want to see if it will leave a scar. It doesn't feel sore, it doesn't feel anything. Jim, who is the proprietor or licensee or just the barman, I don't know which, of the Railway Arms, hasn't said a word, but I believe he thinks I'm someone else. His wife who lent me the library ticket doesn't know me. They think Sandor is a raving queer and I am the second little friend he has taken up to his room.

The curry came and we walked slowly back across the market-place, the windswept open space with the war memorial standing up in the middle of it. In the daytime there are so many people about and so many stalls, cheap sweaters hanging on rails, cheap wicker furniture, tables full of Women's Institute cakes and lemon curd, that you can't see the war memorial. There are dozens of names engraved on it, hundreds maybe. On the step someone has put a wreath of plastic poppies, though November was months ago.

It has got dark. You can't see the green hills and the black woodlands any longer. You can't see the view from our room. The saloon bar is only half full and there are just four old men in the public. The Railway Arms isn't popular because it's not an Adnams' house and you can't play pool there, only worn-out fruit machines. Sandor is paying £7 a night for our room and he says maybe he could afford a bit more.

I sat on the bed and he sat on the chair and we ate our curry. He left half his rice so I ate that too and all the poppadoms. He lit a cigarette before I'd finished. He always does. I thought how much I'd like a room with television.

"Tell me about Garnet," Sandor said.

He hadn't mentioned him since Thursday night and of course I hadn't. I said carefully, "What d'you want to know?"

"I know nothing about him, only that he's the Princess's driver and I know his name."

"He's a big tall guy," I said. "Maybe forty or a bit less. He's got a sort of bull neck and a round head, very short fair hair. I think his eyes are blue. He'd make a good bodyguard." A thought struck me. "Is that what he is?"

"Maybe."

"If you don't know where he comes from, Sandor, and you don't know what he looks like, how do you know his name?"

For a moment I thought he wasn't going to tell me. "How do you think?"

I nearly said, the phone book. I nearly said that, as if you could look someone up in a telephone directory when you don't know their name. "I don't know."

"They've got a post-and-newspapers box at the top of the drive. Did you notice?"

Under the lion, the one that watches, not the one that's holding the man.

"I went over there and looked inside. A few times. The third time I was lucky and their papers were there. *The Times* and the *Daily Telegraph,* as you might expect, with *Apsoland* written on in pencil—misspelled, also as you might expect—and the *Independent* marked *Garnet.* What a fellow like that thinks he's doing reading a quality newspaper I can't imagine."

"Just Garnet?" I said. "How d'you know his name's Ben?"

Sandor never ceases surprising me. I guess—suppose—it's truer to say he shocks me. "I don't know," he said. "It may not be. It's what I call him. I read this survey, said Ben was the most popular name for a male dog in Britain."

He lit another cigarette and said to bring the paper our curry had been wrapped in and we'd stuff it in Jim's bin. And we'd use the phone that's in the passage between the bars. Sandor doesn't like the smell of food wrappings in our room overnight, though he doesn't mind how much smoke there is. We went downstairs and I could hear those yokely voices from behind the saloon door, which was ajar, and someone laughing in a thick gurgling way as if his mouth was full of spit. Sandor gave me the Yellow Pages to hold while he dialed. He'd marked a couple of places, a pub called the Three Tuns and the Lindsey Guest House. The pub couldn't take us, said they didn't take guests anymore, but the Lindsey place could.

"It has to be a twin-bedded room," Sandor said.

He knows how to hurt me. And I'll never get to like it. I'll never get to beg him to hurt me, which may be what he wants. That gave me more pain than cutting my lip with his great-grandfather's razor. He hung up the receiver and said we'd go there tomorrow.

Newspapers are our only luxury, the *Sun* or the *Star* for me and the *Independent* for Sandor. On Sundays I go out and buy him the *Observer* and get the *News of the World* for myself. Sandor says I read the *News of the World* for the dirty bits and the sensation but that isn't really true. I read it because of Tilly. She once said to me that it's the best paper to advertise in because more people read it than any other Sunday paper and it's where solicitors advertise for those who may be going to benefit from wills. If some rich person dies without making a will and hasn't any family, they advertise for his relations. Of course, I don't for a moment think some rich old uncle of mine I've never heard of is going to die and some lawyer is going to want to find me. Of course I don't. But I have other unknown people in my past, don't I, people that I think I can remember? I sometimes think, one day they'll start looking for me.

The evenings in our room are very long. Once or twice Sandor has let me go down into the bar and sit there and have a drink. It was my own dole money I used, so I wasn't depriving him. But now he says he doesn't want me to be conspicuous, he especially doesn't want people to see that my appearance has been changed. It's all right if they don't know I'm the same person, if they don't realize this person with the bare face and the yellow hair is Joe Herbert. But the tandoori man knew something. If he could tell, what would an intelligent member of my own race make of it? Sandor, of course, doesn't count Jim as being intelligent.

So I can't go downstairs. I have already changed the registration plates on the car. I have packed. I have read the *Sun* and all of the *Independent* I can face and there is nothing to do but sit in the chair and look at Sandor lying on the bed, reading. He has propped himself up with our two pillows and the poverty bedspread rolled up under them and he is reading a book called *Nightmare Abbey*. There are sounds, it is not silent here in the evenings. From downstairs comes the tinkle glass makes when it taps other glass or is set down on something hard and cold, the buzz of voices, words indistinguishable, an occasional shout of laughter, hands clapping. They are playing darts, it must be darts night. None of it has the least effect on Sandor, who reads, turns the page.

Once I timed him with his digital watch that shows the seconds moving. His mother gave it to him and he hated it, so I got it. When it is a novel he's reading he takes a maximum of fifty-five seconds and a minimum of thirty-three seconds to read a page, but when it is something—well, heavier, I suppose you'd say—then he takes a maximum of 1 minute fifteen seconds and a minimum of fifty-seven seconds. Timing him and working out the average was quite an interesting way to pass an evening. If he knew he never said. I don't think he knew.

It was just before eleven when he spoke to me. He hadn't said a word for two hours. The bell ringing in the bar downstairs got through his glass wall or else it was coincidence that he put *Nightmare Abbey* down just at that moment. He said to me, "Think of them all down there. What do you suppose they're all doing?"

"Drinking up their drinks and going home," I said. My voice creaked with disuse. Of course I had said the wrong thing again, once more put my foot in it.

"Not in the bar, you fool. Who gives a shit what clods like that do? I was thinking of the people at Jareds."

I looked at him and I realized something: that this was what he thought about—always. It obsessed him. It had ever since we first met. His books distracted him for a while. They were like the aspirins you take when you've got a headache. They kill the pain for two hours and then it comes back. But was thinking of Jareds pain for him or was it pleasure?

He's extraordinary, he's so changeable. His expression was really sad, tragic almost, and suddenly he burst out laughing. It embarrasses me a bit when he does that, I don't know what to do or say. He laughed and then he started singing:

"I come from Castlepatrick and me heart is on me sleeve,
But a lady stole it from me on St. Gallowglass's Eve."

"What's that?" I asked. I can always ask for information, I can always do that. "What you said, gallow-something?"

"Didn't you tell me you're an Irishman, little Joe?"

"So far as I know," I said. "Half, anyway."

"In ancient Ireland and the Western Highlands a gallowglass was a chief's servant."

"You mean that's me, that's what I am?" I said.

He laughed again and said, if I liked, if that was what I wanted. After that he seemed to fall into a sort of dream, lying back and looking across at the window. I won't say "looking out of the window" because there was nothing to see, only a black horizon and a slightly less black sky with lots of stars but no moon. I went off down the passage to the toilet and then down to the bathroom. When I came back Sandor was in bed—that is, under the covers—smoking another cigarette and I saw that he had drawn the curtains.

I turned out the top light. There isn't a bed lamp on my side, but since I never read, that doesn't matter much. I put the digital watch that Sandor's mother had given him on the floor and a glass of water with it and thought that when it was dark in the room I would ease off my upper lip the plaster that I had loosened in the bathroom.

Sometimes Sandor doesn't turn the lamp off for hours but last night he did. His back was to me and mine to him. That's what he prefers. I tried to prize the plaster off with my thumbnail, but the hairs have grown quite a lot under it and they stung as it pulled.

"Stop fidgeting, could you?" Sandor said.

So I lay still and sleepless, thinking about Tilly and wondering what she was up to these days. I wondered if she was still fat or if at last she'd stuck to one of those diets, if she was still with the boyfriend after the one that left her the camper and, come to that, if she still lived in the camper. Sandor would say to me, "Caravan, not camper. You're not American." It made me smile, thinking of that and the way I could sometimes, just occasionally, predict what he would say. I knew what I was now, what I was for him: a gallowglass, the chief's servant.

Four days ago we moved into the Lindsey Guest House. Sandor says most of the people who stay here are not tourists but workmen who come to the district to do a job, building something, for instance, or installing some sort of fancy kitchen or bathroom. They can't drive from and to London every day so they need somewhere to stay where they can have TV in their rooms and a three-course meal at night.

That costs £25 a day, so we don't have the TV or the meal or even a shower but pay £15 for a twin-bedded room that is very small but clean and has a washbasin with hot water. Something rather wonderful has happened to Sandor, or rather, he has made something wonderful happen. When he went to see his mother to get the car, the bill or invoice or whatever it's called for her American Express card had come and she was opening it. On the envelope was an extra bit inside the flap asking the card holder if he or she would like to provide a card for some other member of their family, the cardholder, of course, agreeing to pay the account when it came in. She left it lying about on the kitchen table so Sandor tore that bit off. It didn't show, he said, you couldn't tell it had ever been there.

He can do his mother's signature so that it looks exactly like hers. The printing bit was no problem. He filled it in asking for a card for her son and gave as his address the post office box number he uses in Ipswich. We weren't sure that it would work, but it did. The card came yesterday. He says we should use it all we can for a month. She won't refuse to pay up but most likely she'll withdraw the card as soon as she sees what has happened. So Sandor has put the car into a garage in Ipswich for a respray. We are going to have a color called rowanberry, that being the furthest away from gray.

We can't pay by American Express at the Lindsey Guest House but Sandor doesn't mind about that. He has his income and can manage. What we are doing is buying all sorts of things. Sandor has stocked up with cigarettes in packs of two hundred. We can't use the card in pubs but we can in wine shops, so we have bought bottles of spirits and a case of wine. Sandor thought we might even stockpile petrol but that proved impractical. You can hardly move in our room as it is, what with the bag of registration plates, the bottles, our two new jackets and leather boots, all the paperback books, and—wonder of wonders—my birthday present from Sandor, a tiny color TV with a three-inch by two-inch screen.

We never eat in the guest house but outside, as we always have. There is an Indonesian takeaway place here and the food they do seems more substantial. The trouble is that we are lost without the car. I suggested we walk the mile to Jareds, just to do some more reconnaissance, keep our hand in, but Sandor said you attract more attention to yourself walking in these parts than you would in any sort of car. They'd take less notice of you in a beach buggy or an armored truck than they would of someone on foot.

So last night he showed me his collection of cuttings about the Princess. They were in the case that came open and he snapped at me that the contents were private. There was this magazine cover in his collection—he calls it his portfolio. It was thirteen years old, which means I was only fourteen at the time it came out and I don't suppose I saw many glossy magazines.

Women aren't beautiful anymore, are they? I mean, women in films and on TV and singers and people like that. Real women have never been beautiful as far as I'm concerned. But Tilly once got hold of an old book called the *Picturegoer Annual of 1938* or some such date and there were all these black-and-white photos in it of film stars, Claudette Colbert and Loretta Young and Hedy Lamarr and a lot of others I've forgotten the names of, but the point is they were all beautiful, sort of flawless. An annual like that would be a joke now. Half the actresses on TV have got faces like an old boot.

The only beautiful women left are models and even they are starting to go off, starting to get "interesting" instead. But not thirteen years ago, not when Nina Abbott was the most photographed woman in Britain. That's the Princess's name, Nina. Well, she was beautiful all right. Her face reminded me of some of those faces in Tilly's annual. Very fair and starry-eyed and with a sort of wistful look. Perfect features and not a mark on her skin. Of course she was no more than eighteen. On the magazine cover she was loaded with jewels. There were great heavy earrings like chandeliers hanging from her ears and they were done in diamonds and blue stones Sandor said were sapphires. More diamonds and sapphires were round her neck.

He must have twenty pictures of her from that time, photographs of her in furs and in evening gowns, modeling for some big Paris designer, and more and more magazine covers. They didn't mean much to me. The most interesting was the one from a newspaper of her getting married to the old guy, Prince Piraneso, in Monte Carlo. The picture was ridiculous because she was so young and fresh and gorgeous and he had a face like what Sandor had said, a Gila monster, something horridum, a maxi-lizard in a tailcoat. The heading over the picture was "Perfume Prince Weds His Primrose." Then there were a couple of photos of him and her at parties somewhere in Europe, only the print was in Italian and I couldn't read it.

I kept wondering where I'd seen her before, her or her picture, and quite recently. It wasn't in Cambridge. I hadn't seen her face then. "Does she still look like that?" I said.

That made him laugh. "She's only a bit over thirty and she has all the means money can buy to keep her young. You saw her. Couldn't you see?"

"She was too far off," I said.

They had done a photograph of her for one of his perfume advertisements. Again the writing part was in Italian so I don't know what it said. She was there in what looked like nothing but furs and pearls, though plenty of both because she was covered up to the neck. A cut-glass scent bottle shimmered in the background. Her hair, which was a kind of pale gold like the gold of a wedding ring, was piled up on her head with strings of pearls twisted through it. That was it, I knew it then. That was the tiny picture I'd seen on the powder box in Oxford Street.

Sandor had another picture of her in deepest black at the old boy's funeral. Again an Italian newspaper. He said the English ones took no notice of it, they'd forgotten about Nina Abbott by that time. She was standing in a graveyard full of tombs and pillars and cypress trees, holding the arm of another old man. Maybe it was the one she married next. Sandor had no photo of her wedding to Powell Paton, only a picture of the two of them going aboard someone's yacht in Genoa. He was a big strong-looking guy, maybe only in his fifties, and he was wearing boxer shorts and a straw hat.

"What happened to him?" I said.

"He dropped dead of a heart attack in a house he had at Martha's Vineyard. They'd only been married five months. He left her a lot of money."

"And a lot of jewels?" I said.

"Enough to buy a lot of jewels with. She never went back to Italy. I have to admit I don't know where she went. She lay low. When she reappeared she was married to Apsoland."

"What kind of a name is that?" I said. It had always puzzled me.

"Jewish, I should think. A corruption of Absalom. Do you know that's what you said to me, little Joe, when we first knew each other, what kind of a name is that? What kind of a name is Sandor, you said."

He's being very kind to me at present. I feel like it's Christmas all the time. I wish I could touch him. Not for anything nasty, I don't mean that. I wish I could—well, what I'd like best would be for him to let me hold his hand. Instead I put my new TV on and watched *EastEnders* while he read a medical book called *Cancer Ward*. The plaster has come off my lip and I don't think the razor cut is going to leave a scar.

I look younger without a beard, I know that. The two men staying here who are builders, Sandor says, take me for a boy of eighteen. Kevin, the younger one, told him so and Sandor didn't argue with him. Les, who is fifty, seems embarrassed in our company and perhaps the two of them take us for a gay couple. Kevin is always saying things like, "Live and let live is what I say, it wouldn't do if we were all the same," and "You've got to make allowances in this day and age."

The day before yesterday we went to Ipswich on the bus and fetched the Fiat. It's the color of tomato ketchup and Sandor blinked a bit when he first saw it. He said he expected something a bit quieter. One thing, no one who'd seen the young man with the dark hair and beard driving the gray Fiat would connect him with the fair-haired clean-shaven one in the rowanberry job.

The past two weeks have been spent finding out all we can about Jareds and the people who live there. Sandor has met a man in one of the village pubs whose wife goes there twice a week to clean. Before he even spoke to him he heard him telling a friend that the Apsolands had a foreign couple working for them but the woman couldn't manage that big house on her own. His wife, whose name is Doreen, is afraid of the German shepherd dogs. I am too. I don't like dogs.

Sandor pretended he was looking for a house to rent. He said he'd heard there was a cottage at Jareds that was vacant. Doreen's husband, Stan, soon put him right there. The Apsolands' chauffeur (that was the word he used) lived in the cottage with his young daughter who was at the village school with Stan and Doreen's daughter. He hasn't got a wife, she'd died or run off or something. Stan was moaning because Doreen lives a mile away from Jareds and has to go to work on her motor scooter and it was terrible in the bad weather. Sandor had to buy him and his friend drinks and of course he couldn't pay for those with his mother's American Express card.

I followed Garnet and the Princess again. This time I was much more careful. At first I thought they were going to Cambridge, though it wasn't Thursday, but they only went as far as Bury. All the way I kept three cars behind them and several times I thought I'd lost the Bentley, but it's a conspicuous car and you can see a long way ahead on that A134. To my surprise, when she got out of the car in the car park he got out with her. I mean, of course he got out to open the door for her, but instead of getting back in to wait for her he went with her. If she'd had a shopping bag I expect he'd have carried that but she didn't have one.

I got a closer look at her. Sandor was right, she's still beautiful, she hasn't changed much. She's very slim and she only looks little when she's standing next to Garnet who must be six feet four. It was a lovely day, quite hot for April, and she had a suit on, pale gray with a white shirt, very fresh and crisp-looking. Her hair isn't long or short but cut to hang like a bell to the middle of her neck. She hasn't a fringe. Whatever it was like when she was eighteen it's now the sort of blond hair that's all in different shades together, streaks that are fair and streaks that are pale brown and golden and straw-colored. Tilly used to have hers made to look like that, she's always changing the color of her hair, but I think the Princess's is natural.

There's a walking area for shoppers in Bury. I followed them in there for a while and when they went into a health-food shop I turned back to the car park and drove home. The Bentley overtook me at the only place it's possible to overtake on that road. They hadn't been out long. The Princess was in the back, Garnet sitting up very straight and correct at the wheel. It doesn't look as if they talk much.

Yesterday the weather changed again as it does in April and it was pouring rain. We went out to buy the papers and then to a shop which is just down the road from here and bought waterproof capes, one yellow, one black, with hoods. The man grumbled about being paid with an American Express card but he agreed to take it when he saw it was the only way to make a sale. I put the black one on and Sandor drove me to the outskirts of the village. I was going to walk the footpath that crosses the Jareds land but I wasn't going to cross it, for fear of the dogs. Stan had had a lot to say about the footpath and the dogs, as everyone has when you mention the Apsolands.

I had my hood up and I know I was unrecognizable, which was just as well as the first person I saw was Garnet exercising those dogs. He came over the stile in the hedge that skirts the Jareds land, the German shepherds tearing on ahead of him. The rain had stopped but everywhere was soaking wet and the trees were dripping. The dogs made straight for me and Garnet started shouting and whistling. They obeyed him just at the point when I thought I would have to go up a tree. He called out, "Sorry about that." I lifted my arm in what I hope he took for a friendly gesture.

After that I walked in the opposite direction to the one he was taking. I found that the path branches, one part going across the Jareds land, the way he had come, the other going out to meet the road and passing very close behind the buildings at the back of the house. I hadn't yet been able to see the house because of the trees and the lie of the land. The footpath took me alongside a flint wall that keeps all the buildings inside it, like a picture you might see of a walled city. There was a bit of high ground, a mound, from which the house was at last visible, but only the back of it and that wasn't very interesting. I could make out what must once have been a rather grand sort of greenhouse, stables with a clock on them, and Garnet's house, a courtyard being in the middle of all this.

A woman came out from the back of the house and crossed the courtyard. She was small and wiry with dark hair tied up very tight on top of her head and she was carrying a basket. I had to get down from there. From a distance you can't see who may be behind windows. The glass just looks black. It was then that I heard a shot.

Oh, it wasn't anything to do with me. I realized that almost at once. I was only alarmed for a split second. More shots followed. I was on a public footpath, I had a right to be there. I went over the next stile and through a bit of wood, avoiding the road which comes quite near the Jareds buildings there. In spite of the fact that I was looking about me, I thought I knew what was going on behind and ahead, I nearly bumped into the man with the gun.

He was a tall thin man, though not so tall as Garnet, with a kind of hollowed-out face and a slit of a mouth. I know now it was Apsoland because Sandor showed me a picture, but I didn't then. He must have been taking a day off from his office in London. It was a shotgun he was carrying, a twelve-bore I think, and he was holding it in that way people like him do, bent into two sections and sort of hooked over his arm. *Negligently* is the word, Sandor says. He was wearing a Barbour jacket and green Wellies and a *cap*. The perfect country gent. The only other person I've seen wearing a cap was Dad's dad who was very old and said he belonged to the days when people didn't go out without hats.

He spoke to me. He said, "Good afternoon to you. Bit better now, isn't it?"

He meant the weather. I said, "A bit," and we each went our ways. I thought you could only shoot things in the winter but when I told him about Apsoland Sandor said, no, you could shoot rabbits and pigeons any time. He seemed rather pleased to hear Apsoland was such a wimp but otherwise gloomy.

"We're going to have to get in there, little Joe," he said. "How are we going to do it?"

6

hey gamboled ahead of him across the open heathy land, long-haired, heavy-bodied, pepper-and-salt-pelt shepherd dogs. They were well-behaved with him, docile enough. They came when you called them by those ridiculous names which, whatever Apsoland might believe, were from Scandinavian not German mythology. They sat down more or less when bidden to do so. They growled and barked at every unexpected sound, but that was what they were supposed to do. They were not apparently fierce with the people they knew. Just the same, he wanted as little contact as possible between them and Jessica. Of course she would like a dog of her own but he knew what Apsoland's attitude to that was.

"I think we'd better say no pets, Paul, eh? There's a good fellow."

Paul Garnet disliked being called a good fellow, but he didn't intend to get on his high horse about it. When a man takes a job as a servant he must expect to descend several steps of the social scale. The alternative, not teaching but attempting to teach something, anything, to thirty-five teenagers in an Inner London school, had no longer been tenable. Besides, with the job came the house. A man whose wife has left him to be a single parent to their child needs a house.

Paul lifted his face to the sun. The Suffolk sky, the Suffolk light, he had almost forgotten what they were like in those years away. The enormous sky was full of welling cumulus which shrank and swelled across the blue spaces, which clouded the sun, plunging the heath into gloom, parted and released floods of light. The fallow land was a brilliant, rain-soaked green with dark spots of gorse bushes dotted with gold. It was not this part of the county that he hailed from but farther east, where the winds come in from Sole Bay, shave the fields of shrub and heather, stunt the cringing trees. Paul liked this gentler country, the enormous oaks, the clustering hollies, holy trees, that the superstitious farmer was afraid to cut. Ahead of him the woodland spilled over the rim of the hill in the way Suffolk woods do. Let the dogs in there and he might never get them out again. He called, "Odin! Tyr!"

They didn't come at once. They weren't that good. He called them again and Tyr hesitated. He called them for the third time. Tyr began loping toward him, as idly as a dog running in a slowed-up video. Paul blew the whistle that was supposed to be a kind of emergency button for the dogs, the key to press when all else failed. Odin, who had been investigating with his nose the border of the wood, sprang up, veered, started running.

"Good dogs!" He put a hand out to each peppery-silver shining head, smoothed the silky fur. "Time to go back," he said.

How much use would they be in need? He had heard Odin growl. Tyr's deep bark resounded not only through the big house but could be heard in the cottage as well, his hollow wolf's bay, as might be made by the Hound of the Baskervilles. But Paul had never seen either of them bare their teeth. They had been treated with too much kindness to be savage. Or so it seemed to him.

How would he know? Dogs were usually good with him. His father had always had dogs.

But he did wonder what effect the appearance of himself with these two would have on a caller up to no good. He might be the son of an East Anglian farmer but he looked, his mirror and his ex-wife told him, like an actor cast as an Unterfeldwebel in an anti-German war film. The two dogs provided the necessary touch of brutishness to this picture of a tall, heavily built man with bullet head and egg-shaped face, blue eyes close set, big straight nose and smooth thick lips. He only had his fair hair crew cut because there wasn't enough of it to wear it otherwise, but the Teuton-brute effect persisted notwithstanding.

We are not our faces, whatever the wise ones and the old saws may say. Paul had often thought that, eyeing among his recalcitrant pupils some delicate lad of soulful visage who led riots in the classroom or broke a fellow student's arm. He was peculiarly nonviolent himself, in his ways and tastes.

Apsoland employed him as much as anything for the way he looked. He was sure of that although, naturally, nothing had been said. His looks, his height and strength outweighed those obvious disadvantages of having no wife, having a seven-year-old child and being better educated than the boss. Not that his having been to a university came up at the interview. It had never come up, Paul reflected as he led the dogs back to the footpath that skirted the village and returned the back way to Jareds.

Apsoland hadn't wanted to know what his previous life was. He hadn't asked for references. The salary he was paying, a salary far beyond anything Paul thought he would get when he applied for the job, was to ensure loyalty, safe driving and, he suspected, a willingness to fight if the need came. What were they afraid of, he and his wife? The place was guarded as if it housed nuclear devices or the green eye of the Little Yellow God. Was it outsize paranoia or what you might call justified paranoia—in other words, a real fear with a real cause for it?

The dogs, he thought, the lights that worked on the infrared cell, the gates, the personal transmitters for each inhabitant, the remote-control button, the electrified fence, the extremely sophisticated alarm system, the steel door that closed as it might be in a bank vault—he often thought about them and came to no conclusion. That first time he came to Jareds for the interview he thought he was going to be a driver, handyman and occasional gardener.

"Gardening?" Apsoland had said. "A couple of times a year I have a firm in and Colombo does the maintenance."

Colombo, apparently, also fixed what needed fixing in the big house, played the part of butler, and Maria, his wife, did everything else with help from the village. Paul, though it was never made explicit, soon understood he was to be a bodyguard.

"The idea is that you drive my wife whenever she wants to go out." And he added, "Not just drive her, look after her. Take care of her. Watch over her." The woman must be an invalid, Paul was thinking by this time. He didn't ask, of course he didn't, and Apsoland said blandly, "A touch of agoraphobia." The help wouldn't understand, so he elucidated. "She doesn't like going out alone."

Jessica had been mentioned by then. Her name had brought a frown to that handsome, fair, slightly concave face that was already corroding into a nutcracker shape. A child! A little girl! But on the other hand, this good fellow was so large and fit, bearing all the signs about him of the loyal thug, the prototype hitman and chucker-out.

Paul said, "What if your wife wanted me to drive her in the evenings?"

"Oh, that won't come up. I drive my wife in the evenings." He said it with enormous puffed-up pride. "You mustn't think she's some sort of recluse." He paused, perhaps asking himself if Paul would comprehend the difficult word, then pursued his theme without explanation: "We go out a great deal. Naturally, we have a host of friends in the neighborhood. And we have a home in London. In these circumstances I am always with my wife." He said irrelevantly but as if it were the most natural thing in the world, astonishing Paul, "I collect handguns, as a matter of fact. I've rather a remarkable collection, though I say it myself. I'd be happy to show it to you."

That was when he began to feel persecution mania like a gas on the air or something that put out creeping feelers.

"If by the remotest chance my wife did require you to drive her in the evening, why would that be a problem?"

"My little girl," Paul said patiently. "I wouldn't leave my daughter alone."

"Oh, Maria would be charmed to babysit. She's a tremendously motherly creature, you know how these Latins are."

Paul didn't. The housekeeper he had seen looked young, withdrawn, indifferent.

"There's actually nothing else involved. Oh, if you'd just take the dogs out every day, like a good fellow."

Paul and the dogs were coming up to the Jareds land now. It was a small park that the two houses and the outbuildings stood in. This footpath had been a public one and led close by the area hedged off as garden, led right through the center of the park. Apsoland had taken it upon himself, so Paul had been told in the village, to close this footpath to the public. Great scenes had been made by local people and dog-walkers and the council's footpaths committee. One summer afternoon the path had been walked by members of the committee until Apsoland, to public outrage and horror, had loosed Odin and Tyr.

Now an action was pending, brought by the County Council. "Over my dead body do they open that path," Apsoland was reported to have said. Stan, who was married to Doreen, who cleaned twice a week at Jareds, said Apsoland was planning to install a mantrap, but Paul couldn't believe this. But he did believe in Apsoland's near lunacy at objecting to harmless hikers crossing this plain of gently undulating green with its spreading cedars and drifts of daffodils. The police, who must come by from time to time to check on the gun collection, obviously didn't know Apsoland also had an electric fence.

The two houses lay in a declivity. It was clever the way trees had been planted long ago to conceal everything from the road. He had noticed the first time he came here the subtle arrangement of the buildings, so that as he approached in the station taxi he had thought for a while that the promise of a house to live in was a mere come-on, a bait to lure him here.

He was expected and the gates had been opened from inside the house. The electric cable could be seen running along the foot of the wall. The taxi driver had had a few astonished words to say about the arrangements: the lion and the recumbent man on the gatepost for a start, the corridor of flint walls and the lights that flooded the parkland as they passed the point where the two wrought-iron gates opened into the flint avenue. It was winter and getting dark at four. The house at the end of the tunnel had an imposing Palladian façade slapped on to something much older.

It was a gracious mansion of pale Woolpit tiles with long, dark, gleaming windows, the dome of its porch supported on eight Corinthian columns. And those trees, the cedars and the Corsican pine, the wellingtonias and the swamp cypresses, were older than the façade, had been planted to flatter a seventeenth-century house. Once the oval was reached which the drive made by turning back on itself at the front door, a cluster of gray buildings to the rear became just visible. Later, after he had met Mrs. Apsoland and seen for himself and spoken to her and felt the beginnings of a groping comprehension, but only the beginnings, her husband had taken him out to the cottage that was a very trim conversion of a stable. This house had made up Paul's mind for him. He thought of Jessica. What did the madness of the Apsolands matter?

Now, having taken Odin and Tyr to the back kitchen and handed them into the care of Maria, Paul crossed the courtyard and entered the cottage by the front door. It was 3:15. Mrs. Apsoland had told him to take one of the cars to meet Jessica any time he wanted but today, as was twice a week the case, she was being brought home by the mother of a school-fellow. Not for the first time Paul wondered what on earth Apsoland was up to, paying him this lavish salary and letting him occupy this house rent free for doing so little. For instance, today he had driven Mrs. Apsoland to Bury St. Edmunds where she (and he, necessarily) had called at the bookshop to pick up two new novels she had ordered and at a health-food store which was the only one that kept some vitamin supplement she took. The whole expedition lasted an hour and a half. He took the dogs out for an hour and that was it. Free until tomorrow morning, Thursday morning, when he would be driving her to Ipswich to get her hair done. And then the long weekend would begin—unless she needed him to drive her a trifling few miles on Friday morning.

Paul went into his small but most elegant kitchen which had been refitted by Smallbone of Devizes at the same time the kitchen in the big house was done. Old English oak cabinets with Spanish ceramic tiles on the walls and red earth tiles on the floor, handmade in Mexico. The big fridge also had its front faced in Old English oak. Paul checked that he had milk to give to Jessica and, in the freezer section, ice cream for later. The central heating came from the same boiler as worked the system in the big house. The pipes ran under the flagstones of the courtyard—all very efficient and expensive. There was a large living room, out of which the staircase went up, two bedrooms, and a splendid Smallbone bathroom, the lot done up in the chintzes and wallpaper of Laura Ashley. He liked to think that Mrs. Apsoland had supervised it, though the chances were they had had some interior decorator in.

Thinking of tomorrow, that it was Thursday and on alternate Thursdays he took her to Cambridge to visit her mother, Paul found his mind returning to the matter of the gray Fiat and its driver. Although he had taken the number of the car he had done nothing about it and by now a fortnight had gone by. He stood at the window of the living room which, though invisible from the drive and the flint avenue as the whole cottage was, gave onto the lane that approached the village, a surprisingly short way away at this point, no more than fifty yards. He liked to stand here on the days he didn't fetch Jessica himself and watch the approach of her friend Emma's mother's red Ford or her friend Harriet's mother's black VW.

The gray Fiat . . . He could not have said how far it had followed them. Could he have said it had followed them at all? If he had had to swear to it? He first noticed it behind him some five or six miles the Cambridge side of the Newmarket exit. But it might have been there longer. He couldn't put a spurt on and leave it behind because he had to keep in the slow lane to take the turnoff for Cambridge. But was it following him?

He had said nothing to Mrs. Apsoland. Her husband had never said, but he had implied, that nothing of a worrying nature should ever be said to Mrs. Apsoland. Most of the time they didn't talk, though if there was anything interesting to be seen one of them might point it out to the other.

It had been a shock seeing the gray Fiat parked in the side street behind him. He had watched it go past and disappear. That was when he thought he must have been mistaken. The owner of the gray Fiat must live in this neighborhood. That morning he had had to make a business trip to Ipswich and he was coming home, that was all. She went into her mother's and he saw the Fiat again, and the owner, a young man with a black beard and fuzzy black hair, sitting at the wheel. Anger was what he felt, simple anger. He thought, it's because she's famous, or she was once, quite a while ago, but some of these nuts, they get obsessed with someone who's been in the public eye, it doesn't matter how long ago. So he had got out of the Bentley and challenged the driver, who wasn't going to admit it if he *had* been following, and taken the gray Fiat's number.

At that time, while he waited for Mrs. Apsoland, he had been fully resolved on telling his employer. That must be what they were afraid of, an onslaught of worshippers from former days. Even as he thought this Paul wasn't convinced by his own argument, but he couldn't find a better one. He had driven, not into the town center which would have been blocked with traffic, but to a café in the shopping precinct of this suburb, and had had a sandwich and a cup of coffee. Yes, he would tell Apsoland and give him the number and perhaps advise alerting the police.

They were going out that evening, the two of them. On the way home she was telling him about it, the launch at the Ancient House in Ipswich of the book a friend had written, a party afterward, then dinner with the writer and his wife and another couple. Apsoland was going to try and get home early. In fact he was late, half an hour later than usual. Paul had been determined to speak to him as soon as he arrived but something happened to change his feelings. It was the infrared alarm system.

By the time Apsoland reached the top of the lane in the Jaguar darkness had come and as the car came within the range of the infrared cell, the whole place burst into blazing light—halogen lamps on the gables, on the outhouses, above the porch, inside the circular flower bed opposite the front door. They all shone out like so many moons into the black air, bleached it with brilliance and turned the sky a coppery sparking blue.

Paul and Jessica were at the table having supper. From where they sat they couldn't even see the drive but the light permeated everywhere, a radiant burning blue-whiteness. It made Paul cross. So ridiculous, such a waste of energy—and for what? He was still with the eager fans theory then. If Apsoland wasn't careful he would find the burglar alarm had been activated too and in a moment all the braying and ringing would begin and perhaps the steel door would slide down to create a fortress drawing room. Tell the man about the gray Fiat and it would make things worse. Besides, there was Jessica . . .

Jessica was amazing. She didn't seem afraid of anything. Why wasn't she nervous with her background, life on an inner London street, a poor run-down neighborhood, an indifferent mother, her parents' marriage broken? She wasn't even afraid of the dark, never had been. If he left a night-light burning for her she got up and turned it out. He didn't want her to be afraid, ever. Of course, he meant to bring her up to be aware, to be streetwise, to know about defending herself. And he had already begun telling her what she must fear, what she must watch for. But he hated to think of her becoming one of those women who saw a rapist in every man who walked alone, a mugger in every boy without a tie and a briefcase, burglars waiting in hordes for when the sun went down.

They had been eating her favorite, Chinese. Not takeaway—he had actually tried stir-frying the bean sprouts and mushrooms himself. She laid down her fork and looked up at him and said, "Have Mr. and Mrs. Apsoland got treasure? Have they got jewels?"

"Not so far as I know," he said. "They may have some."

"But there must be bad people who want to steal things from them. That's why all the lights come on, to frighten the bad people."

He hadn't known what to say. Suppose she thought this sort of thing normal? It made him think that perhaps he had been wrong to bring her here. But the house, the house. How else could they have had a house in the beautiful country that was his native heath and which he would have be hers too? Children, when they acquire an adult reflex, will perform it to excess. She blinked at the fierce light involuntarily, then made herself blink artificially while doing a pretend recoil from the window, flinging herself back in her chair. Then she said something rather clever for someone of her years, or so Paul thought.

"If this is going to happen, how will they tell when it's Mr. Apsoland and when it's a robber?"

"I don't know, Jessica," he said, smiling at the word *robber,* which no one uses except children who learn it from fairy tales.

He said to himself that if he saw the gray Fiat or its driver again then he would say something to Apsoland. If not, not. These people shouldn't be encouraged in their paranoia. She shouldn't be. She should have treatment for whatever was wrong with her, he thought, though the words sounded hollow in his head as he wondered what treatment there was and what good it could possibly ever do.

It was the red Ford driven by Emma's mother that Jessica was coming home in this afternoon. He had opened the gates by the remote-control button in his hallway. There was another in the house. A small red car passed between the trees. It was probably Emma's mother's car but not certainly. Strange that he found the only drawback to this house the fact that the drive was invisible from its windows. He wouldn't know if this was the car bearing Jessica until it passed under the archway, a rather odd Italianate structure linking house and former orangery, and entered the courtyard. A small tic fluttered inside him. He was aware of an anticipatory thrill at the prospect of seeing her. His daughter! It was absurd, like a lover.

The red car swung in. Emma's mother was a dashing driver.

The two girls were in the back, the little dark one with round cheeks and fringed bobbed black hair like a Chinese and the blonde, golden-headed, very white skinned. Emma's mother and Emma weren't coming in today. He knew that by the wave they gave him. Jessica got out, banged the car door but not hard enough, the way she nearly always did. He saw her lips move in her favorite oath of the moment: "Oh, piglets!"

Where had that come from? *Winnie-the-Pooh?* She closed the car door correctly this time, ran up to the door, looking back once to wave. The red Ford turned. Her face wore that expression it sometimes had, as if she contemplated angelic hosts, the ecstatic prayerful look of a Millais infant. She was probably only thinking about her tea. When she had her glass of milk in one hand and a chocolate-chip cookie in the other, she said to him, "Daddy, will you sponsor me not to talk for two hours?"

"Will I what?"

"Well, you see, our class hasn't got enough books and the government doesn't give us enough money to buy them, Miss Hunt says, and so that's how we're going to get it. We're going to make silence."

"Keep silence," he said. "You can't make silence."

"Oh, piglets," she said, "you know what I mean."

"Can you really go two hours without speaking, Jess?"

"I'm going to try. Will you sponsor me for ten pee a minute?"

"That seems an awful lot. If you actually do it that'll cost me twelve pounds."

"I know, but we don't know any people here. If you won't do it there won't be anyone and I won't get anything but everybody else will get thousands and thousands."

"Of course I'll do it," he said.

"Oh, good. And do you think we could ask Mrs. Apsoland if she'll do it too? Mr. Apsoland and her are very rich, so she could do it. Can we ask her, Daddy?"

"I don't know, Jessica," said Paul.

Why shouldn't he ask her? She had never said a word to him that was not kind and gentle and generous. She was even timid, as if he were the employer and she the humble employed. He went into the living room to light the fire he had laid earlier. The sun had come out again and the trees cast branching patterns across the flags of the courtyard. He looked up at the back of the pale gray house. She was at one of the windows, not her bedroom, that was at the front, but a window on the second-floor landing. Or so he supposed, he had never been up there.

It was across the rooftops that she was looking, through the trees and to the road, the hills, the wide world beyond. He had often asked himself what she did all day, shut up there. "Shadows of the world appear. There she sees the highway near . . ." But the Lady of Shallott saw things only in a mirror, he reminded himself. He had once tried to teach that poem to the thirteen-year-olds of Holloway. Mrs. Apsoland stood quite still behind her window, gazing, gazing, her eyes on a far horizon as if she yearned for some unseen distant thing. He thought, surprising himself, she and Jessica are a lot alike. Jessica will look like her one day, just as once she looked like my Jessica. Perhaps it was only because they were both fair and both beautiful.

Mrs. Apsoland took her eyes from the treetops and the sky and looked down at him. Their eyes met for a moment before he turned away. He realized he didn't know her first name.

Jessica came in, said, "You haven't lit the fire yet, Daddy," and then, "Can I have a puppy? Harriet's mother dog had puppies. Can I, Daddy?"

7

They would only be home from school for a fortnight, with two weekends included, and he never had much to do on the weekends, starting from Thursday evening. The Monday Jessica spent at Emma's house and the Tuesday at Harriet's. When Wednesday came he had to take Mrs. Apsoland to a rare-plant nursery in Essex, she was buying plants for an alpine garden they were making, and because they were only going to be away for a maximum of two hours, he left Jessica on her own, having asked Maria to keep an eye on her. But the next day was a Cambridge day and he had to ask Emma's mother again, which he didn't like doing.

As well as the alpine arrangement, on which work hadn't yet begun, Apsoland was having the old conservatory restored. He called it the winter garden. They were going to have orange and lemon trees in there. The fuss that was made about vetting the workmen and checking on them Paul would not have believed possible if someone had told him about it. Dealing with the men, it appeared, was to be his job. Before they were allowed to start, the boss, whose firm it was, had to list the names of the men who would be working there along with their addresses, the type of transport they would use to come in, the index numbers of their vehicles and the precise times at which they would arrive and go.

Apsoland himself had dealt with all that. He had taken part of the morning off on Monday, and when the workmen arrived (two in cars and one on a motorbike) through gates opened ten minutes before by Apsoland, he photographed them. Paul, watching from the window with Jessica, could hardly believe his eyes. It was a Polaroid camera, so Apsoland was able to bring him the pictures before he drove off to the station, and also the photographs and the little dossier on each man he had compiled. If a man arrived who was not on the list and not photographed, Paul was to call the number on the top of the sheet.

"In which case," said Apsoland darkly, "help will arrive to assist you in removing the intruder."

"Can we remove someone who's probably just an extra workman called in for some specific task? We could get an action for assault."

"Just do as I ask like a good fellow, will you?" said Apsoland.

Ceremoniously, Apsoland handed the boss a transmitter to work the gates. It all made Paul wonder about something. This excessive care was taken about visitors to Jareds, the infrared cell and burglar-alarm systems were elaborate and complex, there were probably other safeguards he didn't yet know about, but he himself hadn't even been asked for credentials, much less references. It was a mystery. And why the "help" that Apsoland said would arrive? If he really suspected the possibility of burglary or something akin to it, why not the police? "Help" sounded like a bunch of hired hitmen.

But he soon ceased to worry about it. The three men came each day on the motorbike and in their cars and the boss came, they came when they said they would and left when they said they would, and they all matched their Polaroid pictures. Jessica was far more of a problem. He had hated leaving her alone. He began to wonder what he would do next Monday.

On Thursday morning, Maundy Thursday, he did his usual check on the men, then drove Jessica to Emma's in the Volvo. Children make friends very quickly. Jessica and Emma had only known each other since the spring half-term when Jessica had started at the school, but they were already intimates, sharing secrets, giggling together with an exclusiveness that shut out grown-ups. About Emma's mother Sheila he was less sure. He fancied she was rather cold and brisk with him, as if she were summoning up the nerve to say no when next he asked her.

He drove back along the empty lanes, comforted a little by the signs of spring. The hawthorn hedges were coming into leaf. The budding foliage that had been a green spotted veil two days ago was growing dense, becoming a thick rich clothing that hid the branches. They used to call it quick-thorn on the farm, and the new shoots were bread and cheese that you picked off the twigs and chewed. You had to catch them just right, he remembered, when they were more than tiny green sprouts and before they became bitter. On an impulse he stopped the car, got out, and picked a crisp shoot off the hedge. The strong green taste of it brought back childhood, the windswept fields, sheep pastured in a long-disused churchyard, the eroding sea that each year took a few more feet of his father's land.

I was going to do so well, he thought. The first member of his family to go to university, very nearly the first not to work on the farm when he left school. A good degree, a good first job, teaching up north, then Katherine, meeting Katherine, who was also on the staff, and moving to London. When and why did it fall apart? Perhaps it was his fault or that no one with his training and his, well, ideals—pretentious word, but what else?—could exchange teaching for being a warden in a house of correction, sacrificing everything just to keep them quiet and keep them from breaking the place up. The week that Katherine left him was the week one of the fifteen-year-old girls marched up to him without warning and as far as he knew, provocation, and struck him in the face. That was the beginning of last year. In the time that followed he used to say to himself, At least I've got Jessica, I've got her.

It was what other members of his family did, the ones who didn't go to university: they worked on the land or in the building trade or went into what was called "service" in his parents' time but today went under various more dignified euphemisms. He started looking at the ads in newspapers. He went to an agency. The house was going to be sold so that Katherine could have her share and he could have his and the lion's share could go back to the building society. I've made a mess of my life, he often thought, and then he would look at Jessica and revise that. The court had awarded him custody and care of her. Katherine didn't want her, she had loved her daughter before she was born but afterward had been indifferent, he couldn't understand it but it was so. She was going back to university to do a master's degree.

Suffolk, the fact that the Apsolands lived in Suffolk, was what had drawn him. And then when he met them they interested him. He had been a little puzzled, intrigued. As people will, he had formed a picture in his mind of Mrs. Apsoland: showy, made-up, with that funny hair every woman appeared to have who was rich or fashionable or remotely connected with show business, a wild, tangled, teased mass, usually golden. Apsoland had taken him into the drawing room where she was sitting reading. It seemed a little staged, but that might have been his imagination. She looked very young, very ordinary. She was as slim as a teenage girl. Her skin was pale, her eyes very blue. She smiled and he forgot he had thought her ordinary a moment before. He saw that she was very beautiful, exquisite, perfect in the small details, and just as beautiful when the smile had gone. She had a way of holding her head, very slightly to one side, as if she thought carefully before she spoke.

"Has my husband told you?" she had said to him. "We want someone to drive me but also someone to look after me." The voice was unexpected, rich and strong, but gentle. He thought he saw the ghost of a smile on that softly curved mouth. She seemed to understand that more explanation was necessary. Apsoland just stood there, his face a blimpish mask. "I am rather nervous. We're both nervous people. Terrible things happen, don't they?" At least she didn't say she had agoraphobia.

They had been with her only five minutes and then Apsoland had introduced him to the dogs, a less pleasurable experience. Paul had thought about what she said, about someone to look after her, and he had been thinking about it more or less ever since. He was thinking about it as he went into the big house by the back door and, finding no one about, walked down the passage to the drawing room. Creeping up quietly on her seemed to him the worst thing he could do, so he walked with a heavy tread and cleared his throat once or twice. Even so she jumped when he came into the room and as she turned her hand flew to her throat.

"I'm sorry I frightened you," he said.

She smiled, lifted her shoulders a little. "You didn't really. I jump easily." She was ready to go out, even down to the brown calf bag hanging from her shoulder. She had her jeans on again and a white padded jacket. It was cold this morning. "I'm a coward, aren't I? You must think so." She didn't wait for his reply, which would necessarily have been a denial. Her head turned a little to one side. "I wasn't always. I was quite brave once. Shall we go?"

He held the door open for her and she got into the back of the Bentley. As he drove away down the drive he had the notion that great revelations were to be made to him, he was to be enlightened. It was as if he could feel, trembling in the space between them, her as yet unexpressed but energetic need to speak and to confess. But all she said was, "I was upstairs looking out of the window"—the Lady of Shallott, he thought—"and I saw you taking your little girl to school. I thought they had broken up for the Easter holidays."

He had to explain. She interrupted him just as he got to the bit about Emma's mother. "Oh, but you could bring her with us. I'd like to meet her. I don't know any children. Isn't that ridiculous?"

"Are you serious?" he said.

"Serious about her coming with us or serious about wanting to meet her? Both, I suppose. Bring her on Monday, why don't you? Oh, but it's Easter Monday and perhaps I shouldn't ask you to work."

"I don't mind working on Easter Monday, Mrs. Apsoland."

"Ralph's going to the show. I mean, the local agricultural show. He takes being a country gentleman very seriously, you know." She laughed. "I've said I'll have lunch with some friends in Aldeburgh." He realized, though he couldn't see her, that she was quite excited at her own plan. "You could bring Jessica and she could have a day at the seaside. I'll be ages with my friends, I'm sure to stay for tea, and you and Jessica could have a great time. Shall we do that?"

All he could think of for a moment was the gratification he felt at her remembering Jessica's name. He could recall mentioning it to her only once and that was the second or third time he had driven her. Then he imagined taking Jessica round Aldeburgh and, while Mrs. Apsoland was with her friends, driving Jessica north to see his brother who had the farm now. "That would help me a lot," he said. "It's good of you. Thanks."

The role of grateful servant still came hard to him. Calling her "Mrs." while she called him "Paul" came hard. At least he wasn't expected to "sir" and "madam" them. She was silent for a while. He took the back lanes, heading for Lavenham and thence for the Bury road. Once on the major road he started thinking about the gray Fiat, though he hadn't seen it for weeks.

There was going to be no gray Fiat today. There hadn't been since the Thursday before last. And that one time—wasn't it probable that their paranoia had infected him? It was the most catching thing. Apsoland had it in virulent form. She had it too, in a less violent manifestation, but perhaps more personally. He wasn't sure what he meant by that, only that it was as if she was afraid because she had learned fear by experience, but he was apprehensive through taking newspaper and television alarmists too seriously. It was all nonsense, of course, it was all imaginary.

Just as his own nervousness had been, caught from Apsoland like the flu.

She began talking about her mother, whose house on the outskirts of Cambridge they were heading for. She wanted her mother to move nearer to Jareds, buy a house in the village. It appeared she was an only child. Her mother had been over forty when she was born and was old now. Had Paul parents? He told her they were dead, had died comparatively young. His was not a family distinguished for its longevity. Of the next generation there was only Jessica, for his brother was childless and likely to remain so.

"Like me," she said.

No gray Fiat with truculent bearded youth at the wheel, overtaking them or turning up parked in the side street behind. Only empty streets, the blossoming trees in bud, the gardens full of shivering daffodils. He opened the car door for her, waited, watching, while she went up the path. The door opened. As usual he caught only a glimpse of someone thin and straight, white-haired. He got back into the car and drove to the pub where he could get a better lunch than sandwiches and where they had nonalcoholic lager. Easter tomorrow. There was a foil-wrapped, flower-decked chocolate egg on the bar, a prize in some charity raffle. Somewhere, before the shops closed for the holiday, he had better get an Easter egg for Jessica. Would Katherine send her something, a card even? It wasn't like Christmas, of course, or a birthday. She probably wouldn't. Hadn't she said herself, when discarding Jessica, that it would be better for the child to forget her, think of her as she might a dead mother? Sometimes he felt for his ex-wife a pure hatred.

Paul was due to pick Mrs. Apsoland up at three. He found a shopping precinct with a chocolate shop, bought a big expensive egg, all entwined with gilt vine leaves and marzipan grapes, and was back outside the bungalow by five to three. She was always punctual. She came out alone, closed the door behind her. He went round to open the rear door for her.

"Would it be all right," she said, "if I sat in the front with you?"

There was a timidity in her voice that brought him a sting of irritation. What was she playing at, talking to him like that, as if it were he who had the power of yea and nay, hire and fire? He wondered what the reaction would be if he said, no, it wouldn't.

"Of course. Please."

No sooner was she seated than she cleared that up. He thought uncomfortably, she has read my mind. "I'm an awful fool. I ought to realize that I don't have to ask you where I can sit. It must be rather annoying for someone like you to come up against me."

"Someone like me?"

"Someone strong and clever and well educated—a lot better educated than his illiterate employers—who's doing this job because for various reasons it's more convenient. I mean, I'd guess Jessica's the reason, isn't she? You needn't answer that."

He didn't. He said, "May I ask you something?"

"Depends what it is. Forgive me, but not if it's about me and my past life."

She had blushed. He couldn't see her face but he knew she had blushed. "It's not about you," he said. "Not directly. It's this: Mr. Apsoland is meticulous in checking up on those workmen yet he—you and he—took me on without a reference, without a word about what I'd done before. I might have had a police record. You took me on without knowing a thing about me. Why?"

She said calmly, "Oh, we did know about you. We checked."

His hands tightened on the wheel. They were on the big road now, going fast. "You checked?"

"Ralph did. You have to understand about Ralph, Paul. He wouldn't ask you yourself. You see, he wouldn't believe you. People make up references or get their friends to write them, don't they? But it's not just that. Ralph's—what can I say—the very essence of caution, preparedness, watchfulness—well, you could call it paranoia. He lives in it, that's the way he is. That's why . . ."

She broke off with a small dismissive laugh. He must be wrong but he had the curious and rather awful idea she had been about to say, "That's why I married him."

"He sees burglars under every bed, bag snatchers in every crowd. His is the original suspicious mind. If his own mother came calling he'd ask for her ID." Her voice went very low. She almost mumbled. "He's made me worse." Paul wasn't sure if he had heard right. She said in a brighter, more practical way, "Colombo and Maria, for instance, they've been with us six months. Ralph had their pasts checked out, right back to when they left school. As for you, you were just one of about twenty-five people Ralph interviewed. He put private detectives on them. He does that. He's got this firm of private detectives he practically keeps going. They'd go bust but for him. Oh dear, I really shouldn't be telling you all this. But there it is, I've started so I may as well go on. They went into your, well, your anteced-ents, the way candidates for MI5 are vetted before they take them on. For instance, I didn't know whether your parents were dead or not, but you can be sure Ralph knows. And all the rest. Ralph knows."

It didn't make him angry but it astonished him. He thought about it, digested it. Were those private detectives the "help" he was to call if some alien workman arrived? Or did Apsoland have a squad of hitmen too?

"You're cross," she said. "I shouldn't have told you."

"No, it's all right."

"You could be flattered if you like to take it that way. Remember the competition. He picked you out of twenty-five. He's got absolute faith in you."

It didn't appease him. He felt injured. "I'm only the driver," he said.

He must have sounded sulky, for she burst out laughing. It astonished him, her merry, apparently irrepressible laughter, and he laughed too. Then he waited for some comment from her, some reassurance, but none came and they drove on in silence. The road described its great curve by the sugar factory and he took the exit that dipped down and passed under the bridge. It had begun to rain a little. As he turned onto the A134 past the old prison gates he saw a red Fiat following him, remarking on it only because it was a Fiat. Don't catch their paranoia, he told himself. She fidgeted in her seat, pulling at her safety-belt to make it more comfortable. When she moved he could smell her scent that he had been aware of when she first got in beside him and which his nose had grown accustomed to. It was a very light perfume, but dry and spicy, not sweet.

"What would you do," she said, "if you were offered money to betray me?"

"What?" he said.

"I did say that. I did say what you heard."

He understood how very much he didn't want to diagnose her as mentally unsound. He wanted her fear to be justified. "I'm not sure what you mean by 'betray,'" he said.

"You'll know if it happens."

"Mrs. Apsoland," he said, "I hope you won't take this amiss. It's an outdated way of putting it, but I know it's not my place to tell you things like this. You see . . ."

"Go on," she said.

"You said yourself that your husband is overcautious and it's affected you. Don't you think perhaps it's affected you too much? It's true we live in a violent society and crime is increasing—but out here? I mean, when was the last burglary in this village?"

She said nothing. He thought she must be offended but he went on. It would have been wrong for him to leave it there. "I've sometimes thought about the theory that fear of attack leads to attack and I think there's something in it. A woman who walks confidently along a street in the dark and doesn't scuttle when a couple of boys come toward her, it's less likely that anything will happen to her. On a more practical level, word gets round when a house is overprotected and the kind of people who are likely to break in get to know the owners have something worth stealing." Even as he spoke he thought how sententious and glib he must sound.

They had come to a place where the road was up, half its width barred with cones, temporary traffic lights red against them. As Paul put the hand brake on she pointed at a switch on the dashboard and said, as if he hadn't spoken, "That switch, I don't know if you've been told, press it and it locks all the doors and the sunroof automatically." He turned to look at her. It was impossible to tell whether she was serious, but he suspected inner laughter. "When you're at lights or parked somewhere for a little while, just to be on the safe side."

High hedges, a row of Lombardy poplars, empty meadows, and an apron of woodland hanging over the hillside. The man who worked the lights had an orange Day-Glo jacket on. Paul could see her staring at the man, at his broad red face and thatch of yellow hair, past him at the one who drove the roller and the one who wielded a shovel. The lights went green. He heard her sigh beside him.

A minute or two passed before she said, "I knew I'd have to tell you this some time. It's just that I'm not very happy talking about it."

"Don't tell me anything you'd rather not, Mrs. Apsoland."

"Would you call me Nina, please?"

He was very surprised, slightly embarrassed. "Are you sure you want me to?"

"I hate being called 'Mrs.' It would be different if I were a lot older than you or you were a lot younger than me or something. You must know what I mean." He nodded. He couldn't see her face but he knew she was looking at him. "I was kidnapped once." The tone of her voice told him some great internal struggle was taking place. He couldn't tell what. It might have been the effort of lying and pretending the lie was truth or it might have been inhibition on speaking of a terrible event. She said it again. "I was kidnapped." He found himself unable to reply. "It was in Italy when I was married to my first husband. I was Nina Piraneso then. It was in May five years ago—well, nearly five years."

What was there to say? He was glad they were nearly home. He had already opened the Jareds gates and entered the drive. A flock of lapwings, black and white, rose from the parkland as the car approached. Ahead he could see the builders' vehicles—the two cars, the motorbike, and a small truck—all parked on the gravel outside the front door.

"That's why I'm nervous," she said. "That's part of it."

He said, "I see," which meant nothing.

"You didn't answer my question."

"I'm sorry, I've forgotten what it was."

"About betraying me. Now you know why I asked it."

For a while he had felt close to her. Briefly, while they talked, he had felt something like friendship developing. That was ridiculous, of course, they couldn't be close, be friends, and anyway, she had blown it in a flash with her kidnapping nonsense, her paranoia. He repeated what he had said earlier, "I'm just your driver," and added, "there won't be any question of that."

She got out of the car rather quickly. He stood there while she went up to the front door, holding her key. Everything is spoiled, he thought, I should have played along, I should have said "Really?" and "How terrible!" not shown I didn't believe a word. On the step she turned and said, "Don't forget you're bringing Jessica on Monday, will you?" And she smiled at him as if she hadn't a care in the world. Maybe she hadn't.

He drove back into the village and picked up Jessica. She and Emma had made charts for listing their silence sponsors and the amounts they would guarantee per minute. Emma's mother's name, he noticed, was conspicuous by its absence from Jessica's list, but the names of two women he had never heard of were on it, visitors to the house during the day presumably. Jessica's hair was done up in pigtails.

"Emma's mother did it," she said, pulling off the elastic bands and shaking her hair loose in the car. "It fell in the soup and she said it wasn't high-something."

"Hygienic, I expect," said Paul.

"I don't like soup."

"Not with hair in it, anyway."

That made her laugh. She began elaborating the joke, as children of her age will when wit and timing are still mysteries, on hair in soup, hair in soup instead of noodles, instead of onions, fair hair, black hair, pictures of hair on the can. When he had had enough of it he said, "We're going to the seaside on Monday. Mrs. Apsoland has to go, so I'll drive her and you're coming too."

They seldom reacted as you expected them to. A Shirley Temple stereotype would clasp her hands and lisp, "Ooh, Daddy!" Jessica said, "Will she sponsor me, d'you think?"

"You can ask her."

While he got her tea ready he thought about what Nina Apsoland had said, about kidnapping. If she had been kidnapped it would have been in the papers and it hadn't been. He would remember. An ex-model, English, married to a rich Italian called Piraneso. It would have gone on for weeks, these things always did, and the media would have had it and he would remember.

So she was mentally unbalanced or her husband was. Or they both were. That made the question she had asked him no less pathetic, more so rather. Well, would he betray her, whatever that might precisely mean? Would he betray anyone for money?

It was a question, he thought, that people often asked themselves. What's your price? What would you do for a million pounds? Is there really anything you wouldn't do if the price was right and you were guaranteed safety and immunity from the law? Home-baked philosophy, hypothetic speculation of a pointless kind.

Jessica sat at the table and drank her milk. She couldn't get the wrapping off her chocolate wafer, so he did it for her. The face she turned to him was an angel's, gazing at transcendent spiritual glories. Her eyes shone. The tendrils that clustered around her forehead were damp gold circles. A bead of milk trembled on her upper lip, which was red like a poppy petal. "You know about that puppy, Dad?" she said.

"It's no good, Jessica. You can't have a puppy this time. I'm sorry but that's how it is. We have to wait awhile till we know them better and they know us, right?" If we stay, he said silently, if it's going to be permanent. "I'm not saying no, I'm only saying no this time."

"Oh, piglets," she said, and then, "Okay." An enormous theatrical sigh, the weight of the world on her shoulders.

"It's early days, Jess."

She didn't know what he meant. How could she? He thought, she comes outside those speculations. Her I could never betray. The idea is laughable, a stupid joke. I suppose most parents feel like this, it's such a truism you don't even hear it expressed. It would be a pleasure to die for the sake of saving her. You'd run into your death, as to a lover's bed. Someone had said that but he couldn't remember who it was. Shakespeare probably. It was usually Shakespeare.

8

Sandor quoted a bit of poetry to me. It was about two people falling in love and feeling that they hadn't lived before that. They were newly born. What the poem said was something about just being weaned or as if they'd spent their lives snoring in the Seven Sleepers' Den. I like that bit, it's got to do with my love of fairy stories, I suppose. Or else it expresses the way I feel about Sandor. Not that I was exactly asleep before I met him, or if I was it was a sleep full of nightmares, but I hadn't lived or known anything and my head was full of oily water.

He says people can't learn to love if they haven't been loved when they were babies. That's what psychiatrists say. Well, I can't know more than psychiatrists, it stands to reason I can't, but I never had any love until Tilly came along, and I know I've got more love in me than most people, sometimes I feel I shall burst with love for Sandor.

Another thing that isn't true is that being in love means sex, straight or gay. I wouldn't tell anyone this because of the way they all believe that, but I fell in love with Sandor at first sight. I fell in love with him while we were staring at each other, stupefied with shock, on that seat on the Embankment underground station. There's a kind of falling in love that's different, that doesn't mean you want to do dirty things with people, but that you feel about them like, well, God, if there is a God, is supposed to feel about us, or nuns are meant to feel about Jesus. Or like those old servitors and retainers felt about the chiefs of their tribe, gallowglasses faithful unto death.

I don't think you come across this kind of love in the books Sandor reads or the magazines Mum read, so maybe I made it up and it isn't real. You certainly don't find it in the *News of the World*. Do you remember what I said about my reason for reading the *News of the World*? It was because of what Tilly said. The advertisements reach a bigger market than any other because more people read it than any other paper. (A hell of a commentary on our culture, Sandor says.) Of course there is a special advertisement I've always looked for while knowing I'd never find it. It was the one I'd never thought of that I did find. But that's life. What you expect never happens. Either what you don't expect happens or something a bit like what you expected happens. This was a bit like it, I suppose.

I was reading the paper last Sunday in our room. Sandor has finished *Cancer Ward* and started a book about Picasso. He'd done the *Observer* crossword and lit his twenty-fifth cigarette of the day. I'd been counting. I could hardly see him through the smoke. I started looking at the advertisements and broke off to open a window. He looked up but he didn't say anything. I went back to my ads and halfway down the column I found this one:

Joe—where are you? I'm looking for you at c/o Farthing,
25 Grice Rd, London N8—Tilly

The address didn't mean anything. I thought, there have to be other Joes who know Tillys. And then I remembered that the second fellow she'd lived with, the one who went to New Zealand and left her the camper, he was called Farthing, Martin Farthing. This Farthing might be his mother or his sister. Perhaps I'm imagining it but I've got a feeling the family lived in Wood Green or Hornsey, that neck of the woods anyway, which is N8.

When we were out that evening—we had found an expensive place that was prepared to serve dinner on Easter Sunday evening and take American Express—I told Sandor about it. I said I'd like to write to the address and give our PO box number. It was funny but by that time I could feel it growing on me, the real need to see Tilly again, and probably because I wanted it so much I was positive he'd say no. But he didn't say anything much, just lifted his shoulders in the way he has.

"Relations are more of a pain in the arse than an asset, aren't they?" was all he said. I thought that quite ironical when five seconds later he was handing the waiter his mother's American Express card. But by the way he gave me that crooked grin of his and his sidelong look I knew he thought it too.

"What are we going to do next?" I said.

"I'll tell you tomorrow. It seems a small thing but I'm wondering how we can get hold of Garnet's phone number. It'll be in Apsoland's name and not listed."

Next day I wrote to Tilly at the N8 address. It took some careful thought. I couldn't say, Come and see us, or, I'll come and see you, because I was sure Sandor wouldn't allow either of these things. I wanted to tell her about Sandor, at last having someone I could talk to about my life being Sandor's for him to do what he wants with, but although I can think it all right I couldn't get it down on paper. I just wrote:

Dear Tilly,

I am living in the country at present. A friend and me are thinking of going into business together. I am giving

*you this box number because we don't have a permanent
address yet and the phone here is shared. It would be nice
if you could drop me a line and tell me how things are with
you etc.*

> *Your loving brother,*
> *Joe*

I tore it up because when I saw it in black and white before me
I knew I couldn't write to my sister and give her a box number.
So I did it again, leaving out the sentence about not having a
permanent address and giving the Lindsey Guest House and putting in a bit about being happy but missing her. There was
something wrong with the grammar, but I wasn't sure what, so
I left it. Tilly wouldn't know any better anyway. I had never
called myself her loving brother before, but why not start? I'm
not her brother but I am loving. As I've said before, Tilly and
Sandor are my family, only not so much my sister and brother
as my mother and father. Isn't that funny? I'm not quite sure what
I mean by it.

She wouldn't like it. Families make me uneasy but they upset
her, they make her furious. She says most people just have one
set of bad parents but she has had three. And that's true, she
did—her own, then an aunt and uncle who took care of her,
though that's hardly the right description of what they did, then
Mum and Dad. We never talked much about it while we both
lived with them and when I was twelve she went off to live with
Brian. It was in the hospital that we had our real conversations.

She started visiting me regularly in there. It was the best
therapy I could have had, better than drugs, even the doctors said
so. She used to come in the afternoons and we'd talk for hours,
in a corner of the dayroom or outside, walking about the grounds
if the sun was shining. By then she'd split up with Brian and when
she first told me that it upset me a lot. It upset me out of all
proportion to the actual event, which after all was only a woman
who wasn't even related to me parting from a man I'd met a few
times. But I've thought a lot about that, I've had plenty of time

to think in. I've come to the conclusion we mind so much when our friends split up because we sort of equate them with our own parents. Sandor said to me once that the unconscious mind knows nothing of age or time or suitability and I reckon that's right, like most of what he says. I got upset about Tilly breaking up with Brian, like I did later when she broke up with Martin, because my unconscious mind saw them as parents.

My own childhood is all water under the bridge now but it's got something to do with how I feel about Tilly and her boy-friends and how I felt when I saw Garnet and that kid. Tilly and I used to talk about kids and having them and bringing them up. She doesn't like children, and that's an understatement. It's a mystery why people bring them into the world, she says. She's never going to have any. This world is full of misery, poverty, and disease and famine and starvation and who is it you see on the TV suffering most? Children. Children with their bones sticking out of their skin, children with begging bowls, getting their limbs shot off, being abused and battered. Yet people go on having them, more and more of them, and as soon as they don't seem to be having quite so many, governments start screaming that the birth rate's falling and something must be done. Well, we all know what's done.

We used to talk about that and how good the world would be if there were half as many people or less, and another subject was marriage and finding a partner. Tilly's never going to get married either. She's seen three marriages at close quarters and each one was a nightmare. Settling down with one man she loves, though, that's a different matter. You had to try a few out before you decided, she said, and we talked about how stupid it was to say man was monogamous when the only truly monogamous animals are those that get imprinted with the partner when they're very young. Geese and guinea pigs. If you show a young goose a dog or even a teddy bear it can get imprinted with that and never want anyone else. Sometimes I think that's what's happened to me, I've been imprinted with Sandor. Of course it doesn't happen with normal humans, but I'm not normal, at least, I'm not much like other people.

It'll be good to see Tilly again—I wonder if I shall? I posted the letter and one for Sandor when I went out to get the papers. The first one I ever posted for him he asked me not to read the address on it, he said it was one of the rudest things you could do, to read the address on letters people ask you to post, so since then I've made a point of never doing it. He'd gone in the Jareds direction in the car. He said it was Doreen's day to go cleaning there on her motor scooter. When he came back he seemed in a better mood, had had his lunch in the village pub. Stan was in there, talking as usual about Jareds and the Apsolands, but Sandor didn't learn anything new, unless you count finding out that the Garnet child is called Jessica and that she has had Stan and Doreen's daughter down there to play. Garnet drove up to the village to fetch her and brought her back on account of Stan not having a car. Or perhaps on account of security?

Later on I reminded him that he had promised to tell me what we were going to do next. He said he couldn't remember any such promise, he didn't make promises. "Get dressed," he said. "We're going out to dinner."

It was for a final spree on the American Express card. In the last week of the month, Sandor said, the account would come in to his mother and that would be that. He had booked a table in the most exclusive restaurant in the neighborhood. A grand house it was, a mansion that was a hotel as well with every bedroom different and done in historical styles. However, we weren't going to stay in one of them, more's the pity.

Sandor shaved with the cutthroat in his usual graceful way, said something about having to redye the roots of my hair and disappeared to the bathroom. He was in there for ages. When he came back I hardly knew him. He looked wonderful. I had never seen him in a suit before, wearing a white shirt and with a tie. His face looked very smooth and olive-brown, his hair clean and still damp from the bath. He smelled of some pine fragrance.

"What?" he said. "What was that word I heard you use? Perfume is bad enough. What I have sprayed myself with, little Joe, is scent. Scent, right?"

"I can't compete," I said. "I haven't got anything to wear."

"There's no need to sound like a housewife going to a Masonic ladies' night," he said. "Have a bath and put a clean shirt on. You can put a tie in your pocket but they probably don't give a shit. I prefer you to look more casual anyway. It's best to make it clear who's the boss."

The place was floodlit. You could see it from half a mile away. It was like a film set. Sandor was driving. He told me to check that none of the Apsolands' cars were in the car park. That, he said, would have been a turnup for the books, though I couldn't see why. A man in a monkey suit came down the steps to open our car door, the way Garnet does for the Princess.

It was wasted on Sandor because he eats so little. We had five courses but he just picked at his. He said I could have the food and he would have the drink. I couldn't have both because I was driving home and the last thing he wanted was me being done for driving over the limit. It was the last thing I wanted too, not having any license or insurance. I'd finished my lamb and he'd pushed his fish around the plate when he started talking about the Prince and Princess again. He went right into the middle of things, as if we'd been talking about them all the evening. Or as if *he'd* been thinking about them all the evening, and maybe he had.

"After it was all over old Piraneso had a heart attack. He didn't last long, a few months. You saw the picture of her at his funeral."

"Was it the shock of it all?" I said.

"Not shock exactly. Strain would be the better word, I suppose. The kidnappers held the Princess for three weeks. That's nothing in the annals of Italian kidnapping, but I don't suppose Piraneso saw it like that. Some of his neighbors had employed professional negotiators to deal with the kidnappers of their relatives. That's quite usual. But he didn't. I think he wanted it all to be over as soon as possible. By the way, d'you know where the word comes from?"

"What?" I said.

"The word *kidnapper*. It's quite old, not modern, the way a lot of people think. It was first used to describe the men who used to snatch children to work on the American cotton plantations."

The waiter had taken our plates while Sandor was speaking and had come back again to ask us what we wanted for dessert. Pudding, I mean. Sandor says only "pudding" is correct, not dessert or sweet or afterdish. I ordered a thing made of meringue and cream and fruit and Sandor had a crème brûlée. While the waiter was hanging about, because I thought it wouldn't matter if he overheard, I asked a question.

"What about the servants? The ones at what's the name of the place? Rufina? What did he tell them?"

"I don't know," Sandor said, which didn't surprise me. I was only amazed that he knew as much as he did. "I'd guess he said she'd gone to stay with her friend in Rome. She often did, apparently. A woman friend, it's perhaps needless to say, but I expect there were some adventures to be enjoyed while she was away. She was only twenty-six and old Piraneso—well, he was over seventy. She must have longed sometimes for love, for a man of her own age."

I didn't say anything. Why waste sympathy on a girl who marries an old millionaire? She knew what she was doing. "What happened to her chained up in that tent?"

"She only saw the foreigner. Well, he was English like she was. He took her her meals. He waited on her as if he were her servant, he took her hot water to wash in and clean towels. He changed the sheets on her bed. She didn't lack for anything. But he never let her out."

"What did she do all day?"

"Nothing. I don't know. It doesn't matter, does it? He took her books but I don't think she read them and she didn't listen to the music tapes he brought her. They talked. She told him about the truffle dog that was her pet and about living up there at the villa. They talked about Paris, where she had an apartment. She slept a lot. She worried about her husband, or she said she did, wanted to know if he was all right all the time. Piraneso got his proof of life, he got the tape she made, and then he got his instructions from the statue at the Montemario Observatory. There was a letter in the Princess's hand inside the cigarette packet. It was just an appeal to him to comply with the kidnappers' demands and it had obviously been dictated. In fact, the Englishman had dictated it. It told Piraneso to go to Florence on the following day where a room had been booked in his name at the Excelsior Hotel. He was to wait in that room and between six and seven in the evening he would receive a phone call telling him what his next move must be.

"Piraneso did as he was told. The phone call came. It was an Italian. The sum they were asking for the Princess was one billion lire. Piraneso demurred. He doubted if he could find so large a sum. The voice asked him if he would like to receive one of his wife's fingernails, not nail parings. The Prince said they must give him time to raise the money. He was told the room was booked for him for four days and a phone call would be made to it each evening at this time.

"Piraneso set about getting hold of the money, or part of it. The next phone call came and he offered 500 million lire. On the following day he received a fingernail, lacquered pale gold and with blood at the root of it. It wasn't in fact from the Princess's hand. Remember that the younger of the Italians was a medical student with access to a dissection room, but Piraneso didn't know that. The next phone call came and he offered the kidnappers 750 million. They compromised finally at 800 million. Piraneso was to go across the Trinità Bridge and in the left-hand statue on the corner on the other side of the Arno, in a fold of drapery behind the heel, there would be another cigarette packet. Inside he would find his instructions for paying the ransom.

"Sure enough, his instructions were there. He was told to have the money in a small suitcase. The exact suitcase was specified, which suitcase to use, the Englishman having asked the Princess to describe what luggage her husband possessed. He was to take it to a church early in the morning. Eight o'clock was the time named. A Sunday and no one about but a few people exercising their dogs. Florence is full of churches and the streets are covered with dog shit, it's vile. The church they chose was Santo Spirito, very big, very baroque inside, but austere, too. They told him to go into the church and he'd be instructed what to do.

"The church opens at seven-thirty. The heavy outer door stood open and sitting inside the porch was a beggar. Piraneso thought this might be his man. He gave him a couple of coins and the beggar began on that extravagant praise and gratitude stuff, calling blessings on his head and so on. Piraneso was puzzled. He must have thought, what if I give him the suitcase and he's the wrong man? He pushed open the inner door and entered the church. It was empty, cold, silent, and, of course, quite dark.

"He stood in the nave, looking about him. And then a small middle-aged man he took to be the sacristan appeared from a side door. He walked up to Piraneso and said to him in Italian, 'You must not use a flash inside the church.' Piraneso said he hadn't a camera with him. 'You have a camera inside the suitcase,' the man said. 'Let me see.' So Piraneso opened the suitcase, which was full of lire in used notes. The man said, 'I must confiscate this camera,' took the suitcase and disappeared the way he had come."

Sandor lit another cigarette. All four people at the next table turned to stare at him. I can just imagine Sandor caring about that! "Piraneso went out of the church. The beggar was gone. He returned to Rufina where about three hours later he got a phone call telling him to meet a train that got into Rufina station at 3:30, coming from the other direction, not Florence.

"The Princess was on the train. She was alone, dressed as he had never seen her, in a too-large and very shabby black cloth coat, a scarf tied round her head. She was unharmed. All that had happened to her was that her nails had been cut short."

"And she'd been kept in a tent for three weeks," I said, "on a chain."

He shrugged and the dark moody look was back in his face. I had a strange feeling that only a tiny push was needed for him to open his heart to me, make some tremendous confession. But the waiter came up to ask if we'd like to have our coffee in the drawing room. It would be quite all right for "sir" to smoke in there.

We sat down in a room full of gilt mirrors and arrangements of dead flowers and groups of chintzy sofas and chairs. I expected Sandor to go on but he didn't. Our coffee came and a dish of chocolates. "Tell me how you know all this," I said. "I mean, if it wasn't in the papers."

He gave a crooked sort of smile. "I was the Englishman," he said.

I should have guessed. There were all sorts of things I wanted to ask, like was he the beggar in the church porch or was he the sacristan. Sandor loves dressing up, acting. I very much wanted to ask about the money, the 800 million lire. How many ways was it split, two or more? What was he doing in Italy in the first place? I didn't ask any of this because of the look on his face. He looked savage, that's the only word. He was lounging back in that armchair, the picture of grace and elegance in his new dark suit, the hand that held his cigarette in long, long fingers hanging negligently over the chair arm, his legs crossed, not the way women cross their legs, but with slim ankle on knee—and his face was a mask of anger. It was darkened by it, like a guy in the hospital's was with jaundice.

And then a strange thing happened. A new waiter we hadn't seen before came in with Sandor's brandy on a little round tray. He only said a word or two, something about being sorry for the delay, but you could tell he wasn't English. Sandor suddenly started talking in a foreign language to him, talking it as if it was what he had been speaking all his life. The waiter said one word I could catch, *italiano,* and that told me what the language they were talking was. Isn't it funny? Never a week goes by, or even a day come to that, without something happening to make me admire Sandor more. He was smiling by then, all the savagery gone. I suppose I really do feel something like hero worship for people who can speak foreign languages, maybe because I can't imagine doing it myself.

We went home soon afterward. It wasn't far but Sandor fell asleep in the car beside me. He'd had a lot to drink. I thought what I'd really like was for him to go on sleeping so that I could pick him up and carry him tenderly into the house. Of course, that would have been impossible. For one thing I doubt if I could have lifted him, and think what a fuss that would cause at the

Lindsey Guest House! As it was we passed Kevin in the hall and he rolled his eyes round and round at us.

Once we were upstairs Sandor revived. He had a cigarette. There was one question I couldn't resist asking. "Is that why she's so frightened?"

A hint of the black look came back. "Who says she's frightened?"

"Well, that infrared cell stuff and never going out alone. I mean, is it because she was kidnapped? I could understand it if it was."

"It is Apsoland who is frightened," he said very coldly, "not she. Whatever gave you that idea?"

I'd told him, but I wasn't going to say it again. We went to bed quite soon after that but I couldn't get to sleep for hours because of Sandor's dreams. He dreams so noisily sometimes, thrashing about and groaning and quite often saying things like "Where am I?" and once "Who am I?" That night though he didn't say that, but, "I'll give it back, I'll give it all back," over and over.

9

The cherry blossoms sprinkled the woods with white like a thin fall of snow. For a day or two, when the flowers were fully out, when their buds had opened and not yet begun to fade, it was a thick fall, a white blanket. The windflowers underfoot had the same delicacy of blossom, the same transparent pallor. Paul took Jessica walking in the woods and told her the names of everything. They took a wildflower book with them and a book on fungi. He taught her to say "anemones" not "anenomes" and not to laugh at the names of things because they were in Latin and long.

There were woodpeckers in the trees, you could hear the sound of their drilling a long way off, and a flock of long-tailed tits came through, crimson and gray, resembling butterflies rather than birds in their tumbling flight. The new leaves were uncurling now, copper-colored on the cherries, on the beeches the tender pale green of jade. One day they drove into the village and fetched Debbie, the daughter of Doreen who cleaned at the big house, and they fetched Emma and had a picnic at a place by the river where there was a jetty and rustic tables and chairs set out. Emma brought her camera and took a photograph of the pochards with their chestnut heads.

On the two days he had to drive Nina Apsoland—once to Bury and once to Frinton—Jessica came with them. That first time, on Easter Monday, she had sat alone in the back and Paul hadn't liked thinking of her there, isolated and silenced. But from the moment they moved off Nina had turned round and begun to talk to her. Jessica had brought her bucket and spade, had been unable to believe there would be no sand, only shingle. Nina told her there had been sand once but the sea itself had swept it away, and she told her about the lost town of Dunwich, that had once been a great city, and the church bells her own grandmother had sworn you could hear ringing under the sea when the gales blew.

"I didn't know you came from round there," Paul had said.

"My parents moved to Cambridge when I was about Jessica's age, but I was born here. I was born in Walberswick."

After that, on the way back from Aldeburgh and on their two subsequent outings, she had sat in the back with Jessica. Again he had that sense of their similarity to each other. They might have been mother and daughter. Jessica didn't look like Katherine or himself, though a little like his brother the farmer they had been to see, but she looked very like Nina Apsoland. They had the same small, fine, regular features, the same hair that varied through a whole spectrum of golds, the same bright blue eyes. Paul wondered of his daughter, will she keep it? Will she be as beautiful as that when she grows up?

It was Saturday and he had taken her, at their insistence, to spend the day with Stan and Doreen and their daughter. Parking the car, wondering if he would be expected to take Tyr and Odin out even though their master was at home, he encountered Apsoland coming down the front steps.

"I've got something I'd like to show you," Apsoland said.

Paul went into the house with him and into a room he had

never entered before, the study. It was furnished in the correct way, as such places seldom are, with armchairs covered in hide, so fatly padded and tightly buttoned as to look more like polished wood than leather, and with books, purchased surely in lots for the purpose, behind glass-fronted latticed bookcases. All was appropriate, the crimson Turkey carpet and polished oak surround, the desk with one of the more compact computers, mobile phone, television with postcard-sized screen, something that might have been a fax machine—all appropriate but the gun collection.

That was in another glass cabinet, but a plain one with the panes framed in aluminum. Apsoland produced a key, unlocked the door.

They were handguns inside, a .38 Smith and Wesson revolver, as used by United States police forces, a Colt semiautomatic .45, a couple of Lugers from the First World War, a Colt that was much older than that, an original one, Apsoland said, from the middle of the nineteenth century. He asked Paul if he would like to hold a gun he said was a 1918 Schmeisser and placed it in his hand.

"Done any shooting, have you?"

"Not with these," Paul said.

"A man," Apsoland said incredulously, "should be able to shoot."

He began to talk about handling guns, about his own fascination with them from boyhood. Had Paul ever done any clay-pigeon shooting? Paul hadn't. "I'd appreciate it actually if you'd have a go. There's a very decent chap not a mile from here'll give you a lesson if you'd like to book up with him any afternoon. I might come along with you myself, have a bit of a refresher."

Paul had to agree. Any day would be fine once Jessica had gone back to school. Out in the hall again, Apsoland confided that he was considering installing a security screen. This would enable him to see all callers and ask them their business. "Interrogate them" was the expression he used. Returning home, Paul wondered again why Nina had married him. Perhaps he was very kind to her, perhaps he loved her deeply and love given, he knew, sometimes calls forth irresistible gratitude. He hated to think it might just have been Apsoland's money, as it had surely been in the case of the Italian prince.

In the early evening he went shopping for their supper and then fetched Jessica from Stan and Doreen's. At home she had her bath and got into her nightie and dressing-gown and they ate Chinese takeaway out of the cartons on their laps and watched television. He tried to monitor what Jessica watched and turned the set off at news time and when there were documentaries about violence and cruelty. The panel games she loved exasperated him, but they were harmless.

She laughed uproariously at the climax of the quiz show when a blond girl with a Birmingham accent, promised an eighteen-carat necklace as a prize, won a gilt chain with eighteen carrots suspended from it. Perhaps it was something in the quiz which reminded her, for she turned to him and said, "Daddy, who's your friend Richard?"

He said, "What?"

"Your friend Richard. That's what he said. He phoned while I was at Debbie's."

"I haven't got a friend called Richard," Paul said, and then wondered if he should have been so positive. But she didn't seem alarmed.

"Well, we were having our lunch. They have lunch very early, at twelve o'clock, but I didn't mind, I was hungry. The phone went and Stan answered it and he was talking to this person and then he said, 'I don't know, I've got it written down somewhere, but his daughter's here, you can ask her.'"

"Did you talk to him?"

"Yes, and he said he was your friend Richard and could he have our phone number."

"And you gave it to him?"

"Yes, I did, and Stan said I was clever to remember it, but I thought I'd have to be very stupid not to remember because we've been here nine weeks and three days."

"I wonder how he knew Stan and Doreen's number."

"Doreen said that. She said how did he know to phone them,

and we all tried to think but we couldn't. Who's Richard, Daddy?"

"I think he may be someone I taught at school when I was a teacher," Paul said, though he didn't really think that. He would have said, if asked, that he never told lies to Jessica, but of course he did. He told them all the time to save her pain or fear or discomfort. Richard wasn't the name of anyone he knew. He couldn't remember a single Richard among his acquaintances. No doubt all would soon be made clear, for if the man had wanted his phone number and been given it he must intend to phone him.

Jessica went to bed soon after that. He went up with her and waited while she cleaned her teeth and plaited her hair. She could read so well now that he had stopped reading to her. The bed-time-story days were past and Paul missed them, though Jessica didn't. If he ever read aloud to her now he sensed that she was listening not with her old concentration but with a kindly patience, indulging his whim. She got into bed and said, shocking him because it had been so long since she'd asked, because he had thought—idiotically—that she was forgetting, "Do you think my mother will ever come back and live with us?"

Katherine had never been "Mummy" since she left. That loving and special diminutive Jessica had silently discarded, giving no explanation for the change to her present usage. He had tried to tell her he and Katherine were divorced now but she, who understood so much, had seemed to find that beyond her comprehension. He didn't know what to say. The truth was that he wouldn't have had Katherine back in any circumstances. And he felt a deep shame, he often did, that they hadn't tried harder for his child's sake. It was his fault as well as Katherine's.

"I don't think so, Jessica," he said. "But you can go and see her. You can go and stay with her in the summer holidays."

Could she? Katherine hadn't written since they moved to Suffolk. His letter to her telling her that Jessica could read hand-writing now had never been answered. It was becoming clear to him that Katherine wanted to cut herself off entirely. She saw a total rift as inevitable and had no wish to prolong the pain of achieving it. He kissed Jessica good-night and, as he left the bedroom, leaving the door a little ajar, asked himself what had prompted that last lie to her but cowardice. Fifty years ago the counterparts of himself and Katherine would have been kept together by social pressures. Were things better today? He couldn't think so. He had only exchanged uncongenial companionship and respectability for freedom and guilt.

And Jessica? Did children of her age lie awake dwelling, necessarily in a bewildered way, on their family situation, the relations between their parents, on loss and loneliness? Or, puzzled but helpless, did they fall asleep at once? He didn't know, was afraid to know. He stood at the landing window, looking across the courtyard on which fell the light from other windows, in this house and the other.

In the kitchen there seemed to be some sort of confrontation going on between Colombo and Maria. He could see, in the orange glow, mouths working, hands gesticulating. The other windows were empty, most with their curtains drawn, the golden light muted by the cloth, brightness showing only in a vertical line here and there. The Apsolands had guests for dinner. Several times, while he and Jessica watched television, blue-white radiance had flooded the room as the arc lamps burst into light. Maria made some final vituperative remark to her husband, snatched up a tray, and moved from Paul's line of vision.

He thought about the progress of that tray, along the passage and into the dining room—or coffee for the drawing room? And he imagined Nina, in some wonderful dress as he had never seen her, busy with the coffee cups, thin red Chinese porcelain, the sugar bowl filled with little brown chips like quartz, her hands white, her smile gentle and for once unafraid as she paused in front of each guest.

At a window on the first floor the curtains had not been drawn. It was an upstairs hallway where he had seen her once before. Now all he could see was an oval mirror in a gilt frame on the wall behind. In some households, he had heard, the women still left the dinner table before the men. Suppose she were to bring them along there, in front of that oval mirror, to her bedroom? A strange and irrational longing to see her, if only for a moment, possessed him. At the same time he knew this was something foolish that shouldn't be indulged. He drew the curtains and went downstairs.

The question of the man who called himself Richard and said he was a friend had passed from Paul's mind. But it returned in the morning when Doreen phoned to ask if he and Jessica would like to go with them to the 10:30 family service at St. Mary's. Jessica, of course, was longing to go. She was at an age when religious faith makes its first ardent appeal and, besides that, Debbie had replaced Emma, if only temporarily, as her best friend. It was Debbie this and Debbie that and Debbie says and Debbie has, while Emma and Harriet were forgotten—and, happily, the puppies too. Paul asked Doreen what kind of a voice this Richard had.

She had to ask her husband, she hadn't spoken to him. "London, Stan says. One of those London voices."

Not the broad Suffolk spoken by the three of them was what she meant. Jessica would pick it up, Paul thought, and castigated himself for being the worst sort of snob, he who had no real or imagined right to be one. He wouldn't go to church, thanks very much, he said, not feeling it necessary to explain that his parents' faith had left him for good more than twenty years before.

He drove Jessica down to the village in the Volvo. Coming back, he tried to imagine the Jareds estate encompassed by a fifteen-foot wall, calculated roughly the astronomical cost, and made himself laugh. Apsoland he could see in the distance, heading for the stile with Odin and Tyr bounding ahead of him. The cherries, among the clumps of trees, were already shedding their petals which lay in drifts on the green grass like remnants of frost. But it was too warm for frost, the day still, the sun uncertain, the sky a pale mass of cirrus. He drove in under the arch, put the car into its slot in the garage, and walked through the winter garden, looking at what the builders had done. A week should see the end of it, and a week to the end of his role as a kind of immigration officer.

The phone was ringing as he came into the house. He didn't think it might be Stan or Doreen with a query about Jessica, but that it was Nina wanting to be driven somewhere. He picked up the receiver, hoping. There were pips. A silence. A man's voice said: "Mr. Garnet?"

Disappointment made him snap out an affirmative.

"You won't know me so there's no point in giving you my name. I'm in a position to offer you a large sum of money. Two hundred thousand pounds is the figure."

At this point Paul knew he ought to put the receiver down. He didn't. The voice was a London voice, south of the river probably, not educated but far from Cockney. He said, "What do I have to do for it?"

"Not much. It's more what you have not to do. Turn your back and don't look for five minutes, basically."

"Turn my back on what?"

The voice said, "The Princess."

Paul thought he understood but he inquired just the same. "What do you mean?"

"Mrs. Apsoland."

Again he should have put the phone down. He thought, suppose I am being put to some sort of test by these private detectives Apsoland employs? This is exactly what he would do. Then he remembered Richard.

"Is your name Richard?"

The question was ignored. "On Thursday when you drive her to Cambridge you'll call at the petrol station on Newmarket Heath, fill the car, then drive another few hundred yards, when you'll have engine trouble. Take the car into the lay-by, explain you need to return on foot to the petrol station, and leave her. That's all. Two hundred thousand pounds, Mr. Garnet. I'll call you back in fifteen minutes."

The dial tone made a sound like an electric drill in Paul's ear. He laid the receiver back on its rest. I ought to phone the police, he thought, but I can't do that without consulting Apsoland and Apsoland is out with his dogs. I am certainly not going to alarm Nina. But it can't be real, it can't. This is Apsoland's man testing me.

I am being put to the test. This is so much in Apsoland's

character that I wonder he has waited so long before doing it. But would some minion of Apsoland's need to phone Stan and ask for the cottage phone number? Apsoland knew that number as well as he knew his own. He was not so subtle as to reinforce verisimilitude by having that phone call made to Stan. Suppose Jessica had not been there, would Stan have mentioned it? It was the merest chance, on which Apsoland couldn't have counted, that Jessica had been there. It would mean too that he must have counted on Jessica speaking to the caller and telling her father.

Paul, walking through to the kitchen to be out of sight of that phone, remembered the gray Fiat. The caller knew he took Nina to Cambridge every other Thursday because he, or someone connected with him, was the young bearded man in the gray Fiat. It was real. The shock of understanding made him suddenly feel cold. All the reasoning of the past five minutes disappeared. He felt cold, afraid, full of wonder.

Apsoland's paranoia was justified. He had reason for those guns, those dogs, those lights, reason to contemplate building a fifteen-foot wall, for steel doors in the house, for a bodyguard. And she, when she had told him she had been kidnapped once, was very likely not fantasizing. It had happened. The man on the phone was contemplating its happening again. He returned to the living room, aware that he had begun pacing. The wall clock that faced the window told him seven minutes had passed.

Ought he to try to record the conversation? Upstairs was Jessica's combined radio, tape player, and recording device he had given her for Christmas. If he put a tape in and held the microphone close up against the receiver, would it work? He opened the front door and went outside, walked through the arch and looked across the park for Apsoland. There was no one. The sun had come out, it was warm and the still air had a sticky feel.

Paul ran back indoors in case the man phoned early. Eleven minutes had passed. He went upstairs, fetched Jessica's recording machine, and put a tape in. For the first time he thought about the £200,000. It was to him a huge sum of money, but not unimaginable, far from that. He knew exactly what it would buy, here, for him, in his own county. A large, picture-book cottage with an acre, a car, enough left over to bring in a pleasant unearned income. And all he had to do was fake an engine fault, promise her his rapid return, walk away.

Of course he wouldn't do it. He had to live with himself afterward, as the hackneyed but telling phrase went. Besides, what guarantee was there he would ever get the money? No one would do such a thing unless they got the money first. Suppose he got the money first, then what? Of course, they would have to hand over the money first. Otherwise nothing would stop them going ahead with whatever villainy they planned and forgetting his existence. In other words, he thought, you are plainly taking it for granted the money, £200,000 or at any rate half of it, will be handed over before you play your part.

The time had gone by. Sixteen minutes had passed. When the man came on the phone again he would talk about handing over the money. That would be the first thing he would say. A cottage in the eastern part of the county, north of Woodbridge. Saxmundham or near it, perhaps. Jessica could go to a fee-paying school and avoid all those horrors that had driven him out of the teaching profession. He despised himself for wanting to educate her privately, but he knew he would do it if he had the money. The money! It was an enormous sum. Obviously they meant to ask a ransom from Apsoland, which Apsoland would pay. Who would be harmed? He imagined Nina's fear.

Twenty minutes. The man wasn't going to ring back. It was a trick, a test. He thought, I won't just let this go by, I'll have it out with Apsoland, even if it means losing this job. I may be his servant, but he has no right, no one could have a right . . . The phone rang. Paul picked up the receiver and held the earpiece close to the recorder. He put his head down on the table so that he could hear.

"Mr. Garnet? Or may I call you Ben?"

More surprises. "What?"

"Your name's Ben, isn't it?"

"My name's Paul." Why had he bothered to say that? "What do you want?"

"To offer you £200,000, Paul. You've had twenty minutes to

think about it; I gave you an extra five minutes. So how about it?"

He didn't wait for the offer of handing over the money or half of it to be made. Afterward he asked himself, was it because I didn't dare? "The answer's no. I wouldn't even consider it. I'm going to put the phone down now." He did so.

Attempts to play the tape failed. All he got was a soft roaring like the sound a radio makes when you tune it. Paul thought, will they try Colombo and Maria? Or Doreen? Or the workmen? None of those people had the power he had. Why hadn't he waited to hear the man make his offer of payment before the deed was done? He could have played along. Was it really because he was afraid he might have succumbed?

It didn't do to look too closely at oneself in this way. That sort of introspection—what else might he find in there? Neglect of Katherine because he preferred their child over his wife? Feebleness at the core of him, and failure of nerve, a man of six feet four who couldn't keep twenty-six teenagers in their seats and learning something? The stupid self-satisfaction of a man so puffed up with pride at getting a university degree that ambition ended there? None of this was quite true, all of it half-true. The thing to cling to was that he had said no, had never really contemplated saying yes.

Why not, then? Suppose she'd been old and ugly and bad-tempered, what then? Never mind that. He had to decide whether to tell Apsoland. What would the man do? What more could he do? I will wait until they approach me again, Paul thought. If they approach me again I'll tell him. It may be that it was a hoax, a test thought up by Apsoland's detectives, in which case he will expect me, as an honest man, to tell him. The idea of going to Apsoland with a pious face, smugly proclaiming his own honor, his own incorruptibility, brought a tide of anger that he felt actually redden his face. He was hot with anger. No, the private detective's failure would best be proved by his own refusal, his own subsequent behavior. And if the call had been from a genuine kidnapper—well, what could Apsoland do that he couldn't do far better? It was he, not her husband, who was Nina's protector and bodyguard.

The family service would be over by now. He got back into the Volvo, drove through the arch. Apsoland had come back and was standing on the gravel outside the front door with a hand lightly resting on the neck of each dog. And she was there. She had come out, down the steps, and stood hugging herself, a woman not used to the open air. She saw him and waved. Apsoland turned and raised one hand. Paul couldn't help thinking it was the way a high-ranking officer would return the salute of some underling. But she waved and smiled, immediately wrapping her arms about herself once more, a hand on each shoulder, miming an exaggerated huddling, the smile still there and radiant.

In that moment he knew he had fallen in love with her.

He knew it by the blow it struck him. It felt like, though couldn't be, a contraction of the heart. Guilt took over from it in the form of a question: How could I for a single split second have considered betraying her? She even asked me if I would betray her. He said twice, I love her, I love her.

Then he said aloud in the car, as loudly as if there were someone sitting beside him to hear, "You fool, isn't that typical of you to get into the cliché of the chauffeur falling for his employer? All the ridiculous precedents there are and you still do it. Snap out of it, forget it, it's not real, it's loneliness."

Stan and Doreen and the little girls had just got back. They wanted Jessica to stay to lunch again but Paul said no. He said no, no, over again to everyone's protests. Ostensibly his refusal was on the grounds that Jessica mustn't take their hospitality again until Debbie had been to Jareds cottage, but really it was because, selfishly, he wanted Jessica's company, he wanted her with him, not to be alone.

Stan said, "Did you ever hear from your friend Richard?"

Paul said yes, he had, this morning as a matter of fact. Nobody was specially interested. Why should they be? He drove back through the village, silent with Jessica beside him. It would have been impossible for him to say which was the greater shock, the harder to face and exist with, that a kidnapper had offered him a fortune to betray Nina or that he had fallen in love with her. She and Apsoland had gone in when he reached the house. There was not a sign of them. But what sign could there be? A scent of her? A dropped handkerchief?

Through the arch, park the car, and into the house. He half-expected to hear the phone ringing. It wouldn't ring, it was all over. He had passed the test or frustrated a kidnap attempt. Jessica said, "Stan's a plumber, Daddy, did you know?"

What was coming now? "We sang this hymn in church," she said, "and Stan said it was the plumbers' hymn. Doreen said why was it the plumbers' hymn and Stan said because of the bit that goes, 'Praise Him, ye morning stars of light, that fixed this floating ball.' " She looked at him doubtfully, with the smallest of tentative smiles. "It's funny, isn't it?"

Paul, in fact, thought it very funny. He laughed. She looked relieved. "Everybody laughed," she said.

"Do you know why it's funny?"

A hesitation and a frown. "I think so." Her "I think so" meant she didn't. He took her into the bathroom and showed her the inside of the cistern. Now she understood but she had stopped smiling. She seemed to be thinking—about God perhaps. He hoped there would be no questions, not today.

"Come on," he said. "Lunch. And then we'll go for a drive to the seaside, we'll go to Felixstowe." And get out of the house, away from where the phone can ring, away from wondering, if I look out of my window, will I see her at hers?

10

The phone box is on a windy corner outside the post office. I was alone when I made the first call but Sandor had schooled me in what to say. We had a rehearsal the night before in our room. I was me and he was Ben—no, Paul—Garnet, making all the possible replies the man could have made. He did them in this really broad Suffolk accent at first but I laughed so much he had to start again.

It had to be me because I've got an ordinary sort of London voice. Not many people speak like Sandor anymore, not even television newscasters. It's very distinctive. So it had to be me, talking the way you do if you've gone to school in Croydon. Sandor was right, of course, and Garnet gave some of the answers he had already thought of. I left him to think about what I'd said and then I went to meet Sandor in the George. He had a brandy and I had a beer and then we both went back to the phone box.

There was someone in there, so we had to wait and it was nearer twenty-five minutes than fifteen when I got Garnet again.

We stood squeezed up together in the phone box, Sandor and I. It was a long time since I'd been so close to him, felt the warmth of his breath and smelled him. He smells of cigarette smoke and that scent he uses and the sweetness of his own sweat. I might have done better with Garnet if Sandor hadn't been so near. He had his hand pressed flat against that chart on the wall where they tell you what numbers to dial, and it hypnotized me, that hand. So long and big-knuckled and the nails like burned almonds where the nicotine had stained them. Anyway, it was no go with Garnet. He threw me a bit saying his name was Paul. We hadn't allowed for that at our rehearsals, and until that moment I'd forgotten all about Sandor making it up and saying it was a dog's name. I put the phone down and looked at Sandor, I looked into his face which was about six inches from mine, and then he pushed open the door of the phone box and we went out into the street.

I expected anger. I wouldn't have been surprised if he'd hit me. He did nothing, sat in the car, said, "What did he say?"

" 'The answer's no. I wouldn't even consider it. I'm going to put the phone down now.' "

"I heard that last bit," Sandor said.

I said very carefully, I know when you have to be careful with Sandor, "It might have been different if I could have said we'd give him half the money straight away."

"We haven't got it."

I didn't say anything. I drove us back to the Guest House. The feeling of anticlimax was the heaviest I think I've ever known. I wanted to ask Sandor that question again but I was afraid to ask him. One thing about me, I don't mind admitting when I'm afraid. I didn't dare ask him what had happened to the 800 million lire they got for handing the Princess back five years ago.

Had Sandor got through £120,000 in five years? You could, easily, but you'd have something to show for it. Sandor has nothing but his mother's old car and a bagful of registration plates and an American Express card he won't keep for long. Come to that, I didn't know where Sandor had been in those years. It was as if he'd come back from Italy and gone to sleep (the Seven Sleepers' Den) and not wakened till he moved into the room in Shepherd's Bush and found me on the platform at the Embankment.

He didn't speak to me again that night. Since then Kevin and Les went and a pair of old women came in their place. They were bird-watchers on holiday. The funny thing is that both of them are called Joan. Sandor says that they are sisters and their parents loved the name Joan, so they called the second one Joan too in case the first one died. That's what people used to do in olden times when babies died more often than they do now. He says it proves they're a hundred years old.

That sounds as if he'd cheered up, though he hadn't really. Most of the time he lay on his bed smoking and the air in our bedroom went thick and blue. It had got hot, really hot for April, and the birds started singing outside at four. The two Joans ran about very excited, their field glasses bouncing about on their skinny tits. The crazy thing is they kept on about tits whenever you met them, only the ones they talked about were birds with long tails or black heads. Words are strange, aren't they? I never noticed till Sandor told me but I notice now.

When it got to Thursday, the day Garnet was due to take the Princess to Cambridge, I asked Sandor if he'd like me to try again.

"Have you got a hundred grand?" he said.

"It wouldn't have to be that much. We could give him a thousand on account. We could raise a thousand. The car'd fetch that. Or we could buy things on American Express and sell them." I sounded like a child, I know I did.

"The only way is going to be by force," Sandor said.

I'd been watching an old movie about a highwayman on my baby TV. It was *The Wicked Lady* with Margaret Lockwood and James Mason. When Sandor said that, I had a picture of us galloping up to the petrol station on Newmarket Heath and pointing those big old-fashioned guns at Garnet and maybe making the Princess come out and dance with us. I'd seen a film about that too.

"How did you do it that first time?" I said, greatly daring.

"I told you. She used to drive herself about in those days. Cesare drove the car that was across the road blocking her way and Adelmo and I were in the other one."

One thing, I thought, I've learned their names, I know their names now. Father and son, Adelmo the father and Cesare the son, the medical student. Cesare, which is like being called Caesar, the one who blocked her way, and Adelmo, the father, who played the sacristan in the church. Cesare, who was the beggar in the porch, the medical student who pulled the fingernail from a dead woman's hand. Sandor, who sat with her and talked to her while she was chained up, who brought her food and the water she washed in.

"The point is that she was alone then," Sandor said. "She's never alone now."

"So what do we do this time?" I said.

He didn't answer. I suppose he thought he'd already answered, telling me we'd do it by force. As we were on our way back from getting something to eat one of the Joans, the older, skinnier one, called out to Sandor and said there'd been a woman on the phone for him. I don't know what she was doing answering the phone as it's in the private office, but the two of them seem to be friends or relations of the people who run the place.

He must have thought it was his mother acting up about the American Express card, because he went pale and his eye sockets became dark as an Indian's. He said, "Did she leave her name?" And his voice was thick and breathy like someone with asthma.

"She said she was your sister."

The look on his face frightened her. It frightened me and I'm used to him. She said, "Aren't you called Joe?"

I thought he was going to strike her. I'm always thinking Sandor is going to strike people. He turned and went upstairs two at a time.

"I'm Joe," I said. "I'm sorry about that, he's a bit upset."

She didn't say anything, just looked at me the way a teacher at school had once looked at me when someone else in the class that I hung around with put a knife through a picture. Bewildered and indignant and old.

"Was there a message?" I said.

Her voice was very small and nervous. "Just that she was your sister and to say hello."

Tilly must have got the phone number of this place through directory inquiries. Joan the elder couldn't tell me any more. Tilly hadn't left a phone number. I tried to think when I'd last spoken to her. It must have been getting on for a year ago, the last time she came to see me in the hospital. Martin had gone off to New Zealand and left her the camper, which hadn't always been a camper but a mobile greengrocer's he'd converted himself. He and his brother had had a business delivering vegetables to some villages in Kent. Martin put in a toilet and a shower and a kitchen and a foldaway bed. That last time Tilly came to the hospital she drove herself in the camper and parked it in the car park. It was a nice day, I think it was late May or early June, and we walked over to the car park for her to show it to me.

C. W. and M. H. Farthing, Fresh Fruit, Vegetables and Salads was still painted on the side. Tilly seemed to think that was funny, leaving it there, and her new man had touched up the letters with paint. I can't remember the new man's name, but it doesn't matter. She said they were going to Belgium in it. Maybe her man was Belgian or he had a job there or connections with someone in business, I don't know. She didn't leave me an address—how could she?—but she promised she'd be in touch. Tilly had always been heavy, she's a big tall strong girl, but she'd put on more weight since Martin left. She told me she'd been eating for comfort, especially Bounty bars and Marathons, she couldn't pass a shop without buying one of those, but this man of hers had promised her he'd buy her a whole new wardrobe if she'd lose two stone. There were two Bounty bars on the table in the camper, so I didn't feel there was much hope of that.

I thought Sandor would be bound to ask me what my sister wanted or at any rate something about that phone call but he didn't. He'd got his press cuttings and photographs of the Princess out again, spread them out on top of his bed, and he didn't even look up when I went in. He doesn't think about anything but kidnapping the Princess, I'm sure of that, he doesn't think about me except in the way a master thinks about a pet dog. The dog is there and you have to feed it and shelter it and when you haven't anything better to do it's there for you to stroke and talk to. Not that Sandor ever strokes me, actually or—what's the word?—metaphorically. He talks because there's no one else to listen and he can trust me. That's something else dogs are good for, being trusted.

I shouldn't think like this and I don't know why I do. I have to remember Sandor chose me by saving my life. I'm his gallowglass. If I'm his pet dog as well, so what? That look had come over his face that baffles me because I don't know what feelings it's indicating, rage or hunger or pleasure. It's some kind of passion, I do know that. He once told me passion doesn't mean what it does on television, love and sex. It means suffering.

Suddenly there was something I wanted to ask him. The Princess was kidnapped five years ago. They got the money and she was handed back. If it was so successful that he wants so much to attempt it again, why has he waited so long? I'd like to believe it's because he was looking for the right person to go in with him and he didn't find anyone until he met me on the platform, but I don't really think that. Of course, I didn't ask that question. Instead I asked what he'd been doing in Italy in the first place.

Being a tour guide, he said, a courier. He was conducting parties of tourists round Rome and Florence and Pisa. After he left Cambridge he'd been a student of art history at Bologna University but he couldn't get a job suitable to someone with his qualifications. Sandor didn't actually say that, but I could hear it between the lines. As to how he knew Adelmo and Cesare, Adelmo's other son Gianni had been a friend of his at college.

"They were a fine bunch of mafiosi," he said.

He didn't mean real Mafia, did he? No, it was just a term, he said, but they were villains. "They corrupted me," he said, but he had such a funny look on his face, his mouth twisted up in one corner, that I wasn't sure whether he meant it or not. I asked if they'd organized the kidnapping. "Not Gianni," he said. "He had nothing to do with it. He was clean and respectable in those days, or it looked like that, a member of the local commune, the council that is. But when we got the money he wanted his cut. For introducing me to his father, it must have been, there wasn't any other reason."

"Did he get it?" I asked.

"The money?" he said. "What do you take me for?" It sounded foreign, the way he said it, like someone playing a foreigner on TV. "That's enough about them," he said. He put the cuttings and photographs back in the box and fetched the tube of bleach to do my hair.

The room soon stank of ammonia. Sandor handled the stuff a bit carelessly I thought, flicking it around so that gobs of it got on the carpet. Be careful, I said, because I could already see one spot on the carpet where the bleach had landed on a red rose and now it was a pale pink one. The next gob went in my eye. It stung and burned, I'd never known anything like it. The tube said that if you got it on your skin, let alone your eye, to rinse with cold water at once. So I did that but the burning went on. All that mattered to me was that I could still see out of that eye and I could. I don't think Sandor did it on purpose, though it's true he doesn't like being told to take care.

"Don't you worry about the carpet," he said when my hair was drying. "It's a load of shit anyway. Red roses and blue butterflies on a yellow background—Christ God. We're getting out of here. It's time we stayed in a proper hotel."

"Are we?" I said. A neutral response seemed safest.

"At the weekend," he said. "First we'll pay a little visit to my mother's."

When Paul went with Ralph Apsoland to the clay-pigeon shooting range, he was rather surprised that Apsoland, who had taken the day off, should have been willing to leave Nina alone and take her bodyguard with him. But Apsoland had begun explaining before the Range Rover was clear of the grounds. Not only were Colombo and Maria there, but it was one of Doreen's days and Stan had come up with her (on a push-bike, Paul gathered) to assist the landscape gardeners in their task of digging a pond and building a fountain. Tyr and Odin, too, remained at home.

Apsoland spent the short drive deploring the impracticability of building a wall to surround the park and explaining to Paul in great detail the circumstances of the case he had against the County Council in the matter of the footpath. The dislike Paul increasingly felt for Apsoland surprised him. It was jealousy, he supposed, resentment. He told himself he wouldn't mind so much about him being Nina's husband if he were less of an insensitive boor.

It was a gray day, the low clouds sometimes spitting rain. The clay-pigeon range was a bleak meadow with a clump of dilapidated sheds at one end, a lookout tower at the other, and in the middle of the grass a couple of shallow hummocks like tumuli. There was no one to be seen. Apsoland had brought two shotguns with him, a pair of twelve bores which lay side by side on a blanket in the back of the Range Rover. While they waited he talked to Paul about his dog-breeding days and the sad demise of some world champion from liver disease.

Just as Paul was beginning to think he couldn't stand any more and might soon have to pretend illness and a need for fresh air, an ancient estate car, mud-covered, lurched into the field through a wide gap in the hedge. A man in a Barbour jacket like Apsoland's got out carrying a broken shotgun over his left arm.

He introduced himself as Vic and addressed them as "gentlemen." "Now, gentlemen, have you any prior experience with guns?"

This displeased Apsoland. He was one of those people, Paul thought, who ask those who annoy them if they know who he is. Vic evidently didn't know he was a local landowner who regularly shot game on his own grounds. Apsoland said haughtily that he was an experienced shot. It was Paul who needed coaching in the handling of a twelve-bore.

At this point Paul thought he should say something about his previous experience. "It's mostly rifle shooting that I've done. I'd say I was a fair shot." There was no need to mention the silver cup he had won at the rifle club and which now stood on the mantelpiece at Jareds cottage. "This is the first time I've held a shotgun in twenty years."

Apsoland wasn't listening. He strode about, pointing his gun at invisible airborne targets.

"Well, gentlemen, which one of you is going to be first to kick off?"

"Better let Paul here," said Apsoland. "Then, if we have time, he can get two goes in."

Vic showed Paul how to break the gun and load it, neither of which examples were necessary. Paul reflected that it wasn't his fault anyway, he had told them. If they didn't choose to listen, well and good. Vic blew his whistle, signal to a hidden henchman behind the tumulus, and the first clay came flying up. Paul thought, God, I'd better miss it. He waited a fraction too long, fired, and let the clay pass over intact.

Vic said, as Paul knew he would, "Better luck next time." He adjusted Paul's gun, suggested his head was not at quite the right angle.

The next clay came up and this time Paul hit it, breaking the disk into two clean pieces. Vic clapped. "Very good, very good." Paul thought, why the hell should I pretend, I've told him. He took aim and hit the next clay and the next. Now he had hit four in succession, all clean shots that split each clay in half. The fifth shattered the clay and the fragments showered the grass. A flock of pigeons rose into the sky from the distant trees. Somewhere a frightened pheasant cackled and took flight with a rattle of cumbersome feathers.

They were each to aim at thirty clays. Paul hit twenty-eight of his. Apsoland, whom he had rightly assumed to be a good shot, hit twenty-nine. But when they moved to the other range, where the clays came up at a low, oblique angle, first to the left, then to the right, his shooting was less accurate and he missed as many as he hit. Paul on the other hand shot down all but three of his clays. Vic shook hands with them both, but it was to Paul that he said, "Congratulations on a fine morning's shooting."

Paul couldn't help being reminded of one of those stories Jessica was so fond of in which the swineherd or frog turns out to be a fairy prince in disguise. Of course the transformation usually takes place in the presence of the beautiful heroine and to her gratification. Apsoland was miscast in this role. Displeasure made him sullen. Paul wondered if he would tell Nina, hoped he would, saw the transformation as it might be in her eyes—for isn't it still true that women, in spite of themselves, admire a gallant man, proficient with weapons?—and immediately castigated himself for a fool and worse, a pathetic grubber after flattery and praise.

He wouldn't get that from Apsoland anyway. His employer said nothing at all until they were nearly at the entrance to the Jareds drive. Then, in a tone of gruff embarrassment, it was, "Frankly, Paul, I think that was a bit off, giving me the idea the nearest you'd got to a firearm was banging off an air gun when you were a kid."

Paul said nothing. The man must know he had invented that himself. Apsoland waved his key out of the window to open the gates and moved into the flint avenue. All was peaceful. The trees were thickening as their foliage grew, changing from graceful skeletons to impenetrable screens. Past the rise and the curve the house came into view, pearl gray in the slightly misty damp air, a window open upstairs, the landscape gardeners' van parked on the gravel.

"Well, haven't you anything to say for yourself?" said Apsoland like a headmaster.

If he sacks me, to hell with it, Paul thought. I'm not made to be a servant, I waited too long before I tried it. "You ought to be thankful I'm capable of protecting you and your wife. That's what you want me here for, isn't it?"

Apsoland swung the Range Rover round in a swift arc in front of the house. He switched off the ignition and jumped out. Paul got out more slowly and walked round to the rear to take the guns out. Apsoland said, "I'd like it to go on record that I don't care for your tone, right?" When Paul simply nodded, he said, "Clean those guns, will you? And put the vehicle away."

First he fetched Jessica. She had succeeded in maintaining total silence for one hour and fifty-two minutes. It was the first time she had done something that truly surprised her father. A milestone, he thought. This is the first of many things that will astonish me and make me ask myself how well I really know her. He felt proud of her self-control, her determination.

"Well, I congratulate you, Jess. That's perfectly splendid. You mustn't think I'm criticizing in any way, I'm not, but if you could keep quiet for an hour and fifty-two minutes what stopped you keeping it up for the whole two hours?"

"Emma talked," she said. "Emma said something and then Matthew did and some people giggled and there didn't seem any more point. Do you think I was good?"

"You were very good."

"I read my book. It was awful for the ones who can only read a little bit. You owe me eleven-twenty, Daddy, and Mrs. Apsoland owes me thirty-three-sixty."

"Thirty-three?"

"She said she'd give me thirty pee a minute. It was while we were talking on the way to Bury, I don't expect you heard."

He had. He remembered now. And he had thought, she has no idea of money, its value, its buying potential, she has so much: thirty pee an hour, thirty pee a minute, it was all the same to her. She would have offered Jessica thirty pee a second just as willingly.

"Can we go in now and ask her for it?"

His first reaction was to refuse. But he said nothing, he deliberated. It was the best time of day, not yet five, and he had seen Apsoland go out again. He longed to see her. It was more than twenty-four hours since he had seen her, when he had brought her back from Bury and she had left him and gone up the steps where Maria waited, holding the front door open.

For this infatuation, this growing passion, he hated himself. The way it grew was particularly horrible, like a spot on the skin that becomes more and more sore, that instead of drying up and going away is turning into a boil, a carbuncle. But the boil would be entirely painful, whereas what he felt for Nina was pleasurable too, to the extent of silly joy. It was a fatuous happiness he felt when she sat beside him. A voice inside his head sang tuneless powerfully orchestrated melodies. Much of the time he was breathless. When she went up the path to her friend's house and disappeared inside, the closed door, though quietly shut, was a slam in his face.

He sat in the pub, eating his sandwiches, with a horrible feeling of letdown and humiliation. Talking to her in his mind, conducting whole elaborate conversations in which he must supply questions and answers, all the dialogue, was impossible to escape. Try as he might, his very attempts at freedom were requests to her. His struggles not to fantasize their being together were pleas to her to release him. Not that he yet had sexual thoughts. Those he was still spared as he stood there, enclosed in his dreams of high romance, gazing out of the window across the courtyard to her house and her windows, dreams of romance that alternated with self-hatred.

It was all so ridiculous, so trite and above all so unsuitable. He was like the man in the old song who was a servant, who was nothing to his mistress and could never woo her. Better that, he thought, than the modern servant who can envisage a clandestine relationship with an employer and either achieves it or dismissal.

Jessica was waiting for his answer, and not waiting, now that her sponsored task was performed, in silence. The request had been twice repeated and there came an exasperated "Daddy!"

He said, "Yes, all right," and thought, *Did you not see my lady go down the garden singing? Silencing all the songbirds and setting the alleys ringing?*

She came through the arch at that moment. This was so unusual that the idea came to him that he was hallucinating, that the strength of his need to see her had summoned a vision of her. Nonsense, worse than nonsense. She had come, of course, to see the completed winter garden on which the men had finished work about an hour before. Hadn't he talked to them himself, sent the foreman or boss or whatever he was into the house to speak to her, shepherded by Maria?

The double doors, which were on the far side of the glass building and which opened onto a gravel path and overlooked the park, were no doubt locked, for it was to this small side entrance she was coming. She opened the door and stepped inside. The winter garden had been rebuilt in the fashionable Crystal Palace Victorian style with Gothic ironwork. Certain panes of the glass were stained yellow, red, and light blue. The sun made a flickering pattern of pink and amber spots dancing on her arms and body.

She saw him and smiled. The distance was considerable, thirty or forty yards, but she had seen him and smiled. It was enough. He took Jessica's hand and they went outside. Nina came out of the winter garden holding a small stone urn planted with various sorts of cactus.

"Builders are so odd, don't you think? We forgot this when we cleared the place. Wouldn't you have thought they'd have moved it? But no, they must have religiously covered it up with one of their dust sheets every day. It seems to be thriving."

"I made my silence," said Jessica.

Nina seemed disproportionately delighted. Paul noticed, with a small pang, how much more enthusiastic her congratulations were than his had been. "I think you're brilliant. I could no more have done that when I was your age than I could have . . . swum the Channel!"

"Could you do it now?"

"What, swim the Channel? I shouldn't think so."

"Make silence?"

"Ah," she said, "I expect I could do that. I haven't so much to talk about now." He wondered what she meant. He felt obscurely hurt for her. "I owe you some money," she said. She spoke to Jessica exactly as if she were grownup. "Would you mind a check?"

"Would I, Daddy?"

He found himself apologizing for the size of the sum. Even while he was going on with it, floundering about it being an imposition and not necessary, certainly not necessary to pay it now, he was thinking with a rage deeply internal how stupid love makes us, how unattractive, what fools!

"Come into the house," she said.

She sat down at her little desk in the drawing room and wrote a check. Jessica looked about her at the pretty room. I wonder where the steel door comes down? thought Paul. Very lightly, with the tip of her finger, Jessica prodded the rotund cactus and its covering of whitish fluff.

"Do you like them?" Nina said. "Go on, have them."

"Can I, Daddy?" She had suddenly started asking his permission for everything. It was a phase, begun by God knew what.

"Of course," he said. "Say thank you."

She was suddenly indignant. "You don't have to tell me. I know that, I'm not a baby." She picked up the urn with a little effort, it was heavy for her. "Thank you very much, Mrs. Apsoland. And thank you for my check." Her dignity was awe-inspiring.

Paul said, "Come on then. Teatime."

What folly made him hope Nina would say, stay and have tea with me? She probably didn't have tea, no one did any more unless they had children. He heard himself say, unthinking, "Will you want me to drive you in the morning?"

"It's Saturday," she said. "Remember?"

He noticed something then, as they were leaving. She expected him to go out the back way. They had come in by the front door, Maria had let them in; Nina never used the back door, but he and Jessica were expected to leave that way. Colombo was in the kitchen, cleaning silver. He didn't look up as they passed through.

When he had put the kettle on, poured Jessica's milk and put her biscuits onto a plate, he told her to keep the cactus up in her bedroom. If it were downstairs he might be in danger of making a fetish of it. *I remember the wooing of a peascod instead of her, from whom I took two cods, and giving her them again, said with weeping tears, "Wear these for my sake." We that are true lovers run into strange capers.* He carried the cactus upstairs himself, it was too heavy for Jessica; it must have weighed five pounds.

12

I woke up in the night, thinking about that Italian family. Perhaps the money had gone to them, all the 800 million lire, because they'd done most of the work. Or perhaps Sandor had stayed with them after they'd sent the Princess back to her husband and they'd used the money to set up in business together. The business might have had something to do with tourism, maybe a travel agency, but it had gone bust and they'd lost all the money. After that Sandor had had to come back to England. I liked the sound of that, it sounded the sort of thing that might have happened.

There were a lot of questions I still wanted answers to. What had happened to Sandor's share of the money, of course, but others as well. Like, why hadn't he heard a word from his mother about the American Express card? It was May now and she'd have to pay the amount Sandor had run up by the fifth or sixth. I didn't want to think about how much it would be. Every time I calculated I sort of stopped at a thousand pounds.

We were going up to Norwich in the morning but she wouldn't be there. Sandor wanted his leather jacket he'd left there and a silver cigarette lighter she'd once given him in a generous moment. She was going away on holiday to somewhere in Greece, leaving to drive to Heathrow at dawn. I was sorry we wouldn't see her. When you love someone you want to get a look at everyone who belongs to them, don't you? You want to know all their family and friends because it teaches you more about them. I wondered how I'd feel about a woman who could be stern and unforgiving toward Sandor.

Sandor drove the car. If his mother had been going to be home I expect he'd have put his suit on, but since she wasn't and it had turned cold he wore his jeans and that denim jacket lined with sheepskin he had on the day we met. When we'd been driving north a little while I asked him how much ransom were we going to ask for the Princess this time?

"A million, two million," he said. "Does it matter?"

"Pounds?" I said, and my voice sounded quite hollow in my own ears.

"Naturally, pounds. Sterling. What would you like it in? Yen?"

"Two million pounds?" I said. Truly, it was the first time I'd thought of the money in connection with me. Some of that money would be mine, just as some of the first lot had gone to Adelmo and Cesare. I didn't say any more and Sandor wasn't interested, but I thought about it and it didn't seem real.

The house outside Norwich was big and detached, red brick and white plaster with a lot of wood on the outside, but not old like the houses in the country where we lived. It stood on top of a sort of slope that was done in terraces and the path up to the front door was part path and part little steps. Sandor had his key and we started climbing up this sort of path staircase.

He stopped and stared as if he could see something where there was nothing. He might have been seeing a ghost. The front door burst open, that's the only word, and this woman came running out, down the steps, and threw her arms round Sandor. The truth is, I've never seen a woman hug anyone like that except on television. I'm slow, I know that, but for a moment or two I couldn't take it in that this was his mother. His mother had gone to Greece.

She stepped back, said, "Let me look at you," and then, "Oh, what a surprise! What a treat!"

"I thought you'd gone away," Sandor said.

"There's an airport strike in Athens," she said. "We've put it off for forty-eight hours." She didn't seem upset that he'd made it clear he wouldn't have been there if he'd known she'd be home. Her smile was adoring. "Am I glad about that strike! Wouldn't I have kicked myself if I'd missed you, Alex."

Being called Alex would trigger something off, I thought, but Sandor didn't say anything, just sort of smiled half-heartedly at her. He went past her up the steps and was in the house before he remembered me.

"This is Joe Herbert," he said. "Can you give us lunch, Mama?"

She shook hands with me, all smiles. "How do you do, Mr. Herbert? It's always a pleasure to meet one of Alex's friends."

"There you are, Joe," Sandor said. "Can you beat it? It's not you that counts, but being my friend."

I didn't mind. He'd never called me his friend before and that was all that mattered.

The house was nice inside, very comfortable but not grand. The room we went into was full of those things that must make living a very interesting, comfortable business, objects Mum and Dad had never had. There was a compact-disc player and a video recorder, bookcases full of books, plants in a thing she called a jardinière, and a stack of table games in boxes. She got me to sign my name in a visitors book that was bound in white leather. As for her, she wasn't a bit like Sandor to look at except she had eyes like his, deep set and very dark. Her face was heavily made up with white powder and red lipstick and her hair was dyed chestnut red and permed. You could see the corset or girdle thing she wore through her dress, sort of ribs of it, and a bulge where it stopped and her thigh started. She looked awful but she was really nice. I wondered what it would be like to have a mother like her but I couldn't imagine it, not really.

One of the first things she said was, "Are you finding the American Express card a bit of a help, Alex? I've had the account in and I see you've been making good use of it."

I was staggered. It was as if I was dreaming, but I soon knew I wasn't. She really had said that. And she was smiling in a warm way. It was all of a thousand we'd spent, more probably, and she was smiling the way someone might if she asked what you'd bought with a £5 book token.

I thought Sandor'd be embarrassed, getting caught out, and his face had gone a bit dark, which is his version of blushing. But he got himself together quickly enough, looked at me, and winked. I could see it all. He must have wanted to make an impression on me as a sort of defiant rebel who cheats his own mother. And more than that, he must have hated the idea of me thinking he'd had an easy time of it with his parents when the reverse was true for me. Imagine Sandor bothering about what I think! It showed me he's got a weak side to him which just makes me love him more.

His mother came outside with us before lunch to look at the car. Sandor hadn't stolen that either, she'd given it to him. I knew that by her saying she wished it could have been a new one. She seemed delighted, loved the new color. We had asparagus soup for lunch and seafood in a cheese sauce and fresh fruit and cheese and biscuits and wine. The soup and the prawns came out of the freezer and she heated them up in a microwave. It all ran very smoothly. While she was laying the table we had champagne. She brought the champagne in for Sandor to open and he did and it shot all over the room, splashing her and the compact-disc player, but she didn't seem to mind. All through lunch she talked about money, explaining to me I suppose, since Sandor presumably knew already.

She had quite a lot of money her first husband, Sandor's father, had left her and she'd been parting with lumps of it to Sandor ever since. "He might as well have it now, not wait until I'm gone," she said, smiling fondly at him.

What she'd really like, she said, was for Sandor to come back and live at home where she could look after him. But she could understand why he didn't want to do that, he and his stepfather didn't see eye to eye. Sandor cast his up when she said that. She'd have liked to buy him a house of his own or a flat but her means—that was the word she used, means—didn't quite run to that. Not these days, with prices so astronomical.

We drank a lot of wine. I hoped the effects would wear off before we were due to drive back. Sandor had a brandy after his lunch and then another. He got up from the table and told his mother he was tired, he needed a nap, and she wasn't cross or indignant or anything. She just said he must be exhausted after all that long drive, wasn't it dreadful, there ought to be a motor-way to Norwich, and to go and have a nice lie-down on her bed. We were left alone together, the two of us, and I think that was what she really wanted because she brought a fresh pot of coffee and came and sat down beside me on the sofa and started saying some amazing things.

First of all, she simply assumed Sandor and I were having a homosexual affair. Now most mothers, as far as I know, most mothers of her sort of age, in their fifties and sixties, would rather almost anything than that their son was gay. But not Diana, as she said I was to call her.

"It makes me so happy to see him together with a nice genuine person like yourself, Joe," she said. "A really close friendship— relationship, as they say nowadays—is such a support, don't you think? Alex needs support, he's so sensitive. I'm going to tell you something very frankly, you won't mind, will you?"

I said I wouldn't mind. What else could I say?

"Well, then, I'm a very jealous woman. Possessive may be a better word. I just couldn't have stood to see Alex with another woman, wife, girlfriend, whatever. I couldn't have borne it. A man is different, I'm not in competition with a man."

I drank my coffee and had some more brandy because it was

there, though I knew I shouldn't. My head was bobbing about a bit and it felt full of something, but not of dirty water with oil floating on it, never of that.

"So tell me about this business you and Alex are going in for."

The whole thing was so astounding that for a moment I thought he'd actually told her what we were doing in Suffolk, that we were trying to kidnap the Princess. But some common sense came to my aid, perhaps just caution, in spite of all the booze I'd gone through, and I said I thought I ought to leave it to him to tell her. After all, she was his mother.

Then—will you believe it?—she started telling me what a bad time she'd had giving birth to him, in labor for forty-eight hours, had to be cut open and stitched up, and of course having any more children ever again was out of the question. But it had all been worth it just to have him. He looked like his father, she said, the handsomest man in Bomber Command, whatever that means, but his character was like hers, sensitive, vulnerable, too often misunderstood. That was why he had gone to prison, through a misunderstanding. He hadn't meant to hurt anyone.

Another revelation. She assumed I knew and I wasn't going to let on I didn't, that it was news to me. That meant I couldn't ask what Sandor had gone to prison for. All the time she was edging nearer and nearer to me and when she said that about a misunderstanding she took my hand and held it. There wasn't anything sexual in it, it wasn't an old woman getting flirtatious with a young guy, it was just friendly and warm, like a mother. Or what I guess a mother might be like in an ideal world, say, where people behave the way they're supposed to.

Of course I was a bit pissed, I have to be honest. I squeezed her hand back. I liked her holding my hand, it made me feel good, like I wanted to smile and laugh and maybe sing. I did smile, right into her face, and she said some more about being so happy Sandor had found me. Only she called him Alex, she always did that.

"Alex had a nice friend when he was at college in Italy, Joe," she said. "That was in Bologna. He was called Gianni, Gianni Viani. Doesn't that sound funny? Like being called Johnny

Bonny, I always said. He had a second name, I can't remember what. Why doesn't he call himself that, I said to Alex, but Alex thought I was just being silly. I hoped they'd be a team, if you understand what I mean, but he had a very harsh family, very strict. I suppose they disapproved. Italians are all for marriage and the family, aren't they?"

She went on telling me more and more things about Sandor, but she didn't say another word about his being in prison. I'm afraid I dozed off at one point but she didn't seem to mind, she was pleased, she said it was lovely to think I was so relaxed in her home.

Sandor reappeared at about five. Time to go, he said. He'd hardly spent any time with his mother but the funny thing was she seemed quite anxious now for us to leave. She insisted we take food back with us, a chocolate cake and packets of things they call "cocktail snacks" and two bottles of wine. As I was putting it into the boot of the car along with the leather jacket and a new sweater she'd bought for Sandor I saw a man coming along wearing a bowler hat and carrying a briefcase. Of course it wasn't Sandor's stepfather, it was just some neighbor, but it reminded me of what I'd forgotten, that Diana's husband would soon be home. Diana didn't want Sandor to meet him any more than Sandor did himself.

When we were leaving she enveloped Sandor in one of those tremendous hugs. I could see him straining his neck away from her and arching his back like a picture I'd once seen of a man being clutched in the arms of a bear. Or maybe that poor man the Jareds lion has got hold of? She asked if she could kiss me goodbye and I said yes.

Do you know, I don't think I've ever been kissed by a woman before. Well, I've certainly never been kissed by a man, but you know what I mean. I suppose my own mother kissed me but I've no recall of any of that. Mum never did and Tilly and I never got into the way of kissing, I don't know why. Diana didn't kiss me on the mouth but on the cheek, holding me by my shoulders. She smelled sweet and powdery like a cake, like a Victoria sponge.

"Goodbye, Diana," I said. "Thank you for having me."

That made Sandor laugh and he was still laughing as I drove away. He said it was what children said, but I couldn't remember I'd ever said it when I was a child. I wanted to ask him what he'd been in prison for and why but as usual I was afraid to ask. Suddenly he barked at me, "What did my mother say to you?"

"She was very nice to me, Sandor, I think she's a wonderful lady."

"Christ God," he said, "there you go again. I'm not in the mood for translating and I don't give a shit about what you think of her. What did she say?"

For once I wasn't going to let him get it all out of me. "She told me about when you were born and about your father and she thinks—she thinks we're—well, lovers."

That got a burst of laughter. "She doesn't know her arsehole from Christmas," he said.

I didn't mention Gianni Viani any more than I mentioned prison, but I thought about him, I couldn't get him out of my mind. The truth was I was jealous. It hadn't occurred to me to be jealous when Sandor talked about knowing him at university, I didn't feel like that till Diana talked about them being a team. Giving him a surname too, that helped to make him real.

The town was silent and deserted when we got back at about eight. It had taken us half an hour to get round Norwich. Wind was blowing the litter about the marketplace and coming in gusts out of the alleys. It wasn't much like May, though the nights were getting light. The sky was gray and stormy-looking but as light as at three. Sandor said we'd eat Chinese. It was the cheapest restaurant anywhere around and we'd been eating in expensive places lately. But not that night. And he didn't say any more about moving into a hotel. It was as if all that was fun when it looked as if he was cheating his mother, but now I knew that he wasn't so it wasn't fun any longer. Well, if that wasn't the explanation, what was?

I kept thinking about Rome where this Gianni and his family came from, the "mafiosi," the bad father and the bad brother and the good one, who wasn't all that good when he started demanding money he hadn't worked for. I'm very ignorant, I don't mind admitting it, but I somehow thought Bologna where the university was and Boulogne were one and the same. I knew Boulogne was in France because I'd been there once on a day trip, a coach and ferry trip with Mum and Dad to buy cheap booze one Christmas.

In the morning, when I went out to get the papers, I paid a visit to the public library. I was a bit nervous, but I got myself together and asked the girl if they had any maps of Italy. She found me a big atlas with an index at the back and there— surprise, surprise—was a Boulogne in France and a Bologna in Italy. Next I looked in the travel section and found a book about northern Italy. Bologna, it said, was supposed to have the best food in the country and another good thing about it was that you could walk from one side of the city to the other in a rainstorm without getting wet. This was on account of the arcades which covered up all the pavements. I liked the sound of that, we could do with something like that here.

There was a lot more, mostly about churches as far as I could see, but I didn't have time to read any more. I knew Sandor would wonder where I was and get suspicious. On the way back I thought about Gianni Viani and I pictured him walking about under those arcades, thinking of Sandor perhaps and remembering.

When I reached the street where the Lindsey Guest House was it had started to rain. No arcades here to keep us dry, unfortunately. I ducked into a shop doorway and stuffed the newspapers down the front of my jacket. As I came out and looked along the street I saw a van parked outside the guest house—not a van, a camper. It was green with *C. W. and M. H. Farthing, Fresh Fruit, Vegetables and Salads* painted on the side.

Tilly had come. I started running toward the camper.

13

When I first saw Tilly she was twelve and fat. I was seven. She was tall even then, nearly as tall as Mum, and putting on much too much weight. Mum used to encourage her to eat all the wrong things, chocolate bars and chips, crisps and cakes, she used to be always buying frozen cakes. Most days there'd be a dairy-cream sponge or a black forest cake defrosting on the kitchen counter. I believe Mum encouraged Tilly to eat because she wanted her to get fat and be unattractive to men. Women get like that with teenage girls, they can't face the competition. By the time Tilly was a teenager she was huge, all of fourteen stone.

Mum refused to see anything wrong. When she was talking to other people she called Tilly "a fine girl," which was a way of putting it I suppose. Tilly wasn't even pretty, her face was too big and the spaces between her features were wrong somehow,

I don't know, I can't describe it. She had very thick mouse-colored hair and was so shortsighted she had to wear glasses, though she hated them. Mum, of course, insisted on the steel-framed kind.

A woman Mum knew once asked her if Tilly was a bad case of Down's or if she could read and write. That was heavy stuff, wasn't it? She didn't call it Down's, people didn't in those days. A mongol was what she said. Some people are really cruel, it makes you shiver. Now you'd think Mum wouldn't ever have spoken to that woman again, but no, not a bit of it. You'll not believe what she did. Whenever Tilly did something a bit stupid—we all do sometimes, let's face it—or made a mess of things at school, Mum'd bring it up about that woman and say, "You don't want people thinking you're a mongol, do you?"

Tilly ran off when she was sixteen. That's all rubbish about girls having to be thin and pretty to get men. *Any* girl can get a man, I don't know why; I can't account for it, but it's true. When she's young, that is. *Any* girl. Look at the married women you see about, even they managed to get husbands once. Brian had a good effect on her, he made her use a bit of makeup and dye her hair and change her glasses for the kind with big lenses and pink see-through frames. And she lost weight, though not enough. She wasn't ugly anymore and no one would have said what that cruel woman said.

The strange thing was that when I walked into the Lindsey Guest House that morning I didn't recognize her. I didn't recognize the woman who was standing in the hallway talking to Joan the younger. But she recognized me. She knew me in spite of my orange hair. Of course I hadn't had a beard the last time I saw her and I haven't now.

She turned round and said, "Joe," and then she said, "It's good to see you—wow, it's so good," and though she didn't kiss me because we never kissed, she put her arms round me and gave me a big tight hug the way Diana hugged Sandor.

Joan stood there staring. I stepped back and had a look at Tilly. Of course I knew it was Tilly by then. But the thing was, she'd grown—not beautiful, but smashing-looking, you'd say handsome if she were a man. Her hair was down to her shoulders, tinted a dark chestnut-red, and really shiny and nicely cut. She had dark-red lipstick and brown eyeshadow that made her eyes look chestnut-colored too, and big gold dangling hoop earrings. Instead of trousers which she always used to wear and which made her look awful, she had a long black skirt on and shiny black boots and an emerald-green blouse with a black leather belt round her waist. And she was thin! Well, not thin, but normal-sized, with a small waist and a stomach that didn't stick out.

"What happened to your glasses?" I said.

"I've got lenses now. They're great when you get used to them. I don't know why I didn't have them years ago." She looked me up and down. "Your hair! I don't know if I like it. Whatever possessed you?" She didn't wait for an answer. "Joe, I'm glad you're out of there, that place, I never thought it was a good idea. You haven't got depression anymore, have you? I can see you haven't."

There are a couple of chairs in the hall with a glass-topped wicker table between them that they put old papers and magazines on. It's like a dentist's waiting room but we sat down and just kept looking at each other, we couldn't get enough of the sight of each other, we were like lovers reunited. I think that's what Joan thought we were because she took a last look and tiptoed away. Tilly wanted to know if I ever heard from Mum and Dad and laughed when I said, no fear and never again. She asked how I came to leave the hospital and about my friend I was going into business with and for the first time since I'd seen her I felt a little—I don't know how to put it—a little check, a cold finger touching me inside. How was I going to make this right with Sandor?

I passed it off, I said, "What happened to whatshisname? Are you still with him?"

"Rod? He went back to his wife in Brussels. Good riddance to bad rubbish, that was."

For once, a breakup between Tilly and a man didn't bother me. "He bought me all the gear he promised me first, though," she said. "I lost three stone and he spent £300 on clothes for me, that was the agreement, a hundred quid a stone."

I was going to ask when she'd got back from Belgium and where she'd been living and was there a successor to the man in Brussels when I heard the stair creak, the one that always creaks on the bend, and I looked up to see Sandor coming down. I was still holding the newspapers in my hand, I hadn't taken them upstairs or even put them down on the table. He had on the new sweater his mother had given him, a very expensive, totally black job, long and in sort of ribs with a polo neck, and he looked very lean and elegant. If he goes a day without shaving he gets that fashionable shadow. It suits him, it looks sort of glamorous. He had a cigarette in his hand, and say what you like about smoking being lethal, it does look sophisticated. It looks sexy.

You never know how Sandor will behave. He's capable of awful rudeness. I wouldn't have been surprised, though it would have upset me, if he'd told Tilly to get out, we didn't want her here. But he didn't. He didn't smile either or hold out his hand.

"I suppose you're Tilly."

"That's right," she said. "And who are you?"

"This is Sandor Wincanton, my friend that I'm in business with."

"That's a mouthful," Tilly said. I don't know why Sandor let that pass, and I can only account for his doing so by the fact that she looked attractive, she was really good to look at and tall and dramatic as well. When she got up her skirt swirled and her hair swung out like a big red velvet Christmas bell. She reminded me of something I'd seen on TV called *Carmen,* there were a lot of films called that a couple of years back.

But perhaps what really influenced him in Tilly's favor was the camper. We all went outside to have a look at it. I don't know quite what I'd expected, a tip, I suppose. It wasn't what you'd call luxurious inside but it wasn't a mess either. There was carpet on the floor, the bed was folded away into the wall and it all smelled clean and fresh. It really was a little traveling hotel room, with mini-shower and toilet—Sandor says I must stop calling it that and I am trying; lavatory, I mean, or loo—and fridge in the kitchen bit and oven and electric kettle. A heap better than most of the hotel rooms we've stayed in.

I've got to know Sandor pretty well, I think. When you love someone you study the expressions on their face, and I can tell up to a point what he's thinking. Or at any rate when he's giving something a lot of thought. I could see he was speculating about the camper, about it being of some kind of use to us in our enterprise. He smiled at Tilly at last and said it was a nice little place she had there. Did she want him to inquire if there was a room vacant at the Lindsey Guest House? He presumed she'd be staying for a day or two.

I had that choking feeling I get when Sandor does or says something kind. I have to repress giving a shout of joy, which is what makes the choking, I suppose. If someone asked me what happiness was, what it meant to me in my life, I guess I'd have to say it was that occasional choking feeling I get. But it didn't have that sort of effect on Tilly, of course it didn't.

"I might stay around a bit," she said, "but I'll stop in the camper, thanks. I always do. I'll park it in the car park here if they'll let me or else I'll stick it in a lay-by somewhere."

They wouldn't let her. The people who ran the place were very shirty. "In that case we're leaving," Sandor said, very cold.

"You must do as you please about that."

"We're leaving on Monday," said Sandor. He got me to go round to the call box, phone the George and book two single rooms there. My luck was in because they didn't have two. Their tourist season was beginning, or so they said, and all they could offer me was a twin-bedded room with bath. Sandor couldn't deceive me any longer about not being able to afford it, Diana had made it clear to me just what he could afford, so I booked the room and said we'd arrive on Monday at lunchtime.

After I'd made my phone call I went upstairs and found Sandor in our room. Tilly had gone off in the camper to find a place to park it. He was lying on the bed smoking, writing one of his letters.

"So that's Tilly," he said, and he laughed.

I've said I think I understand Sandor pretty well but I couldn't decipher that laugh. It was the kind of way a person laughs when he sees something on TV that surprises him, but he's not all that surprised really because he knows the world is full of things you can't explain. He laughed and then suddenly he looked sad, sorrowful, and he turned his face away from me and gazed out of the window. I knew he couldn't really be looking out of the window because, unlike at the Railway Arms, there's nothing to see here except a brick wall with *Ind Coope* painted on it in faded letters.

There was a question I had to ask him but I was really scared of asking. If Tilly was going to be here, to stay with us even if she wouldn't be sleeping in the guest house, how much were we going to tell her? Of what we were up to, I mean. If we were going to invent a business it had to be the same one in each case. We were going to have to plan it together, and before she came back. But if I was right and Sandor really did have his eye on the camper, were we going to have to be franker with her and maybe tell her some part of it?

He astonished me. Of course, he often does. "Has she got anyone?" he said.

"A boyfriend, d'you mean? A fellow she's with? No, she's alone."

"You might say she leads a nomadic existence?"

I wasn't entirely sure what he meant. I made an intelligent guess, like he says I have to learn to do. "Yes. She never settles anywhere for long. She's like a gypsy. If you mean, has she got any permanent ties, she hasn't."

"I expect she'd like some money," he said. "Most people would. I expect she could do with it."

"You mean . . . d'you mean we're going to *tell* her?"

"What does 'we' mean? This is my enterprise—remember?"

"Are you going to tell her, Sandor?"

"I'm going to think about telling her. That's all I'm going to do for now, think about it. If I think she might be useful I'll tell her and if I don't, she goes."

14

hadn't forgotten what Diana had told me about Sandor being in prison. Far from forgetting, I'd been thinking about it most of the time. It was always at the back of my mind. Two things I wanted to know: how long had he been in there and what had he done. It could have been for as much as four years, it could have been less. I'd got it into my head that it was for kidnapping someone or even for murder. You don't always serve a long sentence for murder, it seems to depend on what some old judge thinks, not the law. There was a man the other day only did four years though he'd killed his wife, chopped her up and hidden the bits in a cupboard.

Sandor's imprisonment accounted for why he'd waited so long before attempting to kidnap the Princess again. While I'd been in the hospital he'd been in prison, we were both shut up, deprived of our freedom. It seemed to bring us closer together. And now that Tilly had come I saw us as three members of society who'd somehow been squeezed out of it or people on a platform there wasn't room for in the train. The train was full and we tried to get on but the sliding doors closed, pushing us back. None of us had a home, Sandor'd been in prison, I'd been, let's face it, in a psychiatric ward and Tilly was a gypsy or a tinker ranging the world in her house on wheels.

That evening Sandor said he'd take us all out to dinner and he spent a long time going through some restaurant guide the Lindsey Guest House people had. The place he was keen on was one of those where the cooking is supposed to be fabulous and the person who owns it has got famous through being rude to the customers. Tilly had taken a long time finding somewhere to park the camper but she was back by then and all for going to a Trusthouse Forte place she'd passed on her way. Sandor wasn't having that. If it wasn't so out of character and generally unlikely, I'd say he was showing off in front of Tilly, trying to make a really big impression.

Although we weren't supposed to use it, he sort of strolled into the office, which happened to be empty, picked up the phone, and told this five-star restaurant he wanted a table for three for eight in the evening.

"A lady and two gentlemen," he said, and, when there was some sort of objection made, I guess that they would have to see if they could take us at such short notice on a Saturday, "Of course you can take us—that's what you're for, isn't it?"

They agreed to take us. But what seemed to make Sandor most gleeful was that he had managed to make a call on the Lindsey Guest House phone without paying for it. He was smoking cigarettes in a tortoiseshell holder which he must have picked up when he was at Diana's house the day before. We should go across to the pub, he said, it was impossible to relax in our room. The best thing that had happened to this benighted country—that was the word he used, *benighted,* I don't think I'd ever heard it before—the best thing in years was the law changing to let pubs stay open all the afternoon. Tilly laughed and said she couldn't agree more.

They were getting on fine, I thought. You'd expect me to be jealous, wouldn't you? If I could be jealous of Gianni Viani, who I'd never even seen, why not of Tilly? Well, I wasn't, and as it turned out I was right not to be. I've got a romantic streak in me, I suppose, and I had this sort of fantasy of Sandor and Tilly falling in love with each other and it being permanent with Tilly this time. Diana wouldn't like it, but she'd have to adjust, she couldn't always have things her own way. I pictured them falling passionately in love and each of them confiding in me, telling me about it. I'd advise them and be a sort of counselor, I'd be good at that because I knew each of them so well. They'd live in the camper, only—no, they wouldn't, they'd have to have a house because I'd be living with them. Diana would have to buy them a house, a cottage, say, she could afford that. They'd ask me to live with them ("If it wasn't for you, Joe, we'd never have met, you brought us together") and I'd consent if they'd let me—well, be a kind of servant to them so that they needed me, cleaning and cooking and taking the washing to the launderette. I can't cook but I could learn.

This all came to nothing and pretty fast. Tilly and I were going down the stairs on our way to the pub, the one next door with *Ind Coope* on the wall. Sandor'd gone back for his cigarettes that he'd forgotten.

"Is he for real?" Tilly whispered to me.

That made me cross. I asked her what she meant.

"I don't know, I thought he must be acting or, you know, putting it all on or sending me up or whatever. You mean he's serious?"

I didn't say anything. I was hurt. "Never mind him," she said. "God, I can't get over the change in you, Joe. You look so good. You're a different fellow. But you're okay, you're still my Joe."

Sandor caught up with us and we went into the pub. Not many people stay in pubs all the afternoon, or not in these country ones, whatever they thought would happen when the new law came in, and we were alone. Sandor asked for a bottle of champagne. When it came it was Spanish and not very nice.

Tilly talked about what it was like living in Belgium. They'd been on a campsite near a place called Mons, which was where one of Sandor's ancestors got the VC in the First World War. Then they moved up to Brussels. Sandor was somehow related to our ambassador to Belgium. When Tilly had finished he told us about being at Cambridge and some famous writer he'd known there and then about Bologna University and a lot about the history of art. I hadn't anything to contribute. After all, what have I done in my life except get parted from my parents, have the bad luck to wind up with Mum and Dad and get myself put in what, frankly, was a bin? And meet Sandor, of course. That happened, that was the best thing that happened. As I listened to him talking, his lovely voice and the long words he uses and all the things he knows about, old painters and architecture and foreign languages, I felt I knew it must be having its effect on Tilly. That remark she'd made to me on the stairs, it was only because she didn't know him, by now she must have changed her mind.

When we got onto our second bottle Sandor started talking about the people at Jareds. He told the whole tale of the Princess's life and marriages over again, just as he'd told it to me that first time. Only he didn't mention the kidnapping and he put some extra bits in, about the Princess coming originally from a place on the Suffolk coast and her parents moving to Cambridge when she was a child. When he'd talked about her that first time he didn't say he'd known her when he was at college in Cambridge —well, not known but sometimes seen her around. She's two years older and she was already a famous model by then, but she used to come home on weekends to see her mother and father.

Tilly knew all about her, that is, she knew everything the public could know. She had had one of those crushes on her the way ordinary-looking girls do on beautiful famous women who are always getting their pictures in the papers. And the reason why she had in the first place was a really crazy one. They were exactly the same age, her and the Princess, to the day. Once Tilly was reading the horoscopes in some magazine and it gave the birthdays of famous people and Nina Abbott's was one of them. She's a Scorpion like Tilly, and they were both born on 25 October.

She was quite excited that the Princess who'd sort of been her idol was living so near and she seemed to have got the impression that Sandor knew her personally. Well, he did in a way, of course, he'd actually spent a lot of time with her, two or three weeks between the time she was kidnapped and the time she was sent back on that train. But he'd never said anything about this and he didn't now. Tilly kept on saying, "Oh, I'd love to meet her!"

She must have said it three or four times while Sandor was talking about Apsoland buying Jareds two years ago and about the security precautions and so on. Sandor suddenly got fed up with it.

"You're just making a fool of yourself talking like that. I'm not on social terms with them. I'm in it for something else."

Tilly took it from him without a murmur, but I knew she wouldn't always. She's not patient the way I am. She asked him what he meant. He wouldn't say and we went back to the guest house. In preparation for our evening out in the restaurant with the rude owner he got all dressed up in his suit again, and Tilly went back to the camper to change into a green-and-white-striped dress and white shiny shoes. Sandor drove with Tilly beside him and me in the back. He took us past Jareds.

Of course going past Jareds doesn't amount to much. All you can see are those gates and the tunnel of walls and the trees, and the leaves were really thick on the trees by this time. The horse was rushing about in the field opposite, tossing its mane. It was still bright daylight, the sun quite high in the sky.

"I'd love to meet her," Tilly said again, though she ought to have known better.

Sandor just laughed. He told her about Garnet the bodyguard and the dogs and the gun collection.

"But what are they afraid of?"

"Of being kidnapped," he said.

Tilly immediately wanted to know all about it. Without saying how he was involved, he had started giving much the same account as he had given me, when a strange thing happened. We had got past the village and come to a place where the road was up. There were temporary traffic lights working and just one lane, the right-hand, open for traffic. As we came up to it the light went red and Sandor cursed as he always does if a light goes red when he's driving.

The cars that had been waiting in a line at the other end started coming through and the first one was the Jareds coppery-colored Volvo with Garnet at the wheel. Sitting next to him was the little girl with long fair hair I'd seen him meeting from school.

"Look, Garnet and his daughter," I said. "Tilly, look."

"Where?" said Sandor, "Let me see," and I realized he'd never seen Garnet.

"In the Volvo."

Garnet came through quite slowly. He looked at our car and away again. "A great bruiser, isn't he?" said Sandor. "Looks like a prizefighter." He seemed for some reason enormously pleased.

The rude man in the restaurant wasn't rude to us. It was easy to tell which one he was, a short man with a big belly, wearing a green velvet jacket and a bow tie. There was a woman in there with a party and he got furious with her because she asked for her sherry iced. I don't know whether she wanted it out of the fridge or with actual ice in it but he wouldn't let her anyway. He asked if she was from a hot climate or just ignorant. She didn't seem to mind. If I'd been one of the men with her I'd have wanted to get up and hit him. She looked a nice woman, gentle and as if she'd be very kind to children.

Then he had a go at a man who was smoking a cigarette. There weren't any notices up telling you not to smoke but evidently there was an area where you weren't supposed to. We wouldn't last long in there, I thought, I was quite philosophical about it, trying to think where we could go instead. I'd never known Sandor go more than ten minutes without a cigarette and I waited for him to light one and for the sparks to fly in more ways than one. The funny thing was that he didn't have a cigarette the whole time we were in there and that must have been all of two hours.

I'm not all that fond of made-up dishes, things in sauce or layers of things, even when it's so-called amazing French cuisine. Nor is Tilly. I suppose it reminds her, as it does me, of the food we had with Mum and Dad, TV dinners and frozen gourmet. It's sauce, sauce, and more sauce in those, to stop you seeing what you're really eating. I'd have liked a plain steak but there wasn't such a thing available. We had red wine. The rude man came up and chose it for us and, instead of arguing, Sandor just said that'd be fine. When the wine came Tilly clinked glasses with the two of us, grinned and said, "To crime."

"I'm not sure what that means," Sandor said.

"You're aiming to kidnap Nina Abbott, aren't you?"

We both just looked at her. Even Sandor looked surprised. "How did you know?" I said.

And then I knew she didn't know. She was joking. It was the craziest, most outlandish thing she could think of to say. Sandor said very slowly, not taking his eyes off her, "Suppose I said, yes, we are, what would your reaction be, Tilly?"

It was the first time he'd used her Christian name, and the only time he'd included me to the extent of that "we." A little of the warm choking feeling came back to me. "I'd say you were pissed," she said.

We started eating. Sandor said, "I'm deadly serious, you know."

She looked at him. She was holding something up on her fork. It sort of hovered there, poised. "You can't be."

"Why not? Say I'm a terrorist. Terrorists are real, they exist. Why not me as well as anyone else?"

She shrugged. There was a sly look on her face. "Why not *us* as well as anyone else?"

He told her about it then, what we'd done and what we aimed to do. Once or twice he glanced at me as a signal to take up the tale, so I filled in the bits that only I knew about. Tilly took a swig of her wine as if it was brandy and she needed it for shock. Sandor told her about the phone calls I'd made. Then he surprised me the way he does. He said he'd written to her. All those letters he'd written had been to the Princess.

"What d'you mean, you've written to her?" Tilly said. She can be really scathing. It's because life has made her tough. "Setting out your intentions, I suppose?"

"Not quite that. Let's say she knows it's happened once and she was told it would happen again. I've warned her it'll happen again."

"And that's all you've done, walked about the fields and looked at the house? Found out he's got dogs and guns and burglar alarms. Followed Garnet and her in a car and what's more, got rumbled. Phoned Garnet, offered him a cut, and when he said no, given up that line. Written a few letters, moved, resprayed the car, bought disguises. And that's it?"

Put like that, it didn't sound like much. It sounded feeble. I couldn't help thinking that that was due to me, I'd done so little and what I had done I'd made a mess of. Maybe Sandor hadn't chosen wisely when he picked me. I don't know what I'd have done if he'd been hurt by what Tilly said. What do you do when one of the only two people in the world that you love hurts the other one?

"What did you think?" she said. "She'd walk out and give herself up? Say, 'Here's the money, I've brought it for you'? How long were you reckoning to hang around on her doorstep?"

Sandor was shaking with rage. "Shut up," he said. "Fuck you."

Thank God the table's between them so he can't hit her, I thought. I was thinking like that when the coffee came and the rude man came up to ask us how we'd enjoyed the meal. Sandor didn't even answer. It was Tilly who looked at him and said it had been okay, he'd have heard from us if it hadn't been. I wondered what would happen but nothing did. To us that is. He went straight over to some meek-looking people, probably a courting couple, and had a go at the girl for drinking vodka and peppermint.

"It was very obviously a mistake telling you," Sandor said, his voice still vibrating. "That sort of destructive criticism isn't much use to me." He drew in his breath, said coldly, "I only hope we can rely on your discretion."

"Of course we can," I said.

Tilly had that same look on her face she had when she asked me if Sandor was for real. Then she started smiling and shaking her head, the way people do when what they've heard is beyond belief. Sandor dropped the American Express card onto the plate the waiter brought up with a kind of cold precision. He stared in front of him and I could tell he was very offended. The chit came and he signed it. Tilly leaned toward him. I thought she was going to put her hand on his arm but she thought better of it.

"Thanks, Sandor," she said. "Thank you for the meal. It was very nice, I enjoyed it."

He didn't answer. Tilly went to the ladies and while she was gone he wouldn't speak to me. He stood there still as a statue but at the same time like something that's set up to explode. One touch of pressure on the vital spot and the lot goes up. When he's like that I feel helpless, I feel utterly inadequate.

Tilly came back with fresh bright lipstick on and her shiny hair combed. They made a handsome couple, only you can't call people a couple when they're not speaking. Sandor tossed the car keys at me. "You drive."

I was trying to think when he'd last called me little Joe. I understood why he wanted me to drive. That way he wouldn't have to sit next to Tilly. Either he or she would have to go in the back and he saw to it that she did. She didn't speak at all for the first few miles. None of us did. A mist had come up while we were in the restaurant, as it does in this part of the world, and I kept coming into white pockets of it. When we got to the bit where the road was up I had nearly driven into the pole it was mounted on before I saw the red light.

Tilly spoke once the car had started again. Her voice sounded excited.

"I can tell you how to do it," she said, "if you want to know. I've suddenly had this idea. I reckon it's a foolproof way."

Still Sandor said nothing. Risking a reproof from him, though one never came, I said, "Do what?"

"Snatch Nina Abbott."

"Okay," I said. "How?"

"You could forget dogs and lights and burglar alarms. You could forget guns. There wouldn't be any risk. Once the first step was past, and we'd have to work that out, I don't see how it could go wrong."

Sandor turned round slowly and looked at her.

15

The shotgun practice might have been purposely arranged by Apsoland for that particular date because it was a few days before he was due to go away. A short business trip to the United States was planned, going there and back on the Concorde. In the meantime he was assembling, as Paul put it to himself, his private army. Paul even wondered if he had got off so lightly after his undoubted rudeness to his employer because Apsoland simply could not do without him at this particular time. He, at any rate, might have been styled colonel-in-chief of Apsoland's regiment.

His soldiers would be Colombo and Maria, Tyr and Odin. In the daytime the landscape gardeners were to be his territorials, while by night Stan and Doreen had consented to come and stay in the house during Apsoland's absence. These precautions Paul saw as excessive but he no longer saw them as absurd.

There had been no repetition of the phone calls. He half expected something to come through the post, but nothing had. The chance encounter, if it could be called that, of Saturday evening surely meant nothing. Not every Fiat on the road was keeping him under surveillance. Besides, the red one waiting at the temporary traffic lights had been driven by a man he had never seen before with a girl he had never seen before sitting next to him. There might have been someone in the back, but he couldn't be sure.

Paul was learning that paranoia is more easily caught than a cold in the head.

"When Stan and Doreen come," said Jessica, "can Debbie come and stay with us in our house?"

"I expect so. If you like. She'll have to sleep in your room."

As soon as he said it he realized it was hardly a threat. Jessica looked ecstatic, she had on her expression of a young saint contemplating the heavenly host. She said, as children will before they lose this charming habit, "I love you, Daddy," sat on his knee, and wound her arms round his neck.

"I love you too, Jess," he said, but even as he said it he thought of saying those words to a grown woman and wondered if he would ever say them again. It seemed to him sometimes that he must utter them to Nina, "I love you," whatever the consequences might be, whatever disgust or anger they aroused.

When he had driven her to Ipswich the week before, she had sat in the seat beside him but had hardly spoken. The intimacy of the previous week, the conversation as it might be between old friends, was over. Nothing had been said about the purpose of her trip. All she had said during the first ten miles of the journey was that it was nice to see the sun again. They were coming up to the turnoff for the Orwell Bridge when he heard her draw in her breath like someone desperate for a smoke inhaling on a cigarette. He waited for the exhalation. It was a long time coming. When she spoke it was to plunge into the middle of things, as if there had been much preamble.

"I was so frightened, Paul. It went on for years. You see, I knew in a way it had been my own fault, I'd invited it. I should have been more careful, more prudent—it would have made no difference in the end."

"When you went out driving on your own, do you mean?" He believed now. He had had no problems with belief since the second phone call.

Beside him he felt her shrug. "I wish I could tell you everything but I can't, I can't utter the words. I can't even tell Ralph this much. He just says, 'Don't think about it. I'll look after you.' What's the use of people telling you not to think about something? It's not as if you want to. You'd stop if you could."

Katherine used to say that, "Don't think about it," when he fretted about thirty more years as a teacher, when he worried about the place they lived in. Nina reverted to what she had begun to say at first.

"I was so frightened and so—well, mad. I thought I was losing my mind, I'd have promised anything, done anything. I don't think it showed, my fear, not by then. You can get to a point with fear when if saving yourself depends on hiding it, you'll hide it. And you'll do things that aren't in your nature, things which would revolt you, because self-preservation is the strongest of all instincts. Sex, hunger, they don't even come into it. And you'll say anything. Oh, the things I said!" She stopped. He drove on but he seemed not to breathe. "They did things to me. Oh, that doesn't matter, it might have been worse. When they released me they put me on this train. I don't know where it was, somewhere between Rome and Florence, a local train that stopped at every station. One of them got on the train with me and traveled nearly all the way. He got off at the station before Rufina and before he left me he took off the dark glasses they'd taped onto me and the scarf they'd tied round my head and—he kissed me and said, 'We'll meet again. It won't be long.'

"I was in a first-class section of the train, only it's not separate in Italian trains, just a sort of better section of the ordinary class. I was alone. After he'd gone I was sick. I threw up, I mean. Over and over, in the carriage. It was terrible. And then we got to

Rufina and Barney was there, my husband, I mean, that they always called the Prince, though he wasn't one really, not what we mean by a prince."

Paul had taken the car into a multistory car park. He disliked them because they seemed to him places which were potentially frightening to someone as nervous as Nina and now, of course, he had the added disquiet of believing her fear justified. Where he would once have dismissed apprehensiveness as ridiculous, he now felt a real sense of alarm on these dim levels, low-ceilinged, squat-pillared, the cars ranked in long rows and offering easy hiding places. But there was nowhere else to go, no street spaces. He parked the car as near as he could to the exit lift.

She was facing him, looking at him. He thought, if she begins to cry, and she looks as if she is going to cry, I shall take her in my arms—how can I not?

He spoke, to keep himself from touching her. "What did he mean by that, about meeting again and it not being long?"

"I don't know," she said, but something in her face told him she did.

She opened the car door and got out. For once she hadn't waited for him to do it for her. He escorted her into the lift and they went down in it together, not speaking. It was shopping she wanted to do, in a department store. She was wearing a primrose linen skirt and a silk sweater in the same shade, the color of the fairest strands of her multi-blond hair. It had been a long journey to buy what she wanted, a pair of Dior tights and a special sort of hand cream. The cost of the hand cream astonished him. They had to cross a busy street to get back to the car park. He wouldn't have touched her without her invitation, in spite of those dreams of tears inspiring kisses, but at the pavement edge she took his arm, curling a small white hand into the crook of it.

"There," she said, "now we'll run!"

It was the first contact. For some reason they hadn't shaken hands when first they met. Up in the lift, standing very close together, and the hand back in the curve of his arm as they walked through the quiet dimness to the car. As she stepped in she turned, smiled up into his face, "You're good to me, Paul."

This time he said nothing about being only the driver or that it was his job. They were leaving the big road, turning into the hinterland before she spoke again.

"He left me alone for three years, more than three years. There were letters before that. The world wasn't big enough to escape, not the whole world, Australia, America, all over Europe. I used to think sometimes, if I went to the moon it wouldn't be far enough."

"These were threats to kidnap you again?"

He thought she nodded but he couldn't see. You had to keep your eyes on the road constantly in these narrow lanes. "Then they stopped. Till five months ago. In December they began again. I had the last one last week."

From seeing her as beyond his reach, his unattainable lady, he had contrived to move himself and her, like pieces on a chessboard, into a position of possible confrontation. Contemplating telling her of his feelings, approaching her, was no longer absurd. Foolhardy it might be, but it was possible. What would come after he had scarcely thought about. He was avoiding an "after" where arrangements must be made (even though they might only be arrangements for him to leave), money be considered, plans rejected and others adopted.

Apsoland had left for Heathrow, driving himself in the Jaguar. Because he was going so early in the morning, Stan and Doreen had had to come up the night before. Maria, who hadn't much English, nevertheless managed to tell Paul that she had prepared for them the other bedroom in the annex where she and Colombo slept, the wing of the house that stepped out almost to join the stables and his own cottage. Maria's own initiative, Paul thought, or more probably Apsoland's orders. Stan and his wife were doing him a favor, very likely at great inconvenience to themselves, but still they were to be relegated to a "servants' wing," though there must have been at least four spare bedrooms in the house.

These things and allied matters troubled him. Was it because he believed that if she saw Stan as a menial she would see him in the same light? She had called him better educated than herself or her husband. It was true, he was—but did that make a difference? Only money, he thought rather bitterly, would make a difference.

Everyone had got up early. Nothing could have made Apsoland's position as the "master" clearer than this concerted effort of his household to be up to see him off. Not that there was any sort of assembly in the courtyard or on the gravel outside the front door, but Paul, without being asked, brought the car round through the arch and Colombo was waiting with the two suitcases. One of these was full of documents, he hastened to assure them both, lest they should think him a vain man to take so many clothes for two nights.

Nina stood at the drawing-room window, waving as the car moved off. She smiled at Paul, she seemed to linger there as if she were waiting for him to come up to the window and speak to her. He resisted the temptation, he would see her later to drive her to Bury. In the meantime he drove Jessica to school, took Tyr and Odin across the park and out on to the heath. The sun was strong, the air soft, and in the wood the ground was the color of a sunlit sea where last week all had been a pale unfolding green. The bluebells had come out. Their scent was sweeter than hyacinths and less cloying. It was difficult to accept, on a morning like this, that there were callous and brutal things in the world, that the innocent suffered and men existed who wished harm to Nina and planned her exploitation.

He phoned her, as he had got into the habit of doing, to tell her he would bring the car round in five minutes. She said, "Listen, I've had an idea. I mustn't say it on the phone, you can imagine why not. I'll tell you in five minutes."

He couldn't imagine at all. His heart was beating hard. She sounded . . . almost merry. The frightened girl who had talked of no escape anywhere on earth was gone. He had never heard her so lighthearted nor with that impulsive note in her voice. It was difficult not to make the link between this new delightful mood and Apsoland's departure. The front door opened before the car drew up. She was in a pale-blue cotton dress and sandals. She looked very young.

"What I was going to say to you—shall we have lunch together? Somewhere nice? Somewhere we can eat out by a river? I can think of lots of places. Shall we, Paul?"

He nodded, unable to speak.

"I'm only going to have my hair cut, it won't take long. I expect you're disillusioned because I don't go somewhere smart in London, but oh, the hassle of that!" She got into the car as lightly and quickly as Jessica would, turned her face up to him. "It's not a bore for you, is it? I just thought you might quite like the idea. For a change, you know. I couldn't say it on the phone. I didn't want Colombo to hear."

Her mood changed on the way home. There seemed to be a gradually encroaching melancholy. All through lunch, in just such a place as she had named, tables on a riverbank terrace by a stone bridge, she had been light, warm, casual. She had asked him to tell her about himself but he too had kept it light, at that sunny table, dappled by those willow leaves. While he spoke, though, he had been thinking all the time of making some sort of declaration, of choosing as his time the pause that must come. But there was no pause.

Once, when he had spoken a little ruefully of what must look like a failed life, of starting afresh from nothing, she had for a moment or two laid her hand gently over his. It was a very brief touch. She had reached across, almost as if to pick something up from the table, the rose perhaps that had fallen out of its vase. But the rose had been bypassed and his hand located and her fingers laid on skin that was as sensitive to her touch as to burning or ice. But he had said nothing.

In the car she smiled no longer. She hardly spoke. He opened the door for her and she got out wearily, stiffly, like an old woman who needs a hand or a stick. His hand was there but she didn't take it. On the steps, though, she turned.

"Come into the house a moment. You haven't to fetch Jessica yet, have you?"

"Not for ten minutes," he said, and he followed her in.

"Wait a minute," she said. "Wait here." Her tone was not so much peremptory as imperious.

He stood in the drawing room, in the middle of the Chinese carpet, ivory and blue, and looked out through long windows across the park. The sight of it unnerved him because of what she had and what she hadn't. It was a small cardboard box she held in her hand when she came back into the room. She took off the lid and handed it to him.

The box contained a single fingernail, varnished pale gold. The tip of it brutally cut off, and ten nail tips in the same color, all of them as crudely sliced as if with kitchen scissors or even a knife.

"They're your nails?"

"The cut-off bits are." She shuddered, an uncontrollable reflex. "The other—I don't know where that came from, but I can guess. One of them was a medical student. I expect he's a doctor by now. What a thought!"

She began to cry, her head bent, she cried without touching her eyes. A sob made her shake. He put the box down on a chair and took her in his arms. The time had come to say what he had planned but he said nothing. He held her close to him and she felt delicate and small and warm. Because she was so small it felt natural to bend his head and touch the top of her head with his lips. She remained in his arms for a few seconds only, then disengaged herself, said, "I'm all right now," with great composure.

"Put them away, those things," he said. "You ought to throw them away. It would be best."

"You're right. I will. Of course I will. Nails are dead anyway, aren't they? They're dead from when they grow out of your fingers."

He found himself nodding, said the only thing he could think of, "I must go and fetch Jessica."

"Of course you must."

Somehow he got out of the room and the house and into the car. He hardly saw Jessica as she came down the steps and along the path with Harriet and Debbie. They were simply three little girls, one of whom meant more to him than the others. He was stunned, dazed, he was recovering from a concussion. Holding Nina and feeling her close against him, a powerful emotion had lighted up him and her and darkened the rest of reality. He had to grope his way out of it. For one thing, he had to remember he was meeting Debbie as well as Jessica. Debbie was staying with them. And it seemed, though he had forgotten this as he had forgotten so much today, that he had promised to take Harriet home.

Harriet's house seemed full of puppies. There were in fact five. Of course the girls had to stay for ten minutes to play with the puppies while Paul and Harriet's mother drank tea. Debbie had to be admonished for her rough handling of the fat little roly-poly dogs, but Paul found he had no need to caution Jessica, who held the puppy she was cuddling with the most circumspect gentleness. I mustn't neglect her, he thought, I mustn't let myself be deflected from my care for her.

What had he expected when he reached home? That Nina would be waiting to greet him? Of course she was nowhere to be seen. He remembered that she had told him she expected guests, those Aldeburgh friends, to keep her company for the evening. The first real pang of jealousy came when he thought of those friends, invited instead of him. She could have asked him. A moment's thought showed him she couldn't have done that, not with Stan and Doreen in the house.

It was with those two, Debbie's parents, that he must naturally pass his evening. They were nice people, it was the least he could do considering the number of times Jessica had been to them. He happened to be outside, checking on the departure of the land-scape gardeners, when the car with the Aldeburgh people arrived. Nina came down the steps to them and he turned away quickly so that she shouldn't see him watching. Ten minutes after Stan and Doreen had gone back to their room in the annex, the Aldeburgh people left. Paul was indoors but it was dark by then and the whole cottage was lit up with that bluish-white light as the car entered the area subject to the infrared sensor.

After their departure all was dark and silent once more. Clouds which had come up during the evening covered the moon. He went outside and walked through the arch to the front of the house. No lights showed. Nina must have gone straight to bed once her guests had left. It was absurd that he had no idea which were her bedroom windows. Did they have separate rooms, she and Apsoland? He resisted speculating. The only light was in the annex. It might have been in Stan and Doreen's room, or Colombo and Maria's. Paul stood for a moment, listening to the quiet, the calm, velvety, rather warm silence. When it was broken by the thin distant shriek of an owl, he went indoors and to bed.

16

Jessica grumbled at having to brush her hair, she whined, there was no other accurate word for it, making the movements mechanically and, after a while, ineffectually.

"Debbie doesn't have to. Why do I?"

Debbie's appearance spoke for itself. Her ginger hair was nearly as short as Paul's.

"You say you want it long," said Paul. "You have to get the tangles out somehow. Have it cut if you don't like it. I don't mind, chop it off if you want."

"I want the kind that's long and never gets tangly."

Paul laughed. "I dare say. You'd want cherries without stones and a rose without a thorn."

"You can get those," said Debbie. "Thornless roses, I mean. We've got one in our garden."

"Okay, I give up. Come on, or you'll be late."

He drove them to school in the Volvo. It was Cambridge day. Because of what Nina had said and because of the phone calls, he half expected to see the gray Fiat following them, but they had an empty road behind them all the way to Bury. She was dressed up today, in a pale-apricot linen suit with a black-and-white blouse and very shiny high-heeled black shoes. It made her seem remote. She made no reference to what had happened the day before in the drawing room. He hardly knew in what terms she could have referred to it. She had a curious gift of maintaining tranquil silence without seeming stand-offish or cold. Miles went by and they exchanged no words. As they entered the A45 she said lightly that her husband had phoned the night before to tell her of his safe arrival. She, for her part, didn't like flying and intended never to go in an aircraft again.

That was the tenor of their conversation on the way back too. Small talk was made and she told him something of the lives of the friends who had visited her the evening before. Dull episodes, he thought, of interest only to those who knew those people intimately. It was plain to him that having said—and done—too much the afternoon before, she was now regretful. She was closing the gate in the wall between them, the gate which yesterday had opened so generously.

All she said when they separated at the front door was, "Thanks, Paul," though the parting look she gave him puzzled him. It was unsmiling but with something yearning in it, perhaps something of a plea.

Doreen had picked the girls up from school, and they had walked back together. Paul felt guilty for Jessica, who looked tired after her long school day. He had told himself firmly not to think of Nina, not to dwell so obsessively on the situation he was in, but this was too hard a task. It might be that he would have to go away. If his position was to be that of a hopeless lover, living so to speak on her doorstep, with nothing to console him and nothing to cure his obsession, the only thing might be to leave. And if Jessica had to move on again, change her school again, leave her new friends—well, so be it.

In the evening, while they were having supper, the phone rang. Paul had taken their used plates out into the kitchen and was occupied in a task he still found difficult and awkward: taking an apple pie he had baked from frozen out of the oven and sliding it onto a dish. He usually burned his fingers or knocked bits off the pie. Jessica answered the phone, he heard her saying the number very correctly, but he was sure it must be for him. She was too young yet for her friends to phone her. But when he went back into the room, the receiver was in its rest and Jessica was very composedly discussing with Debbie the rival merits of dogs and cats as pets.

"Who was that, Jess?"

"A lady."

He thought at once of Nina, but no . . . "Did she give her name? Why didn't you tell me?"

"She said she was your friend Richard's wife." Jessica now spoke with a child's exaggerated patience when confronted by incomprehensible adult insistence. The impact that sentence had on her father she ignored. Perhaps she didn't notice it. "She said, 'Is that Jessica?' and I said, 'Yes,' and she said, 'My name is Anne, I'm Richard's wife.' I didn't know what to say, so I didn't say anything, and she said, 'Don't bother to call your dad, I expect he's busy.' Oh, and she called me 'dear.' I said I wouldn't call you if she didn't mind and she said, 'Just tell him I'll ring again or Richard will and give him my love.' "

Paul was very anxious, since she seemed not to have noticed the initial effect on him, not to show Jessica how much this call had alarmed him. His lips felt stiff, he spoke calculatedly, "Anne, yes. Oh, yes."

"She's going to ring again, Daddy."

Was this woman one of them? He supposed so. She must be connected with the man he had seen at the wheel of the gray Fiat. On the other hand, he had no real reason to believe that the phone call offering him money had anything to do with the man who called himself Richard. Or therefore with this woman Anne.

Wasn't there a possibility that Richard and Anne were genuine law-abiding ordinary people he had known in the past and somehow forgotten?

The connection between Richard and the phone caller existed entirely in his own mind. Considerable relief resulted from thinking like this. Now he came to think of it hadn't Katherine once had a close friend called Anne?

Very much later the phone rang again. Because it was ten to eleven and past the time any friend would ring, Paul thought at once of the caller who had offered him the £200,000. But when he picked up the receiver he heard the short-long-short-long bell that is the signal a call is coming from a pay phone. The sound went on for thirty seconds and he put the phone back.

Again there was no moon and the sky seemed even darker than on the previous night. He walked outside but no farther than the courtyard. Not a light showed in the back of the house, nor in the annex. Perhaps because he felt more than usually guilty about Jessica, felt that lately he had been neglecting to put her first, he looked inside the room where the girls slept before he went to bed. The night before they had stayed awake giggling and talking until past midnight, until how late he didn't know because he had fallen asleep himself, but now they were growing used to each other's company and they were tired.

The covers had come off them and each one lay asleep in a welter of toys and books and bits of clothing, Debbie on her stomach, Jessica sprawled in an absurd and inappropriate attitude of abandon, legs apart, one arm behind her head, the other outflung, silky golden hair spread about, tangled again. Paul rolled her sideways, covered them both up. The tape player was still on. He turned it off, went to his own room, and fell asleep at once.

His room was at the back, on the side of the house that overlooked the meadow beyond the boundary wall, so the phone awakened him before he saw the light. For a moment, surfacing sluggishly, he was tempted to let it ring. But he went down and at the bend in the stairs saw the bluish-white radiance that streamed in at the windows. He ran the last bit to the phone. It was Stan.

"Paul? We never made an arrangement, I mean, what to do if anything happened. I'm sorry if I woke you. It may be nothing's happened. But the light has come on and I think I've seen someone. Well, no, that's not right, I know I've seen someone."

"I'll come. I'll get dressed."

Immediately he thought of the two phone calls, the one from the woman calling herself Anne, the other that had never got through. It was probably coincidence that those calls had come a few hours before the arrival of this intruder. The light would last for five minutes from the time it was activated. Paul put on jeans and a sweater. The gun Apsoland had insisted on Paul's keeping in the cottage was in the back of the wardrobe. He hesitated, then took it out and put a handful of cartridges into his pocket. At the foot of the stairs he picked up a torch from the hall table.

Stan was at the back door with Colombo. He spoke in a whisper.

"The light coming on woke me. It makes our room as bright as day. I looked out and I saw someone in the park, running, a man. He'd run through the gates in the flint avenue."

Colombo was looking at the gun under Paul's arm. Paul said, "Is Mrs. Apsoland awake?"

"Not so far as I know."

"She take sleep pill," Colombo said.

Did she? How would he know? Through his wife, Paul thought. His wife cleaned the bedrooms, probably looked in the bathroom cabinets. While they were standing there the light went out. There must be a way of turning it on manually but Paul didn't know how. He walked through the arch with Stan and Colombo following him and crossed the path of the sensor. The lights blazed.

The park was bathed in their radiance as by the most brilliant moon. The light silvered the turf so that it seemed frosted. The whole landscape, though the air was mild and soft, looked cold like midwinter. The shadows of the great trees were dense designs of blackness on that silvery-white. The lamps made the sky itself radiant, a mass of complex and mysterious pearly cloud. Colombo had gone in. Paul and Stan stood in the sensor's path, maintaining the flow of light.

"Which way did you see him go?"

"Into the wood." Stan pointed to the right where a finger of woodland came close to the Jareds boundary hedge. "They call it Wolves Wood, don't they?"

Paul didn't know, he had never heard it called anything. It was an extended branch of the bluebell wood where he had been the day before with the dogs, one of the arms of the horseshoe. And now as he turned back to look at the house, to wonder if the light would awaken Nina, the two German shepherds appeared through the arch, feebly restrained by Colombo, who had them on a double leash.

"I let them go free?"

"I don't see why not," Paul said. "It's hard to say what good they'll do but they won't do any harm."

Instead of making for Wolves Wood, Tyr and Odin frolicked around the three men, Tyr even bringing a stick to Paul for him to throw. "Perhaps one of us should take a look at the wood," Paul said. "I'll go if you like, I've got the gun."

"We all go," said Colombo.

"Well, hardly. While he's got all three of us out of the way, his mates can have a go at the house, don't you think?"

Colombo shrugged, clearly disappointed. He and Stan made their way back to the arch and the courtyard. Calling the dogs, Paul set off across the park. The lights stayed on. Colombo must have done what was necessary to make that happen. Even so the wood looked very dark and impenetrable from a distance.

There was no gate in the hedge, but a gap in it that looked as if often used in the recent past. Paul pushed his way through, the dogs following. The drifts of bluebells were silvery when he shone his torch, their scent more powerful than by day. It was silent in the wood, not a quiver or crackle, not a bird sound. He saw the first running snare before he had taken more than a step or two into the trees, the length of string attached to a tree root at one end, a noose at the other, and, inside the circle which would tighten when pulled, a scattering of corn.

Paul pulled the string off and put it in his pocket. Guided by his torch he found three more snares and disarmed them all. He didn't know who the pheasants belonged to, Apsoland perhaps, but he hated this illegal and out-of-season means of catching birds by enabling them to strangle themselves. Tyr and Odin sniffed everywhere suspiciously. Perhaps they smelled the intruder—who could tell? Paul called them and returned through the hedge into the park.

The lights went out just before he stepped on to the gravel. This reactivated them. The sudden darkness followed by the renewal of light must have frightened Tyr, for he gave a low growl, threw his head back, and began to bay like a wolf. Paul tried to quiet him, clipped the leash onto his collar, stroked his head while talking softly to him. All the while Odin, jealous, was pushing himself against Paul, jumping up, trying to lick him. At last Paul got them both quiet and on the leash and was able to bring them back through the arch to the back door.

The door was unlocked but there was no one about. Stan and Colombo had evidently gone back to bed. So much for Apsoland's elaborate security. If the man Paul now knew to have been a poacher had in fact been a kidnapper's decoy, his partners could have walked into the house in Paul's absence and taken Nina without arousing anyone. How, for instance, did Stan know, if up in the annex he could even hear, that the man who had walked into the back lobby and thence into the kitchen was Paul and not some intruder?

Tyr and Odin had a room to themselves, a place that had once been a scullery or boot room, with two wooden beds like large drawers and a bowl of water on the floor. He shut them in, crossed to the door that led into the hall and listened. The door was open, the passage beyond and the wide hall at the end of it a tunnel and cavern of darkness.

Not a sound. No one had heard him come in, or, if they had, were taking for granted it was he. Paul understood that Stan and

Doreen's presence in the house was quite useless, and he began to be angry. What would you have to do to bring them down? Fire a gun? Scream? He walked along the passage into the hall, his eyes growing accustomed to the darkness. Glass and silver gleamed a little, there was always a scrap of light. At the foot of the stairs he stopped. He could hear something now. Not Colombo or Stan bestirring themselves but a whimpering, the soft moaning a frightened child might make.

At once he understood. They might not suspect, even if they could hear, that it was anyone but he who had come in, but she did. She had heard his deliberately careful tread, sensed the surreptitiousness of it, feared the absence of light.

He ran up the stairs, calling, "Nina, Nina, it's me, it's only me."

It was the bedroom over the portico with the two central windows that was hers. She came out, barefoot, wearing a white toweling wrap. There were tears on her face and her eyes were wide with terror. Light poured out of the bedroom into the upper hall.

She said, "Paul, oh, Paul," threw herself into his arms, and clung to him.

"I'm sorry," he said, "I'm so sorry."

"I've been so frightened, I thought I'd die of fright. I thought it was them and I'd rather die than go to them again."

"Colombo said you'd taken a sleeping pill, we thought you were asleep."

"I didn't take one. I felt happy, so I didn't. It was the dog barking that woke me and the lights were on and when they went out I heard you come in, only I didn't know . . ."

"It was only me. There's no one there, there's nothing. It's all right, everything's all right."

He helped her back into the bedroom. He had an impression of lavishness—white, pink, gold, rather predictable. The two windows were covered only in curtains of heavy lace which hung to the floor. She held him, clinging to his arm with both hands.

"Nothing like that's ever happened before, not ever. Those lights have never come on at night."

"It was a poacher, setting running snares in the wood."

"How do you know? How can you tell?"

"I saw the snares, Nina. I took the dogs to the wood and saw the snares and took them out."

"They could have been put there at any time. They could have been put there in the day." It was true, but he didn't think so. "He said he'd come for me, in his letter he said he would. You won't leave me, will you, Paul? You'll stay with me?"

What was she asking him? She held his shoulders and, looking up into his face, brought her mouth very near his. He was very aware that she was naked under the robe. "I'll stay in the house, if that's what you want." It sounded stiff, cold, because it was a substitute for what he wanted to say: I love you, I will stay forever.

"Stay *here* with me."

In a moment he would begin to tremble. "Put some clothes on and we'll go downstairs. I'll make you some coffee."

He saw the beginning of a smile, saw it spread to her eyes.

Five minutes ago it seemed as if she would never smile again. "Don't be silly, Paul. You know what I'm saying. I'm inviting you to stay here with me—here!"

Then he knew. "I've fallen in love with you." He had said it at last.

She didn't seem surprised. He had imagined her astonishment, but there was none. "I know," she said. "Of course I know and I'm so glad!"

17

It was just after five. He had slept for perhaps three hours. A blackbird singing awakened him, or the light of dawn, softer, gentler yet stronger than those artificial lamps. It crept through the thick, regular folds of the lace curtains as they shivered in a little breeze from the open sash. Nina lay deeply asleep, her face calm, almost grave. One hand lay palm-upward on the pillow as if it had moved a little from the cheek it cupped while she slept. Paul could see a tiny mole on one cheekbone that he had never noticed before, the pink indentation in an earlobe where the earring passed through, in the many-shaded fair hair a single silver strand, coarser and wavier than the rest. He laid a kiss on her cheek, another, very lightly, at the corner of her mouth. Then he got up. When he was dressed he went back and kissed her again. This time she said very sleepily, "Paul?"

"I'm going, I must. It's light now."

A finger reached up to touch him. She closed her eyes again. He went down, heard one of the dogs whimper but ignored it. His shotgun, albeit unloaded, lay on the table. The back door was still unlocked, as he had found it and as he, in spite of all his inward criticism of Stan and Colombo, had himself left it. He was as bad as they, or worse. But self-reproach was ridiculous at this stage of things. He would have defended her after all, with his bare hands, fought to the death if necessary.

Come on, you fool, he said silently and walked out into the cool still morning. The sun was rising, a red orb in a dressing of dark cloud, into a sky that was pale and distantly bright. He had not been so aware of birdsong, the diversity and volume of it, since he was a boy. The windows of the two rooms in the annex were shut and their curtains closely drawn. The flintwork of the walls, the stone flags, all looked clean as if they had been secretly washed by night.

He let himself into the cottage. At least he hadn't left the front door unlocked. There was no sound. He looked into the girls' room and saw them lying asleep, as he had left them. But if one of them had woken up, had had a bad dream, say, and come looking for him? He found himself unable to think, that is, to rationalize. It was not that he was tired. He felt fresh and vigorous, sleep being something to be indefinitely postponed. It was rather that events of the past few hours, excepting for that short period of sleep, had been all feeling, all emotion and activity and wonder and astonishment. Thought had not been there, or rather, had been rejected. And now he was out of the habit of reflection.

But not of recall. She had offered herself to him sweetly and responded to him with passion. While they made love—and he had not previously thought of making love, in all his knightly dreams he had not reached that point—she had said, clearly and plainly, not whispering or hesitating, "I love you, Paul." Just before he might have begun wondering if she would ever say it, she had said it. What now? What next? But thought was not possible, not needful. He threw himself into a chair and gave himself up to remembering.

Later when he went to wake the girls up he felt a momentary dread of reproach from Jessica. Where were you, Daddy? I looked for you but you weren't here. He knew that Jessica had been relegated to a secondary place in his life and that even if she reproached him, even if she had been afraid in the night, this wouldn't weigh heavily with him or for long. He even found himself thinking that too much attentive care wasn't good for children. The rough and tumble of life suited them better, "healthy neglect" had been the term for it in his own childhood.

But in any case she said nothing. She and Debbie had both slept long and soundly. A spelling test was lined up for them at school that day, twenty difficult words to spell, and over their cornflakes at the kitchen table they chanted to each other litanies of nouns.

"Who's going to collect us?" she asked him on the way to school.

It wasn't a reproach, it was an exaggeration to call it that. She was asking a simple question. He was sure she had forgotten the long walk of the previous afternoon, which now seemed to him years in the past. Before he could reply Debbie reminded her that she and her mother were returning home that day, only her father remaining at Jareds. Apsoland would be back on Saturday evening.

"So you'll come, will you, Daddy?"

Her insistence on knowing made him feel she was pressing it home too hard, even punishing him. "I or Emma's mother or someone." He was unable to stop himself saying rather sharply, "You haven't exactly been let down in the past, have you? Yesterday was the first time you ever had to exert yourself to walk."

Her dignity dismayed him. Once or twice in the past, when reproved, she had whined, tossing herself this way and that, making faces. But now, when he pulled up outside the school and turned to look at her, he saw her sitting quite gravely in the corner of the seat, her expression resigned, sad. A pang struck him. He wanted to hug her—but here? In front of all these children and parents?

"Off you go," he said. "Goodbye, Debbie. See you soon."

Jessica was no sooner gone than forgotten. He drove back to Jareds faster than usual, not until he reached the park being struck by the thought that he hardly knew what to do next, that she had made no plans for them, promised nothing. Thinking had come back, though, that had returned to normal. Friday—he had never in the past had much contact with her on a Friday. But surely today he could go into the house to see her? Surely he must. By the front door or the back? A flicker of dismay touched him as he drove through the arch.

He went into his house and began to reason it out. Five minutes of that and he found himself restlessly pacing. Suppose she should behave as she had yesterday morning, with that distant gentleness? But a kiss only had preceded that, hardly a kiss, it was different now, the world had changed since then. His pacing had taken him back to the kitchen when the doorbell rang.

She stood there smiling. She had never called on him before. Nothing could more effectively have emphasized how things were different. He took her by the hand to draw her in, closed the door, and held her in his arms.

Life must follow its regular course. The landscape gardeners had to be checked, their vehicles noted, the dogs had to be exercised. Nina said she would come with him when he took them across the heath to Wolves Wood.

"But you never go for walks."

"I used to. It's years since I've had anyone to go with. Things are going to be different now that I've got you. My whole life is going to change."

"Is it?" he said. "Is it? And mine, is that going to change?"

"You'll see."

He met her in the courtyard and she had the dogs with her. Up till then, he realized, he had seen her almost as an invalid. It was because she was indoors so much and so sheltered. She wore jeans, a zippered jacket, trainers. Her grasp on the dogs' double leash was more efficient than Colombo's. He expected to have to suit his pace to hers, necessarily walking far more slowly than usual, but she strode along like a fit woman who walks every day.

"You're never going to be my driver again," she said. "We'll just go out in the car together. I might even drive myself. Would you mind?"

"I don't think I should mind anything."

She gave him a sidelong look. "Let us hope you may be preserved from such a state of insensibility."

"Well, I shall be." He laughed. "You'll preserve me from it."

"Let's go out for the day. Let's go to some great house and walk about the gardens hand in hand. Shall we?"

The dogs disappeared into the wood. Paul and Nina walked carefully along the path, avoiding the bluebells. He showed her where he had found the snares. "I'd like to meet that poacher, I'd like to shake hands with him and thank him. If it hadn't been for him last night wouldn't have happened."

"Not last night," she said, "but it would have happened."

"I should like to kiss you. There's nobody to see but Tyr and Odin."

"And they only speak Old Norse," she said.

They went to Ickworth, saw the silver collection and were conducted through the rooms. Then, as she had proposed, they walked hand in hand about the gardens. He had entered a state of disbelief of what was happening to him and found himself constantly stealing glances at her, as if, since he last looked, she might have vanished or been transformed into someone quite different. The sensation of being locked inside a dream he knew was common in situations such as this, but all the same he couldn't admit there had ever before been a situation quite like this.

While they were having lunch in the dim quiet dining room of a restaurant in Bury, she laid down her fork, put her head a little to one side, and said, "You're waiting to be disillusioned, aren't you?"

It was precisely true, but still he said, "Why do you say that?"

"There are things you're waiting for me to say. I know it, I can feel it."

"Perhaps there are."

"We have to talk?"

He laughed, but uneasily. "I was thinking, your husband comes back tomorrow."

"Yes, I was going to say, why not live in the present? And then I realized that I don't myself, I live in the past and the future always, I'm living in the future now. But perhaps that isn't so bad."

He made himself say it, and firmly, "It is if it excludes me."

"Paul," she said, "listen to me. You *are* waiting for me to disillusion you. You think I'm going to say we have to keep this from Ralph, or else I'm going to say it was lovely but that's it, it's over."

"Are you?"

"I'm going to say I'll tell Ralph at the first possible opportunity. Or when you tell me to, whenever you tell me to. Why have secrets? There's no point." Her face hardened. "People keep these things secret for economic reasons. I don't need to do that." She didn't specify, went on, "I haven't any children, I've nothing to keep me with him. We can just go when you like."

Coming all at once like that, it was a little too much for him. The climate of dream and disbelief was suddenly overpowering. "Nina, do you mean all this?"

"You don't want to deceive him, do you? You don't want some clandestine thing, an adulterous intrigue? Imagine how it would be, it would be grotesque, with me running into the cottage as soon as Ralph had gone to work—or maybe we could take a room for the afternoon at the Post House?"

"Being disillusioned of one's disillusionment," he said, "is necessarily a slow process," and then he couldn't restrain himself from asking, all in a rush, "Why did you marry him?"

She could be crisp and sharp when she liked. He would never have suspected it. He was getting to know her. "I married Barney, my first husband, for money. He was a millionaire and he was old and unlikely to live long. Not very nice, was it? I married Powell because I thought he could look after me and by then I was very afraid. He had a lot of money too, but that wasn't my reason. I thought he was strong and perhaps he was, not strong enough to stay alive though. Some time I'll tell you how I met

Ralph, but for now it'll do to say he'd been bitten by the safety and self-preservation bug. He knew more about looking after someone whose life was threatened than anyone else I was likely to meet. He wasn't just paranoid—paranoia was his life. That's what he'll be doing now, telling some tycoon how to turn his apartment into a bank vault."

"I thought he was a stockbroker."

"Ralph?" She burst out laughing. "Oh, dear, that's funny, because I'm quite sure he'd like people to think he was. Perhaps he fosters the illusion just a bit. No, he's head of an immensely prosperous and flourishing firm that deals in—what does he call it?—domestic security."

He said somberly, "You were that afraid?"

"I was lonely. There had to be someone."

That was all she was going to say. There had to be someone. How many others had there been, that she hadn't married? He imagined a procession of young men, poor men. The rich old ones she married. It wasn't the first time she had paid the bill for a meal they had shared, but the first time since he had made love to her. That changed things. He wondered if she was paying with Apsoland's money. There was nothing, for the moment, that he could do about it. In the car she put her hand on his shoulder, laid her cheek against his arm.

"Would you laugh if I said I've never been in love before?"

"Not if it were true," he said.

He took her home first, then drove back to the school. Jessica was late coming out. Among the women waiting at the gate was Doreen and he wondered, as people in his situation do wonder about the opinion of their acquaintances, what she would say if she knew. Presumably, if Nina meant it all, she would soon know. This little world would know. Jessica came out at last with Debbie and Emma and, in spite of his resolve, his heart sank a little. At present he wanted only to be with Nina, alone with her. Doreen's request, coming at that moment, was the answer, coincidental and awesome, to an unuttered prayer.

"I was thinking, could Jessica come back for the night with us? That'd really please Debbie."

Paul told himself he wouldn't have agreed if Jessica had shown the least hesitation. She had never before stayed a night away without him or Katherine. But she was already jumping up and down with enthusiasm.

"Yes, Daddy, yes, I can. I can, can't I?"

He went back to fetch her nightdress and dressing-gown, clothes for the morning, the indispensable hairbrush. For the night of liberty she was giving him he would have driven ten times the distance. Coming back from Doreen's house he was overtaken by a gray Fiat and a moment or two later met a red one coming toward him. Both cars were driven by women and he told himself he was being ultracautious, but he couldn't help remembering the phone call from the woman named Anne who said she was Richard's wife.

Nina came down the front steps as he brought the car in. He told her where Jessica was.

"We'll go out," she said. "We'll be together the whole evening and you can come back here tonight." A thought struck her. "Will you miss her?"

"Of course I won't. She's all right, she's fine. It's only one night."

"I don't know, you see. I don't quite understand how people feel about their children."

He beckoned to her and when she brought her face up close to the car window, whispered, "I can't stay the night. Not with Stan there."

"He won't know—and who cares if he does? Who cares?"

First they went to a small, quiet restaurant. He agreed to it because he thought it would be cheap, in which belief he was wrong. She had suggested a palace of a place whose stately façade was floodlit or else a restaurant where the food was wonderful and the proprietor, who she knew, had a reputation for being rude to awkward or naïve patrons. It was all too bold for Paul, who was still surfacing from his dream state.

Small and secluded the restaurant might be, but she had dressed herself gorgeously for him in dark-green-and-blue-shot silk, a dress with a little short skirt and huge puff sleeves. The jewelry she wore he had never seen before, a necklace of emeralds and pearls in a gold setting, emerald and pearl earrings, but the wedding ring was gone and her hands were bare.

"It's not too soon to make plans, is it?" she said. "I shall tell Ralph—only when you say I can, of course—and you must tell Jessica." For all her deferring to his decision, she had an imperious way about her. It delighted him. "And then we'll—just leave! There'll be nothing to keep us. We'll leave and drive away, over the hills and far away. It'll be so good to leave fortress-Jareds, I can't tell you, I hate it so. It's only you being there these past months that's made it bearable. Do you know, Paul, now that I've got you I don't think I'm going to be frightened. I sort of trust you to look after me the way"—she spoke with childlike naïvety—"I never did the others."

It was as if a cold fingertip touched him. He flinched from it a little, said, "Nina, when you say we'll go, where will we go? I haven't got a home except the cottage here, Jessica's at school here . . ."

"Oh, I've a house in London. It's a nice house, it's in South Kensington, only we hardly ever go there. Ralph always got too nervous about me being in London. We'll go there. Paul, don't look like that, it's mine, if that's what's worrying you. Did you think it was Ralph's, did you think all this"—she made a sweeping gesture, then brought her hands to her shoulders, her neck, where the emeralds were—"Ralph paid for? I'm much richer than he is. I'm really very rich. I'm not exactly sure what makes a millionaire, how much you have to have, I mean, but I'm sure I am one."

He stayed the night. The lights were out in the annex, the dogs shut up in their room. This time he checked that all the doors were locked and bolted. She took him into the drawing room and showed him how the doors and windows could be closed off with iron gates. It was done simply by operating two switches, concealed as a safe might be, behind a painting.

"It's Ralph's specialty," she said, "only not many people have it done because it's awfully expensive."

"I knew about the gates," he said, "but I thought they'd be latticework."

"Like in a jeweler's? D'you know why they're not? Because you can fire a gun through latticework. Nothing but the impregnable for us. It's the same in my bedroom." He noticed she didn't say "our" bedroom. "There you are, my darling. If Ralph changes his mind and comes home tonight and you're in bed with me, we can just press the switches and shut ourselves up behind iron walls."

Not that night but the following evening, as was the arrangement, Apsoland returned. Paul and Nina had been out all day at Southwold while Jessica remained at Doreen's. It was too cold to swim in the sea but not too cold to walk on the sands and sit outdoors to eat.

"I'll tell Ralph on Monday," she said, "if that's all right. I must warn you, he may want to knock you down. Shall you mind that?"

On the way home they picked up Jessica. Nina didn't come in with him but remained in the car. If Doreen noticed her sitting there in the passenger seat she said nothing. Jessica jumped into the backseat, but this time Nina didn't join her there. She resumed her holding of Paul's shoulder, her nuzzling of his upper arm, in spite of the child's presence. When they were at home and in the cottage he expected a comment or a question, and getting none made him more uneasy than if she had asked. Once or twice he caught her eyeing him with a puzzled gravity.

Apsoland's return was expected any time after six, but Paul didn't hear him come and it was far too light for the infrared sensor to be activated. The news that Nina's husband was home reached him by means of a phone call which Jessica took. She handed him the receiver.

"Put the Jag away, would you, like a good fellow?"

Paul had to assure himself of two things: that Nina wasn't even in the room with Apsoland when he made that call and that he was still, after all, the man's paid employee. But just the same he asked Jessica what Apsoland had said. Her reply in other circumstances might have been very funny. She put on Apsoland's plummy barking voice. It was a creditable imitation, he hadn't known she had this gift for mimicry. "Paul Garnet there, is he?"

"No hello to you or anything?"

She said with a charity beyond her years, "Well, he doesn't know me. We haven't actually been introduced."

Sunday he devoted to Jessica and missed Nina nearly unbearably. It was still hard for him to believe that what she had promised would happen. Such things don't happen between the Lady of the Strachey and the Yeoman of the Wardrobe. And this continuing disbelief was fostered by her total disappearance, her vanishing into and hiding in, it seemed to him, the vastness of the house. Apsoland he saw, walking the dogs beyond the flint wall and into the wood, Tyr and Odin running for the sticks he threw. Inevitably, he had his shotgun hung over his arm. Silhouettes of Maria and Colombo appeared early in the kitchen window and some elaborate cooking routine seemed to be in progress. The master's homecoming, Paul thought.

Of Nina he saw nothing, though he returned often to a front window, until Jessica asked why he kept staring at the house, what was there to see? She had learned card games at Doreen's and had him playing snap with her and beggar-my-neighbor half the day.

"It's a long time since we heard from my mother," she said before she went to bed.

There was something uncanny about the way children sensed things. He felt the sort of dismay hints of supernatural happenings bring to someone alone in an old isolated house. She had seen Nina touch him, take his hand when they parted. Jessica could know nothing of sexual love, but some deep-lying instinct showed her this restrained behavior as a threat to the family she no longer had but which she yearned, as the parent-deprived child always will yearn, to re-establish.

"Will it be you fetching me or someone else?" she asked him in the morning and he sensed an admonitory note in her voice.

She was binding him to her by his own guilt, and somehow she knew about that guilt too.

"It's Emma's mother's day," he said, "or Harriet's, not mine. Somebody will fetch you, Jess. Does it matter?"

She said very firmly, looking him in the eye, "I like it best when it's you."

She had done her hair in two plaits, not very evenly. He decided it would be a mistake to redo them. Probably no one but he would notice the crooked parting down the back of her head. When he got back to Jareds he had the same feeling as he had on Friday morning, he was still waiting to be disillusioned. This time Nina phoned him.

"Come over to the house, Paul. Please come now, as soon as you can."

Of course he thought something was wrong. The real dissolving of his fear began when he came to the house, when, watching for him at the window, she let him in at the front door, and had her arms round him in the hall.

"Let's go upstairs. Now. Please, Paul. I've had thirty-nine hours without you, I counted, thirty-nine hours. I've told Colombo and Maria I don't want to be disturbed. They think I'm having the morning in bed because I'm not well. Oh, Paul, I'm going to have the morning in bed, aren't I, and I'm very, very well indeed!"

He wasn't nervous about the confrontation she must have with Apsoland that evening and had given the permission she rather absurdly asked for. But he would have preferred being present at it himself, which she wouldn't allow. Taking an active part in that kind of meeting of wills and conflicting interests was always better, he thought, than waiting elsewhere for news of the outcome. He knew he must brace himself for Apsoland's arrival at the cottage, for his bursting in upon them, and although he could face that steadily for himself, he was apprehensive about the effect on Jessica.

She should be home shortly before four, brought by Emma's

mother or Harriet's, but he no longer stationed himself to watch for the car at the only window from which the road was visible. At this crisis in his life he could contemplate only Nina and their future, attempt to imagine a year hence when they would all three be used to living together, by which time Nina and he might even be married. Did she have marriage in mind? A qualm came briefly when he remembered the promises he had made to himself to bring Jessica up in the country. But perhaps Nina would not insist on London. Thinking like this brought him, as it had begun to do, up against her money.

Sooner or later he must make up his mind what his attitude to her money was going to be. It would be no use bumbling along, pretending it wasn't there. His lifestyle—and Jessica's—would inevitably change hugely. Any job, for instance, that he had would be for fun, like a hobby.

Was it really going to happen, all of it? When he was with her he believed it but when they were apart the recent past became a fantasy, something he had imagined because he wanted it so much. Yet if he were to wake up, come back to consciousness after a lengthy and incredibly vivid dream, would the recovery of real life altogether surprise him?

He became aware that Jessica was late. It was 4:15. He shook himself out of that other life. Would she go home with Debbie without letting him know? Doreen would certainly let him know. He picked up the phone and dialed Emma's mother's number, confidently expecting no reply. The phone was by that window from which the road was visible, and he waited to put the receiver back at the moment he saw the car. Sheila answered after the fourth ring.

"It wasn't my day." The aggrieved note in her voice was unmistakable. He had done something, or left something undone, but what he didn't know, and she was the kind of woman who would prefer nursing a secret grievance to bringing it out into the open.

"Did she go with Harriet, d'you know?"

"It's no good asking me. I knew it wasn't my day. It wasn't my responsibility."

There was no reply from Harriet's mother. It had never happened before but it seemed just possible that Harriet's mother had gone shopping on her way home and taken the children with her. More likely, Paul thought, it had been his day but he had forgotten and poor Jessica was even now trudging home on her own.

It was perfectly safe, there was nothing to worry about, broad daylight on a fine warm day, a rather long walk for someone of only seven but along a not very busy road with wide grass verges. By this time, even at no more than two miles an hour, she should be nearing the entrance to the Jareds drive. It wasn't worth getting the car out to meet her. He thought how horribly alarmed he would have been if it were Nina who had gone out somewhere and was late getting back, what fears it would have given rise to—only Nina never was out alone.

He must open the gates. It could be done from inside the house or he could walk down the flint avenue. Not from inside, not this time. The park seemed peculiarly empty. Lately rabbits had begun appearing in ones and twos and there were nearly always birds, pigeons, a covey of red-legged partridges, magpies—one for sorrow, two for joy, he remembered the old country litany—flocks of starlings. But there was not a bird to be seen, not a rabbit. No wind ruffled the now dense leafage and the silence was absolute.

The green spread of the park lay bathed in soft sunshine, hazy enough to color the distant woodlands violet-blue. The sky was a very pale blue, sprinkled all over with small transparent clouds like down. If she were walking she would be here by now. He looked at his watch: 4:35. It was an hour since she had come out of school—fifty minutes at best. He asked himself how he could have said she was perfectly safe, she was only seven, and for the first time a chilly apprehensiveness touched him.

There was no sign of her. In both directions—and you could see a long way—the lane was empty. In the field opposite, the bay horse stood cropping the creamy fronds of fool's parsley. As he went back to fetch the car a magpie flew from the trees that sheltered the house and, flapping its tail up and down, perched on the roof of the winter garden. It was alone and remained alone. Paul said to himself, let there be another, just one more, one more to make two for joy, and castigated himself for a superstitious fool. The next step was to go out in the car and look for Jessica, never mind birds and omens.

As he walked in at the front door the phone began to ring. Harriet's mother, he thought. Thank God. The car had broken down. Of course. He picked up the phone.

A voice he had never heard before, a voice of positively aristocratic exquisiteness, said, "Mr. Garnet? We have Jessica. Don't call the police, will you? We'll kill her at once if you do. None of us is particularly fond of children, so we shall have no qualms."

As if a hand held him half-strangled, Paul spoke so hoarsely as to be inaudible. "Who are you?"

"I beg your pardon? I didn't catch that?"

"Who are you? What do you want with Jessica? I've no money, I can't pay ransoms."

"Oh, it's early days to talk about ransoms. In any case, we'll worry about that. At present we're only interested in negotiation."

"What do you mean?"

"I'll come back to you," the voice said, "in thirty minutes."

18

What a lot of anomalies there are in life! Sandor has just taught me that word and I'm finding it useful. For instance, you would expect people like me to be fond of children. I had a bad time as a child, none of the people who were supposed to be my parents showed me any love. So you'd expect me to have a fellow feeling for children who have a bad time of it, you'd expect me to care, but I don't. What I feel is much nearer indifference, a sort of, "I had to put up with it so why shouldn't they?" And it's likely that if I ever have children of my own, which is possible, most people do, I'll treat them just as badly as I was treated, for that's the way of the world.

Tilly feels much the same. That's natural too. Only somehow you think a woman is going to be different. Well, that's another mistake, that women are gentler, kinder, softer, sort of more squeamish, than us. They aren't. It's men that have put that sort of thing about to make up for being the bosses. You don't feel so guilty if you can persuade yourself your slaves are morally better than you, Sandor says.

The red light was shining into the car onto Tilly's face. When I turned round and looked at her I thought, Medusa. Sandor was reading a book about a lot of old Greek stuff one day and he told me stories out of it, he told me about this woman Medusa whose face turned people who looked at her to stone and whose hair was made of snakes. Tilly's eyes glittered and her hair seemed to writhe as the light changed to green. I had to drive on. She began telling us about this plan of hers, and with a kind of relish, as if she was hungry and describing the sort of meal she'd most like to have.

"You know, Tilly," said Sandor, "I really believe you'd stop at nothing."

I don't think I've ever before heard admiration in his voice for anyone, but I heard it then. By rights I ought to have been happy that they were making up their quarrel, were getting friendlier than they'd ever been, and I was, I was. But people are anomalies and I had an uneasy fear of being left out in the cold. I've been out in the cold, you see, I know what it's like. It's not an empty dread for me like it is for so many people.

That's why I wasn't sorry when we separated for the night, Tilly to go to the camper and Sandor and I to our room. Next day we moved into the George and a big room with a bath and color television and a little fridge disguised to look like a cabinet but containing liqueur miniatures and cans of beer and what Sandor said was the most expensive champagne he'd ever seen at £15 the half-bottle. Tilly came up, wearing a bright red dress, very low cut, and gold jewelry, emerald-green patent sandals, and a belt to match, four inches wide with a gold clasp studded with red and green stones.

The colors she wears are bright enough to hurt the eyes. I don't know if it's her taste or the man's who bought clothes for her for losing weight. When she was at home with Mum and Dad and me she always wore fawn and navy and brown because Mum said that if you're mousy bright colors overpower you. Tilly's nails are painted scarlet with the kind of varnish that's got silvery bits in it. We didn't drink the expensive champagne but had a bottle of the wine we'd bought, with some macadamia nuts from the fridge.

Tilly said she'd need a couple of days to get an idea of Garnet's movements and the child's. Her idea was to do the snatch on Friday if everything worked out. She'd do the snatch herself and then she reckoned she'd have done her bit. When I told her I'd been Richard on the phone to Garnet she laughed a lot—she always laughs when we talk about all our preliminary work—but said she'd be Richard's wife, she'd be Anne.

"Kids are all told not to talk to strangers these days," she said. "And they're told why not. I should have been so lucky. All Mum told me was the worst thing I could think of would happen to me. I had this pal at school whose gran had had her leg amputated and that was the worst thing I could think of happening, having my legs cut off."

"I thought they'd put electrodes on me," I said.

Sandor said nothing. That sort of confirmed for me that he'd been happy when he was a kid, Diana had been a good mother to him and he'd had his father then. It was funny because that made me think, I wonder what made him go to the bad? We think these things without meaning to, without our will being involved. Once, not long ago, if someone had told me you can know a person's bad yet love them just the same, I'd not have believed them.

Tilly said she'd make sure this kid Jessica got to know her name so that she'd go with her when the time came. I don't think Sandor much liked Tilly having it all her own way. He sort of took command after that. Tilly could make one phone call to Garnet's, saying she was Anne. She could keep on trying till she got Jessica. Kids of that age love answering the phone, he said, though how he knew that I don't know. When we'd got Jessica he'd do the phoning to Garnet.

Where were we going to keep Jessica? Hardly in the George Hotel.

"The caravan, of course," Sandor said.

He talked as if it was his and he had a right to do as he liked with it, but Tilly didn't seem to mind. What I had hoped for, but dismissed as being as unlikely as anything you could imagine, looked as if it might actually happen.

"You know something, Joe?" Tilly said to me when we were alone that night and Sandor had gone off to phone Diana, "I fancy him. It's that sort of dark, brutal brooding look, I've always fancied that sort, but the chance of it never seemed to come my way."

For all I'd thought of them together, it'd been love I'd thought of, silly me, not what was going on in Tilly's head. I always think of love, like the poor always think of money.

"Sandor's not interested in women," I said.

"What is he interested in then, men?"

"He's not interested in sex," I said.

Tilly started keeping watch at the school where Jessica went. She could soon tell there was a rota of mothers and of course Garnet himself dropping off and fetching their kids, only it didn't seem very regular. Once she went in the Fiat, another time in the camper and parked it across the road, then in the camper but left it in a side street and walked past the school and back at the crucial time. I was sent to scout around for a place to park the camper while Tilly made the snatch and to find somewhere to keep the camper when we'd got the kid in it. It was Thursday evening when she phoned Garnet's house and by a piece of luck got the kid the first time she tried. What did she sound like, I wanted to know, was she a nice kid? Tilly said she didn't know what I meant. A kid of seven was a kid of seven was a kid of seven.

The snatch was planned for the next day. Tilly had thought that some other kid's mother was coming to fetch Jessica but it didn't work out that way. Garnet came and instead of taking Jessica home with him, she went off with the woman who cleans for the Princess and goes to work on a moped. There was nothing more to be done till Monday. I asked Sandor, when the time came, how much money were we going to ask for. I was sitting on my bed with a can of beer from our fridge in my hand and he was in the bathroom, shaving.

"You can leave that to me," was all he said, but I felt rather uncomfortable. Not for myself, I knew I could trust Sandor, but more for Tilly, who was doing all the work.

"Is it going to be a million, then?" I said, though I was nervous about persisting.

"I said you can leave all that side of it to me."

"What if he won't play?" I said.

He affected not to understand what I meant, the way he does sometimes if I use slang to him or expressions like that. "Do I follow you?" he said.

I don't know why I had to think of what Tilly had told me about the Princess sitting in the front seat of the car next to Garnet but I did and, anyway, I was considering all possible eventualities.

"Suppose he's screwing her?" I said.

It's not a nice word, I know that, but there aren't any words for it that are nice. The way Sandor reacted seemed to me out of all proportion to the offense. I wasn't even looking at him at that moment, I was drinking my beer, my head half-turned away from the bathroom door. The next thing I knew I was being yanked up off the bed with Sandor's arm holding my neck in a fireman's lock and the razor sort of glittering an inch or two from my face.

"I'll cut your fucking throat," he said.

I could hardly speak, he'd got a stranglehold on my windpipe. I wanted to explain to him that I'd only meant the Princess was the sort of woman who went with a lot of guys, all those husbands and Sandor himself had hinted there'd been "adventures" in Rome. What could "adventures" mean but men and sex? But I couldn't say it, I could only gasp his name over and over, "Sandor, Sandor, Sandor . . ."

He didn't cut my throat. Perhaps he wouldn't have cut me at all if I hadn't put my hands up to try and pull his arm away, I had to, I was suffocating. He drew the razor across the back of my right hand, a long clean cut from the root of the little finger to the lower joint of the thumb.

Like that first time, it didn't hurt for a while, but it bled dreadfully. My beer had spilled all over the floor and the blood just dripped into the pool of it, golden beer with a crest of scarlet foam. It was surreal—Sandor's word. I held my hand under the cold tap and put lint on it and plasters. It began to throb then, as if there was a heart inside it, beating away.

Sandor'd gone out, I don't know where, but when I saw him again he said Tilly was coming over and we were all going out to eat in the grand place with the floodlighting. She arrived dressed in white, which you can't exactly call a bright color and yet in some ways is brighter than any other. It was a white suit she had on, tight and with a short skirt. She'd made her hair redder and her lipstick was the color of the geraniums in the pot on the reception counter.

"What have you done to your hand?" she said, and when I told her there'd been an accident with Sandor's razor, she flinched away from me and said not to get any of it on her.

The blood had come through all the lint and plasters. I had to do it again and tear up one of the hotel pillowcases to make a bandage. Sandor drove and Tilly went in front with him. I could tell at once they were changed, the way they were with each other. Tilly was making all the running, though, Sandor just accepting, not going so far as to push her away when she touched him but not returning her long sexy looks either.

Sex bothers me. For one thing, I find it embarrassing. I can't help feeling the world would be a nicer place without it. It makes me uncomfortable and when it's really heavy—I mean watching it—it upsets me. Of course you'd have to have some, for the race to go on. I suppose we all want that, but I don't know why we do, because surely what's important is us and being here and now. But taking it for granted the race must continue, people could do it just for that, like animals do. Animals have really got it right there. Sex is dirty however you look at it, or I suppose so, with all the sticky stuff and mess and smell. God or whoever meant it to be used like any other necessary dirty function, spitting out phlegm, for instance, that clears your windpipe, or shitting, that cleans your gut, meant it to be used for getting something over with and then put behind you. What is nice isn't sex but holding someone and cuddling them and sitting up close to them with your arms round each other. That's what's nice. It must be.

Tilly's got used to sex. For her it's the way she communicates. I mean, even the couple of times she's given me a hug since she arrived here she hasn't been able to help pushing her stomach at me and rubbing my chest with her tits. I could see she wanted to do that with Sandor, and more.

We didn't go mad on the drink, just had a bottle of wine between us and some brandy afterward. The Italian waiter was there and of course as soon as he saw Sandor he made a point of serving us all the time. Sandor and he jabbered away nineteen to the dozen, and I could see Tilly liked that, she liked Sandor demonstrating something he was good at. Having something to admire about him made her want him more. Sandor called him Giovanni and he called Sandor *signore* but I couldn't make out any of the rest of it.

On the way back we passed the camper. Tilly had parked it on a bit of waste ground where they'd pulled down an old building and were going to put up flats. It was only a few hundred yards from the George. She asked Sandor if he noticed anything different about it, and he asked her where had the letters gone that said about fruit, vegetables, and salads?

"I used two cans of spray paint on it," Tilly said.

In the white mercury vapor that makes these towns so grim and cold by night the camper looked a sort of greenish-khaki color all over, but you couldn't really tell. When we were in the George car park I got out first and had to wait awhile for them until they'd finished kissing in the front seat. They did some more kissing after they got out, with their heads bent over at right angles to each other, and grabbing and gobbling as if they were going to eat each other up.

I suppose I should have known what would happen. If I was tactful, if I'd even guessed, I'd have stayed downstairs in the bar or something. The truth is I thought these things took longer, I thought the process would be slower. All the lipstick and pancake stuff and blusher was sucked off Tilly's face but it hadn't transferred itself to Sandor's. I suppose they'd licked it all up and swallowed it. You see what I mean about sex being dirty? I followed them upstairs and I really thought Tilly had just come in for another drink, I expected Sandor to get me to phone for room service to bring champagne.

He stopped me while I was closing the door. "Come on, little Joe," he said, "you can't be that thick. Give us your space, will you?"

Strange way of putting it, wasn't it? "Get out," he said when I didn't seem to understand.

"Okay, but get out where?"

Tilly said, "You can sleep in the camper for tonight. I'll give you the key."

That's how I came to be walking back across the marketplace, under the clock tower, between the few remaining parked cars. The sickly light bathed everything and took out the colors, the way it does. It was like looking at television on an old mono set. And it was rather cold. It's often colder in May than it is in March. Everything was closed, even the pubs. The market had been on all day and bits of squashed fruit and fruit rinds and rotten vegetables and cabbage leaves people had trodden on were everywhere. Nobody had attempted to clean it up and I doubt if they will. It'll just get trodden in and stuck on the soles of shoes and ground into car tires unless the rain comes to wash it away. The only other human being apart from myself was an old woman wrapped in a blanket and sitting on newspapers in the church porch.

I told myself I was the gallowglass going back to barracks but all of it made me start feeling a bit low just the same. I could say I felt as if I'd been rejected but that wouldn't be accurate. I *had* been rejected. The strange thing was that I didn't want to be doing with either of them what they were doing with each other and it didn't make me jealous. I didn't, as a matter of fact, want to think about what they were doing except to hope it was all over by now. I found the camper and unlocked the door and once I got inside I began to feel a lot better. It was bright in there when I put the light on and the heater and it smelled nice, of perfume and makeup. Tilly had left the bed down and there was a duvet on it and pillows all covered in red-and-blue-patterned stuff. Clothes were everywhere, the ones she'd decided not to put on, and there were pots of cream too and hair-coloring stuff and sprays. I could see the camper was like Tilly's own beauty center.

It had a funny effect on me. A nice one, though. I can't help wondering what sort of distant memory, from that early child-hood I think I can't recall at all, all that woman's stuff called up. Because I was soon seeing Tilly and Sandor as my father and mother again, only more strongly, and that was only a step to thinking that it was all right for them to be doing what they were doing, because parents did, mothers and fathers did. They were playing at mothers and fathers.

First I hung up all the clothes and put them into the little cupboard. I tidied up the pots and jars, having that strange feeling you sometimes get of I-have-been-here-before. Then I undressed and lay down in Tilly's bed and put out the light and pulled the duvet over me, being very careful with my sore hand. It was a lovely way I sent myself to sleep, by imagining I was tucked up in a cot in their room and they were asleep in the big bed only a yard away from me. I even fancied I could hear their gentle regular breathing, but I think maybe I dreamed that.

It worried me rather, how I was going to get into our room in the morning. But it's always the way, the things you worry about don't happen and the things that do happen are those you never gave a thought to. The key to our room was hanging on the hook in reception, so I just asked for it in the normal way and went upstairs. Of course I thought they'd both gone out somewhere, but when I let myself in I found Tilly in bed.

"Where's Sandor?" I said.

She didn't know or anyway she didn't say. I could see she hadn't anything on but when she sat up she pulled the sheet up right around her neck. This was the old Tilly. I don't mean the old old one who was fat and sullen and with raggle-straggle mousy hair, but more the one who used to come and see me in hospital.

"I found out what he went to prison for," she said.

"What d'you mean?" It was the last thing I expected.

"I found out what he went inside for. He told me."

"What was it?" I said.

She laughed, a cynical sort of laugh. "Well, it wasn't rape, I'm telling you."

I didn't know what she meant and I'm not sure if I do now. She went on laughing. Then she stopped and the laughter was wiped off her face as quickly as turning off TV. "Causing actual bodily harm in the course of robbery. I may have got that a bit wrong, but it was more or less that. He cut someone with a razor, an old man, trying to get him to open a safe." She was looking at my hand, making me want to put it behind my back.

"Sandor being Sandor made a right cock-up of it. I mean, reading between the lines, Joe. I drew my own conclusions, anyone with a bit of sense would. For one thing there was two hundred quid in the safe, not twenty grand, and for another the old man wasn't so old. He opened the safe, but while Sandor was having a peep inside he sounded the alarm. Sandor got five years but he didn't serve that long."

"Why did he tell you?" I said. I suppose I really meant, why had he never told me?

She turned her face away, gave me a sidelong look that had things in it to make you shiver, nasty things in her eyes. "How about to get him going when all else failed? What d'you reckon to that? I wouldn't put it past him to try a spot of S&M, only not with me, not bloody likely." She tugged the bedspread off and wrapped it round her. "I'm going to get up, Joe, and have a bath and then I'm going to have a look at your poor hand and see if I can make it a bit more comfortable for you."

Sandor had taken the car and been to see Diana, who was back from her Greek holiday. He didn't go all the way to Norwich but met her for lunch in Diss. When he came back he was driving her car, a nearly new Vauxhall Cavalier in light blue. He'd persuaded her to exchange it for the Fiat. I don't suppose it took much persuasion. She'd do anything for him, he only had to ask.

He and Tilly must have got their sex urge out of their systems. I've heard it said that this is what can happen if you're very randy for someone. Do it and do it a few times, make a pig of yourself, and it'll all be done with and you'll feel better. However you look at sex, it's not attractive, is it?

Monday morning and I changed the registration plates on the Cavalier just to be on the safe side. Sandor and I went along to the camper in the afternoon to station ourselves there, hand the Cavalier over to Tilly, and have a look at her disguise.

She'd put on a flowered cotton skirt and a pale blue T-shirt and sprayed her hair brown. There's some mousse stuff you can buy to spray on wet hair that'll do that, though it's sticky afterward and comes off on everything, but Tilly didn't care about that. It did the job for the time being. She had on no makeup but pale pink lipstick and she wasn't wearing stockings but had sandals on her bare feet.

Tilly pulled an awful face when she looked at herself in the mirror but I thought she looked quite nice. She was going to blend in with all the other mothers. That was what she looked like, someone's nice warm young mother. It spoiled it a bit for me when she put sunglasses on and I guess it must have for Sandor too because he said, "All this elaborate disguise really isn't necessary."

"Not for you maybe," said Tilly, and she made quite a speech. "The kid's not going to see you, since I hope you and Joe are going to get stockings over your faces before I get back here. But unless we kill her she's going to remember the lady with the flaming red hair and the legs and the long red nails, isn't she? So she's not going to get the chance, seeing as I don't want to be mouse-haired and flat-footed the rest of my life, I'd rather be that way for three days or whatever it's going to be. Because, frankly, I may not be mad about kids but I'm not into killing them. You said I'd stop at nothing but that's where I stop. So just for once in your life, one of your projects had better work out. Right?"

While she was speaking Sandor had turned aside. He actually yawned. I don't think he heard much of it because he went on as if she hadn't spoken. "Garnet won't tell the police, therefore it doesn't matter who sees you or in what particular aspect of your colorful personality they see you. And after Garnet has done what he's asked, he and his daughter won't be in a position to tell the police or anyone anything. They'll be in this up to their necks as much as we will—more."

"I hope you're right," was all Tilly said.

It was time for her to leave. We arranged where we were all going to meet in an hour's time. Sandor and I sat in the camper, looking at the pair of stockings Tilly had left for us to put over our heads. We didn't put them on, not at that stage. Sandor said, "I shouldn't have done that the night before last, little Joe. It was a mistake."

I think that's the first time he'd ever admitted to me that he'd done something wrong. It marked the start of a new intimate stage in our relationship, or that's how I saw it. I felt warm inside. Lifting up my hurt hand and feeling the soreness of it with my fingertips, I looked up at Sandor.

"Christ God," he said, "I don't mean your bloody hand. You asked for that and you deserved it. I mean screwing your sister or whatever she is. Don't look at me like that, like a bloody dog holding up its paw that someone's trodden on."

I got into the driver's cab and he got into the seat beside me and I drove to the place we'd fixed on, a long track that goes down to the river and crosses it by a footbridge and a ford. There's never anyone down there. It was quiet. The river flows gently over a bed of yellow pebbles and the water is full of weeds like long green hair and leafy things that might be watercress. Flowers were out, tall stems with pink bells hanging from them, and in the grass yellow buttercups and white daisies. The trees are quite thick there but there's a place where they part and you can look up a long avenue of them where the grass between is green and lush and cows are there cropping it, all silent and ordered and rather mysterious. Birds don't sing in the afternoons, except cuckoos and they sing all day. There was this cuckoo that went on and on making its noise, as if it was taunting me. It got on my nerves anyway.

Sandor said, "I wouldn't bet much on that bird's chances if you'd got a gun, little Joe."

Maybe, but I'm not so sure. I don't think I'd kill anything. Because if you do that you take their life away, don't you? And that's the end of it, they don't have any more, it's the end of things for them forever. If more people thought of that, of what it actually means, they wouldn't talk so much about killing. But I didn't say any of that to Sandor. The cuckoo started up again and must have flown right over the camper, they keep on singing while they're flying, Sandor says.

We put the stockings over our heads. I don't know how it made me look but Sandor reminded me of a film I'd seen on television of soldiers in the First World War wearing gas masks, though a stocking isn't much like a gas mask. I suppose it had the same effect of making the face disappear and a man without a face isn't human, is he?

It was 3:20 when we got there and the time passed slowly. Sandor hardly spoke after he'd said that about shooting the cuckoo. I thought about what Tilly had told me and the old man Sandor had cut while trying to rob his safe. Was it a shop or a bank or what? Was it a private house maybe? It didn't make me feel any different about him, any more than it had made Diana feel different. Love doesn't care about that stuff. I'm an expert on love, you see, the way an astronomer can be an expert on a star that's so far away he's never seen it.

It was five to four when the blue Cavalier appeared, heading quite slowly down the drive toward us. The kid called Jessica was sitting in the front passenger seat beside Tilly. There was no way of crossing the river except by the ford and Tilly came through slowly, across the concrete ramp that lies two or three inches below the surface of the water. The kid laughed as the wheels went through the water and made the spray come up. She didn't know then, she didn't know anything had happened, she thought "Anne" was taking her home.

I didn't like the feeling that gave me, but so what? She wouldn't be in ignorance for long. The puzzled look on her face probably started from the moment Tilly fetched her out of that car all among the trees and walked her over to the camper. She must have known things were wrong when she came in and Tilly shut the door behind her. And she saw us, with our masks on.

She didn't cry out or scream or anything. She looked at Tilly and back at us and put her lips together in a funny tight sort of way. Her eyes are very large and greenish-blue and her hair is—well, was—in two plaits long enough to reach to her waist. She turned to Tilly and said, "Why have they got those things on their faces?"

Tilly didn't answer her, no one did. Tilly said, "Sit down. Go and sit down there on the other side from them."

I suppose any kid would have said it. I wonder how many times I've heard kids say it in TV serials. "I want to go home."

All the time we'd been waiting—well, off and on—I'd noticed the scissors lying there on the countertop between the cooker and the fridge, a big pair of scissors with long blades and orange-colored handles. They hadn't been there on Saturday night or I'd have remembered. The kid, Jessica that is, didn't move after she'd said that about wanting to go home, she just stood as if she was stunned. Tilly was behind her. She picked up the scissors and cut off Jessica's two plaits in a single rapid movement.

I gave a sort of gasp. Although he didn't make a sound, Sandor turned his head sharply away as if he'd seen something that hurt him. Jessica, bewildered, slowly brought up both hands to feel the cut-off ends of her hair, the stumps of her hair.

19

Thinking of Jessica's terror, her need of him, and her inevitable dreadful bewilderment was so bad that it made him groan aloud like someone in physical pain which would be unendurable in silence. Some power of the will was brought into use to stop him dwelling on that again.

At first, whatever they might say, he had been adamant about calling the police. Hadn't he in the past condemned out of hand those people in his situation who obeyed the commands of— terrorists? For these kidnappers were terrorists, however small might be their scale of operations and however base their aim. But in the half-hour before the second call came he had not phoned the police, he had only waited for that call. Attempting to be very honest with himself, he understood that the accent in which the voice spoke carried with it some implication of authority. Those were the tones in which authority spoke, government, the law, deriving from a famous public school, a great university. You believed what that voice told you, no matter how many times in the past it had let you down.

"In the morning your instructions will be in the letter box. Wait until after eight. Jessica is quite safe while you obey us. We don't want money, we want you to do something for us. Remember we don't want her, we don't even like children."

Those remarks could be taken in two ways, one reassuring, the other barely to be thought of. Instead he considered the police again. Could he tell the police without Jessica's abductors knowing? Without having even any vicarious experience of his present situation, he understood that he was plunged at once into the typical plight of the kidnap victim's parent. In such a person's mind kidnappers take on superhuman, almost supernatural, qualities, all-knowing, all-hearing, their spies behind every corner, up every tree. Stealthily and invisibly they have bugged every room, tapped every phone, and the telescopic lenses of their video cameras reach impossible distances.

Paul actually looked up the phone number of the nearest police station and dialed the first three digits of the number. The room became full of eyes. The breathing was audible of the listener who crouched with ear pressed to the wall. He fancied as he dialed that he could hear unfamiliar mechanical sounds inside the earpiece. He put the phone back.

It wasn't yet six. He had fourteen hours to wait before they told him what to do next. And there was nothing he could do, nothing to do. Eating, opening a book, going out—all seemed equally grotesque. He could contemplate drinking, getting drunk to the point of oblivion, but it wasn't to be seriously considered. They had said he would hear no more from them before eight in the morning, but he refused to trust to that. If they changed their plans they would phone, if some new idea came to them they would phone. In the kitchen he had two cans of beer and a half-bottle of whiskey, unopened. He poured himself a small amount of whiskey and drank it neat. It made him feel no better, but no worse either. His head swam. The whiskey, effecting a gradual change of consciousness, seemed to have brought him a degree of disbelief, a feeling of, this can't be happening to me and Jessica.

Someone to tell it to would have been a help to him, someone to be there, be here, sitting in the other armchair listening. There was no one. His aloneness had never been so acutely felt. It wasn't until he heard her voice that he remembered Nina, remembered her existence. When the phone rang he thought it was the kidnapper with the smooth, suave, authoritative way of speaking. The shock of hearing her silenced him, for a moment he was unable to answer her.

"Paul, are you all right?"

It was the time to tell her, yet he never seriously considered it. He lied and said, "Yes, I'm all right."

"Ralph just phoned. He's going to be late. He actually asked me to phone you and tell you. So that you'd look after me. I thought that was funny in an ironical sort of way." He heard her light deprecating laugh. "Poor Ralph," she said, and then, "Paul? What is it? If you're worried I can be overheard, Colombo and Maria are both in the kitchen."

He could see their silhouettes through the kitchen window. They had put the light on, though it was barely dusk.

"Shall I come over to you? I know Jessica's there but we could just be together, the three of us."

He summoned up the strength to answer her. "Not this evening, Nina." A hint that all might not be well escaped, he couldn't stop it. "Bear with me. Don't ask me."

She asked him. Of course she would. "But what is it? You're not well, are you? Or is it Katherine? Is it something with Katherine?"

"Nina, please don't ask me. Let's not talk now. Please."

"Paul, what is it? Are you ill?"

He made a superhuman effort. "I'm fine. Really. Jessica . . ." What had he been going to say? He said it again, just the name. "Jessica." She received it as if he were trying to tell her something Jessica mustn't hear.

"All right," she said. "I'll see you tomorrow. I only wanted to say I shan't be able to tell Ralph tonight, not if he won't be home till late. I don't want you to think I've chickened out."

"I wouldn't. I don't mind. It doesn't matter."

A mounting madness, it sounded like. He couldn't even say goodbye to her, words failed, it was as if he had come to the end of all possible reserves of words. The phone went down and he stood looking at it, certain she would ring back. She didn't. There was a deep silence.

He went into the kitchen and poured another small whiskey. There was no possibility he would be able to remove himself far from that phone. Even the kitchen was too far. He lay in the armchair, taking sips of the whiskey. While it was actually in his mouth, beginning its journey down his throat, its warmth brought him a kind of hope. It will be all right, it will be all right. But after that there was just a fuzziness and then, gradually, a spreading of panic through his body. It came from powerlessness, from enforced inertia. There came a need to pace, which he resisted. He lay back in despair.

The house lights blazed up just after ten. Apsoland was coming home. Paul thought the phone might ring then and Apsoland demand the Jaguar be put away. He didn't always do that, sometimes it stood outside all night. After half an hour Paul knew he wouldn't phone. An upstairs light came on in the house, the window that was on the rear wall of the upper hall. No one had drawn the curtains. He saw Nina pass along the hall on the way to her bedroom. She paused and looked out of the window toward his house. Before she could catch sight of him, he turned away and went back to the kitchen where he hacked off a slice from the new brown loaf and ate it dry. It was eleven hours since he had eaten anything. When he had poured himself another inch of whiskey he went upstairs and fetched a blanket to cover him while he tried to sleep on the sofa.

It was quite dark, even with the curtains open, now that all the lights in the house had gone out. From the distant wood an owl called, a thin unearthly shriek.

Sleep of a different kind from anything he was used to had come fitfully. Each episode lasted ten minutes or less, sometimes filled with dreams, sometimes with very bright or very dark images. But all of it was shallow. He was acutely uncomfortable, his body ached and sweated. With the light, which came impossibly early, before five, he lost all hope of recapturing sleep.

There was a dull beat inside his head. He washed his face and hands under the cold tap in the kitchen. An almost superstitious fear of going far from the phone still possessed him. They might be up there now, approaching the mailbox, or they might have been there already or were still preparing to come. Strong, black instant coffee was the only thing he could contemplate ingesting. The idea of it was even a tiny comfort.

If they kill her I will kill myself, he thought. It was his first real thought of the day. Then, although he hated it, he shuddered his way into it, he pictured her, where she was now, in some dirty uncomfortable room, locked in, but with a bed no doubt, with blankets. At least it wasn't cold. She would sleep. Children slept in spite of what happened to them, in spite of fear, unhappiness, pain even. Sleep was so natural to them, they were still without those visitations of misery at the horror of the world or the desert with no oasis that lies waiting at three in the morning. Hungry children, sad children, abused children, all had the solace of sleep. She would sleep—and she would wake up.

He found he was crying. It was the first time in his adult life, so far as he could remember, the first time since he was ten or eleven. The lachrymal glands, unused for so long, still knew how to do it. He stood weeping with his head held back, as if that would stem the tears. Presently, he drank his nasty bitter coffee.

There was nothing to do, no way of passing the time but by thinking of Jessica. He thought of her and it made him cry. And then he discovered something, that he might as well give himself to his unhappiness, he might as well think of her, remember her, ache and long for her, because anything else was a denial of her and a loss of reality and of being human.

At five minutes to eight, with tears dried on his face and still in the clothes he had worn all night, he went outside and began to walk to the gate. Rather than keeping inside the flint walls, he walked on the grass. It was drenched with dew. The morning was cool, hazy still, the sun weak. A hare, startled by his tread, leapt from behind a tuft of long grass and bounded away. He thought, let them be kind to her, at least let them speak kindly to her. For the first time he remembered the woman who had phoned called Anne. There was a woman among them. Let Anne be kind to her.

He had to enter the flint avenue, there was no other way of escape from the park. What a place! What folly! The electric fence awaited poacher and the law-abiding alike. He entered the avenue by the wrought-iron door and walked to the gates, opened them, passed through to the mailbox which was underneath where the watching lion stood.

The post had come. Two envelopes with typewritten addresses for Apsoland. A parcel for him with an address in Northampton that had nothing to do with him. His instructions. Why would instructions be in a parcel?

Before he had got it open he thought of what it might be. It was as if everything his body did stopped, his heart, his breathing, the course of his blood. Only his fingers worked, tearing at the sticky tape, the reused brown envelope from which the original label had been stripped, the newspaper inside. The plaits slithered into his hands. He gasped as he held them. His skin goosepimpled. The hair smelled of her, sweet powdery little-girl smell, and where one of them had been cut off near the crown was one of those snarls, the tangles that were almost the only cause of argument between them.

He turned his face aside and retched. Bile came up into his mouth but that was all. He was clutching the hair, a pigtail in each hand, as if holding on tight to all he had of her. The lion that held the man in its claw-grip stared at him with its blunt stone muzzle lifted. A car coming down the avenue made him look up. It was Apsoland in the Jaguar. Paul thrust his child's hair into the pockets of his jacket, picked the wrappings up from where they had fallen onto the ground.

Apsoland put down his window, said, "Tell Colombo you've

fetched the post, will you, like a good fellow? Save him an unnecessary journey."

Having nothing to say, Paul said nothing, looked at him and nodded.

Uttering something incomprehensible about leaving the gates open for the plant suppliers, Apsoland drove on. Paul went back up the avenue. There had been no instructions with the hair. He understood what they were doing, they aimed at making him sweat in suspense. They succeeded. For some reason at this point he remembered what Nina had said about a fingernail. She had also said it wasn't her fingernail. Were they the same people who had taken Nina? And was it possible they had taken Jessica by mistake for Nina? Someone had got it wrong, been told to snatch the girl with the fair hair?

But they had cut off her hair. If only she wasn't frightened, he thought, if only they did it while she was asleep. There was no end to his terrible imaginings. He saw her holding on to her hair and the two plaits coming away in her hands.

Once in the house again he thought, should I tell Katherine? Should I try to get hold of Katherine and tell her too? She's Jessica's mother, after all, in her strange way she must have some love for her. Not yet, not yet. Wait by the phone, don't leave the phone. That's how instructions will come, by phone. When they feel they have softened me up enough.

They have, they have. I wish I could tell them so.

The phone rang. He jumped for it. The voice was Colombo's. The plant suppliers had arrived with stock for the winter garden. Did Paul have instructions for checking them out? Mr. Apsoland said he did. Colombo refused to take any responsibility on his own initiative.

Paul remembered. He had an envelope somewhere. It was on the bookcase. If it had been physically possible for him to laugh he would have laughed. There were two small photographs of the passport type inside the envelope, a sheet of paper with names and descriptions typed on it. The irony of it, now the danger was past! It was too late. But he went outside, leaving the front door open so that he would hear the phone. The plant suppliers' truck was parked on the other side of the arch. Maria stood talking to the driver, who was still sitting in his cab.

Paul thought, suppose they've taken Jessica to distract my attention, and these are the rest of them, come for Nina. It would be quite a clever way to do it. But the faces matched the photographs, the descriptions matched. Paul nodded to them, told them to go ahead and unload. He went back to the house, to the phone.

The two men came through the arch, pushing trolleys laden with plants in pots. The plants they brought were orange and lemon trees, plumbagos and a selection of those houseplants which are so common, so universal, that everyone recognizes them and no one knows their names. He took Jessica's hair out of his pockets. Looking at it was almost worse than his first sight of it up at the mailbox. He shut his eyes, thought, I must keep it, it may be all I will have of her.

Nina came through the arch. She was wearing the pale-blue cotton dress he liked so much. The two men were putting the plant pots on shelves in the winter garden and she followed them in to stand and watch them. Paul could see that she was talking to the men. Once she laughed. He turned away, looked at the phone. The clack-clack of her heels on the flagstones told him she was coming to the cottage. He opened the door, let her in, and closed it quickly. As soon as the door was shut she had her arms round him. He thought, suppose she wants me to take her out somewhere? She had promised he would never be her driver, in that sense, again.

She said, "I'm sorry about yesterday."

"Why should you be sorry?"

"I meant to tell Ralph. It turned out to be rather an anticlimax. I know you were cross with me, I could tell."

"I wasn't cross," he said.

"I'll tell him tonight. Listen, what will you do about Jessica? About her school, I mean. You'll have to notify them."

Now was the time to tell her. He wasn't alone, he had Nina, his partner, his natural confidante. With her it could be shared. He could tell her and she might help him. Somehow, before he even began to think of this, he had known he wasn't going to tell her. She would be extremely frightened, but that wasn't the reason. She was talking about arrangements. He need not give notice to Apsoland because, after all, it was for her he had been engaged. She seemed to be making some kind of joke about being engaged. He was unable to smile.

They sat side by side on his sofa. The plant suppliers could have seen them, or Maria could have, if they had looked toward the window. Nina seemed indifferent to what they thought. She held his hand.

"I wanted to have the whole day with you and then these people phoned last night. They're relations of mine—well, very distant, but relations. They're on holiday here and they want to call, I had to ask them to lunch. Paul, I'm very sorry, but it's only one day."

"It doesn't matter," he said.

It was a reprieve. He wondered how he would handle it if the phone call came now. All he could do was continue to hold her hand, squeezing it tightly. She said, "All the time you've been here I've gradually been getting less and less afraid. My confidence has been growing, it's made me tell myself not to fantasize and get things out of proportion. What harm can it do me if a madman writes to me and tells me he'll take me away? He can't, not with you here. All Ralph's fences and gates and lights haven't done for me what you've done."

"I haven't done anything," he said.

"You've been here. You've been big and strong and sane and reasonable—and I love you."

He held her in his arms in the half-dark of the hall. It was a comfort, small and inadequate but a comfort, to hold someone and feel the pulse of another body, the pressure of flesh, the gust of breath. As she separated herself from him and the door closed behind her, he thought, why doesn't the phone ring, why don't they phone?

The plant suppliers had gone, the truck had gone. He saw that Nina, instead of returning immediately to the house, had gone back into the winter garden and was examining all her new, dull plants with a tender regard. They reminded him of the floral decorations in the foyer of a hotel or conference center. She seemed very far away from him. I hardly know her, he thought. Who is she?

The words had been spoken aloud involuntarily. It was as if the phone bell answered them, or they had invoked it. He picked up the phone, gave his number and heard someone breathing.

"Who is it?"

"You don't need my name." It was the man who had offered him the £200,000, the other voice. "Did you get the parcel?"

He would have liked to scream abuse. "Yes," he said quietly.

"I expect you recognized her hair. We didn't think a covering letter was necessary. She's okay, a bit miserable, but that's to be expected. No doubt you remember my friend said something to you about doing something for us?"

"I'd be ashamed to own someone like that as my friend."

"That's silly," he said. "Insulting us isn't going to get you anywhere. Don't you want to hear how to get Jessica back?"

"Of course I do."

"You can have her back tomorrow. Would you like that?"

Even for Jessica's sake he wasn't going to let this man torture him for his pleasure. "Tell me what I have to do." He spoke sharply. It seemed to have a swift effect.

"Give us the Princess. That's the exchange. Give us the Princess and you can have Jessica."

"Who?" he said. It would have taken some thought for Paul to know who he meant and he couldn't think.

"Nina Abbott," the man said. "We want her in exchange for Jessica."

20

Mum's old father that we were supposed to call Grandad used to come and see us sometimes. He'd come for Sunday dinner. Dad would go and fetch him in the car from the old folks home. Grandad had bow legs like a jockey and a bent back from arthritis. Once, about fifty years ago, he'd been a farm laborer, as they were called then. "Agricultural workers" is what they say now. Grandad used to talk about the country, Hampshire it was, I think. In fact, that was all he ever did talk about.

He said you couldn't go anywhere in the countryside. It was trespassing. Gamekeepers would shoot you on sight if you didn't get your leg caught in a mantrap. Dad said he must have been talking about a hundred and fifty years ago, but Grandad insisted. He said the only people who could go where they liked were fox-hunters and people hunting hares with beagles. Well, it may or it may not have been like that in Grandad's time but it isn't like it now. For one thing, there's not a soul about. Farming is all mechanized and though the chances are you won't meet anyone, you just might see a solitary man driving a tractor or some kind of agricultural tank thing, but he'll be shut up inside his cab with his fags and his sandwiches and his beer and his headset on.

If they want to kill the weeds they send a helicopter over to poison them with spray. Most of the time the fields and the woods are deserted. They're like the towns at night, only they're the same by night and day. In the country it's only the roads that are crowded, the open land is left strictly to nature, or what's left of it. That's why it was so easy for us to keep moving the camper to hiding places.

The first night we moved about twenty miles north and parked inside a wood. It was very deep country. We passed through a village with all the usual stuff—a church, a couple of pubs, village hall, tarted-up big houses, and the usual silos and corn stores on the outskirts. After that there was nothing for miles. Our wood was in a valley, approached by a track from the road. You couldn't see a house in any direction, you couldn't see a church tower.

Tilly had got everything organized, even food supplies. She grilled sausages and we had tinned potatoes and frozen peas with them. Jessica was asleep by then, which was just as well because we couldn't have eaten in front of her and kept the stockings over our heads. She refused to eat anything but said she'd have a cup of cocoa. Tilly was very pressing about that cocoa, which wasn't like her. I understood why when Jessica fell asleep. Tilly had mixed up a sleeping pill in it. They were capsules really, so Tilly took one apart and mixed up the powder with the cocoa and sugar and milk.

I've said I don't like kids and that's true. They're boring, aren't they? They're boring to be with. All those questions they ask and the way they don't know about things you've known about for years, it gets you down. But just the same I felt funny with Jessica there. I felt—well, I suppose embarrassed is the word. I know

Sandor and Tilly didn't feel like that. Sandor didn't take any notice of her, she might not have been there as far as he was concerned, though he would have reacted fast enough if she'd tried to get out. Tilly was like I imagine the superintendent of a home for delinquent kids would be, brusque and tough and very firm. I could see the point of that. After all, we weren't in it for cuddling her and telling stories. But I was embarrassed, I felt awkward. When she looked at me I was glad she couldn't see my face, and not just for the reason we wore the stockings, either.

So I was glad when she went to sleep. Tilly said that if she'd never had Seconal before, which seemed likely, she'd probably sleep on and on into the morning. That made me feel better, that she'd have long periods when she wouldn't know what was happening to her. It was a relief to get those stockings off. Having those things pulled down over your head and neck for three hours and more makes you wonder how women get on with putting them on their legs. I suppose it's different because legs don't breathe.

Once Jessica was asleep Tilly started talking about the money we'd get. Sandor said why worry about that now when we hadn't even got Garnet to agree yet.

"Because I've done a hell of a lot of work," Tilly said. "This has taken a lot of organization and I'm the one that's done it. It's my camper and I've got the responsibility of her, at least for tonight I have. I want to get it settled here and now what my reward's going to be."

"Sandor said something about two million," I said.

"Okay, little Joe, if you're happy with that, you keep two million in your head, right?"

"But is that what we're going to ask?"

"It may be," said Sandor, "but we don't know what we're going to do till Garnet says yes. And we know even less what we're going to do if Garnet says no."

With that Tilly had to be content. But she wanted to hear all over again what had happened the previous time, so while we were eating our sausages Sandor told her. About old Prince Piraneso and the Vianis and Adelmo Viani meeting the Prince in the church and taking the ransom from him.

"What did you do with the money?" Tilly said it sharply, like a whip cracking.

"I beg your pardon?" When Sandor talks in a slow drawl like that it makes a shiver run down my spine.

"Your share of the loot, it must have been more than a hundred thousand quid, what did you do with it?"

"Is that any fucking business of yours?" But Sandor was in a good mood and he said it quite mildly. He laughed a little. "You must be accustomed to a very modest lifestyle, Tilly, if you think I could live on that for five years and have anything at the end of it."

But he'd been in prison for getting on for four of those years, hadn't he? And his mother kept him, always had. I could see Tilly was thinking that too but she didn't say any more. It was dark by then and very quiet. We had a bit of a shock when lights suddenly flooded across the camper ceiling. It was so unexpected. I think we all had a vision of policemen in uniform and a couple of them in hats and raincoats running through the trees and making a sort of onslaught on the camper. But the lights died away and after a moment or two I went outside to look.

It never occurred to me till afterward that the police might be squatting down behind trees with guns cocked, waiting for me to emerge. I'm glad it didn't because it would just have been more pointless fear. The wood was empty and very dark. I walked a little way toward the track, gradually getting used to the dark. When I got to the edge and there were just open fields beyond I saw the twin taillights of a car or van a mile away where the track wound down to the bottom of the valley. That was what had passed the wood on its way to some farm down there.

As I turned back I could hear something in the distance. I'm not superstitious, I don't believe in ghosts or anything, but I could hear birds singing and birds don't sing at night. While I moved I couldn't hear it. It was only when I stood still and really concentrated on listening. The sounds were very pure and cold and in a way like scales being played on a toy piano or one that hasn't enough notes. They were like that, yet I knew it was birds making them, and they upset me in a way I couldn't have explained and can't now. The nearest I can get is to say they made me yearn for something I can't identify and wouldn't know what to do with if I had it.

I was afraid I might start to cry if I spoke. Luckily, I didn't have to say anything until Sandor and I were on our way. We'd been prepared to stay the night in the camper but now that Jessica had had the Seconal there didn't seem any need. Tilly said she'd be all right alone, she'd be fine, and we could deliver the hair on our way back. We wrapped it up in the center pages of the *Daily Mirror* and put it in an envelope Tilly had found with some other wastepaper in a skip. The address on it was Northampton which we thought a good touch just in case Garnet called the police in.

The birds were still singing. They'd moved nearer. I looked at Sandor but it was too dark to see his face. I could sense he was listening too. His feet sort of faltered and he stood still, his head a bit on one side. The cold notes trickled out of the darkness but for all that they didn't seem in the here and now. It was as if they were in one world and we in another and sometimes there was a bridge between the worlds or a barrier pierced through.

"What is it?" I said. "What's making it?"

"Nightingales."

So that was all. I thought they'd disappeared, all died out, an extinguished species, as Sandor says. Was that the sort of sound made by the one that sang in Berkeley Square and Mum had on a record? Somehow I'd always imagined a song with a tune. We went back to the car where we'd left it among the trees and I drove us back. By the time we got to Jareds we knew Garnet hadn't told the police and therefore most likely wouldn't do so. The place would have been swarming with police and police cars and there would have been lights everywhere. All was as dark and still as in the nightingale wood. I got out of the car and put the parcel inside the mailbox.

Branches hung with big dark leaves overhung the entrance by those closed gates and covered up that treacherous electrified fence. One of the leaves patted my face and felt like a cool damp hand. The lions were heavy gray shapes but the one that had the man in its paws, the car lights played on it and it was as if it moved a bit, tightening its hold. As we drove away Sandor looked back and was just able to see a pinhead of light glittering down by where the house must be.

For the first time in weeks he told me a story that night. I was in bed watching TV. Sandor picked up the remote-control device—isn't it funny there isn't a name for those things?—switched channels, and then turned it off. He often does that without asking me, and it's natural I suppose if he wants to go to sleep. But he wasn't going to sleep. He looked happier and younger. Some of the darkness had left his face.

"Once upon a time," he said, "there was a goddess of the sea called Thetis who was married to a mortal man named Peleus. All the gods were present at the wedding except Discord, who was not invited and who revenged herself by throwing among the assembled gods a golden apple on which was inscribed the words: 'For the fairest.' "

"Who was the fairest, Sandor?" I said.

He smiled. For a moment he didn't answer. Then he went on with the story about the three goddesses who each thought she was the most beautiful and how they found a fellow called Paris to judge the beauty contest. They all promised him rewards for choosing them but the reward Aphrodite, the goddess of love and beauty, promised was the most beautiful woman in the world to be his wife, so Paris picked her.

"I thought the goddess was the most beautiful woman," I said. "How could there be two?"

"The one Paris was promised was the most beautiful mortal woman," said Sandor. "Mortal means she could die. Goddesses can't die. That's all for now, we'll have another installment tomorrow."

I've bought us two hoods with holes in them for eyes and mouth. Sandor says they look like the kind worn by the Ku Klux Klan. Ours are made of black material though. I bought them in a joke shop in one of the towns we passed through on our way back to nightingale wood. The man had wonderful things, I could have stayed in that shop for hours looking at dog and cat masks and skeleton suits and hands made to look as if they'd been chopped off at the wrists and purple birthmarks to stick on your face and green and red contact lenses to change the color of your eyes. As well as the mask I bought a toy gun. The man called it a replica, a genuine Colt look-alike, but it can't have been, because it only cost £2.25.

Before we left the George and Sandor checked us out with the American Express card I phoned Garnet. Sandor wrote down what I had to say. Garnet was very rude but I suppose that's to be expected. I enjoyed telling him we wanted the Princess. For one thing, I haven't got anything against the man, he's an ordinary working-class fellow like me, he's not rolling in loot the way the people he works for are, and I liked the idea of showing him his troubles were over and he could have his kid back. The other reason was it was so dramatic, announcing it to him and putting the phone down. It was like on TV, the last words spoken before the commercial break. You're sitting on the edge of your seat all through the ads for Persil and Hamlet cigars, wondering what the person those words were said to will do next.

I'd told Garnet Jessica was a bit miserable because Sandor wrote it down on the paper, but in fact when we got back to nightingale wood she was still asleep. She'd been asleep for fifteen hours. I didn't want her to wake up. I don't mean I wanted her to die or anything, just go on sleeping so that I wouldn't have to talk to her or meet her eyes.

Tilly said she was sick of being a nursemaid and it was someone else's shift coming up. She wanted some fresh air and a few hours' freedom. So I drove the camper, Sandor sat inside with Jessica, and Tilly took the Cavalier. We were going eastward, nearer the sea. It was just a matter of finding another deserted place with small lanes and high hedges and another bit of wood. A suitable spot was found by Tilly after about fifteen miles.

It was pine forest here, miles and miles of it. I drove up the sandy track and parked the camper where some trees had blown down in the gales and left an open space. Jessica had wakened up in the meantime. As I came up the steps and opened the door, careful to put my hood on first, she was asking Sandor if she could have a drink. I found a can of Sprite in the fridge and peeled the top off for her.

She was heavy-eyed, as if she could hardly hold her eyelids up. I didn't know what to say to her and I felt embarrassed all over again when she said thank you to me for the drink. Tilly and Sandor went off together, she to get her hair done and have a coffee and look at the shops, Sandor to find us a new hotel and make the next phone call to Garnet. I was alone with Jessica. I didn't like it but it had to be. What I would really have liked to do was get Tilly's scissors and trim her hair so that it looked nice, not all uneven the way Tilly had left it. But I thought of how she might feel if I approached her with the scissors in my hand—I mean, it would seem like a masked man with a weapon, wouldn't it? It would *be* a masked man with a weapon.

She didn't speak to me, she didn't look at me. If she'd cried at all since Tilly brought her to the camper I hadn't seen her. When the bed was down the whole camper seemed full of bed. Jessica had seated herself on the side of the bed that was against the wall. She sat with her back to the wall, her fists in her eyes, rubbing her eyes. Sleeping in her clothes the way she had and not washing and having her hair chopped off had left her looking a mess. Suddenly, she took her hands from her face and said, "Can I go to the toilet?"

I nodded and pointed to where it was. The hood I absolutely had to keep on, I knew that, and yet I'd have given anything to have taken it off and not have her see me like that. While she was in the cramped little toilet cabinet I pulled the clothes off the mattress and put the bed up inside the wall again. The place looked a bit tidier and there were seats to sit on. There was a table like the kind you get in train carriages. I found some sliced bread and a carton of Flora and some sugar-free jam that I suppose was part of Tilly's diet. Break the ice, I told myself, speak to her, say something, anything. What was the matter with me that I was scared—yes, *frightened*—to speak to a kid of seven?

She came out. I said, "There's some breakfast if you want it."

The bread got a look and I got a nod. I saw then that she was afraid to come too near me. I pushed a paper plate toward her—Tilly only had paper ones. She took a slice of bread, spread Flora on it but not the sugar-free jam. Maybe she was wise there. She took her plate and sat as far from me as she could get. I don't think anyone's ever been afraid of me before, so I suppose that's something.

She didn't say a word until she had finished her bread and drunk her Sprite. Then she spoke in a way that didn't seem typical of a seven-year-old to me.

"Are you friends of my mother's?"

"What?" I said. "What d'you mean?"

"I mean, have you brought me here to give me to my mother?"

I didn't follow that at all, but I thought she might feel easier if I called her by her name. "Jessica," I said, "I'm sorry, but I don't understand what you're talking about. I don't know your mother. Your mother's with your father at Jareds, isn't she?"

She shook her head. "They had a divorce. I thought you'd brought me here because my mother wanted to get me away from my father. Isabel's father did that, you see, he had someone steal Isabel and take her to France where he lived and her mother had to get her back and it took yonks and cost a lot of money but they got her back in the end." She couldn't have seen I didn't understand but she must have sensed it. "Isabel's a girl I know, a person at school, at my other school. I thought my mother had got you to do what Isabel's father got those people to do."

"No," I said, "no, nothing like that."

In a minute, I thought, any minute, she's going to ask me why we've brought her here, and if that's not the reason, what is. But she didn't ask. She said, "What can I do?"

"Pardon?"

"It's boring, not doing anything. Is there something I could read?"

There was the remains of yesterday's *Daily Mirror* that we'd wrapped her hair up in. Tilly isn't any more of a reader than I am. Jessica said, "Well, can I have a pen and something to draw on?"

I hunted about and found two sheets of writing paper with *The George Hotel* on the top that Tilly must have nicked from the desk in our room. There was a red ballpoint on the window-sill over the sink. Jessica sat on the bench against the wall and rested the notepaper on the table and drew pictures. She wasn't very good, you could see she'd never make an artist. It was pin men she drew and people made out of a big O and a small O with spider's legs sticking out. But I thought I'd found the way to entertain her and keep her quiet, or she'd found the way. And then, when she'd covered both sides of both bits of paper with her scribbles, she put the pen down and sort of lolled and drooped her head and said, "I want to go home now."

I didn't know how to answer her. I just shook my head. I went on shaking it as if somehow that would make things better.

"Please take me home now."

"You can go home tomorrow," I said, though I'd no idea if this was true.

She began to cry. It was terrible, it was so awful, like the end of the world happening and no help for it, no help. Everything that had ever happened to me when I was her age and younger seemed to come back, my own tears shed in buckets, in gallons, and forgotten long ago I'd thought, but not really forgotten, not ever. She sobbed with her head on the table and then she lay facedown on the bench and cried some more. I understood what had happened, how she'd been very brave and made an effort with her drawing and tried to be strong, but she was only seven.

I thought then, what are we doing? Why are we doing this? But what could I do? I couldn't drive her home to her father. I stood to get my share of £2 million. Anyway, she'd be all right, I knew she would. If she remembered it all her life—well, she'd remember it all her life. I had my own things to remember, worse than hers if this was all she was getting, and I was still here alive and well, wasn't I?

After a time—a very long, horrible time—she had her thumb

in her mouth like a baby and she went to sleep. She'd cried herself to sleep. It wasn't like a drugged sleep, so I had to be careful getting myself something to eat. I didn't dare take the hood off but pushed bread and some dried-up Cambazola I found through the mouth hole.

Tilly and Sandor were back by three. The hairdresser had done Tilly proud, washed out all the brown mousse stuff, cut her hair a bit, and styled it in the way Princess Diana has hers, sort of all swept back as if it's windblown. When she left she was wearing the cotton skirt and T-shirt but she'd changed that for a very short dress in bright hot pink and white tights with pink roses on. I guessed Sandor must have come through with the American Express card.

She looked grim, though, not a bit pleased with her appearance. And the darkness had come back into Sandor's face. He even seemed thinner, more gaunt. Tilly glanced at Jessica, asleep on the bench, but Sandor didn't look at her. He'd found a hotel, not in the nearest town, but on the road between two villages, a converted country mansion called Bollingbrook Hall, and booked a double room for us. Tilly and he went up to the room and he made the phone call to Garnet.

"He said no."

I had a quick glance at Jessica. "You mean Garnet said no to exchanging the Princess for Jessica?"

"That's what I said. For Christ's sake why do I have to translate everything? I wasn't inviting him to dinner, was I?"

That was when Jessica started to wake up. She sat up and saw us all there. Tilly looked fashionable and sexy, but she was very bright, face and clothes and hair, and I suppose she could have been frightening to a child. Jessica slid along the bench to the far end in the corner and sat there with her arms crossed over her chest. It was as if she was trying to push herself back into the wall and disappear.

21

If they had waited he might have said yes.

The opportunity, the offer, just after the miserable realization had come to him that his feeling for Nina was weakening, might have resulted in a desperate clutching at the proffered straw. She was rich and could be ransomed, for the second time, with money. Probably he would not even have thought of these things, would have thought of nothing but the chance and the answer, and have gasped, "Yes, anything, anything!"

But the ultimatum had been delivered and the phone immediately put down. Paul did nothing. He stood paralyzed, gazing across the walls, the parkland, the road, with unseeing eyes. The phone was still in his hand, the steady buzz of the dial tone making quite a loud sound in that silent room. He put it back on its rest, performing the action clumsily, like someone with damage to the central nervous system.

He should have gone to the police when it first began. Nearly twenty-four hours ago now that was. If he had done that they might have found her by this time. But even thinking of it brought back that sensation of eyes watching him, ears hearing, a bugged room, a tapped phone. He hadn't gone to the police, he had been too frightened for Jessica's safety to go to them, and now it was too late. It was within his own power to get Jessica back, by handing over, in her stead, the woman he was in love with—but a woman whose husband could afford to pay a ransom without much feeling the loss of it. A simple and clear-cut decision to make.

The voice had said nothing about phoning again but he supposed he would hear from one of them in the course of the afternoon. He went across to the house, fetched Tyr and Odin, and took them out across the park. It was a fine warm day, a little misty and humid, the lawns a clear emerald green, the woods bluish and mysterious in the cloudy light. It seemed at one remove from him, as if he carried reality about with him inside his head, and all this was a dream or a hallucination. The blackbird's song sounded as if it came from behind glass. He imagined Jessica. She was in a dirty room with a blanket but no sheets on the bed, food in paper bags, water in a cracked cup. He had seen something like it in a television serial.

A car coming up the drive made him catch his breath. It was only Nina's friends, come early for lunch. He called the dogs, called them again patiently, caught their collars, and snapped on the leash. The car parked outside the front door and a woman in a wide-brimmed white hat got out, followed by a man in a dark suit. Very formal, not his world. Colombo came down the steps, then Nina herself.

This time there was no leap of the heart, no shiver down the spine. He saw her throw her arms round the woman's neck, be drawn into the man's embrace and kiss him on both cheeks. And these were the people she hardly knew, hadn't seen for years, couldn't put off. He was aware of what he was doing. He was convincing himself she was worthless. In self-disgust he turned away, pulled by the dogs toward the door in the wall, the courtyard, the kitchen door. Maria opened it, took them in impatiently. She had an apron on, her sleeves rolled up and flour on her hands. Her small sallow face looked pinched and harassed. Paul, before he could stop himself, was thinking of the unfairness of it, how hard this woman worked as perpetual cook and housemaid for someone who could be called, with absolute truth, the idle rich.

He would give her in exchange for Jessica without a qualm. He would give everyone in the world for Jessica, but he was only being asked for one and that one was easy. It was nearly over. By the evening it might be over and he might have Jessica back again.

His change of heart occurred in the early afternoon. He had been making scenarios in his head, one-act plays in which he would drive Nina down some country lane and bump a tree trunk or dip the Bentley into a ditch or pretend it had broken down. Perhaps he could even do something to it to *make* it break down. He would tell her he had to get help but to sit and wait for him, she would be quite safe.

That went against the grain. He didn't think he could quite do that, tell her she would be safe and go immediately to give a signal to those who were waiting for her. How would he appear to himself after that, in his own eyes? What excuses could ever be found to restore his self-esteem?

But what else was there to do? When he gave her in exchange he must do it that way or some similar way. He could drive her to Bury or Ipswich and lose her in the crowd. Why would that be different from his original idea? If, for instance, he left her sitting in the car in the Bury car park and said he must go back into the town for something he had forgotten, would that be different? He would still know what must ensue, he would have arranged it in advance. If he sat with her and waited for them to come, let them hold him up at gunpoint while they took her, why would that be different?

The truth was that no way he or they might devise could be anything but a foul, dishonorable betrayal. That he loved her or didn't love her or despised the way she lived made no difference. That he might do it to get back his only child, his daughter, made no difference. He doubted now if he could physically do it, if he was capable of such blatant treachery, and this not because he was pure and incorruptible but because he was a coward who lacked the nerve to look a woman in the face and lie and lie so blackly.

The phone rang. He picked up the receiver and said, "Garnet," in a voice he hardly recognized as his own.

It was the one who spoke in velvety tones, the voice of an actor in a Shakespearean tragedy. "I expect you've been thinking about the proposition we put to you this morning."

"Yes."

He was taking it for granted Paul would agree. "The best thing will be to select a venue where you can hand over the Princess to us and we'll return Jessica to you. Not a main road, of course. Some quiet lane. I'm open to any suggestions you may have yourself, it may well be that you not only know the local terrain better than we do, but you also have a fair idea of where you're likely to be able to take the Princess without arousing suspicion."

A business deal he made it sound like, setting up the venue for the conference. "I can't do it," Paul said. His voice came as a hoarse whisper, that of someone recovering from an operation on the throat. He coughed. "It's not possible for me to do what you ask."

"I beg your pardon?"

"You asked me if I'd thought about the proposition you put to me this morning. I've thought of nothing else. You didn't ask me what my answer was. You took it for granted."

"Look, Garnet, I think you know what the alternative is. You've already had Jessica's hair. I'm sure I don't have to remind you of that. If that hasn't convinced you we shall have to take the next step."

"You must think of something else."

"There's nothing else that we want. Do you understand that, Garnet? Do you? I'll give you your last chance. Your last phone call comes at nine tonight."

Paul went upstairs and packed everything he possessed, all his clothes and Jessica's, into suitcases. There wasn't a great deal. Whatever happened, after tomorrow, he would never return here. He knew that. He should not have meddled with these people, entered their alien world. He was a teacher, not a body-guard. This country retreat, apparently peaceful and lovely, was more the abode of violence than the streets of North Islington and the schools of Holloway. Knowing the danger, he had had no business to keep Jessica here.

A sense of impotence and uselessness possessed him. He had nothing to do and there was nothing he could do. The panic had gone and he was strangely calm. He wondered, in an almost detached way, how long he would hold out against their threats, how long he would stick to his refusal.

At four the phone rang again. A fresh threat or a new proposi-tion? It was neither, but Emma's mother Sheila asking how Jessica was. Of course, they would all suppose her ill. He told her it was nothing much but she wouldn't be back at school that week and said goodbye before she could ask more questions. The front of the big house was invisible from where he was but if he happened to be looking out at the right time it was possible to see a car pass on the other side of the arch.

This happened now. Nina's friends were leaving. Paul thought, all I have to do is tell her. Once I have told her that I've been asked to hand her over to these people it will be too late, I will have burned my boats. Once I've told her, I will never be able to give her up and get Jessica back. Have the courage, he told himself, to go over to the house now and tell her.

And Jessica? Did he have the right to all this self-indulgent courage and integrity when it was Jessica's life he played with? They wouldn't kill her. There would be no point in their killing her. And if they mutilated her? He could hardly utter the words in his own head. To apply that word to Jessica marked the death of something in him, as if he might never be the same man again.

Somehow, with no reason, he believed totally that the exchange could be effected. They meant what they said. They wanted Nina and they didn't want Jessica. They wouldn't kill Jessica. That was all very well but why wouldn't they? Why not? Somewhere a child dies needlessly every day.

These thoughts chased themselves round inside his head. The bravado that had made him say no was dwindling. He had no doubt he wouldn't be able to repeat it when the phone call came at nine. Only if the whole thing were taken out of his hands, if Apsoland were brought into it and perhaps the police, if she knew, if he had some support or just some other viewpoint, could he utter no again when the caller spoke to him at nine.

It was clear to him that he couldn't go on as he was. To keep Jessica safe and not embroil Nina he could only stall, and stalling was mere postponement. He left the house and crossed the courtyard to the back door. Colombo opened it before he touched the handle. He followed the man along the passage, across the hall. I won't tell her until Apsoland comes home, he thought. There will be screams and tears and terror and I can't face that alone. She was sitting on the window seat, reading a magazine, but when he came in she jumped up and ran to him as if Colombo wasn't there.

Nina put her arms round him and kissed him. He held her and the thought came to him that he would like to do this forever, hold her like this and not speak, not change, only lie down and hold her, perhaps until they grew old. Yesterday it had been he who had broken away. Today she did. She looked at him and he thought how pretty she was, how lovely, every tiny detail perfect, no flaws. Her hands were like a goddess's hands in carved ivory.

She said gravely, "You look very ill, Paul."

"I'm not ill."

"Something has happened to you."

It was his chance. He didn't take it. They sat down close beside each other on the window seat. The park out there looked like one of Gainsborough's landscapes, as still, as timeless. On the lawn, a little way away, a brown bird was pecking at something in the grass with its long curved beak.

"That bird, what is it?"

"It's a woodcock," she said. "He and his mate or she and her mate live in the wood. He's lovely, isn't he? Look at his beak."

"Nina, what time do you expect"—he hesitated, uncertain what to call him—"your husband home?"

"About six-thirty, I suppose. It's usually around that time." She gave him a sidelong look, half-smiling. "Not getting cold feet, I hope?"

He had no idea what she meant.

"I'm teasing," she said. "Don't look like that. I know you're not. But you needn't be nervous about it, nothing will happen. I won't even tell him it's you if you'd rather not. I could say 'someone else' if you like, that's the classic way, isn't it?"

Then of course he remembered. It was this evening she was going to tell Apsoland about them. The arrangement seemed made a hundred years in the past or never to have been serious.

"Paul, something *has* happened. I can see it in your face. I'm serious now, I'm not teasing. What's wrong? I do have to know. Don't you want me to say anything to Ralph? Is it that you want us to wait?"

What happened next he had not envisaged, would never have imagined. He found himself holding both her hands, then gripping her shoulders. Apprehensiveness came into her eyes, leapt there like a flame.

"Paul, you have to tell me, tell me what's happened. Have you heard from them? Have they asked you to—to give me to them?"

In a moment she would begin screaming. She would fall on her knees and beg him, she would tell him she would rather die than go to them. He looked at her and closed his eyes because he couldn't bear to look.

22

Bollingbrook Hall is the best hotel I've ever stayed in. Not that that is saying much because I never stayed in any hotels at all before I met Sandor. There was as much difference between it and the George as between the George and the Railway Arms. In the front hall was a huge flower arrangement that I knew must be made of wax and silk flowers it was so enormous and so fresh-looking, but when I tweaked a rose petal it came off in my hand and it was moist and cold and scented.

Sandor asked for the key to our room and a funny thing happened. The girl gave him a key with the number 23 on it and Sandor said, "Not that one. It's the key to my other room I want, number 24."

Of course I, being me, silly me, thought he had booked two single rooms for us and I'd be alone. I didn't dare ask, he was in his blackest mood. But the girl took the 23 key back and gave him 24 and we made our way up to the room. If there's anything wrong with the place it's that there's no lift. Even the George had a lift. But you could see it would have been hard to put one in here, what with the beams and carvings and low ceilings and steps up and steps down. It's all carpeted in jade green, very deep and soft, and curtains like girls' flowered skirts and vases of flowers everywhere and plates with red-and-gold birds and dragons on them up on the walls. Every bedroom has a name from famous Suffolk people, Sandor says, though I'd never heard of any of them, and the name is on the door on a little sort of plaque with gold decoration round the edge.

Our room is called Thomas Gainsborough and the mysterious number 23 is Millicent Fawcett. I don't know what it's like inside but ours is—well, *magnificent* is the only word. We've got two four-poster beds with sort of canopies on top and curtains you can draw and pillows with flounces. There are about twenty different lamps and lights, a coffee table and blue satin armchairs, a bowl of chocolates and a bowl of wrapped sweets and— amazement—a cut-glass decanter of sherry. Of course we have our own fridge and TV and radio and in the bathroom there's a hairdryer.

"I could stop here forever," I said.

That was later when Sandor's mood was good again, when he was what he calls jubilant. "You should see number 23," he said. "The bed in there has satin sheets."

But when we first arrived it was only seven and he still had his phone call to make to Garnet. Tilly was alone in the camper with Jessica and she'd moved it to within a quarter of a mile of Bollingbrook Hall. From our bedroom window you could actually see the bit of woodland where she was hidden among the trees. I'd fetched them in fish and chips and when she'd had hers—she was hungry by then—Jessica got the powder from another sleeping capsule in her cocoa and that put her out for the night. Tilly didn't really have to do anything except be there.

Sandor went into the bathroom and started shaving. Where

he'd cut my hand across the knuckles was healing up, but it was clear I'd have a scar there forever. It didn't worry me much. One day if, God forbid, Sandor and I weren't together anymore, I thought how I'd have my scars to remind me of him. But I didn't want to think about that. I unpacked our things and hung them up in the cupboard which had hangers covered in blue satin and an electric trouser-press and I set Sandor's books out on the antique desk, *The Golden Bough* and *Nightmare Abbey* and the medical book and the one he was reading called *Hadrian the Seventh* and a new one I hadn't seen before that was a guide to "the best hotels" in East Anglia.

Bollingbrook Hall was in there with five stars beside it. Sandor hadn't picked it by chance, he knew what he was looking for. He came out of the bathroom in the white toweling robe that the hotel provides for guests to put on. I should think they must get an awful lot of them nicked. Sandor looked very glamorous in his. He made me think of a playboy in a French film, the kind that were made in the sixties that they show on TV. Even what he said was like a film.

"I'll kill her with this if I have to."

It was the razor. I wasn't sure if he meant it, I know I couldn't kill anyone, but the last thing I wanted was to antagonize him in his dangerous mood.

"There won't be any purpose in it," he said. "No doubt that's what you're thinking, that it would be pointless. I don't give a shit. It would be revenge and then I'll cut my own throat."

There was nothing to say. "I'm going to phone my mother," Sandor said. "Keep her sweet."

As I've often thought, Diana doesn't need to be kept sweet. She'd go on loving Sandor if he never spoke to her, if he spat in her face. She and I, we love him in the same way. But I sometimes wonder and I hope it's not treachery to think it, that it makes Sandor feel stronger, more real if you like, to make believe they've got a relationship like a normal mother would have with a son who's—well, I can say it in my secret thoughts, a wastrel, a black sheep. There'd be threats in that kind of relationship, and don't-darken-my-doors-again, and the son making up to the rich mother—in other words, the kind of thing Sandor pretends he's really got.

But we all have our weaknesses, don't we? God knows, I'm feeble enough and I don't even pretend otherwise. Sandor phoned Diana and although I couldn't hear more than the murmur of her voice I could imagine the loving things she said. Then we went downstairs, Sandor very sulky and grim-faced, and had dinner in the dining room. There was a candle on the table and a rose in a cut-glass vase.

All he said—or all he said in English—while we were eating was that Diana had had an insurance policy come up. *Mature* was the word Sandor used, I think. She was sixty or something. She'd told Sandor he could have it, it was for him, she'd been looking forward to it for years because it meant she could give him a lump sum. Getting on for £20,000 it was. I'd have expected that to cheer him up but it didn't.

The waiter who brought us our starter and our main course— or my main course, Sandor didn't want any—was an English boy with a Suffolk accent. But he must have gone off duty or been busy at another table because when we came to have our sweet— sorry, pudding—it was the Italian from the floodlit place.

Of course they were soon jabbering away. I couldn't understand a word and somehow I knew Sandor wasn't going to bother to explain, but I sort of guessed he'd left or been fired and had got a job here. Quite a coincidence. At least it was someone for Sandor to talk to and take his mind off Garnet and Jessica and the mess it looked as if we'd got ourselves into.

He was as silent as ever when we walked back to our room. There was fifteen minutes to go before we were due to phone Garnet. The time went very slowly. It always does when you're waiting to do something important. At two minutes to nine Sandor had a look at the instructions which told you how to work the phone, get an outside line, that sort of thing. It was a copy of the kind of phone they used to have a hundred years ago, white with gold decoration on it.

Sandor dialed the number. I suddenly started thinking about

killing Jessica. It wouldn't be so bad if he'd do it while she was asleep—but, I don't know, it would be bad, I didn't think I'd be able to stand by while that went on, it would be very bad. I heard the phone ringing in Garnet's house, and then I heard it stop and his voice.

Sandor said, "I'm going to remind you what will happen to Jessica if you don't agree to this exchange, Mr. Garnet. Evidence of the first stage will be in the mailbox at eight in the morning."

Only he didn't get to "eight in the morning" because Garnet cut in. I couldn't hear what he said, only that it must have been yes, yes to everything, because Sandor started talking about arrangements for handing Jessica back and getting the Princess handed to us, and he was so pleased he could scarcely keep the excitement out of his voice.

We walked down to tell Tilly the news. The sun had just set and the sky was still blue above but a sort of violet-pink on the horizon. It was warm still and everything felt soft and gentle, the little breeze was like a kind hand stroking your face. All the birds had gone to roost for the night but the wood pigeons went on making their soft whispering cooing noise. The tree tops seemed full of them. We startled a pheasant and it gave its clattering shout, like a fist punching on paper, and rose up in front of us on wings that never seem strong enough to carry that big shiny coppery body.

Thousands of gnats were dancing in the air, and breaking off from their dance to bite me. Sandor lit a cigarette and that helped to keep them off. It was dusk by the time we got to the wood and the sky had become that violet color all over.

The light inside the camper showed like a star between the dark tree trunks. I trod on a stick, it made a sound like a shot—well, an airgun, say—and Tilly opened the camper door and looked out.

She was still wearing the bright pink dress and the floral tights. She made me think of one of those flowers you see in expensive florists', the kind that are red and pink and fleshy and perfumed and always seem to be gleaming out of a background of black earth and leathery leaves. Sandor surprised me. He went up to her and hugged her. He didn't kiss her but held her tight in his arms. I knew that wasn't because he wanted to sleep with her again or she with him but because he was happy.

Jessica lay on the bed in her drugged sleep. Her face was flushed and there was sweat on it in tiny beads. Sandor lit a cigarette and gave one to Tilly. I noticed she'd done her nails and put transfers on them, silver hearts on the bright pink varnish.

"So he's going to play, is he?" Tilly said. She sounded like the gangster's girlfriend in a TV kidnap drama.

"Of course," Sandor said. "He was bound to. I had a brief failure of confidence and now I can't imagine why. Now listen, this is how it will be. He's driving the Princess to Stowmarket in the morning. There's a church up there in the heart of a wood. It used to be the chapel on a private estate. He'll take a turn on the left that's an unclassified road which leads to the church. He'll tell her there's something wrong with the car and that's the way to a garage. The road comes to an end at the church gates. That's where the car's going to break down."

"Did he go along with that?" said Tilly in the same tone.

"He'd have gone along with anything."

"It could be a trap."

"All the way along there could have been traps but there haven't been. I think I know why there haven't been and why there won't be now. We'll see if I'm right."

I think Sandor wanted Tilly to ask how he knew but she didn't ask. She doesn't rise to his provocations the way I do, but then our feelings for him are quite different. What she said was, "It's time we had a serious talk about the money, the ransom."

"We can do that when we have the Princess," Sandor said easily.

"No, I don't reckon we can. Once we've got her, pretty well as soon as we've got her, we have to set in motion our approach to her husband. Which reminds me, do we have his phone number at his office, wherever that is?"

Sandor shook his head, not impatiently exactly, but the way

someone does when he thinks the question irrelevant or boring.

"Well, I suppose it's in the phone book. The thing is, Sandor, they don't have London phone books out here. You have to go to a library or something. I mean, we ought to do that on our way to your church in the morning. I'll do it. You tell me the name of the firm and I'll do it."

"I don't know the name of the firm," Sandor said. "I do know but I've forgotten. It'll be among my papers somewhere."

"You find it so that we have it for the morning, right?"

"Tilly," he said, "I'm running this operation, is that okay with you?" He didn't sound cross, only mildly amused. "We'll do it my way. I don't know the name of Apsoland's firm because we don't need to know it. The Princess will pay her own ransom— that is, when the time comes, she'll instruct others to pay it for her."

"So that's your game, is it?" Tilly sounded even more like the girlfriend in the movie. With a fresh one of Sandor's cigarettes stuck to the corner of her mouth, she looked the part too. She must have got that habit from Mum, you never see young women do it, do you, as a general rule. Mum used to stick a cigarette to her lower lip and talk with it there so that it waggled about. "Two million it's going to be, is that right?"

I could tell Tilly was really worried about the money. She'd worked for it, taken risks, borne the heaviest responsibility for Jessica, and lent her camper.

Sandor said, "That'll be up to the Princess. It'll be what she considers she's worth." There was a dreamy look on Sandor's face. His eyes were on Tilly but I thought the dreamy look was the way he might be if he was with a woman he was really in love with. "Maybe everything she has, her whole fortune—how about that?"

"Suits me," said Tilly, and she seemed satisfied because she said no more and we only stayed about five minutes longer.

We'd be back at nine in the morning, Sandor told her as we were leaving. It had got dark and I listened for nightingales but there weren't any in that wood, only silence and a feeling of something dense and oppressive. I heard nothing, though I could see eyes, twin gleaming points, two pairs of them, among the brush at the roots of trees. We walked back along the path across the fields as the moon came up, a round ball as red as the sun had been.

In our magnificent bedroom we drank sherry from the cut-glass decanter. Sandor got into the toweling robe and lay in one of the blue satin armchairs and told me some more of the story about the man who judged the beauty contest and how the goddess Aphrodite sent him to a place called Sparta where the most beautiful woman in the world lived and was married to the king. When he got there he stole her away and they sailed to where he lived in Troy, but the beautiful woman's husband was furious and called all his friends together. They had an arrangement, Sandor said, like the Monroe Doctrine, whatever that may be, he laughed when he said it, that an attack on one was an attack on all. So they raised an army and started a war on Troy that went on for ten years.

The dreamy look came back to Sandor's face, and he said a bit of poetry that I made him write down for me.

> *What were all the world's alarms*
> *To mighty Paris when he found*
> *Sleep upon a golden bed,*
> *That first dawn in Helen's arms.*

After that we both found sleep upon our golden beds, or our blue-and-pink-and-white-flowered beds, I should say. Sandor pulled the curtains round his and shut himself in. It was like him being in another room and it made me feel shut out but there was nothing I could do about it. I lay there thinking how Sandor had talked in a fatalistic sort of way and that was when I thought for the first time that as soon as he got the Princess, Sandor meant to kill her.

It was the waitress bringing our breakfast, knocking on the door first, that woke me. I didn't know Sandor had ordered it, he'd never done that before. The woman pulled the curtains back and I expected sunshine to come flooding in, but it was raining. It looked as if it had been raining for a long time and quite a high wind was sweeping the tops of the trees where the camper was.

I put my little TV on—as far as I'm concerned even some hundred-quid giant-screen job can't compete with it—and the weather forecast was for steady rain giving way to high winds and squally showers. Sandor got up and I could tell he was terribly excited. He was trembling with excitement, but he had two cups of coffee and when he'd had a bath and an expert shave with his cutthroat, he seemed calmer, though he walked about the room brandishing the razor in a way that made me a bit nervous. We still had more than half an hour before we were due at the camper and he went off, saying he had something to see to.

The chambermaids must have made an early start on room 23 next door because I could hear someone moving about in there. You couldn't hear much, you understand, because the sound-proofing was really good, but light switches going on and off you could hear and if furniture was actually moved. All that was just audible this morning. Sandor came back and he had the key to 23 in his hand. So maybe it *had* been him in there, though I couldn't imagine what for. He had a strange look on his face. There's a look he has when he's going to say something awful— well, awful to *him,* daring, an admission of something shocking. As we were in the Cavalier, driving to the wood, he said softly, "You know how Tilly keeps fretting about the money?"

I nodded.

"You know how she wanted to know what happened to the money I got that first time, the Italian money?"

"What about it?" I said.

"I gave it back."

"You *what,* Sandor?"

"I gave it back. To the old man and her, all of it. All my share, that is. I wanted Adelmo and Cesare to do the same, but I might as well have talked to a brick wall. Well, a brick wall that knows how to handle a knife, if you see what I mean. Gianni had turned up by then and he said if I didn't want it I could give my share to him and we fought, I mean really fought, not with words, and I came back to England. That's why I turned to crime, as they say. I needed something to live on."

I thought of Diana, but I know Sandor by now. And maybe a lot of it was not wanting to be beholden to her. He said, "I hit an old guy in a shop, I knew he wouldn't stand up to me. I went in there with a stocking over my face like the way we did the other day. Hurting him was the last thing I had in mind. He spoke so nicely to me, quite pleasantly, saying okay, to take it, he knew he didn't have a choice, it was insured anyway, and it wasn't his business, he only worked there. He even made a sort of joke when he was showing me the safe on the lines of if you can't beat 'em, join 'em. And the next thing I knew he was putting his foot on the alarm button. I saw red, it made me so mad, it was like a betrayal, him being nice to me just to deceive me, it was so false, so I slashed him with the razor."

"Sandor," I said, "why did you give it back? I'm not talking about the old man, I'm talking about the Princess. Why did you give the money back?"

"The operation had failed, hadn't it? I didn't think I'd a right to it in the circumstances."

Failed? When they'd got the ransom money, all of it that they'd asked for? We'd got to the camper by that time and anyway I knew it would be useless asking any more. Tilly had got Jessica up and washed her face and hands and trimmed her hair. It looked quite nice, as if it was meant to be that way. Jessica wasn't flushed anymore, she was very pale, and she looked about as listless and indifferent to everything as a kid could without actually being ill. Of course she was half-asleep still, her head lolling. She wasn't sucking her thumb but sort of chewing on her knuckles, hunched up as far into the corner of the seat as she could get.

I expected Tilly to be back in her drab disguise but she was dressed up to the nines. That was Mum's expression for someone who'd gone over the top with her clothes. Tilly had the white suit on and a scarlet silk shirt with gold charm-bracelet charms sewn all over it and scarlet shoes and lots of gold jewelry. What I was thinking but not really believing she confirmed by whispering to me while Sandor had gone out to the car, "I'll be facing the competition today, shan't I?"

23

Very early in the morning he had loaded all their property, his and Jessica's, into the boot of the Volvo. Whatever might happen today, if he recovered her, if some fresh terrible thing happened, if he had to wait more barely endurable days, he would never return here. The place was already hateful to him. Those voices that had spoken on the phone, *this* phone, had spoiled it. They had destroyed the things that might have made for good memories.

But he tidied the house. He must leave it as he had found it. Apsoland's gun, the twelve-bore, he broke and laid aslant the kitchen table. Before they left he might change his mind and take it with him, but he thought not.

The sun was rising, a dark red fireball, from a bed of thick gray cloud. He watched its progress, its growth in strength. When he saw it set would he have Jessica back with him? The light in the kitchen of the big house was switched off and Tyr and Odin were let out into the courtyard. Paul saw Maria standing in the doorway with a cup of coffee in her hand.

He went out to close the garage doors. Maria lifted up her cup, mimed an offer to him, and he nodded. She brought the coffee out to him, gave an exaggerated shiver and wrapped her arms round her chest. In her scraps of English she gave him to understand that where she came from summer mornings were warm.

Paul drank his coffee, followed her into the kitchen, and fetched the dog leash. He had never taken the dogs out so early before, but they were unlikely to object. Dew covered the grass with a pearly sheen. From the wood a cuckoo began to call. He walked down to the stile and climbed over it onto the heath, the dogs galloping ahead, sparring sometimes, rolling over, Tyr once somersaulting, in a mock fight. In the dark wood the bluebells were over, their flowers shriveled, their scent like something sweet that has fermented. He thought of the day he had come here with Nina and they had been so happy.

Clouds had rolled up out of the west to cover the clear greenish sky and hide the sun. They carried a wind with them, the kind that gusts and whistles. Entering the wood was always a risk because of the chance of a dog disappearing. This time it was Odin who vanished. Paul called him and whistled, tried to encourage Tyr to find him, followed the wood round to its long fingerlike extremity where, on that miraculous night, he had discovered the running snares. It took him so long to find Odin, to call both dogs to him and secure them on the leash, that by the time he arrived back Apsoland was getting into the Jaguar, about to leave for the station.

No doubt it pleased Apsoland to see his dogs exercised so early. From the interior of the car he grinned at Paul and gave the thumbs-up sign. Paul thought, an hour and a half to go before we leave. A few drops of rain began to fall. He handed the dogs to Colombo and asked him if Mrs. Apsoland was up yet. Colombo nodded, said with a grin, "Have somebody kidnapped Jessica? I not see her about since I don't know when."

The inquiry staggered him in its innocent accuracy. Paul

turned back, managed a kind of smile, a stretching of the lips. The steadily increasing rain provided an excuse to dive for the house. The phone was ringing too. Snatching up the receiver, he expected one of those men's voices announcing a change, a postponement, some new condition. It was Nina.

"Come over to the house, Paul."

They left an hour earlier than they intended. He drove down a lane she knew of, an unmetaled road, and parked the car.

"Sit in the back," she said.

He looked at her with so much doubt and caution, almost with dismay, that she broke into laughter.

"What did you think I meant?" Her laughter was merry as if she had no cares, no awful future. "Oh, Paul, it's more comfortable in the back. Let's face it, I'm not used to little cars."

In the back she took his hands. "Listen, it's not so bad as you think. I was afraid, yes, of course I was, but I wasn't that afraid anymore. It's Ralph who's paranoid, he infected me with it. Oh, I'm grateful to him, of course I am, but I don't think even you understand how obsessed he is with danger and threats. It's his life, it's as if he believes life can only be lived after every precaution has been taken to make it safe. I was just an excuse. And you have to consider what a gem I was for a man like that, a nervous woman, a soon to be very frightened woman, who would put myself into his hands absolutely and agree to all those absurd things. Steel doors in my drawing room, those lights, the dogs, a bodyguard." She squeezed his hand, loosened her hold and brought it to her lips. "Paul, Paul, think how many men would be made happy by keeping a sleeping beauty in an impenetrable wood."

He said, "What will happen to you?"

"Nothing much, probably. I should have handled this years ago, I could have. I was so relieved to have escaped, as it seemed. The demands stopped, there was silence and peace. Once I met Ralph it was too late, and when I got a letter last year and then another, the fear began to come back. But it may be an empty fear, it may all be groundless. You say they cut off her hair?"

He nodded.

"I see it as my fault. That's why I'm doing this, as much as for Jessica's sake. I'm doing it to resolve things once and for all. It's what I should have done long ago."

"The nearer we get to it," he said, "the less sure I am that I can let you do it."

"You can't stop me!"

"I can drive us to the police now. If I have you with me I think I could do that. Things are so different, Nina, when you've an ally, when you've one person to support you."

She turned her face away. "You mustn't do that."

"But you say your fear may be empty and nothing much will happen to you. Doesn't that mean Jessica's really safe?"

"You're talking of crossing them. He may be all right, Alexander. Did I ever tell you that's his name, the one who got so angry when they cut my nails? He won't hurt me. It's the others, the Italians, I never heard their names, but I don't want to think of Jessica in their hands. Not if you disobey them—don't look like that. She's safe enough if you do what they ask. They want me, you know that."

She got back by climbing over the seat, but he walked round. She had jeans on and a checked cotton shirt. For the first time he noticed she wore no makeup, no jewels. He asked her why she had brought nothing with her, not even a handbag.

"I couldn't think of anything I'd want, except an umbrella. I brought an umbrella."

Rain blinded all the car windows. They sat inside walls of water. He took Nina in his arms and kissed her. Then he started the car, switched on the windscreen wipers and followed the signs for Stowmarket. Nina didn't speak for a while. The rain was so heavy that visibility was poor and sheets of water lay across the road in places. He joined the B1115 north of Kettlebaston, drove up a straight stretch with no side lanes which went on for so long that he began to wonder if he had inadvertently passed Great Finborough without noticing it. Then he found himself in it, a tiny place, no more than a village for all its ponderous name, and had to turn round to go back the way he had come.

The turning, signposted to unheard-of villages, was plain to see this way. The rain had eased a little. It was a narrow lane he took between high hedges of luxuriant summer growth, gleaming and dripping with water. Dog roses, flat pale pink faces, glimmered against the drenched foliage. No houses, no farms. A dipping lane that rose and fell and rose again between that hedge avenue, an embroidered double hem of dark green, fields on either side of sharp brilliant emerald, woods that loomed behind a bluish veil.

He thought of the evening before. Expecting hysteria and despair, he had told her what was asked of him and her reply had been ready, spontaneous, immediate, without a second's hesitation. "You don't have to give me up. I'll give myself up."

He thought he had misheard, just as he did now when she whispered to him, "This way." But she really had said that, as she really had said those other things the day before. A sign with an arrow pointed: *To the Church,* and he began to feel sick. He slowed and looked at Nina. She was very pale but she smiled at him. They were four minutes before their time. Both had looked simultaneously at the dashboard clock. She laid her hands on his arm.

"You must keep the car. When you have Jessica take the car and go at once. You said you won't go back to Jareds. Where will you go?"

"To my brother. I can't think of anywhere else."

"Tell me where he lives."

He told her the address and she wrote it down. As she wrote he was aware of her arm shaking. The road became a narrow lane. Woodland came down to the verges first on one side, then on the other. The overhanging trees dripped water onto the roof of the car.

"If I hadn't told you but just brought you here, if I told you the car was going wrong and I was looking for a garage, wouldn't you have been suspicious by now?"

She said simply, "I trust you, you see."

"But they can't know that."

"I don't think they know much about people's feelings," she said. "They don't have emotions like we do, they're different, so they can't understand."

Was that true? "It's what psychiatrists call affect," he said.

The lane led past an old overgrown churchyard. He could see gravestones erect or toppled among the long grass. A sign pointed ahead: *To the village.* The church gates were closed. No vehicles anywhere, no gray or red Fiats. The rain had stopped, leaving behind it a misty silent stillness.

"It was a church last time," she said, "where Barney had to go. Not this sort of church though, about as different as could be."

The church was small, built of flints and with a round flint tower. Part of its roof, the bit over the chancel, was thatched. Paul knew little of architecture, less of ecclesiastical history, but he sensed that this church was special, even unique. A porch of gray stone, once intricately carved, now weathered to dereliction, showed benches inside, a large black chest or box, a door of black oak that might be just ajar.

Not looking at him, staring at the windscreen down which water had begun to trickle now the wipers were off, she said in a small low voice, "Are we ever going to meet again?"

"You won't want to. Not after what I'm asking you to do for me. You may even hate me." What a cowardly way to do it, he thought. Here we are at the eleventh hour, the crunch, and I still haven't the guts to speak out straight. "I may not want to." He imagined her stricken face, not looking at it. "It's that you'll have done too much for me. That happens and it's—it's death. And," he said, "and—when Jessica was gone, when they took Jessica, I forgot you, Nina. I stopped caring about you. It was terrible but it's true."

"But you remembered me again. You remember me now, it's come back now." She held on to his hands. "Listen, when I was with them, Alexander and the Italians, when I was with them, I didn't care about anyone or anything but my own skin. I'd have given anything, promised anything, said anything, to get away.

I *did* promise things, Paul, awful things. But it didn't mean anything afterward. We can't judge ourselves by how we act when we're terrified."

"Where are they?" he said. "Why are they late? They're five minutes late."

He understood suddenly that even here and now their desires were different, he longing for them to come, she dreading their arrival. Back there I kissed her for the last time, he thought, but it wasn't the last time, this will be, perhaps forever. She felt small and cold in his arms, tense with anxiety. He kissed her lips, slowly and very tenderly.

"We'll meet again," he said. "We'll try again."

"I can hear a car."

A small blue sedan had appeared over the brow of the long lane ahead, suddenly visible in the misty rain. It slowed as it approached and he could see that there was only one person inside, the driver. His heart seemed to dip a little. They had said a blue Vauxhall Cavalier which would turn into the lane behind his car. The driver was a man, young, pale-faced, with yellow frizzy hair. The car passed them, it was nothing to do with them or with Alexander and the Italians. It vanished from view behind them, the way they had come.

"It's a coincidence," he said. "I've a feeling, a presentiment they aren't going to come."

"Do your presentiments always prove sound?"

"No," he said.

"Well, then." She was looking in the wing mirror on her side. "That car's coming back."

It passed them, went ahead, and turned into the little muddy open area that was a kind of car park for the church. There it sat, blue as a piece of sky, but today the sky was gray with moving clouds. This was the sign. Paul felt a sick tension mounting inside him. Jessica hadn't been inside the blue car, there had been no one inside but the fair-haired man he wouldn't be able to identify.

"Goodbye," she said. "Well, it won't be goodbye. I love you. I'll see you soon."

"Of course it won't be goodbye."

When he saw the car he was to raise the bonnet lid, get out and look under it. Then he was to explain to her, talk to her, say anything he liked to convince her, before walking off and not looking back. Once out of Nina's sight he was to turn across the car park and enter the church by the only one of its three entries which would be unlocked, the west door.

Things wouldn't go entirely as they had planned them, but he got out of the car and raised the bonnet lid. Jessica hadn't been inside the blue car. He said that twice to himself as he looked unseeing at the engine. Thin spatters of rain stung his neck and the backs of his hands. He put his head inside the car window.

"I'm not going to walk away from you. I can't do that."

"It's a condition," she said.

"I can't help that. Jessica isn't even in the car."

"No, look—"

A van was coming over the top of the hill, along the lane, toward them. Paul got back into the car. The driver of the blue Cavalier probably had no idea whether he was there or not. The van, large, patchy green, turned into the car park, disappeared from his view behind the church, backed until it again emerged, until he could see the driver. The driver's head turned in their direction and Paul saw that he or she wore a hood. Visibility was poor and he thought it unlikely the driver could make out anything through their windscreen. The sky had grown very dark and the green leaves and grass livid.

He wasn't supposed to be there. By now he should have been on his way down the lane and doubling back to the church. They had said nothing to him of what they would do. Come to the car and take Nina? He watched the van. He reached for her hand and held it. The driver of the van sat there staring, very likely seeing nothing but the rain and the outline of the car, waiting.

Nina snatched her hand away, threw open the car door and jumped out. Paul let out a shout of dismay. The car door slammed as he reached for her. She walked a few steps and stopped to put up her umbrella. He couldn't believe it, that she was putting up her umbrella. Holding it very straight, walking quite calmly, she moved toward the van, not looking back once.

The man in the hood got down from the driver's cab. He was wearing his hood while he was in the cab but he had taken it off before he came outside. Paul saw someone tall and dark and thin who held one hand up to shield his face. Nina didn't look at him until she reached the van, which couldn't be a van but must be a camper, for it had a side door. Then she turned her face toward him and slowly furled her umbrella. The man opened the door and handed her inside.

There had always been silence, but now it seemed deeper. The camper had a grid like a face, lights for eyes, radiator mustache, fender mouth. It sat beside the church watching Paul. The rain that was gray and fine, just too heavy to be mist, fell lightly between him and it. The blue car had moved forward out of sight.

Open the door, he said, send her out. Then he said it aloud. Nothing happened. A car door closed behind him, more than a click, a restrained slam. He heard a footfall on wet sand. He opened the door and got out of the car. Though all their lives depended on it, he couldn't have sat in there a second longer.

A man in a hood. Not the man who had admitted Nina to the camper, but the driver of the blue car. He gave a gasp when he saw Paul, but he was holding a handgun, so he must have been half-prepared.

"You're supposed to have gone," he said.

"As you see, I haven't."

"We want the car." He pointed with the gun at the Volvo. "You can have the Cavalier."

"Where's my daughter?"

"I don't know," he said. "In there. That's for them, not me. I'm just here to take the car."

Paul hit him. He didn't think about the gun or he didn't care. He struck out with his fist and all the force of thirteen stone of muscle behind it. The gun didn't go off. The man let out a yell, staggered, and fell to the ground. Paul thought of kicking him but he restrained himself. He picked up the gun, which wasn't loaded, which might be a toy.

Someone had opened the door of the camper. It opened outward. Not Jessica but a woman came out. She had a hood over her head which made her appearance even more grotesque, the swollen bust and broad hips and thighs crammed into a tight white suit, the patterned tights and high-heeled scarlet shoes. She hadn't seen what had happened, he was sure of that. The man on the ground began to get up when he saw her, holding his jaw.

She said to him, "Are you okay? Did he do that?"

The man said nothing. "Animal," she said to Paul. She got into the Volvo and started the engine, put her head out of the window. "Get in there. You'd better start praying." For a moment he had no idea what she meant. The Volvo reversed and swung forward, the tires screaming. He had to jump clear before it roared away up the lane.

He walked toward the church. The door inside the carved porch was locked and the rusty old latch rattled in his hand. He had forgotten what they had told him, he had forgotten everything. Round the church he walked, stumbling, coming face to face with the camper's grid-face, aware that it was moving, slowly turning. A little Gothic door under a canopy of ivy was unremittingly locked, had been locked perhaps for a century. His trousers were soaking from the long wet grass. He took hold of a gravestone's curved top to steady himself. Then the west door was open, creaking a little as it swung infinitesimally on its ancient hinge.

She was sitting at the end of a pew, crouched in the corner of it, her arms round the bench end which was a carving of a cat. The way she held it was the way she held a toy in bed at night, the dark gleaming oak of the cat's body pressed against her cheek. He said in a hoarse voice, a voice she might not recognize as his, "Jessica!"

The look she turned to him was terrible, white, shocked, and with something else that might have been dreadful reproach or simple lack of understanding. But she was seven, she had learned some social necessities, and he saw that what she was trying to do as she slowly got up was achieve a smile. It was a small ghastly stretching of the lips. He held her very tight and close. She was breathing shallowly, very quietly. His hand felt the cut ends of her short hair. Oh God, he prayed, let nothing lastingly awful have happened to her, let her not have been hurt in her mind, have lost the power of speech.

He lifted her up in his arms the way he had when she was a tiny girl. Her cheek felt damp against his. A confused impression of the interior of the church swam in front of his eyes in blues and crimsons, dark wood and soaring gilded angels. Flowers in a vase were wilting, past their prime. He hooked back the heavy swinging door with his foot, came out into the mist.

The man he had hit had gone, the camper had gone. He could see it making its way up to the brow of the hill. He and Jessica were alone in the middle of nowhere, without possessions, with nothing.

But the blue car was there. He carried Jessica across the church-yard, between the gravestones, through the sodden grass. One of the stones said, in deeply incised black letters, *Mary Anne Frost, born 1888, died 1894, Suffer the little children to come unto Me.* He heard himself sob. Jessica was looking into his face now, her eyes wide open. Her voice hadn't changed, her speech wasn't slurred.

"I'm tired," she said. "Can I go to sleep in the car?"

24

It's true that you see stars when someone hits you like that. I saw galaxies and lightning flashes, the zigzag kind, not the branched. When people get hit in TV westerns they just stagger a bit and come back with all they've got. Maybe they get hit again and they still come back. Real life isn't like that. Being hit on your jaw by a great heavy bloke like Garnet jars you right through your body and it's a pain like nothing you've known before.

I didn't want to get up, I just wanted to lie there and die. Anyway, I was sure things had gone wrong. The Princess had gone off somewhere and he'd stayed, that's what I thought. It was Tilly coming out that made me get myself together and make a gigantic effort. I staggered over to the camper and there was the Princess inside with Sandor.

When I saw them sitting there looking at each other, Sandor

with his hood off, I just stood there and stared. I was holding my own hood in one hand and the other was up to my jaw.

"What's happened to your face?" Sandor said.

"Garnet hit me."

It was horrible what happened then. They both started laughing. *Both* of them, that was what was so mad and crazy and *wrong*. If Sandor on his own had laughed—well, he's got a cruel sense of humor, I know that, I can take that. As for the Princess, she had a right to laugh, you might say. But both of them . . . I didn't say any more. I sat down and nursed my jaw.

"I suppose you're unfit to drive," Sandor said.

"I wouldn't be safe to drive."

He shrugged his shoulders but still he didn't get up and move. He couldn't take his eyes off the Princess. It was as if we had all the time in the world. She wasn't really all that worth looking at either when you saw her close-to, no makeup and her hair wanted washing, jeans and trainers and a shirt Tilly wouldn't have been seen dead in. But Sandor wouldn't be looking at her for her beauty or lack of it, I knew that. He was looking at her because we'd got her, we'd done it and he was pleased. I just hoped I wouldn't have to be there when he killed her.

After a minute or two he did get up and went round to the cab. The Princess said to me, "Is it possible to get a drink in this thing? I mean a drink of water. Could I have a glass of water?"

The only glasses Tilly had were for wine. I was pouring the water when the camper suddenly started with a lurch and I spilled a good deal of it on the floor. The Princess was watching me curiously. She thanked me for the water and then she said, "Where are the Italians?"

I knew what she meant, but I didn't let her see. Anyway, I thought it couldn't be a very good idea to chat with your captive. It wasn't a social occasion.

"No Italians here," I said shortly, to show her I didn't want any more nonsense out of her. And I stayed up that end of the camper, the rear end. Tilly had a mirror over the sink and I could see that my face had already started swelling up.

There are windows over the rear wheel and I stationed myself at one of them. Tilly had disappeared. I suppose Sandor had told her where to make for. Were we all going to live in the camper now? It seemed to me we were heading for the coast, the way we'd come. The endless green fields and the gray villages rolled past and there were plenty of handy places to stop and park but Sandor didn't stop. I realized he must have a rendezvous with Tilly somewhere.

I was looking out of the window, trying to guess where we might be heading for, when the Princess gave me a shock.

She touched me on the shoulder. I nearly jumped out of my skin.

"I'd like to go and sit in the front."

"What?" I said.

"In front. In the driver's cab."

"You can't go anywhere," I said. "You shouldn't even have come down here. If you move again I'll have to tie you up."

For a moment I'd a feeling she was going to laugh, but she didn't. She shrugged her shoulders and went back to the bench she'd been sitting on. It had begun to rain again and it was hard to see much. We seemed to go on for miles through dripping fog. All this countryside looks much the same to me, fields and woods and hedges and lanes. Sometimes you see a couple of bungalows and sometimes a farmhouse. It beats me how the people know where they live, how they can tell one village from another, except that they've got signs up with their names on. For all that, even I couldn't fail to see we were approaching the place that was the last village before Bollingbrook Hall.

The Princess was sitting there, up in the corner where Jessica had sat, and she picked up one of Tilly's magazines. I think she wanted me to see how cool and indifferent she was but she didn't deceive me. She wasn't reading the magazine, she had her eyes on it, that's all, and they were unseeing eyes.

The next thing Sandor was turning in at the Bollingbrook Hall entrance. They must have come to some arrangement while they were alone in here that she'd go quietly, wouldn't scream or make a fuss. That was what I thought at the time. But I couldn't see what was in it for her. Sandor hadn't a gun and Garnet had taken my replica. There was nothing to stop her, as far as I could see, from telling the girl or the man in reception that these people were holding her against her will. Maybe she would, maybe she'd deceived him.

The Volvo wasn't in the hotel car park. Tilly hadn't come back. Sandor got down from the cab and came round to open the door for the Princess. For the short walk to the door she put up her umbrella again. It was a golfing umbrella, the sections all different colors, red and blue and yellow. Sandor asked for both keys, 23 and 24. The Princess stuck her umbrella in a pot thing they kept for the purpose, it was full of wet umbrellas, and I thought, now she'll say something, now she'll tell this guy, the undermanager or whatever he was. Of course she will, what has she got to lose?

She didn't say a word. We went upstairs like three friends on holiday, a bloke and his girlfriend, say, and the bloke's brother. Something like that. Sandor held the Princess's arm. Well, he sort of held her elbow, he had his hand under her elbow, and she let him till we were at the top. Then she lifted her arm away from him and put it across her body.

Outside number 23 that was called Millicent Fawcett, Sandor said to her, "This is your room. I think you'll find it's comfortable." I had never heard him speak so humbly. He had never been so considerate. "I've got you some clothes—for the night, that is. I've got you a nightdress and a dressing-gown. And there's a toothbrush and toothpaste and things like that and I got you some scent. I remembered the scent you use."

She looked at him. It must have been at least ten minutes since she'd said a word. "I don't use it anymore, Alexander."

"If you'll tell me what you do use," he said, "I'll send out for it."

That means me, I thought. But she shook her head and held out her hand for the door key. Sandor wasn't having that. He unlocked the door himself, let her enter the room, then followed her, quickly shutting the door behind him. I went next door to Thomas Gainsborough and sat in one of the blue satin armchairs and wondered what to do next. My jaw felt stiff, I thought I might not be able to eat anything. But I could still drink. I poured myself quite a lot of sherry from the decanter into my tooth glass because the sherry glasses were too small. I think I could get hooked on that stuff, I really do. The fact is I'd never tasted it before we came to Bollingbrook Hall.

You couldn't hear a thing through the wall. I imagined they must be haggling about the ransom she was going to pay to free herself. Or even that he'd killed her and so skillfully that she hadn't uttered a sound. But they do something to the walls in places like this to make them soundproof. After a bit I turned on the TV, though all that was on was kids' cartoons. In the middle of a Yogi Bear rerun there was a knock at the door. I didn't know what to do, I even thought for a moment it might be the police, it might be Garnet setting the police on us. I crept up to the door, listening. Then Tilly's voice said, "It's me, Joe. Let me in."

"Has he asked for the money yet?"

How was I to know?

"Has he got her to phone her bank or get hold of someone who'll get the money for her? It takes time to get that amount of money, Joe. Where is she, anyway?"

I cocked my thumb at the wall. "In there."

Tilly said slowly, "I don't believe it." She looked at the four-posters up against the wall, at the bed tables, one with the phone and the other with the radio. "She just walked in and she's in there?" Tilly's face had gone very red. "Christ," she said, "I've been driving round and round for bloody hours. I've been to both the places we were at when we had Jessica, I've been to the wood down here. And all the time you were here and she just walked in like she was your *friend?*"

The wall answered for me. It started thundering, fists banging on it. Then the phone rang. You don't know what to do in a hotel when the phone rings. Your friends don't know you're there so it has to be the management asking questions you can't answer. Tilly picked up the receiver. I don't know why it came to me then, like a flash of light, that Tilly and I were on one side and those two in there on the other. Maybe it was just the two rooms and the wall between, maybe that was all. I could hear what Sandor said. He spoke to Tilly as if she was the hotel operator— no, worse than that, he'd have been more polite to an operator.

"I want to talk to Joe."

She said, "Charming," and handed me the phone.

"Come in here," Sandor said, "and her too if she likes. Let 'em all come." He sounded very strange, sort of hysterical.

We went into room 23, both of us. It was like Sandor's and mine but more feminine, rose-pink satin and rose-pink velvet. The bed wasn't a four-poster but a divan in an oval shape with a pink-and-white silk coverlet and piles and piles of pink-and-white frilled pillows. Spread across these pillows, laid there sort of tenderly, more the way a lover would do it than a maid, was a nightgown of white satin and lace and a white satin robe. There were three vases of flowers—well, one was a basket and it was full of roses, it dripped roses, and rosebuds on long stems thrust their way out of a cushion made of roses. The air was scented with them, that smell that isn't like any other the way the smell of strawberries isn't like any other. There were some of those too. They were in cut-glass dishes on the trolley some hotel servant must have brought up, and there were plates of smoked salmon and slices of pale-orange melon and a bottle of champagne in a silver bucket.

Neither of them had eaten or drunk anything. The Princess sat in one pink satin armchair and Sandor in the other. He jumped up when we came in. The Princess said, "I won't say any more alone with him. It's useless. I need a witness."

"You've got two," said Tilly, and she took her cigarettes out of her scarlet handbag and put one between her lips. It was then I suppose I really noticed that the room smelled of roses and strawberries, not of smoke. Before she could light the cigarette Sandor snatched it out of her mouth. She shouted at him, "Hey, you, what the hell d'you think you're doing?"

"No smoking in here," he said. I couldn't believe it, I couldn't believe this was Sandor. "This is Nina's room and she doesn't want smoke in it."

"And who the fuck does she think she is, dictating to us?"

The Princess was looking at Tilly with a curious expression on her face. I've seen women in jeans, women who might be men from the way they dress, look at smartly dressed, well-groomed girls like that before, as if for some reason they thought being a mess was superior to being tidy and pretty. The Princess looked at Tilly not exactly with a smile but with a tiny spark of amusement in her eyes. Then her face blanked over and she sighed.

"I have to tell you something," she said. "Listen to me. Alexander and I . . ." I could tell it was hard for her to say it. "We were together a lot when he and his friends kidnapped me. It was his job to look after me. We were alone together a lot."

Sandor gazed at her. He sat there, holding the cigarette he'd taken from Tilly and, unconsciously I think, pulling it to pieces. He had his eyes on the Princess and down in his lap his fingers shredded paper and pulled tobacco. His skin is dark, he's got a dark face, but the color had gone out of it and he was very pale.

"He fell in love with me," she said.

Suddenly it seemed very still and silent in that room. You could have heard a pin drop, as they say, only you never see pins anymore, I haven't seen one since I was a kid. It was silent like everyone was holding their breath. Then Sandor spoke, in a very strange upset kind of voice.

"We fell in love with each other."

I could feel Tilly's tension across the four or five feet that separated us. I could smell the roses and the strawberries.

"No, Alexander," the Princess said. She sounded gentle and firm, like a primary-school teacher. "No, that's not true."

Like a kid might say it, "You promised," he said.

"I know. I know I promised. What I did was wrong, I know that now. You'll do anything to be free, say anything not to be hurt. I'm a coward and I was afraid of my—the way I look being injured."

"You did love me."

"I *said* I loved you." She corrected him and it was like hitting him. He flinched. "You said you were in love with me and you asked me if I was in love with you and I said yes."

"You showed yes," he said.

"I know, Alexander, I know. I know what I did. I'm not making excuses for myself. I promised to see you again, to be with you, live with you, whatever. I said that if you'd let me go I'd come back to you. I promised—and I broke my promise." The Princess seemed to have aged while we watched her, lines were growing on her face. She and Tilly are the same age but she looked older, for the first time she looked older. "Alexander took me home on the train," she said to us. "We made a rendezvous. We were going to meet in Florence, at a table, a specific table, in the Piazza della Signoria at Rivoire's, at nine one evening, ten days afterward. He said, the money you've paid, I'll give you back my share. I didn't care about that, I didn't care about anything except getting away and being free. I said, I'll meet you outside Rivoire's at nine on the eleventh. You see how I remember all the details?"

"You never came," he said. "I'd given you back the money. I waited. I waited past midnight, I waited and waited, and they closed and took the tables in and everyone went home."

"Didn't you know by then? Didn't you understand?"

"I wrote to you. I wrote you hundreds of letters. Your husband was dying, he died, and I thought, once that's past she'll come to me. You married another old man and I still went on loving you. I expected you to keep your promise. What was marriage to you? Fidelity never meant anything to you. How many times did we make love in those four days we were together, Nina? How many times?"

She went red. "You're going to say I put up a pretty good imitation of enjoyment, aren't you? It wasn't imitation. I enjoyed you, Alexander. Why not? You're young. You look nice."

He got up. "Is that all?"

"That was a great deal. To get out of there, to be free, I'd have gone to bed with the Elephant Man."

He walked over to the window as if he was going to open it, they were French doors to a balcony, but he didn't open them, he came back and stopped behind the Princess's chair. She looked up at him and then away. They reminded me of an old photograph Mum's father had of a young couple posing for a wedding picture, she sitting, he standing behind her sort of protectively, only the clothes were wrong.

"Did you really think I'd come after all these years?" she said. "Did you still think I wanted you when I didn't answer your letters? I burned all your letters, Alexander. Some of them, the last ones that came, those I didn't even open. I burned them unopened. Did you really think I wanted to come to you?"

"Apsoland guarded you," he said. "Like a bloody Crusader, like a eunuch in a harem."

"If a woman wants to get away, she can get away from anything," she said, and I remembered Sandor'd once told me a story about that, only I suppose he'd never applied it to his own life, his own wants.

Tilly hadn't said anything for ages. Her voice was very abrupt and angry when she spoke. "What's all this to us? What does it matter what she did or promised? That's all in the past, that's water under the bridge. You wanted us in here, so what for?"

"Because talking to him on my own was useless, because he won't say anything but that he loves me and knows I must love him, deep down I really love him. But it isn't true, I don't, I can't, and I wanted someone in here to hear me say it and make him take no for an answer." She drew in her breath. "Then we can see what happens next."

"We can't make him do things," I said.

She spoke to Sandor. "Who are these people? Are they your friends?"

"They're nothing. Nothing to you. Nothing to me."

I felt panic when Sandor said that. It was as if everything was pulling away from me, like the tide on the beach drawing back with a cold roar and rattling of stones.

"When you came here and that fellow guarded you in a fortress, when you didn't answer my letters, I knew you had to be rescued. I knew you were waiting for me to rescue you and I got them to help me. That's all. That's all they are."

Tilly had gone white under all the stuff she'd put on her face.

I saw the color leave her face when Sandor said that about us being nothing to him. She loves clothes, though she's never been able to afford nice ones. She got up and took hold of the nightgown and the robe on the bed and hurled them across the room. They hit the window with a soft slurp and slithered onto the floor in a glossy milky pool. She picked up one of the vases and then pulled the flowers out and poured out the water onto the carpet.

"Stop that!" Sandor said, taking a step toward her.

"Don't you touch me, you bastard! You said, what happens next, you, Nina Abbott, or whatever your name is. Well, I'll tell you what happens. You get us a million pounds sterling." I noticed, sadly really, that she'd cut the ransom in half, she was weakening. Tilly only looks and sounds strong. But is anyone strong when it comes down to it? "You get it or get someone to get it. In used twenties and fifties, and then when we've checked it out we'll think about letting you go home to your open prison."

Things were never like that in the Via Condotti. I felt a bit embarrassed for her, she sounded so amateurish.

"I've already offered Alexander money," the Princess said. "Not a million, I must tell you, but money. He was insulted."

Tilly didn't understand. "Anything less than a million *is* an insult. There's no point in wasting time like this. You have to get on the phone right now and fix it up with someone to get the money for you."

"How would I do that? I'll do anything within reason." I really believe she meant it, she was genuinely sorry. "I'd like to make things right," she said.

Then an awful thing happened. Sandor came round from the back of the Princess's chair and fell on his knees in front of her. It was terrible seeing him who'd been so proud and arrogant brought low like that. He knelt at her feet and told her he loved her and begged her to stay with him and the two of them would go off together somewhere and be together and be happy.

"Oh, Nina, I've loved you for so long, I've given up my life to you, I've worshipped you, I can't give you up. I've worked for this for years, I've thought of nothing else, when I was losing heart I thought of what you promised and I knew you meant it. I knew that though you'd weakened and other people had worked on you, once you saw me again and I got you out of there, I knew you'd love me. What's happened to you, Nina? You can't have changed, you can't. I remember how we were, how we loved each other, nothing could change that."

"Come on, get up," she said. "Alexander, get up. You're making a fool of yourself. You didn't *know* I'd love you. How could you know something like that? It was in your mind. It was wish fulfillment."

He jumped up and shouted at us, "Get out of here, the pair of you! Leave me alone with her."

"You asked us here," said Tilly, "and now that we're here we're staying. I'm not leaving you here to let her go and us never see a penny of that money."

Sandor ignored her, he was feeling for something in his jacket pocket.

"You used us," Tilly said. "You roped us in to help you and now you're doing the dirty on us. You have from the start, telling all those lies. This was supposed to be a kidnap and you've turned it into a bloody lovers' reunion."

Before the Princess could get a word out, maybe to deny that stuff about lovers, Sandor moved behind her chair. She gasped because his left arm suddenly hooked round her neck, pinning her against the chair back, and the thing in his right hand which flashed and caught the light along its silver blade was his cutthroat razor.

"Alexander," she said, "Alexander, what are you doing?" And then she couldn't get any voice out because he was holding her too tight in the crook of his elbow.

"We're going to die," he said, "the pair of us. You first, then me. That's all there is for us, that's the best way."

25

She couldn't see that wicked blade but she could hear it in his voice. Perhaps it was a gun she thought he had. Her face went stiff and white with fear. She wasn't beautiful anymore. They say beauty is skin-deep but really it's fear-deep. Being frightened makes you ugly. She put up her hands to try to pull his arm away but she couldn't. She was small and weak and her little white hands didn't even shift Sandor's arm a millimeter. He brought the razor round and held it in front of her eyes and she started whimpering.

Tilly said, "She's not going to die till she's fixed for us to get the money. You make her do that and then you can kill her. The best thing to do with people you kidnap is kill them first and talk after."

"Tilly," I said, silly me, "Tilly, you can't, you mustn't."

No one took any notice of me. When do they? Tilly went up

to the Princess and stuck her face right close up to hers as if the razor wasn't there, as if the razor wasn't between them. "Tell me who to phone."

The Princess didn't speak. Perhaps she couldn't. She closed her eyes.

Tilly yelled at her. "Tell me who to phone. I'll get the number and bring you the phone, right?"

"Sit down," Sandor said. "Sit down, or I kill her now."

If it wasn't who it was, Sandor, my Sandor, I'd have said the light in his eyes was madness. I've seen plenty of it, I ought to know, madness in the eyes of patients in the hospital, the ones who sit in corners talking to demons, the ones who think they're the Ayatollah or that Gorbachev's in love with them. But you can be wrong, even psychiatrists can be wrong, and Sandor wasn't mad, just driven over the edge by pain sometimes, and which of us isn't?

I saw Tilly retreat. The razor flicked in front of her face. It was like an animal I'd once seen in a market, driven back by a probe. Sandor dropped his head and spoke to the Princess. She cried out. Her head was bent right back by his arm but she managed to cry out. And in that moment the phone started ringing. I knew what it must be, I reckon we all did, the management calling up to find out if we were all right, what with all the shouts and cries and things crashing. No one answered it but it distracted Sandor's attention. He loosened his hold just a tiny bit, he must have, he looked away and the Princess started screaming.

Tilly got behind with the big vase she'd emptied in her hands and she brought it down on his head with all the force she had. He staggered and fell against the trolley, grabbing at it, and the cloth came off and all the glass and silver and food went crashing to the floor. Sandor fell over and the trolley went over on top of him. It was awful, the noise, the crash, and the screams.

I ran to him. I heaved the trolley out of the way. The vase was only thin china and it had broken into a hundred bits. Sandor lay on the floor. He'd cut his wrist on the razor when he fell and it was bleeding. Tilly stood there shaking, staring down at him, with the remains of the vase in her hands, the base and a jagged bit shaped like a dagger.

It was a good thing someone came to the door just then because otherwise I wouldn't have been able to control myself, I wouldn't have been able to keep from punishing her for what she'd done. As it was, I had to open the door. It was the undermanager. I tried to say everything was all right, there'd been a misunderstanding, when a voice behind me said, "Excuse me."

The Princess had the Volvo key in her hand. The undermanager stepped back, looking at her. Sandor had sat up. She looked back at him.

"You never took the chain off, Alexander. It might have made all the difference."

She said it sadly. I don't know what she meant. She walked past me, quite lightly, you couldn't say she pushed past me, and she was holding her head high, though there were tears on her face and I could hear her breathing quickly. She walked down the passage and disappeared round the bend at the head of the stairs.

"There's been an accident," I said to the undermanager.

"I can see that." He was looking at his broken crockery and smashed vase and melon with Sandor's blood all over it, at the mayonnaise on the carpet and the cutthroat razor impaled in a plate of thin brown bread and butter. "I'll send someone," he said, "to get things cleared up." Hotel staff don't tell you off whatever you've done. That was something, among all the rest, I learned that day. "Would you require medical attention, sir?" he said to Sandor.

Sandor had got up by then. He didn't reply. He'd wrapped one of the hotel's white damask serviettes—sorry, napkins—round his wrist and the blood was pulsing through. The undermanager contented himself with a last look of horror round his wrecked room and then he went, leaving the door open as if he was thinking people like us had no right to privacy. Or maybe only that they'd hear us better with the door open if we got up to anything more.

We didn't. There wasn't any reason to. Sandor opened the

windows on to the balcony and stepped outside, kicking bits of vase and broken flowers out of his way as he went. I was behind him. I never felt more like hugging him in my arms and comforting him than I did at that moment.

The sun was shining. It was warm and humid. We watched the copper-colored Volvo come out from the car park and move slowly down the long drive toward the road. At the gates it waited for a tractor to pass and then a couple of cars, before turning to the left and vanishing from our view. Forever from our view. Sandor leaned on the rail and surveyed it all, the green, the emerald-green, and the dark-green ribbon hedges, the woods that look blue and the great arc of sky that is blue. I came and stood beside him, going cautiously for fear of him, but he spoke very gently. He spoke very sadly.

"Oh, little Joe, oh, little Joe . . ."

While we were standing there, looking over the balcony, Tilly must have gone too. Anyway, the room was empty. I quickly picked up the cutthroat razor and wiped the butter off it. In Sandor's present mood, a permanent mood now I thought it might be, I wasn't going to leave him alone with that. I'd throw it away the first chance I got.

D'you know, it was only one o'clock. All those things had happened and the world had changed and it was still only one o'clock. The funny thing was, I can't remember it ever being one before and me not ravenously hungry. I couldn't have eaten a thing. The smell of the food in that room made me feel a bit sick.

After a while Sandor came back and a chambermaid came in to deal with the mess. He picked up the basket of roses, handed them to her and told her to keep them. "For clearing up my shit," he said.

We went back into our room but I think we both knew we wouldn't be staying any longer. Our stuff was all there in the cupboards, including Sandor's new suit, though we'd left our wine stock and that bag of registration plates and all the pictures of the Princess Sandor called his portfolio in the boot of the

Cavalier. Sandor'd forgotten that and I wanted it to stay that way, him not remembering, at any rate for the present. What I did remember to take with me was my mini TV, that and the cutthroat.

Sandor didn't pay the hotel bill. "We're coming back here, are we?" I said.

"Maybe. Who knows?"

But he'd forgotten we hadn't got a car. He asked them at reception how we could get to the nearest British Rail station. Was there a bus? Of course they'd had plenty of provocation from us, you can look at it that way, and maybe that was an excuse for their looking down their noses as if a bus was something they'd never heard of or perhaps just possibly a form of transport one of their cleaners might use. A taxi was suggested, but you can't pay taxi-drivers with an American Express card, or not out in the sticks you can't.

The Princess had left her umbrella in the stand. I recognized it, all those bright jolly colors, but I don't think Sandor did. He was in a state of staring at things and not seeing them. We went out and started walking. My jaw had come up to quite a size and Sandor had his wrist still bandaged up, with blood soaking through the linen.

"Walking wounded, little Joe," he said.

"You ought to go to a doctor with that. You ought to have stitches."

"It doesn't matter," he said, and then, "I shan't *bleed* to death."

I asked him where we were going on the train, but before I'd finished asking I'd guessed. "We're going to Diana's are we? Of course we are." I liked the idea, I had trust in Diana, in her making things better.

"Where else is there?" he said, and then a car came along and offered us a lift. There's a lot more of that on country roads than there is in a town or on a motorway. Sandor said it's because people driving in the country and seeing someone walking think the chances are they come from the next village anyway, they're like neighbors. The drivers aren't afraid of them.

I wish I didn't have to think about what happened after that, but I do. I can't stop seeing it over and over, and maybe it's good for me to do that, to think of it and see it so that I can believe it, so that it's real.

Sandor bought us two tickets for Norwich. It was coming up to 2:15 and the stopping train was due at twenty past. We went up onto the platform. He said, "Do you remember the first time we came here and we saw the express go through?"

"That wasn't here, Sandor," I said. "That was south of here, that was nearer London."

"It's all the same," he said. "It's the same train. I wonder how fast it goes. D'you think it goes at a hundred miles an hour?"

Before I could answer that I didn't know, how would I know, the voice came on the station announcing system: *Will passengers on platform two stand clear of the edge, please. Stand clear of the edge of the platform, please.*

You can hear it coming a long way off. It roars like a live animal. We hadn't stepped back, not then, you only need a second to do that. If you can think of a cross between a guided missile and a dragon, that's what it's like, that train, the intercity express. It tears the air in two, it shakes the platforms, it makes the people gasp and laugh.

Sandor looked at me. He smiled a bit. He said, "It's a great train." And then he jumped.

26

The driver must have started applying his brakes the moment he saw Sandor, but the train still took a long time to stop. I was flung back by the blast of it and I was screaming. If I'd known what he was going to do I'd have gone with him, I swear I would. But I didn't know, I thought we were going to Diana's, silly me, and by the time the train was charging over him, crushing him to nothing human, fusing what was left of him with its wheels and the shiny silver track, by that time it was too late to jump.

I don't know what happened next, what they did, because they took me to hospital. To be treated for shock, they said. It was sorrow, really, but there's no treatment for that. There's no injection you can have that will dry up the tears that fall out of your eyes. There's no tablet you can take three times a day with meals that'll lower your high grief pressure.

Tilly found me there. She read about it in the paper, about Alexander Wincanton's companion being taken to hospital after the "accident," and she came and took me away with her in the camper. I was sinking into a new depression, what I always knew would happen if Sandor and I were ever parted, I could feel it closing in on me, or rather, drawing away from me, for it was more like a loss than something happening. And then I began to feel the oily water swinging about inside my head, slurp this way and slurp that. It's funny what saved me—my tiny TV that Sandor bought me when he first got the American Express card and pretended he'd had to play a con trick on Diana to get it. All the rest of our stuff was gone somewhere, left in the hotel, lost on the road, in the boot of the blue Cavalier, but Tilly had rescued my TV and kept it for me. I thought, well, I'll always have that to remind me of him and that he did like me, he did need me. I was his, you see, because he'd saved my life. If I'd managed to save him from going under that train, would he have become mine?

I've got my TV and I've got his cutthroat razor. I never threw it away like I meant to, though what use it'll ever be to me I don't know. It's not that I'd ever dare use it to shave with and anyway I'm growing another beard. That's a help to me too, giving me something to hide inside again.

"I hope you don't mind me asking," Tilly said, "but were you and Sandor having a gay relationship?"

"Whatever makes you think that?" I said. "Sandor wasn't that way, you know that. I mean, you *ought* to know that."

"Frankly, Joe, it's on account of the way he was with me that I ask. But I guess maybe he just loved Nina Abbott and he wasn't interested in anyone else. D'you reckon he was mad? I mean nutty as a pecan pie, bonkers, out to lunch?"

Have you ever noticed what a lot of words for mad there are? More than for sex or a man's thing or a woman's. "Don't ever say that," I said. "Don't ever say it."

She never has and that was a month ago. A lot of things have happened in that month. We drove the camper a long way from there, down into Essex and through the Dartford Tunnel into

Kent and found a caravan site where we're living now. It's a nice smart site, a field with new young trees planted all along the sides of it, near enough to the village pub and the shop. Tilly's got a job working the bar. She says I'll have to look for a job too and I know she's right, but somehow I can't imagine it, it would be too strange. I go in the pub every night and have a chat and I've learned that the local people didn't want the caravan site, but the council said they had to have it to encourage tourism. It suits me. If I lived in a house now, in one room in a house, reminders of Sandor would be too painful to bear. It was always in a room that we lived, squalid rooms and super ones, but always a single room.

There's only one bed of course. At first I pushed myself right up to the edge on my side so as not to touch Tilly. I remembered what had happened when I touched Sandor. But Tilly isn't Sandor. I wish she was, but wishes aren't horses to ride on to the land of your dreams. She isn't my sister either. She lay beside me for a bit and then she rolled over and put her arms round me and, well, now we're living in a full sexual relationship. Or so she says and it must be if she says so. Having no prior experience, I wouldn't exactly know. Is this what Mum and Dad did, and my parents before them, and Tilly's?

It's a funny thing to get so steamed up about, wreck worlds and kill yourself—for *that?* No better than a good meal really and not always so good. You can't imagine someone threatening to kill people and kidnapping them and committing suicide because he couldn't get stir-fried chicken for his dinner. Tilly says it's not like that and I've got hold of the wrong end of the stick. What she doesn't understand, what no one seems to, is that what's the wrong end of the stick for others may be the right end for you.

In the mornings when Tilly's at work and in the evenings before I go down to the pub I sit alone in the camper and think about Sandor. Sometimes I think about him so intensely that I can conjure him up. I close my eyes and open them again cautiously and then I see him sitting in the shadows on the end of the bench where Jessica sat and where the Princess sat on the day we took her to Bollingbrook Hall. But when I reach out to touch him—I sense he wouldn't mind being touched now he's a ghost—he fades away and I'm all alone in the pale sunshine or the summery dusk.

I know I'm too fanciful, I remember what Sandor said about wishing he had my imagination, but I can't help wondering if he's found the Princess where he is now that they're both ghosts. I wonder if she loves him where they are and she's forgiven him for the chain, and if he's forgiven her for stealing his heart from him on St. Gallowglass's Eve.

What happened to her I learned from my TV, just the bare facts, and then Tilly brought the paper back with her from work. It was one of those so-called quality papers that have every fact and every detail and more dirt than the ones they call gutter press.

Apsoland had been interviewed and gave them the whole story. He didn't know about the past, of course. It was amazing what that man didn't know, for all the stuff that came out about him, having this firm of private detectives in his pay, for instance, and being the country's foremost expert on security. That's what the paper said he was, at any rate. It was plain he'd never heard of Sandor and didn't know where his wife had been the day we kidnapped her, or rather, the day she gave herself up to us. The day after that was the last time he saw her.

He went off in his Jaguar to the station in the morning the same as he always did. Nina had told him she'd be driving up the coast to return someone's property to him he'd left in her car. There was nothing about who this someone was, but I guess it was Garnet. After all, we changed cars, didn't we? He had to take the Cavalier, on Sandor's orders, so that the Volvo could be left for the Princess. Well, my theory is that Garnet had all his stuff in that car because as soon as he got Jessica back he meant to get the hell out. Only it didn't work so easily.

Apsoland didn't like Nina going alone, but she said Colombo would be with her. Their driver, he said, meaning Garnet, had left them the day before without warning. When Apsoland came home that evening the house was empty, the whole place was empty. Imagine that house deserted, the whole place deserted, and the warning system disarmed.

Of course it wasn't dark at nine o'clock when he got there. It was a spooky sort of dusk, the sky covered with black clouds, and everywhere wet. Rain had been falling all day. The lions were sitting on the gateposts with water running down their heads and dripping off their chins and the poor man who was going to be eaten had a pool of water between his ruff and his neck.

"Come on, you can't know that," Tilly said, but I can, I do.

He opened the gates with his magic key. Up the avenue he came, between the flint walls, and he knew something was wrong when he passed the halfway point and the lights didn't come on. That place, an example of security to all—but there's no such thing as security, is there, there's no safety in this world—the front door was open, the windows were open, the back door was wide open. His dogs came running up to him as he got out of the car. The phone was ringing, the sound pouring out of the house, out of the open door, as if it had been ringing for hours with no one to answer it.

"Your imagination's working overtime again," said Tilly.

"How else would it be?" I said. "I can picture it, I know I'm right. Those dogs'd have been running round him, jumping up, wanting their food, while he was desperate to get to the phone, pushing them away, shouting at them to get down."

"Okay, have it your own way," she said. "And then he heard a voice he knew, a voice he'd heard every day for months on end and never suspected, never given a second thought to."

"I don't know about never given a second thought to. It says here he checked everyone out, he had these private eyes go into all their ancestors."

"Antecedents," she said, and she's right. Now that I haven't got Sandor to teach me and correct me I'm forgetting the education he gave me and the words I was taught.

"People don't really have them," I said, meaning antecedents, "not if they've never been caught out doing anything criminal.

Those two didn't have a record. I don't suppose anyone knows what we know about them."

"They were so near and yet so far. Suppose Sandor had seen him? What then?"

"He didn't," I said. "I saw him a couple of times, but how would I have known?"

Apsoland didn't tell the papers that part, about recognizing the voice, that came later. He didn't tell them the voice asked for £2 million or his wife would die. At that time he didn't even tell them what the voice called his wife, not Nina Abbott or Mrs. Apsoland but the Princess.

He waited two days before he told the police. By then he'd handed over half the money. He'd been instructed to take it to a church in a village, not the one where we left Jessica, but a place beginning with an H like so many of them do up there, Hinxton or Hintlesham or Heveningham, one of those. The voice said, give us half and the Princess'll talk to you on the phone.

"Always churches," said Tilly. "I wonder why."

"Because that's what they do. That's what they did when it was Sandor and Adelmo and Cesare. You could call it their trademark."

Apsoland left his million there in a suitcase that he had to put on the floor of the pulpit, a funny little eight-sided room made of oak up a flight of steps. But he never spoke to Nina, there was no phone call. The Princess was dead by then, she'd been dead all along, shot through the head with a gun from his precious collection and buried in Wolves Wood. A shallow grave, the paper said. It must have been shallow because it was Apsoland's dogs that found her and dug her up.

Colombo and Maria, they called themselves. Well, that's what they *were* called. By the time the police were told they were in Italy. They had to be extradited, if that's the proper word, and brought back here. It takes months and months actually getting people up for trial, but they've already appeared on a charge of murder and plenty of other things in the court where there's a magistrate, not a real judge.

I thought how amazed Sandor would have been. I mean, if

he'd known that all the time he was working out how to kidnap the Princess, his old mate was actually living in the house making his own plans.

"What did they say his full name was?"

I did my best to get my tongue round the Italian. "Giovanni Colombo Viani. Sandor's mother said he never liked being called Gianni Viani, and he had another name he thought of using. Well, he did use it, didn't he? Of course he wasn't married when Sandor knew him. He was just Gianni Viani, the one who wasn't in on it but wanted his whack of the money just the same. Well, that's what Sandor said."

"You're always talking about Sandor," she said. "Don't you have any thoughts of your own? Don't you have your own feelings?"

My sister, my spouse. I don't know where I got that. Not from Sandor, from something in my distant past I don't know about, maybe. Who knows where all the rubbish in your brain is dredged up from? Bobbing about like empty cigarette packs and juice cartons on a pool of oily water.

Yesterday I had a letter from Diana. She wants me to go and see her.

"And take your live-in lover," said Tilly.

She thinks I could get Diana to adopt me like a son now that Sandor's gone. And perhaps I could, perhaps it's meant, inevitable. Tilly's thinking about the money, all that insurance money she's got coming.

But what I'm thinking is that it would be a way of being close to Sandor for the rest of my life.

It would be a way of being him.